What Happens in France

What Happens in France

CAROL WYER

CANELO

First published in the United Kingdom in 2019 by Canelo

This edition published in the United Kingdom in 2019 by

Canelo Digital Publishing Limited
57 Shepherds Lane
Beaconsfield, Bucks HP9 2DU
United Kingdom

A CIP catalogue record for this book is available from the British Library.

Print ISBN 978 1 78863 528 8
Ebook ISBN 978 1 78863 276 8

Look for more great books at www.canelo.co

Printed and bound in Great Britain by Clays Ltd, Elcograf S.p.A.

Prologue

March – Four Months Earlier

Bryony Masters clattered down the hospital corridor, handbag swinging wildly on her shoulder, skirting round patients and staff as they ambled without direction in front of her. She flew past the bookshop with paperbacks on a rotating stand and buckets of colourful flowers prepared in bunches for visitors to purchase. Her heart smashed against her ribcage. Tears had blurred her vision and the signage was incomprehensible: Cardiology, X-ray department, haematology, paediatrics, ENT, Wards 1–11. Where was Intensive Care? She drew to a sudden halt and cast about. A woman dressed in white trousers and tunic with hair scraped from a round face in which were set kindly, silver-grey eyes, noted her distress and approached her.

'Can I help you?'

Bryony nodded, not trusting her emotions. 'Intensive Care,' she blurted before the tears could flow.

'Come on. I'll take you.' The woman spun on her heels and walked beside Bryony, her calm demeanour exactly what Bryony needed. She talked all the while, her singsong voice anchoring Bryony to the here and now, preventing panic from taking hold of her.

'It's not far, just down this corridor and on the left. You meeting anyone here, or are you alone?'

'My mother. She's here.'

'Then, she'll no doubt be in the waiting room. We'll head there first and you can meet up with her. That's where all relatives wait. There's a coffee machine and water and even biscuits.'

Bryony strode beside the woman, the smell of disinfectant and something medicinal that was omnipresent in these places assaulted her nostrils. *Please let him be okay*.

The woman drew to a halt and gave her a smile. 'The waiting room is just there.' She pointed out the blue sign over double glass doors. 'Someone will be inside to answer any questions you may have.'

'Thank you,' Bryony said as the woman turned to leave. She adjusted her handbag, now dangling from her forearm. Her mother would need her to be strong. She pushed open the doors and spied the figure huddled on the front chair, hands cupped around a plastic cup, head lowered. She froze. Was she too late?

'Mum.'

Her mother looked up at the sound, issued a cry and, dropping the empty cup to the floor, hastened towards her daughter, throwing her arms around her waist. Bryony hugged her tightly, letting her cry.

'Is he...?' Bryony couldn't bring herself to speak the word.

Her mother pulled away, eyes shining with tears and shook her head. 'No. It was a severe stroke but the doctor managed to give him a clot-dissolving tissue plasminogen activator, within what he called the 'golden hour'. It might just have saved his life and prevented any more brain cells from dying. He's going to be okay but we don't know what state he'll be in. He might never regain his speech or walk. We'll have to wait and see how well he recovers. He'll need lots of therapy and there's always a chance he could have another stroke – and if he does, he might not be so lucky next time. Oh, Bryony, what would I do if I lost him? I couldn't bear it!'

'It's okay, Mum. He's survived before.'

'That was different. A stroke is different to a nervous breakdown.'

'He'll make it,' Bryony said, although her head was in turmoil. 'How did it happen?'

'The stroke?'

Bryony nodded.

'He was looking through some old photographs we keep in the cupboard. He was on the floor, going through them and I was in the kitchen making dinner when I heard a groan. I went running and found he'd keeled over.'

'Photographs?' Bryony asked warily. A buzzing began in her head. This was her fault. Her father had collapsed and suffered a stroke because of her. 'Which photos?'

'Hannah,' said her mother as tears trickled down her pale cheeks, leaving two shining trails.

Bryony enveloped the frail woman in her arms, wondering if she could hear the loud hammering of her heart. Hannah. Of course it was Hannah. Bryony had to fix this, once and for all. It was now or never. There might not even be enough time left but she had to do everything she could to make things right. She had to find her sister, Hannah, before it was too late.

Chapter One

Thursday, 6 July – Afternoon

Bryony drew up outside Melinda's house. The gaily coloured yellow front door stood out boldly among the row of identical houses, all of which had brown doors. The door was much like Melinda herself. Melinda was a one-off and she didn't much care if others thought her odd or different. It was one of the things Bryony loved about her. In Bryony's opinion, her friend's front door was far more inviting than the others in the street. Someone – no doubt Sean's father – had planted clumps of marigolds in the garden. A grinning garden gnome in a ridiculous costume and bright red hat dangled his rod into the flowers. The wooden sign hanging from a nail on the front door read: 'Forget the Dog. Beware of the Wife,' adding to the impression that this was a house filled with fun and frivolity.

Bryony rang the doorbell and waited. The door opened wide and there stood Melinda, a huge smile on her round face as always. Her smooth chestnut bob clung to her head like a helmet but her large brown eyes sparkled with youthful enthusiasm.

'Come in,' she said, wiping her hands on a faded tea towel. 'You've arrived at just the right time. I've finished putting the final touches on the casserole and it's ready to go in the oven. We'd best go in the kitchen. Freddie's off school. He had a temperature this morning so I let him stay at home. He's been playing with his Lego again and there are bricks everywhere in the lounge. I daren't clean in there. Sean had to fix the vacuum cleaner last time because I hoovered up several yellow bricks and they got stuck in the pipe. Anyway, I've finished my housewifely chores and am ready for a glass of wine. Make that a very large glass of wine. Care to join me?'

'It's only one o'clock,' protested Bryony.

'And? You haven't got to go back to work, so why not?'

Bryony laughed. 'Only a small one. I have to drive, remember.'

Melinda led the way into the kitchen, a friendly space that oozed warmth and contentment. The fridge was covered with plastic letters spelling 'Freddie', 'Mummy' and 'Daddy'. Several drawings had been added to the side of it: one of a large sun shining over a house, one of a large dinosaur and another of three stick figures holding hands. Plastic animals adorned the shelf above the sink and a piece of pottery showcasing the small handprint of a child took pride of place; next to it stood a photograph of a grinning boy with dark hair and chocolate-brown eyes who looked exactly like his mother.

Melinda swept away small pots of herbs into a cupboard and extracted two glasses from another, all the while moving plates and pans into the sink so they were out of view. Bryony sniffed the air. It smelt of warm dough and lemon essence. A rack of scones stood cooling next to a sponge cake. Melinda had indeed been busy.

The bright room was dominated by a huge dining table protected by a plastic, floral tablecloth. A chubby face peered out from under the table.

'Hello, Briny.'

'Hello, Freddie. What are you doing under the table?'

'I'm not under the table. I'm in a boat. This is my sky,' replied the boy, solemn-faced, pointing to the underside of the kitchen table. 'It's night-time. I've been travelling all day. I'm sailing to Zanzibar.'

Bryony lifted the cloth to get a closer look. Freddie was seated in a large cardboard box, his mother's egg whisk in one hand and red spatula in the other, 'paddling' from one end of the table to the other. He wore a pirate's hat made of newspaper and somebody had painted a black moustache under his nose.

'Are you looking for treasure?' asked Bryony.

The boy shook his head. 'I'm looking for a new country to live in. Daddy says he's fed up of this one,' he said then set about rocking his body to make the box slide along the floor. Melinda shrugged her shoulders in a display of astonishment and passed a glass of wine to Bryony. Melinda took a sip and sighed with pleasure. Freddie crawled out from under the table and handed Bryony his whisk.

'Mummy, I'm going to get my dinosaurs. They want to go to Zanzibar too,' he shouted as he scurried off.

'Zanzibar?' Bryony said.

'I've no idea where that came from. Maybe it was from one of his bedtime books. I expect it's sunny there and the roads have no potholes. Sean spent an hour complaining about the state of the roads last night. He hit an extra-large pothole on his way home. I don't think the van's

6

too damaged but Sean wasn't happy. He went on about England being a third-world country and grumbled that we should all move to a better one. He wasn't serious but obviously our little earwigging child decided he was.' She slugged back the remainder of her wine. 'I needed that. It's been a long day. I envy these younger mums. It's tough racing after a hyperactive five-year-old when you're well into your thirties.'

'You do a fantastic job. Freddie is a credit to you. He's a well-balanced, healthy boy and that's all down to your parenting skills. You're always there for him and you spend loads of time with him. You're a fantastic mother.'

Melinda blushed. 'Being a mother wasn't exactly what I planned but it is the best job ever,' she admitted.

'Who'd have thought the career-minded, hard-nosed Melinda Ashbrook would become a full-time mother, eh?'

'Less of the hard-nosed, thank you. I loved being a crime scene investigator but I'm so lucky to be in a situation where I get to be a stay at home mum.'

Singing from the room next door indicated Freddie had now abandoned his plans to row to Zanzibar and was watching television.

Bryony regarded her friend, whose face had taken on the look of maternal pride that accompanied a child's achievement. There was no doubt that Sean and Freddie had transformed her. Bryony recalled the first time Melinda had brought Sean back to their flat, eyes glittering with mischief but still nervous in his ill-fitting suit he'd worn to impress them both.

Sean had succeeded in exposing Melinda's gentler side that hitherto had been well and truly concealed. Being the only daughter in a family of four boys, and the youngest sibling to boot, she had learnt to stand up for herself at an early age and give away nothing in the emotion department. Her brothers had signed up for the Armed Forces but Melinda had followed in their grandfather's footsteps, studied forensic science, and become a crime scene investigator with the police force.

Bryony had all the time in the world for her friend. Without her, Bryony's time at school would have been even more horrendous than it already was. Melinda had been her friend and protector on more than one occasion, and in return Bryony had offered her unwavering affection and friendship that would always stand the test of time.

Melinda pointed at the small television screen on the wall above the kitchen table. 'Ooh! Turn it up, Bry. It's Professor David Potts, the gorgeous host of *Mate or Date?* Now, I wouldn't kick him out of bed. He could charm me with that Irish lilt of his alone. Makes me go weak at the knees thinking about it.'

'Behave yourself, woman. You're happily married to Sean. If anyone should be thinking about such nonsense, it's me.' She pointed the remote at the set. 'You're right though. Professor Potts is absolutely divine. Lovely accent, piercing blue eyes, charisma. I wouldn't want to be on a dating show but I'd happily spend all night listening to him explain the Theory of Relativity or even the offside rule in football. He is one very sexy man.'

Bryony turned up the volume and both women watched Professor Potts talking about the importance of protecting elephants in the wild. Once it was over, Melinda turned off the set.

'I'd definitely trade in Sean for that man. He makes my toes tingle.'

Bryony laughed again. 'That's never going to happen. You and Sean are soulmates. I can't imagine you ever trading him in. You and he are great together.'

'We are, although some days I feel like I need an adventure – a whole new sexual adventure. A girl can dream, can't she?'

'Get a grip, woman. You two should spend more time together, without Freddie. Remind yourselves of what it was that attracted you to each other. Freddie arrived so quickly after you got together you didn't have many opportunities to enjoy life as a couple. Why not have a date night? I'll babysit Freddie for you.'

'You and your sensible suggestions. You're right, of course. We ought to light candles, play soft music and rip each other's clothes off with unbridled lust but to be honest we're both a bit tired these days. My mind is willing but my flesh is wobbly and not up for it. Talking of babysitting Freddie – he'll be staying over at my mum's at the weekend. He loves Granny Brigitte. She cooks him pancakes and lets him eat jelly beans. So, do you fancy coming around for booze, crisps and a bit of a murder mystery game?'

Bryony shook her head. 'Shouldn't you and Sean be enjoying some time together? Alone.'

'Nah, honestly we're fine. I'm crazy about Sean. And we see enough of each other. If I needed time away with him, I'd take it. The grandparents are always willing to have Freddie. It's me. I don't like parting with Freddie or being away from him.'

Bryony felt a small pang of envy. Although she didn't begrudge her friend any happiness, she would like to have experienced the same herself.

'A murder mystery night will do us both good. Sean bought me the game for Christmas. It'll give us the chance to open it at last. Go on. Remember the fun we had when we did them way back in Birmingham?'

'Okay. Why not?'

Melinda beamed at her. 'It'll be a hoot. Maybe I'll arrange it so I get to be the elegant lady of the manor who is looking for a bit of rough and passionate sex with the gardener. Don't worry, I'll make sure Sean is the gardener,' she added, shutting her eyes and tilting her head back, playing out her fantasy in her mind. 'He could be one of those beefcake sorts – strong, silent, muscular. I'm liking this idea already.'

'Is it a murder mystery night or a weird sexual fantasy version of events?'

Melinda ignored the comment and said, 'We could all do with a fun night. I'll phone around and arrange it. I'm sure I can rustle up a few guests at short notice. There's the new chap, Lewis, who moved in a couple of months ago.'

Bryony's mouth opened in surprise. 'You're trying to match me up with someone again, aren't you?'

Melinda giggled. 'Might be. And why not? You're young – thirty-six is still classified as young – free and single. He appears to be on his own too. He's renting number forty-one, the Shepherds' place. I've waved hello but not spoken to him. Sean met him at the gym a couple of weeks ago. They both like running, so Sean's enjoyed having someone to talk to while he jogs along on the treadmill. It makes the time go quicker. He says Lewis is a really good guy with a quirky sense of humour.'

'That's a good start. I bet he won't like me though. The last guy I went out with said I surrounded myself with an invisible, impenetrable force and I frightened him.'

'When you stop trying to do a million things at once, you might actually meet someone. You're always too occupied to get involved.'

Bryony pursed her lips but gave up the idea of arguing. Her friend was right. She wondered if she didn't deliberately keep herself occupied to avoid meeting men. She rubbed at her forehead, her fingers lightly grazing the scar there, hidden now by a fringe but still evident when her hair fell away from her face. 'Okay. Count me in for the party. I could do with a laugh.'

'Great! I'll get onto it immediately.'

Bryony sipped at her glass of wine. Freddie was singing along to the television. She allowed the feeling of homeliness to envelop her.

'I baked a cake for your dad,' said Melinda, after a moment. 'It should have cooled. I'll finish it off and then you can take it with you. You are going around this afternoon, aren't you?'

'Yes. I'll be able to see them more often now school's over.'

'You finished?'

'Tomorrow. I've got one last class and then that's me done until September. Which brings me onto the reason for dropping around. I want help with an application for a game show.'

'Really?'

'It might be a way to help me find Hannah.'

'Have you been sniffing whiteboard markers again?' said Melinda. 'How on earth are you going to manage to do that?'

'It's the first show of its kind and will attract thousands of viewers. You must have seen adverts for it on television – *What Happens in…*'

'It's *that* show! They've been showing those ads every night. It's all very mysterious. "The ultimate challenge and adventure,"' she said in a deep voice, quoting one of the voiceovers.

'That's the one. You know I told you Hannah was bonkers about game shows, well, I think she might watch it and I want to be on it. The trouble is I've left it a bit late and today's the last day for applications. I started to fill in the form online and got stuck. Can you help me?'

'You downloaded the application?'

Bryony rummaged in her bag and brought out a few sheets of A4. 'I spent ages last night staring at the screen trying to think of ways to make myself sound interesting enough for the producers to invite me along for audition but I couldn't, so I've printed off what I've written so far for you to check.'

'Hand it over.' Melinda took the form and read the title. '"Contestant Application for *What Happens in…*" It sounds exciting already. They give any clues what the show's actually going to be about?'

'It's all hush-hush. I only know it's an exciting new game show, unlike any other, for people who really want a challenge and to make a name for themselves.'

'That's pretty much the same as they say on the adverts for it. What have you put so far? Name, address – yadda-yadda-yadda. Ah, here we are. "Tell us some interesting facts about yourself?" And you've answered… I run an annual quiz at a private school. Are you for real?'

'What's wrong with that? The school quiz *is* my baby. This is a game show. I thought they'd like to know I enjoy quizzes.'

'Hell-lo!' Melinda put on an American accent. 'You can do far better than that. Give me that pen.'

'What are you writing?'

'That you dived with sharks, abseiled down the Shard dressed as a monkey, and sat in a tub of cold baked beans wearing only a bikini, for charity.'

'You think they'll be interested in that?'

'More than in you running a school quiz, yes. "Why do you think you'd be a good contestant?" Easy. "I am a quizzer and love anything that is game related. My best friend thinks I'd be perfect for the show as she says people will underestimate me and not realize I actually live up to my nickname of Miss Masterbrain." I reckon that'll get them curious about you.'

'Melinda, I can't write that. I sound like a complete show-off.'

'No, you don't. That's why I put "My best friend says…" You need to stand out from all the other thousands of applicants if you want to be on this show, so do as I suggest.'

'I can't.'

'Okay, I'll complete the online application for you.'

'No, don't do that.'

'Well, either you write word for word what I put down here, or I will. You know I will. In fact, I'm going to stand over your shoulder while you type it out. You can use my computer.' She pursed her lips and put her fists on her hips, reminding Bryony of the fierce little girl she'd once been. She grinned at her friend.

'Okay. You win.'

'Good. Now, what about this question, "Why do you want to be on the new gameshow *What Happens in…*?"'

'I struggled to answer that. Do you think I should tell them the truth?'

'Absolutely. You need a good story to get on it; something that will resonate with the producers and the public, like candidates on the *X-Factor* or similar who have sad stories to tell. You have to be truthful.'

'I thought something along the lines of, "I've been searching for my long-lost sister, Hannah, for many years. Last month our father had a serious stroke and is desperate to see her. I hope that, like me, Hannah still has a passion for quiz and gameshows and watches *What Happens in…* Being on the show might also give me a chance to make a nationwide appeal to the public and ask her to come home before it's too late." What do you think?'

'We'll rephrase it but yes. I think you need to be upfront about this. After all, it's the actual reason you're applying for the show.'

'I really don't know how best to phrase everything, even though I'm an English teacher. I need to get on this show and don't want to fall at the first hurdle. I don't want to screw up the application.'

'Don't worry. We'll make you sound like the most amazing, interesting contestant ever. So much so, they'll be desperate to have you audition. You told your folks about it?'

'I've only told you. I don't want to jinx it. There's no point in saying anything unless I make audition or more importantly, the actual show.'

'Fair enough. We'll keep it between ourselves for now. Right, let's big you up some more. Can't have you sounding the slightest bit dull.'

Bryony threw her friend a warm smile. 'Thanks, Melinda.'

'It's nothing. That's what friends are for.'

Bryony raised her glass. 'To friendship,' she said.

'To friendship, success, and lots and lots of wine,' replied Melinda, draining her glass.

Chapter Two

Bryony extracted the key from her handbag, unlocked the familiar front door and called out.

'In here,' came the reply. Geraldine Masters had once been a tall, elegant lady with golden-blonde hair swept back in a perfectly coiled bun. Time and events had taken their toll. Her mother's hair was now white and wispy. The bun was no longer neat and some errant strands had escaped to hang limply down her drawn face. Bryony noted her mother was becoming more wizened each time she visited. Fresh wrinkles had appeared on her once unblemished forehead and her eyes were bloodshot.

She stood in the kitchen, stirring a large pot of chicken soup. Steam curled above her head, bringing with it delicious aromas of lemon and tarragon that filled the room. Gurgling from her stomach reminded Bryony she had not eaten since breakfast, and had drunk nothing other than the wine at Melinda's. She placed the cake on the worktop.

'Melinda's baked a cake for you.'

'She's a sweet lady. Thank her for me. Her little boy is such a charmer, isn't he? He's growing up fast. I saw her in Derby the other day. They were shopping for new wellington boots for Freddie. You want some soup, love?' asked her mother, ever the carer; ever the strong woman who carried her husband through tough times.

'Later. I'll go and see how he is first.'

Her mother's eyes were red-rimmed with blue-grey smudges under them. Her face was drawn, worn out by fatigue. Bryony's heart ached. Her mother did not need any more sorrow in her life. She had suffered enough. 'How are you?' she asked gently.

'You know. Okay. The same. You know,' came the reply. Her mother emptied the soup into a cream-coloured bowl adorned with tulips, the pattern faded over years of use. Bryony looked about the familiar kitchen and her heart sank. It was also looking dated. The walls were in desperate need of a fresh coat of paint and the scrubbed worktops required updating, yet it only seemed a few years since they had all moved into the cottage in an attempt to start anew. Time was a cruel thief, robbing each of them of their youth and even their home of its energy and appeal.

Bryony held out her hands. 'Let me take it to him.'

Her mother handed her the bowl. 'He was awake all night. He was crying. I didn't know what to say to him.'

Silence filled the room; unspoken words flew between them then Bryony set the bowl down on the kitchen table and held her mother, who was choking back tears. After a few moments, her mother pulled away and dabbed at her swollen eyes. 'Thank you. It's hard to stay strong some days.'

'You're amazing,' said Bryony. 'You've always managed to support and look after us in spite of everything. This'll get easier. He'll get better. And I'll help you both.'

17

'There's only one person who can truly help him and I don't believe she is here any more. If she were, surely she would have been in touch by now. All these years. All these long years,' she said, wiping her eyes with the edge of her yellow gingham-checked apron – a gift from Bryony. 'Why wouldn't she try and get in contact?'

'I don't know,' said Bryony with a pang. Her mother was right. It was heartless to have made them all suffer like that. Another voice in her head whispered that Hannah had good reason not to find her way home. 'I'm still hopeful I'll be able to find her. I'll track her down. Don't give up hope, Mum. Sometimes, it's all we have.'

Her mother regarded her with soft, dove-grey eyes. 'No, I have more than hope. I have you.'

Bryony kissed her gently on the cheek and took the soup to her father. He was slumped in his usual chair, eyes open but unseeing, lost in a tangle of memories. His face twitched on hearing the door open and he turned his head towards the sound. Expectation flitted across his face, and in a reedy voice he asked, 'Hannah? Is it you?'

Bryony felt a familiar pain in her chest. She took a deep breath and in as normal a voice as she could muster replied kindly, 'No, Dad. Hannah isn't here. It's Bryony.'

The light in his eyes extinguished. He nodded dumbly and dewy-eyed, accepting his bowl of soup.

–

As her father dozed in the lounge, Bryony sat with her mother in the kitchen. A frail figure, pale veined hands cupping her teacup, she poured out her concerns to her daughter.

'The speech therapist worked with him again this morning but he's still slurring his words so badly, I can barely understand him. He gets frustrated when no one can comprehend what he's saying and then angry. I don't know how to handle it when he's like that. I'm scared it'll bring on another stroke and this time it'll be a fatal one. I want him to get better so much. Oh, Bryony, what if he doesn't?'

'He'll make it, Mum,' said Bryony softly. 'You've both been through bad stuff before and survived.'

'He's not as strong as he used to be, and he's become so confused. You can see that. He talks endlessly about her. He asks when she's going to visit. I don't know whether to tell him Hannah left years ago.'

'Maybe it would be best not to. At least give me some more time to see if I can find her. I've got my blog for her and the page on Facebook. I keep hoping somebody who knows her will see them, or she will and get in touch.'

'I don't understand how that works. I know what these sites are but I can't see how it might get Hannah back.'

'It's along the idea of putting up a lost and found poster but you do it on social media rather than actually putting up posters. It worked for a friend of a friend's dog. Hector was stolen from her front garden but the police couldn't do anything. His owner – Lexi – set up a page and asked her clients to share it. By the end of the first day it had been shared by hundreds of people, including some England rugby players and Ant and Dec, who tweeted about it to their thousands of followers. The newspapers got hold of the story and so did GMTV, who invited Lexi onto the show to share her story and to ask viewers to look out for Hector. A couple of days later, two people turned up at Lexi's house with her dog. The thought was that whoever had taken Hector had been frightened off by all the publicity and abandoned him. It's surprising who knows who on social media, and once something like that gathers sufficient momentum, it really attracts the attention of the press.'

'The press was involved before and it made no difference.'

'That was the local press. I'm aiming for national press and maybe even coverage on nationwide television. If the right person gets involved in this, then it'll work.'

'I'm sorry, love, but I don't think you're right. I don't want to hurt your feelings but you're being naïve or probably placing too much trust in this approach. I can't imagine an old forgotten case of a sixteen-year-old who ran away thirty years ago, would cause a sensation. It didn't attract sufficient attention when we tried to find her even back then because lots of young girls and boys run away – too many. Some don't even leave goodbye notes like Hannah did. She wasn't forced to leave, or kidnapped or—' Her mother stopped, anger making her voice rise. She continued, resignation softening her words, 'She upped and left and hasn't contacted us since and although for many, many years I hoped she would, I now think she might not even be alive. I appreciate you want to help your father but you've set yourself an impossible task.' She sighed, a sound filled with heartache and sorrow. 'I drove her away. I should have been there for her when she needed me. I believed she was a normal teenager with moods and quirky behaviour and I didn't spot the signs she was unhappy. She never hinted there was any real problem. I failed her, Bryony. She obviously couldn't talk to me, and for that I blame myself. I was far too wrapped up in work and your father's career. I was so intent on supporting him, I failed my daughter.' She stopped again. This time the tears trickled down her face, down the creases that had recently appeared.

Bryony had borne witness to her mother's suffering and her father's decline over the years. At first, both of them had believed Hannah would walk back into their lives. Derek Masters had kept up the appearance required of an important headmaster at a large school. He taught his sixth form classes and ran his school like a tight ship, but as time passed and it became increasingly unlikely that Hannah would return home, cracks in his demeanour appeared.

The police had written Hannah off as a runaway. After all, she had left a note saying she was leaving and had taken some personal belongings with her, and they did not consider the possibility that she might have been abducted. Her parents were less convinced and had hired two detectives at different times to track down Hannah. Neither detective found evidence she was alive. Hannah had simply vanished.

Both her mother and father eventually began to fear the worst – that their daughter was dead. Her father could no longer maintain his front. The responsibility of looking after 400 children, ensuring their well-being and educa-tion when he could not look after his own daughter, was too much to bear. Worry ate away at him and eventually he had the breakdown that saw what was left of their fractured family move to a village outside of Derby and where he was confined to the house for many months with Geraldine caring for him.

Once he began to mend, Hannah's name was mentioned less often. Gradually, her mother's tears dried up and she took employment in a local hospice where she helped care for those who were terminally ill by reading to them or visiting and chatting with them.

Bryony too erased the painful memories that followed her sister's departure, although on occasion, she would stop dead in the street, convinced she had spotted her sister – another woman with blonde hair and grey eyes – and scurry after them only to recognize at the last moment that she had made a mistake.

Bryony buried her self-reproach deep within herself. She studied hard. She went to university, made some new friends and lived a life without her sister. Each time the memories rose to the surface she drove them back, although sometimes she would shed a tear with Melinda. The year before, she'd suddenly decided to look once more for Hannah. She'd begun the quest, set up the blog and hoped, but then in March, her father had suffered a serious stroke and suddenly it became imperative to find her sister.

Bryony held her mother's hand and squeezed gently. She felt the acrid taste in her mouth as guilt stirred in her stomach. Her mother wasn't at fault. Nor was her dominating, demanding father. She knew there was only one person to blame for Hannah's leaving, and that was Bryony.

Chapter Three

'Searching for Hannah'

Dear Hannah,

Today I finished work at lunchtime. I only had one group of children to teach. Because I mostly teach examination-year classes, I find myself free quite often this time of year. The GCSE and A-level students have left school and it feels odd without them.

One pupil who shall remain anonymous here, a tricky individual renowned for disrupting classes, completed William Golding's Lord of the Flies and actually enjoyed it. He stayed behind after class to tell me it was the first book he had liked and asked if I thought there were any more books like that he could try. Little achievements such as this make my job as a teacher worthwhile. I can see why our parents loved teaching so much.

I borrowed a copy of Albert Camus' L'Étranger from the French department to read. I haven't tried any of his works before. I wonder if you have kept up your French and still speak it. Sometimes, when I shut my eyes, I imagine I am listening to your sweet voice singing 'Frère Jacques' as you did when you sang me to sleep some nights when I was frightened.

After school, I visited my good friend, Melinda, whose suggestion it was that I write this blog. She wondered if you'd ever try to search for me or look me up, and pointed out that one of the most obvious ways in this age of technology would be to Google my name, in which case you'd find this blog and the Facebook page I've set up for you. Since then, I've tried hunting for you on various social media sites and used numerous search engines, but only drawn blanks. You don't seem to have any online presence, at least not as Hannah Masters.

Anyway, Melinda is planning a murder mystery dinner party for the weekend. I'm to play the character of Tilly Poole, an unmarried twenty-nine-year-old kitchen hand who works in a top restaurant. I'll have to borrow one of mum's aprons and wear a dark skirt. I hope I don't have to cook. That's something I'm no good at.

Melinda helped me with something this afternoon which I hope will lead me to you. It's a crazy idea I came up with, but if I manage to pull it off, it might bring you back to us. I'll tell you more about it if it comes to fruition.

Dad continues to make progress but it's frustrating for him and he asks for you repeatedly. If only you would read this blog and understand how much you mean to us all, Hannah. Mum and I aren't sure if he will make a continued recovery and are anxious he'll suffer another even more serious

stroke. He needs to see you, Hannah. He needs
to see you soon.
  I fervently hope you read this and contact me.
  Hannah, I love you and miss you every day.
  Please come home.
  Your loving sister, Bryony

Bryony read the post again and published it. She'd set up the blog a few months before her father's stroke, and although it had attracted visitors, it had yet to attract Hannah.

In the early years, her parents had tried more conventional routes to find Hannah. They'd contacted journalists, given interviews on local television and hired detectives. Each fruitless attempt drained her parents further and Bryony watched their optimism ebb. Initially, she too had believed Hannah would return home but as time went by, Bryony began to hate her sister for abandoning them and causing such pain. In the end, she shut off from her emotions and continued life without giving her too much thought.

Her father's stroke had jolted Bryony into further action. She'd made efforts before but now she had to undertake a more determined effort and was intent on seeking alternative ways that might help locate her sister, should she still be alive. Hence the idea of applying for *What Happens in…* Bryony was pinning much on getting onto the new game show. Truth was, she was rapidly running out of alternative ideas and ways to track down Hannah and now she was running out of time.

Chapter Four

Saturday, 8 July – Evening

The black dress hadn't been worn for some time and Bryony was surprised at how short it was. She tugged at it, willing the hem to cover her knees, but it stayed firmly halfway up her thighs. She should have checked before the evening. There had been enough time for her to buy a new one. She tied the frilly white apron over it and decided she looked more like a maid than a kitchen hand. She removed it with a huff of annoyance and attached a plain cream apron instead. That would have to do. With a bit of luck no one would notice how short the skirt was and they'd all get so drunk they wouldn't care about how silly they all looked.

Melinda flounced into the kitchen wearing a large hat and a coat with the collar turned up and carrying a notepad and pen. Bryony looked her up and down but couldn't work out the outfit.

'I give up.'

'I'm Jessica Snobbs, a food critic. I write for an important newspaper – my column is "The Golden Grub" – and whatever I say goes. Chefs are scared witless of me. I have a formidable reputation, and tonight I shall be dining at Chez Vincent.'

'Why the hat? I didn't think food critics wore hats.'

'I thought it made me look important. It was that or a monocle.'

Bryony guffawed.

'I didn't allow enough time for the event. This is all I had upstairs. I could hardly wear my Agent Provocateur knickers, or my everyday comfy outfit of tracksuit bottoms and baggy top. If you think I look bad, wait until you see what Sean's wearing. I've never seen a chef dressed like him.'

'Where is Sean? Is he getting ready?'

'He took Freddie to Granny Brigitte's house an hour ago. He should be back soon. He'd better be. The others will be arriving in ten minutes. I've invited the neighbours – Tina and James. They're a nice couple. They usually keep to themselves but were quite keen to come along. I don't think they go out much. Tina's an artist and works at home most of the time. I don't know what James does but he can't work far away. He dons Lycra shorts and cycles there each morning.' She rolled her eyes. 'I've prepared the first course. It's my speciality – 'pâté maison' and toast. After we've eaten it, we'll get the murder mystery game board out and find out what happens next. I hope I don't get bumped off. It'll mean I'll have to lie on the floor while Sean ruins the second course. It's steak and he always overcooks it.'

'It'll be fine. You can supervise from the floor. Pretend you're the voice from the grave.'

'Or the voice from the gravy,' Melinda suggested, earning a groan from her friend. 'There's six of us in total. Should make for a giggle.'

'Is Lewis coming?'

Spotting the glint in her friend's eyes, Melinda said, 'He is. But I have bad news. I'm afraid he's not your type.'

'How can you say that? He might be. He might be exactly my type.'

'No, sweetie. Lewis has been pretty cagey about his love life but I pestered Sean to find out more about him. He knows I'm always on the hunt for suitable singletons to invite to dinner to meet you. Sean's not as good as me at extracting information but he did discover that Lewis isn't keen to get involved in another relationship at the moment. He's recovering from a bitter split with his partner of five years who walked out on him for another man. It was completely unexpected and knocked Lewis for six. He's sworn off relationships for the time being.'

'That's very sad but surely, given time, he'll get over it and—'

Melinda shook her head. 'I'm not explaining this very well. His partner's name was *Maxwell*,' she added by way of explanation.

'Maxwell,' Bryony repeated. She furrowed her eyebrows, a fake attempt at dismay. 'Alas! Maybe he isn't my type after all. Shame. I was looking forward to getting to know him.'

'You can get to know him. You just can't get drunk and drape yourself over the poor man and try to play tonsil tennis with him. You'd scare him rigid.'

'I wouldn't ever do that!' protested Bryony, flushing deeply.

Melinda chuckled. 'I know you wouldn't. You're far too well-mannered for that sort of behavior, drunk or not. If you did go wild, I'd be the first to try and capture it all on video and post it onto YouTube for your students to snigger at.' She laughed at the expression on her friend's face. 'You old prude! Maybe you *should* let yourself go once in a while. Not with Lewis though. I'll have to go back on the hunt for you since you're hopeless at the whole dating game thing. Fancy a glass of wine? Sean was unsupervised at the supermarket and bought loads of plonk. There are some bottles of Hungarian red out in the utility room. Knowing Sean, it'll be a super-strength, brain-numbing vintage that cost next to nothing. We can uncork a couple and let them breathe.'

'I am not prudish. I'm merely reserved, shy, and even a little old-fashioned. I can be a goer when I'm with the right person.'

Melinda smiled at her friend. 'I know that. I shared a flat with you, remember? I'm only kidding. There's nothing wrong with you at all except you're a bit shy in front of potential hunky dates. I have a totally different approach to sharing a man. I'm all for launching myself at him and making sure he can't get away.'

Bryony laughed. 'Poor Sean. You certainly had plenty of practice getting boyfriends in the good old days behind the bike sheds.'

'Oh yes, it was *the* place to hang at break and lunchtimes. If you hadn't been such a goody-goody you could have joined us.'

'Yeah, I'd have been a huge hit, wouldn't I? There wasn't a boy there who'd have wanted to be seen with "Frankenstein's other monster". Besides it was the only chance I got to sit down quietly with a book while you lot were being rebellious outside.'

'It's amazing what you can learn in a library, especially when you have it all to yourself. I certainly learnt a thing or two in that school library and I don't mean from books,' mused Melinda.

Bryony chuckled. 'You naughty girl. Who'd have thought you'd have turned out to be such a responsible citizen?'

'That's because I had you as a friend. You made me mend my errant ways. I only played up at school when others in the class were messing about. It was easier to be one of the gang than to be an outsider.'

'Don't I know it?' Bryony added quietly. 'Right, you flirt, I'll fetch that wine.'

Bryony walked to the utility room at the back of the kitchen and flung open the door, turning to face her friend and continue the conversation when something caught her eye. Her hands flew to her mouth and a muffled gasp escaped. Slumped on the floor of the pantry was the body of a man, his eyes open in fear, mouth distorted. A trickle of blood ran down the side of his head. Bryony slammed the door shut and screamed.

–

'I'm sorry, pumpkin,' said Sean, a devilish Cheshire Cat grin on his face. He put out a meaty paw to rub his wife's shoulder. Square-shouldered and muscular from weight-lifting, Sean looked most un-chef like in a long, striped butcher's apron and a baseball cap and shorts. His round face was clean-shaven and his eyes sparkled with energy.

Melinda tasered him with a look before saying, 'You should have known better.'

'It was only a bit of fun. I thought you'd both find it hilarious.' He waggled his heavy eyebrows.

Melinda fought back a smile. 'We might have done if it hadn't been so damn convincing. My heart is still hammering.'

Lewis grinned winningly. 'I was pretty convincing, wasn't I?' He winked at Bryony.

'Don't push it,' she growled assiduously, avoiding his eye. Lewis Scott was now standing in front of her; his tall frame leaning against a kitchen worktop, hands splayed behind him. She noted his clean clipped fingernails and elegant fingers – the hands of an artist or pianist. She studied his relaxed pose and cursed her stupidity. A dribble of crimson make-up ran down one side of his head. It had been applied crudely and she wondered how she had been taken in. Screaming was out of character for her and now she felt rather ridiculous in spite of the sisterly support from Melinda.

She looked Lewis over, drawn to his topaz-brown eyes. They were clear and luminous. Under the strong light in the kitchen they were dark gold in colour and, fringed by long black eyelashes, were very beautiful. His angular face sported a hint of stubble. Physically he embodied everything Bryony liked in a man – a muscular body that was not too fat and yet not too lean, long legs and dark, naturally wavy hair that reminded her of Gerard Butler. She looked up again to study his face. A smile played at the corners of his mouth. His easy manner was infectious. She turned towards Sean, who now looked like a scolded puppy, and conceded defeat. To be fair, the men had pulled off the stunt with aplomb. She thumped Sean good-naturedly on the arm.

'You win. I fell for it. You convinced two hardened, wise women with your act. Be warned though, at some point I shall be sorely tempted to retaliate.'

Lewis gave a mock bow. 'I accept your challenge.'

'Twit,' muttered Melinda, wagging her finger at her husband.

He kissed her on the cheek then chuckled and said, 'I don't know about "wise women". You were so busy jawing you didn't hear the van pull up or us sneaking through the back door and hiding in the utility room.'

'Quit while you're ahead,' warned Bryony.

'Yes, or I might hide your little choo choo set,' Melinda added.

Lewis struggled to suppress a grin.

'It's my son's set,' Sean said by way of explanation.

'It may be Freddie's but that doesn't explain why you were in the spare room playing with it while he was watching television.'

Sean shrugged it off. 'I wasn't playing with it. I thought Freddie was going to return and so I was keeping it going for him.'

Melinda snorted. 'Lewis, I hope you appreciate what you've let yourself in for. It's going to be a mad night. And we haven't started on the Hungarian red yet.'

Lewis stretched to his full height and smiled. 'Sean warned me it could get crazy here at times when you got together but I thought it sounded a lot of fun. Hope I got the costume right.' He whipped out a soft white baseball cap and a black striped apron from his back pocket where they had been hidden. 'I watched a cookery show and this seemed to be the sort of gear chefs wear. I found the apron hanging on the back of the Shepherds' kitchen door.'

Melinda smiled. Lewis was wearing white jeans and a white shirt, which looked freshly washed and ironed.

'You look spot on. This, everyone, is Georges the sous-chef.'

'Georges is my sous-chef. This is beginning to get interesting,' said Sean. 'So, Lewis, I mean, Georges, let's see how you feel about us all later this evening after Melinda's bossed you about and somebody is dead on the sitting room floor.'

The doorbell rang out, interrupting the banter.

'I'll get it. It'll be Tina and James. Action stations, people. Time to get into character. And Sean, behave yourself,' called Melinda as she left the others to answer the door.

'Of course, my little commandant,' Sean replied once she was out of earshot. He turned and spoke to Bryony, 'I notice she didn't tell you to behave.'

'No, she didn't, did she?' replied Bryony thoughtfully before grabbing and brandishing a wooden spoon. 'So, watch out! I have a weapon and I'm not afraid to use it. On either of you,' she added, fixing Lewis with a look.

He threw his arms up in the air. 'Save me, Sean. We have a crazy chefette in the kitchen.'

'Mate, you're on your own. Every man for himself,' he shouted, running to the other end of the room. 'I warned you these two were lunatics.'

Chapter Five

'Searching for Hannah'

Dear Hannah,

What a crazy night I had last night. I went to the murder mystery party at Melinda's house as planned. She had a board game version of several plots and had chosen one set in a restaurant. It was a complete laugh from start to finish. This one was set in a restaurant called Chez Vincent and involved the murder of a chef. I played the part of a kitchen hand who is terrified of the volatile chef and who is fired for burning the cakes. James, who played an ex-con employed to wash up, was actually the murderer and 'stabbed' the chef with an extremely sharp Sabatier chef's knife belonging to Georges, the sous-chef, played by Lewis, a new neighbour.

Lewis is cool and we had a crazy few minutes messing about in the kitchen, behaving like kids and then had such a laugh.

Sean (who played a very convincing bad-tempered chef) was murdered after the first course. He went to get some wine and after a while we decided he had been gone too long. We discovered him lying in the kitchen with a knife by his side and blood on his apron. Don't worry. It was fake blood. We dragged him back to the lounge so he could hear us then we had to work out who had murdered him and why. To be honest, after the second course and several bottles of wine, no one could remember who they were supposed to be and we all kept dissolving into giggles.

Lewis played his part brilliantly although he spoke his lines like a character in the television show 'Allo, 'Allo! Sean and I kept sniggering at him. Sean got told off by Melinda because he was supposed to be dead but kept snorting with laughter. Lewis shrugged his shoulders in mock Gallic annoyance at the questions we asked him, and when he went into a panic about losing his 'leetle sharp kneeves', none of us could keep a straight face. He was most entertaining.

Lewis had to rush off afterwards but he's going to come to Melinda's next party. She's planning another one for a few weeks' time.

Tomorrow, I've got the important audition in Birmingham. Cross your fingers for me.

If you are reading this, Hannah, please, please contact me.

Your loving sister, Bryony

Once she'd published her post, she reread the email she'd received the day after submitting her application to *What Happens in…*

Dear Bryony,

Thank you for applying to be a contestant on the fabulous new game show, What Happens in…

We are very pleased to be able to invite you to an audition for the show. This will in take place on Monday 10th July 12:00 p.m. at the Royal Theatre, Broad Street, Birmingham.

We look forward to seeing you there.

Kind regards,

Laura Perry Producer, What Happens in…

There was no further information about the show in her email and she studied the advert on the game show website for clues as to what might be expected of her:

Are you a quizzer? Do you like challenges?
Are you better than the rest?
We are urgently seeking lively contestants for a brand new, game show – What Happens in…
This show takes place over several days and will be unlike any other quiz show on television.
Only the best will remain and go onto the next challenge and ultimately win the prize of
£10,000!
Filming takes place in France in July.
Have you got the brains to take on this exciting new quiz? Then apply now.

She read it again even though she knew what it said by heart. There was nothing to help her prepare for the audition. She'd have to rely on intelligence and enthusiasm. Bryony wouldn't be there for the same reasons as the other contestants. She wasn't interested in winning the loot. She had a greater prize in mind – finding Hannah – and being on a game show that was going to be broadcast day after day on national television might just help her do that.

Chapter Six

Monday, 10 July – Morning

The train drew into Birmingham New Street station, releasing a bad-tempered wheeze as it came to a standstill. Passengers fidgeted by the doors, waiting for the green light to illuminate and allow them to escape. Doors flung open and people were propelled from the stuffy carriages. Bryony, sandwiched between a large gent wearing a three-piece suit and a woman in killer heels whose skirt barely covered her backside, tumbled out onto the platform and joined the crowds racing to the exit to begin their day. The audition started at nine and she had calculated the journey by taxi would only take ten minutes. She followed the signs to the taxi rank. Outside, rain poured from the leaden skies. A sea of umbrellas filled her vision and her heart sank. A queue of at least 100 men snaked along the pavement in front of her. She joined the end and checked her watch. Only thirty minutes remained. The people in the queue shuffled forward one space.

'Excuse me? Why are there so many men here?' she asked the four men in front of her. They gave her a bemused look that suggested she really ought to know the reason they were waiting. 'Cricket, love. It's the 20/20 match at Edgbaston.'

'In this weather?'

'It's only a shower,' replied the man. 'It's supposed to clear up according to the forecast.'

His colleague intervened. 'If you need to get to work, I'd phone in and let them know you'll be late. We've been here thirty minutes already.'

'I have to get to an audition,' she continued, her brain thinking over the possibilities open to her.

'What sort of audition?' asked the man, interest flickering in his eyes as he tried to place Bryony.

'For a new game show.'

The man's interest faded. He was obviously not talking to a celebrity. 'I'd walk to it if I were you. It'd be quicker than hanging about here. Good luck.'

She thanked him and darted away from the queue, punching the address into Google Maps on her mobile phone as she scurried down the road. If she ran, she might make it in time. The thought didn't appeal. Running was definitely not her strong point.

Bryony squelched through puddles and scooted between people as she sprinted towards the theatre. Every few minutes, she checked her progress. It was hopeless in the rain. Large raindrops plopped onto the mobile's screen and made it almost impossible to see the route. She drew a deep breath. The British weather was not going to get the better of her. She shouldered her bag and jogged towards the library. By the time she reached the park behind it her breath was coming in ragged gasps. She slowed to a trot and ploughed on, uncomfortable in her wet shoes – her best ones – that had filled with water. The familiar pain in her hip was becoming noticeable. She would pay for this folly later. She rubbed at it and threw a glance at her phone. It was not much further. She thought of the reason she was auditioning and dragged onwards, trousers splattered with brown water, hair plastered to her head.

The theatre came into sight at last. She slowed to catch her breath, arrived at the front door and entered the building. The entrance was filled with hopeful candidates for the show. Men and women of all ages looked up as she stood in the foyer, rain dripping from her jacket and puddling around her feet.

'Hi,' she said to no one in particular. 'It appears to be raining cats and dogs and I think I might have stepped in a poodle,' she added, earning a few smiles. A girl in her twenties approached, her face welcoming and bright.

She studied a clipboard. 'You must be Bryony Masters?'

Bryony nodded, aware of the looks she was now attracting.

'We were about to cross you off the list as a no-show. Bad journey?' the girl asked.

'You could say that. There were no taxis and I had to do an impression of Usain Bolt to get here on time,' mumbled Bryony as her eyes lighted on a grinning face she recognized. *What's Lewis doing here?* He was leaning against a wall chatting to a slim young man with ramrod posture, lean physique, coffee-brown eyes and pale blonde hair. There was an aura of a matinée idol about Lewis's companion, even dressed as he was in a baby-pink jumper and jeans. Lewis twiddled his fingers at her before saying something to the young man who looked up and also waved at her. She returned the gesture and turned her attention to the girl; her name badge stated she was 'Laura Perry – Assistant Producer'.

'Laura, would you mind if I nipped to the toilet to dry off a bit? I'm in danger of flooding the entrance at the moment,' she added, pointing at the damp footprints she had trailed in.

'Go ahead. We're still setting up, so sign in at reception, collect your name badge and get sorted out. It's horrible when you run late, isn't it? We left at four this morning to get here and we're not ready. I need to get a photo of you.'

Laura manoeuvred Bryony against the far wall and snapped her camera before Bryony could protest.

'It's only for identification purposes. No one important will see it.' Laura showed her the image.

'Thank goodness it won't be my next passport photo,' replied Bryony with a grimace. 'Although, it might be an improvement on the one I currently have.'

Laura's lips twitched upwards. 'You look fine. Honestly. See you in a few minutes.' She disappeared through a door marked 'Private'. The wannabe contestants resumed their conversations. Bryony squelched to the toilet where she struck a contorted pose and attempted to dry her hair under the hand dryer. It was hopeless. There was little warm air and the dryer kept shutting off. She gave up and ran her fingers through her flaxen locks, trying to lift them from her crown. They adopted a tousled, fresh-out-of-bed look. Her mascara had run slightly so she had smoky, smudged eyes adding to the effect that she had only recently tumbled out from under the duvet after a night of hot sex – *if only!* Hopefully her intellect would see her through this process and the producers would ignore her looks. She patted the insides of her shoes with some scrunched-up toilet roll and sighed. They were ruined. Her hip throbbed. She wondered for the umpteenth time if she was doing the right thing by auditioning. A tapping at the door alerted her to the fact she needed to get a move on. Outside stood a middle-aged woman in an ill-fitting black dress over which she wore a leather biker's jacket. The effect was spoiled by the evident bulges of undergarments that squeezed her stomach so tightly it ballooned under her breasts, making her appear to be wearing several small tyres around her midriff. Her hair had been expertly cut into a short, severe style that did not suit her lean face, and the black-framed glasses she wore accentuated her sallow complexion.

'Sorry to disturb you. I need a pee. I'm so nervous and my Spandex is squishing my bladder. I think I bought a size too small. This is the fifth time I've had to go to the loo since I left home. Do you mind?'

'It's not a problem. I'm done.'

Bryony returned to the entrance and attached her name badge. As soon as it was fixed in place, she started towards Lewis but felt a light tap on her shoulder. She turned to face the woman who had scurried into the toilets.

'Can I ask you something?' asked the woman. 'Do you think I've captured the Helen Mirren look?'

Bryony smiled and politely responded, 'That's who you reminded me of.'

The woman beamed at her. 'Yes. I bought this outfit especially for the audition and I had my hair cut at a top salon. It cost a fortune. It'll be worth it when they select me to go through. It was my husband who remarked on my resemblance to Dame Helen. Have you heard the latest? The presenter is going to be Anneka Rice? I'll need a few more outfits I think for the actual show if I'm going to be standing near her. She's so glamorous.'

'Really?' Bryony's pulse beat faster. Hannah had loved watching Anneka in the 80s.

'I overheard the producers discussing it. I think it's supposed to be a secret for now, so don't say anything to anyone. I do admire Anneka Rice.' She tugged at her skirt. 'Sure I look okay?'

'You look very nice. I wish I'd made as much effort,' replied Bryony, who was wearing dark blue jeans and a checked red shirt she had owned for a few years. If the producers were looking for stylish people in flash outfits, they wouldn't choose her. Bryony had already noted the woman in a slinky red dress with skyscraper red heels. She was far more striking than Bryony, as was the girl with purple hair and the lady who was wearing a trouser suit and striped tie. The non-look-a-like Helen Mirren suddenly became talkative and insisted on telling Bryony how much she knew about literature and nature. Bryony was itching to get away and talk to Lewis but couldn't escape from her.

She was relieved when Laura reappeared and invited them in for the audition and she could get rid of the woman at last. Those who were seated stood as one and shuffled after Laura like obedient sheep, leaving behind an atmosphere of damp clothes mixed with anticipation, nervousness and excitement. Lewis and the young man drew level with her, and Lewis halted in front of her.

'Good luck, Lewis,' said the man. 'And you, Bryony,' he added, glancing at her name tag. She detected a transat-lantic drawl.

'You too, Oscar.'

The young man rushed ahead to catch up with those in front. Lewis trailed behind with Bryony.

'I certainly didn't expect to see you here. I see you ditched the idea of wearing the cute kitchen maid's outfit for the audition?'

'Yeah. I decided to go for the drowned rat look instead. How come you managed to dodge the rain?'

'I took one look at that ridiculous queue for taxis and worked out I'd be late if I waited in it, so I was a bit naughty, walked back inside the train station to where the taxis drop off, flagged one down and asked the driver to bring me here. I told him it was very urgent and he let me jump in there rather than join the queue outside.'

Bryony mentally kicked herself. She should have done the same.

'Ever auditioned for a game show before?'

'No, it's my first one,' she replied.

'I know quite a few people who've done this,' he whispered. 'A word of advice – don't try too hard to answer the questions correctly. They're not looking for geniuses. If you know the answers, deliberately get one or two of the questions wrong and make a real show of disappointment when they reveal the answer. They're searching for the most entertaining contestants not clever clogs ones. It isn't *Mastermind* or *University Challenge*.'

'Oh. Okay. Thanks for the advice. I could do with some help to get through,' she replied.

'Also try to be enthusiastic and unique. It's good to be dissimilar to the other participants. Although it might be a good idea not to chase anyone around the room brandishing a wooden spoon, even if they enjoy it,' he added as an afterthought, a smile tugging at his lips. 'Stay animated, talk to the crew and most importantly, be yourself.'

'That will surely make them discount me.'

'Far from it. Break a leg,' he murmured with a conspiratorial wink as they entered a large conference room. Chairs lined the room on one side while a team of three people – two young women and a man – sat opposite them. It looked like the biggest group interview Bryony had ever seen. She took a seat in the middle. The woman in the leather jacket dropped down beside her.

'Hi again. I'm so excited. My husband assured me I would be brilliant at this quiz. What do you know about geography? That's my weakest area of knowledge. If it's a question about countries or television shows then I'm going to be stumped. I tried learning about the characters of all the soap operas because that sort of thing always comes up, doesn't it? Oh, I forgot to introduce myself. I'm Daphne.'

Bryony wished the woman would let her gather her thoughts.

'Hi Daphne. I'm Bryony,' she responded, pointing to her badge. The woman laughed nervously. Again, Laura came to the rescue.

'My apologies for the delay in getting started today. So, welcome to you all. I'm Laura. Sitting next to me is Jackson and hidden behind a pile of application forms is Helena. We're part of the production team and have been out and about all month interviewing potential candidates for the fantastic game show *What Happens in…*'

A man in his early forties with a neatly trimmed ginger moustache and dressed in a shirt and trousers that looked to be two sizes too large for him cheered.

'Congratulations on being selected for this audition. We've been inundated with applications, so to get to this position is an achievement in itself. Unfortunately, we won't be able to choose you all, so if you don't get through today, please keep checking your emails as we might choose you for a show at a later date.' Laura turned to Helena for a moment.

Daphne nudged Bryony. 'Some of these people don't look like they know very much about anything,' she hissed. 'I reckon I'll ace it.' Bryony ignored her. Lewis was looking relaxed, his arm casually draped over the back of his chair as he listened to the bug-eyed lady, who was leaning into him and talking in a hushed whisper.

Laura nodded to Helena and continued, 'We'll start by asking you to say a little about yourselves and what you'd do if you won any money. Keep it short, sharp and punchy. Try and pretend you're at the start of show and the host is asking you to introduce yourselves. I'll get the ball rolling for you.' She gave a cough, stood tall and spoke. 'I'm Laura, twenty-eight, from London. I'm the assistant producer on the fabulous game show *What Happens in...* I enjoy watching football even though I'm a Crystal Palace supporter and have had to suffer a few disappointments. I'd use any winnings for a down payment on a flat, although with house prices as high as they are in London, I'll probably need to go on every quiz show there is and win all of them.'

There were a few titters in the room. 'So, we'll go from right to left and begin with Debbie. Please stand up, Debbie, and tell us about yourself.'

Debbie rose and tugged at her red silk dress that sat snugly on her lithe frame. Bracelets jangled on her arm as she wafted her perfectly manicured hands nervously.

'I'm Debbie. I'm thirty-six. Actually, I'll be thirty-seven tomorrow. I'm a beautician and I live in Sutton Coldfield. I have two teenage children and I like... I like...' Debbie looked about anxiously. 'Horse riding and yoga. I would spend any money on a new horse. Mine is getting too old to ride,' she continued then sat down.

'Thank you, Debbie. Jim?'

A man in his sixties rose, standing to attention as he spoke. 'Good morning. My name is James, known to everyone as Jim. I'm retired now but I used to be in the army. I was in the catering corps and I still enjoy cooking today. I'm a whiz at making Yorkshire puddings and roast beef. I don't have any hobbies unless you count looking after two grandchildren every afternoon as a hobby. And yes, I'd spend all my winnings on them.'

There were a few more laughs. The next contestant rose. It was the beautiful young man who had been talking to Lewis in the lobby.

'I'm Oscar, from America, New York, but now living in London. I should have been at the London audition but I'm performing in Birmingham so these kind people let me come here today. I'm a professional ballet dancer. I have a little pug dog named after the late American rapper Biggie Smalls. My Biggie Smalls has his own Facebook page, Instagram and Twitter accounts, so I post about what he's been doing. He's very trendy and enjoys posing in hats, jumpers and jewellery, so I'll spend anything I win on buying him new outfits to wear for his fans.' Oscar bowed and sat down.

Bryony zoned out and wondered what exactly she would say. The room became very small as she felt pulled back in time. Back to the day of the accident that changed their lives…

–

It's so sunny it's like someone has turned on a lamp outside. She squints as Hannah holds her hand and pulls her to the gate. They're going to the park. Hannah is in a bad mood.

'You're such a brat,' she says. 'You always get your own way because you've been ill. I didn't want to take you to the park and now I have to.'

Bryony doesn't feel guilty. Hannah often gets cross with her when she has to look after her and soon gets out of her bad mood.

Hannah is very irritated. She won't even look at Bryony as they go down the path but Bryony doesn't mind. Hannah will cheer up when they get to the park. Bryony is wearing her new duffle coat. It's sunny but it's cold outside and the air nips at her nose and her eyes, making them run. Mummy made sure she tied Bryony's scarf on properly in case it blows off. She doesn't want Bryony to get ill again. Bryony has been off school too much recently, recovering from an illness that has left her struck by another condition – one that makes her twitch and her muscles jerk uncontrollably. She can't afford to catch a chill on top of all her other problems.

As they leave the house, Rob rounds the corner and Hannah slows to a reluctant halt, grumbling, 'That's all I need. It's your fault, Bryony. If I'd stayed inside he wouldn't have dared talk to me.'

He's wearing a beanie hat and the collar of his coat is turned up. He puts out a hand, rests it on Hannah's shoulder. 'We need to talk,' he says.

Bryony forced the memory into the back of her mind. Panic rose in her chest and she struggled to fight it. She could do this. She ought to try and be witty. The truth alone was not going to get her on the show. Before she knew it, she had returned to the present and Daphne was standing up. She tugged at her jacket.

'I'm Daphne, a head teacher from Nottingham. I'm a member of a local quiz team called "The Head Teachers". I'd spend any winnings on a new kitchen for my house. It needs updating.' She sat down looking very pleased with herself.

Bryony got to her feet. 'Hi everyone. I'm Bryony, from Derby. I enjoy murdering people.' There was a gasp then someone sniggered. Bryony smiled. 'For the record, only at murder mystery parties. I also like tackling challenges that scare me so I've abseiled down the Shard and earlier this year I dived with sharks – they're quite scary although the sight of me in a mask and a wetsuit might have given them a shock too.' There were some more chuckles. 'I'm searching for my sister who ran away from home years ago and I'm hoping she'll watch the show, see me and get in contact. Our father is very ill and we need her to return.' The room went quiet and Bryony wondered if she'd just said the wrong thing. She aimed at levity again. 'If I won any money, I'd spend my winnings on some new shoes,' she added, looking down at hers. They had curled up slightly as they dried out. 'Lots and lots of expensive shoes,' she continued, earning some laughs. 'And some waterproof boots.' She plopped back down on her seat, glad the initial ordeal was over, and listened to the other contestants, keen to hear Lewis.

He soon stood up and smiled a warm smile at Laura before turning slightly to address the room. 'I'm Lewis, originally from London but I migrated to the Midlands area because of its famous Balti triangle.' He paused and rubbed his stomach. 'I'm addicted to hot curries. I'm also a petrol-head who is into antiques, so I enjoy hanging out at classic car auctions and car showrooms until they boot me out for wasting their time and for drooling over all the cars. If I won any money I'd actually love to buy a vineyard in France and a classic Citroën 2CV although if I only won a little amount, a bottle of French plonk from the supermarket and a die cast model car would do too.'

The purple-haired girl grinned at him and gave him the thumbs up. 'I enjoy a decent curry too,' she whispered to Bryony. 'I think that bloke will go through. He's got charisma. I wonder if he has a girlfriend.'

Bryony shrugged in a non-committal way. Lewis certainly had what it took to charm people – exuberance and an easy manner.

Laura came forward once more. 'So, that's the introductions over. Thank you, everyone. Next, we need you to do a timed general knowledge quiz. You'll find a list of questions under your seats. Please pick them up but don't turn them over until I tell you. You'll have two minutes to answer all twenty.'

'At last,' muttered Daphne, wriggling about on her seat, unable to reach her paper thanks to her constraining underwear.

Bryony bent forward and passed it to her before picking up her own. Daphne took it without thanks, turning it over immediately and reading the questions, lips moving silently, brow furrowed with concentration.

'Jackson, are you ready with the timer?'

'All ready,' he replied. 'You may turn your papers over and begin now.'

Bryony glanced at the first few questions and suppressed a smile. These were easy. She started scribbling then remembered Lewis's words. But what if he was wrong? She needed to get on this show. She read, 'What was Barbados named after?' She wanted to answer it was named after the many bearded fig trees on the island but instead she wrote, 'The shape of the island – like a beard,' and moved on to the next question. She hoped she was right to place her trust in Lewis. Much was riding on this. More than several pairs of expensive shoes.

Chapter Seven

Monday, 10 July – Late Morning

Papers collected, Daphne sat upright in her seat. 'That wasn't too bad,' she crowed. 'I'm so pleased I knew that Maddy Hill plays Nancy Carter in *EastEnders*. I've never even seen the show. It goes to prove what a little swatting up can do,' she announced to anyone who was within earshot.

Bryony had spent too much time writing incorrect answers for the most difficult questions so she did not appear to be a quiz boffin. She was not sure now if she had performed strongly enough to even come across as average. The last thing she wanted was a post-mortem on their performances. She gritted her teeth and made what she hoped were the right noises of encouragement.

Laura took over and announced they would be filmed while playing a quiz game. 'It's time for some fun. This is only a bit of nonsense so we can see how you perform under pressure and how you interact with your fellow contestants. Don't take it too seriously. Come on, guys. Get that energy flowing. Let's give a little cheer.'

The hopefuls cheered. Oscar whooped extra loudly.

'That's better. Right, let's start with Oscar, Jim and Debbie. Come on up and stand in front of the camera.

Jackson is going to transform into our genial host for this game.'

Jackson bowed, coughed and in a deep, theatrical voice said, 'Hello and welcome to the most popular quiz show on television – *Contestant Panic!*'

The contestants chuckled at the name. Oscar bounced from foot to foot as if limbering up for a dance.

'Let's explain the rules. You each have three questions to answer.'

The people in the room were glued to Jackson. Laura turned the camera around so she could film the reactions from each of them.

'Every correct response wins your team a thousand pounds. If you don't know an answer or get the question wrong, your teammates will have only ten seconds to come up with the correct answer. For every second your team takes to respond, one hundred pounds will be wiped off that one thousand pounds.' He stopped to check everyone understood. He was met with nods. 'Helena has a stopwatch.' Helena waved her mobile phone with countdown application at the ready.

'If your team guesses the answer correctly, the money that remains will be added to the total fund. If your teammates get the answer wrong or fail to respond within the ten seconds, you will hear a man with a deep voice shout, "Counted out," and you will be eliminated along with the thousand pounds. You must answer all your questions to be "counted in" and be part of the final team. Do you all understand?'

The trio nodded enthusiastically again but to make double sure, Jackson ran through it one more time. An air of tension and excitement filled the room as everyone fell silent, waiting for the mock quiz show to begin. Laura spoke up. 'Oscar, if you could move a few inches to your left so the camera can pick up all of your expressions. That's lovely.'

Oscar crossed his hands in front of his torso and his face took on the serene look of a man used to performing in front of others.

'Okay, here we go. Oscar, what did Christopher Cockerill invent in 1955? Was it the telephone, the hovercraft or the bagpipes?'

'Oh my goodness! That's tough. He sounds Scottish so it could be the bagpipes. Maybe that's too obvious. Was it the telephone?' asked Oscar.

'You're saying Christopher Cockerill invented the telephone?'

'No. Yes. No. Yes, I am. I hope my team know the answer if I'm wrong,' said Oscar, flapping his hands in panic.

'I'm sorry. You are wrong.'

Helena held up her mobile and shouted, 'Ten… nine…'

'Hurry up, team. You need to help him,' Jackson urged.

'Eight… seven…'

Jim tugged at his moustache. 'Hovercraft. I'm confident it was the hovercraft.' Debbie gave a helpless shrug of her shoulders.

'Six… five…'

Jim called out, 'Hovercraft.'

'Hovercraft is the correct answer. You had four seconds remaining on the stopwatch so you have added four hundred pounds to your fund. Well done. Oscar, here's your second question. Who composed *Peer Gynt*? Was it

Wolfgang Amadeus Mozart, Frédéric François Chopin or Edvard Hagerup Grieg?'

Oscar smiled. 'Easy. Edvard Grieg.'

'Correct. Bravo. You now have one thousand and four hundred pounds in your final pot.'

Oscar performed a perfect pirouette on the spot.

'Your third and final question: which fruit is a cross between a tangerine and a grapefruit? Is it tangergrape, tangerfruit or tangelo?'

Oscar looked puzzled. 'Tangerfruit.'

'No. You're wrong. Team? Have you any idea?'

Debbie mumbled, 'I've not got a clue.'

'Ten… nine…' called Helena.

'I'm sure I've seen one in the supermarket. I think it's also called an ugli fruit. It's a tangelo,' declared Jim.

'Correct. You had eight seconds remaining so you added eight hundred pounds to your fund making a total of two thousand, two hundred pounds. Oscar, you are through to the final round. Up next, it's Debbie.'

Debbie tossed her hair back from her face and glided forward to face Jackson. Behind her, Oscar jigged up and down. Debbie adopted a sexy pout and stared at Jackson.

'Debbie, here's your first question. Which planet is nearest the sun? Is it Mercury, Jupiter or Venus?'

Debbie's face went blank for a second then she said, 'Oh, I learnt these at school. There's a way to remember them – my very easy mother just sat on uncle Ned – m is for Mercury.' The room exploded into guffaws.

Jackson struggled to maintain a serious a face. 'That's the first time I've heard that particular mnemonic. However, it has earned you one thousand pounds.'

Daphne leant into Bryony and muttered, 'I teach my pupils the mnemonic "my very easy method just SUN". Simple really. Any idiot should know that. These questions aren't very difficult.'

Debbie's face glowed. She re-adopted her pout.

'Question two. The patella is commonly known as what? Is it the elbow? Is it the shoulder blade? Or is it the kneecap?'

Debbie's face broke into a smile. 'My husband injured his playing football and had to have an operation on it. It's the kneecap.'

'Correct. You have added another thousand pounds to the fund. Here's your final question. You're doing great, Debbie. You haven't needed your team to help out yet. Okay, originating in Mexican culture, where on the body would a *huarache* be worn? Is it on the foot, on the head or on the arm?'

Debbie's lips quivered as she tried to pout and think.

'The head,' she replied at last.

'No.'

'Ten,' called Helena as the digits on her phone counted down.

'I've never heard of it,' muttered Oscar to Jim.

'Me neither. I'm stumped for an answer. We'll have to guess.'

'Three... two...'

'Arm!' yelled Oscar.

Jackson held the card containing the question at arm's length. His face displayed no emotion. Debbie bit her lip.

Daphne shook her head. 'Wrong,' she whispered.

'Debbie, I'm very sorry but you have been counted out. The answer I was looking for was foot. Huaraches are woven leather sandals'

Jim's face was a picture of woe. 'Oh no. Sorry, my dear.'

'Debbie, I'm sorry. You added two thousand pounds to the fund, making a total of four thousand, two hundred pounds for your team but you have to stand down. Sadly, you have not been counted in.'

Debbie returned to her seat, disappointment etched on her face.

Jackson resumed his role. 'Up now, it's Jim.'

Jim stood erect, chest out, arms by his side as if in readiness to salute Jackson. His moustache looked like it had been starched into place.

'Question one. Which mammal is responsible for the pollination for the most bananas in the world? Is it a tapir, a monkey or a bat?'

Jim was motionless for several seconds. Oscar looked perplexed and shrugged his shoulders at those watching.

At last Jim said, 'I can only think it must be a mammal that flies if it pollinates the flowers on a banana plant, therefore, it must be a bat.'

'You are absolutely correct. Way to go, Jim.'

Several people applauded. Oscar bounced up and down and gave a cheer.

'Question two. What was Walt Disney originally going to call Mickey Mouse? Was it Willie? Was it Jerry? Or was it Mortimer.'

'I know this. I watch a lot of cartoons with the grand-children. Some people think it was Willie because the first cartoon to star Mickey Mouse was called *Steamboat Willie* but that's not the case. Walt Disney wanted to call him

Mortimer Mouse but his wife asked him to change it to Mickey. And I believe the name Mickey was actually taken from Mickey Rooney.'

'What a terrific answer, Jim. You are spot on. You have added another one thousand pounds to your team's total. Now, here's your third and final question: Nosocomephobia is the fear of what? Is it shadows, night-time or hospitals?'

Jim's moustache twitched as he fought the smile threatening to spread across his face

He spoke with authority. 'It's a common fear. President Richard Nixon suffered from it. Nosokomein is the Greek word for hospital. It's the extreme fear of hospitals.'

'You are... correct!' shouted Jackson, waving his card with gusto and encouraging the observers in the room to applaud. 'You have fantastic general knowledge. You have also added three thousand pounds to your pot making a grand total of seven thousand, two hundred pounds to play for in the final round. Congratulations.'

Oscar bounced on his toes, leapt in the air then did the splits on the floor, causing everyone in the room to applaud once more. He brought himself back up to a standing position and shook Jim's hand formally, and they both returned to their seats.

'Jim was quite knowledgeable,' muttered Bryony's neighbour. 'I knew the answers too though.'

Bryony considered the advice she had been given. Surely Jim would be the perfect candidate for the show. Lewis couldn't be right about them choosing people who did not shine intellectually. It was a quiz show, after all. She didn't have too long to deliberate; Jackson asked for the following three team members and she'd been put in the same team as Tonya, the girl with purple hair, and Lewis. She stood and took her place in front of the camera and Jackson. It was now or never.

Chapter Eight

Monday, 10 July – Night

Outside Bryony's apartment block, a hefty marmalade cat squabbled with an equally well-built black one. The music that had been pumping through the ceiling all evening had ceased and the young couple living above her had turned in for the night. All was quiet apart from some soft murmurings coming from a television set somewhere else in the block and the hissing duo currently engaged in conflict on the fence that ran along the front of the apartment block. Propped up in bed, laptop on her knee, Bryony continued to type. Her hip ached, the pain dulled slightly by the adrenaline of the day. Disregarding the throb, she read through her latest post on *Searching for Hannah*.

> *Dearest Hannah,*
>
> *How I wish you'd been with me today – you'd have loved the audition for a new quiz show* What Happens in… *It was one of our dreams, wasn't it? To be on a game show like Blockbusters or Crackerjack where we would have been giddy with excitement at winning a pencil. Sometimes, you made up little quizzes for me and we played our*

own version of a television show. You'd pretend to be the hostess and put on a funny voice:

'Next up, we have Miss Bryony Masters from Derby. Bryony, to win a carrot: what is the name of Winnie the Pooh's tiny friend?'

I would giggle and squirm and try to guess the answer. If I got it correct you gave me a sweet or a new colouring pencil. How I loved those games!

I can still feel the frisson of excitement as the old television set came to life and we heard, 'It's Friday, it's five to five it's... Crackerjack!'

Your enthusiasm was infectious and I shared in it even though I was too young to respond to the questions on the show. But you, you always knew the answers, and how we laughed when the celebrities got covered in gunge for guessing incorrectly. I can still hear you yelling answers and giggling at Stu Francis saying his catchphrase, 'I could crush a grape!'

You taught me so much and made me want to learn more. I wanted to be exactly like you – top of the class, A-grade reports, a top scholar. The teachers already had you earmarked for Oxford or Cambridge University even though you hadn't sat your GCSEs. You really were my heroine.

You'd have been amazing today. I have a decent amount of general knowledge but you'd have stolen the limelight. You always were the shining, outgoing one.

So, to recap, I summoned up the courage to apply to be a contestant for What Happens in... and was invited to audition for it. We were twenty potential contestants crammed into one room. We were all a little stuffy and reserved when we first arrived but as the morning wore on we regressed and ended up behaving like schoolchildren.

We completed written quizzes, and had such a laugh, participating in a crazy made up television show that would have had you in stitches. Funny, you think games are only for children but adults come alive when they play them too.

I was on a team with Lewis, who I've written about before – the gay guy I met through Melinda – yes, it was a shock to find him at the same audition. Lewis looked very suave. He wore dark brown trousers paired with a stylish, dark brown and copper striped jumper. For the first time, I noticed his hair is not as dark as I first thought. When the light catches it, it reflects streaks of copper and auburn. He has one of those smiles that knocks you off-guard. It certainly worked on Tonya, a Brummie girl who fell in love with him as soon as she saw him. When he announced he liked eating curries, I thought she was going to rush over, drop down on one knee and propose to him. She stood out with her vibrant purple hair and matching contact lenses. Apparently, she has lenses and wigs in a variety of colours. I was glad she didn't wear her shocking pink ones. I think that might have scared the life out of a few of the more elderly contestants.

I didn't chat to Lewis for long as he spent most of the time with an American ballet dancer called Oscar who was sweet and engaging. He has a tiny, *black, pug dog that has a huge fan base on social media. Oscar was so excited he pirouetted every time he got an answer correct. At one point, it looked like he might leap into Jackson's arms.*

We were asked quite a variety of questions. Lewis played it very cool. He claimed he didn't know that France's third-biggest city was Lyon. After the audition, he told me he had visited Lyon several times and was well aware it was the third-biggest city but he decided it would look better if he played dumb, relying on his teammates to come up with the answer. It gave him the chance to rush over and high-five us. I told him he had taken a bit of a chance. If we hadn't known, he'd have been out of the game. He gazed at me for a moment, his cognac-brown eyes searching mine, before replying, 'I had faith in you. You're a very clever lady.'

Purple-haired Tonya was bonkers. She got all her answers wrong although I don't think it was on purpose. She spent most of the time pulling faces whenever we were asked a question. Afterwards, she confessed that she was only at the audition because one of her friends had dared her to apply for it.

The audition attracted a variety of people. I suppose that's because there's been so much publicity surrounding it on television. The adverts to apply for What Happens in… *have captured a lot of interest. It's odd given none of us actually know what format the show will take. It's all very secretive. I sat next to a woman, Daphne, who told* me Anneka Rice is going to present the show when it airs, which would be amazing because I know how much you used to love her show *Treasure Hunt*. When it was Daphne's turn to go in front of the camera, she froze. She couldn't answer a single question. Her mouth flapped open and shut, in spite of prompting and help from Jackson. She left immediately after her performance. I felt sorry for her. It's awful when your confidence deserts you like that. I should know. I've had more than my fair share of such moments.

Anyway, to cut a long story short, I'm now waiting on tenterhooks to see if I get picked. Given they have been holding auditions throughout the country over the last month and we were the last group to be seen, I'm trying not to raise my hopes, even though I really want to be selected. You see, I'm going to use it as a platform to gain nation-wide interest in my beautiful, missing sister. The contestants who do well on each challenge, stay on the show. Imagine if I could tell everyone who watches it every day about you? I'm convinced I'd be able to track you down.

I know you are out there somewhere. If you are reading this, Hannah Jane Masters, please let me know. I shall never give up hope. Even if I fail to make *What Happens in…* One day, somehow, you'll find this blog and understand how much you are missed.

Please forgive me and come back.
Bryony

She re-read her words. This was her fortieth post on the blog. Ordinarily, each was filled with cheery conversation – thoughts and hopes she'd like to share with her sister and recollections of their time together, rather than the more recent, urgent posts that were appeals for her return. She would go through this one again in the morning and make some adjustments before pressing the publish button. The statistics graph showed 185 people had visited the blog since her last post. *Searching for Hannah* was gradually increasing in popularity. At first, it had seemed a crazy idea to write a blog for her sister but the more Bryony had considered the idea, the less crazy it had sounded. Millions of people wrote blogs, and having an online presence was the norm these days. The odds of Hannah finding the blog were long but the ploy might yet pay off, although time was no longer on their side.

Bryony could fight her thoughts no more. She closed her eyes and allowed the memory of the day that changed everything to play out, and like a well-watched film it rolled in her mind's eye…

–

As they leave the house, Rob rounds the corner and Hannah slows to a reluctant halt, grumbling, 'That's all I need. It's your fault, Bryony. If I'd stayed inside he wouldn't have dared talk to me.'

He's wearing a beanie hat and the collar of his coat is turned up. He puts out a hand, rests it on Hannah's shoulder. 'We need to talk,' he says.

'Not now. I have to take Bryony to the park.'

'I'll come too and we can chat.'

'No,' she says, her lips pressed together as she does when she is in a stubborn, bad mood.

Rob and Hannah are going out together. Bryony is not sure what that means but when Mummy and Daddy are out at night, Rob comes over to watch television while Hannah is babysitting. Bryony likes Rob. He doesn't laugh at her when she has one of her twitching turns. He's kind and always brings her sweets. She likes the little cola cubes that come in a paper bag. She knows Hannah likes him because she's seen them kissing on the settee. They didn't see her though. She sneaked downstairs to ask for a glass of milk one night but when she saw them lying on the settee and kissing, she tiptoed back upstairs.

It's quite chilly. Bryony is getting bored. Hannah and Rob are still talking. Rob hasn't brought any sweets with him today and they seem to have forgotten all about her. They are talking in low voices and Bryony can't hear what they're discussing, but she can tell by the way Hannah is standing that it's serious, grown-up stuff. They're not holding hands and kissing like usual.

Bryony's feet are beginning to get cold now and she wants to go to the park. She likes the roundabout best. She likes the way the sky spins around and around, faster and faster when she holds her head back, eyes wide open on it. She pulls her hand away from Hannah's.

She tilts her head back and spins as if on the roundabout, arms outstretched. The clouds whirl around her head, leaving her breathless. She stops, dizzy, and spots Tubs over the road. Tubs is a small, black Labrador puppy that lives in the house opposite. It looks as if he's escaped from his yard again. He's always getting out and running off to find someone to play with. Sometimes he appears in their front garden and Hannah has to take him home. He's an affectionate, happy dog. Whenever he sees Bryony he jumps up and licks her nose. She loves Tubs. She *wants a dog exactly like him. He would be a good friend like Timmy the dog in 'The Famous Five' books she reads. Bryony does not have any friends. Children think she's weird now. She has moments when her hands open and close for no good reason or her eye twitches or her shoulder jumps about. They've started to call her horrible names. If she had a puppy she wouldn't care about the children.*

At the moment, Tubs is chasing a plastic bag. The wind is propelling it down the road and he is pursuing it, tongue lolling out and ears back. Bryony stops her spinning and heads towards the bag. She will catch it and play tug of war with Tubs. She runs out into the road; the bag is not far away. She hears a scream behind her. Tubs stops chasing the bag and stares at her in wonder as she is suddenly lifted high into the air and propelled upwards towards the powder-puff clouds, weightless.

Bryony is confused. She can feel the air whooshing past her ears and wonders if she's on a swing in the park with Hannah. And then, the sun goes out.

Chapter Nine

Tuesday, 11 July – Morning

The shiny, white Volkswagen Polo pulled up outside number thirty-two Aspen Drive. Bryony felt a sense of sadness as she surveyed the front of her parents' house. It had been her home for much of her life but she felt like a stranger when she visited these days. Her mother opened the door before Bryony reached it and greeted her with a tired smile.

She spoke softly. 'Come in, sweetheart. He's up and in the sitting room. He's been looking forward to seeing you. I'll make some tea.'

Bryony hugged her mother. She felt even thinner than she had the week before and as fragile as glass. Bryony imagined if she squeezed too hard, Geraldine would shatter.

She headed for the living room. Her father sat dwarfed in the large, leather winged-back chair he had always favoured, a blanket over his knees and an open book placed precariously on his lap. His eyes were closed, his breath almost silent, and a tiny sliver of drool dribbled down one side of his mouth. She picked up the book to replace it on the table in case it tumbled.

His eyes fluttered open. 'Hannah?' he mumbled. 'Is that you?'

'No, Dad. It's Bryony.'

'Bryony,' he said, her name coming out slurred. 'I thought you were at work.'

'I don't have any classes today, Dad. Term is over. I came to see how you were.'

He looked puzzled. He scratched at the grey stubble on his chin and cheeks. His thin grey hair stuck up on his head. Bryony had never seen him so unkempt.

He struggled to speak. 'Not good.'

Bryony felt her soul crack. To hold back the tears she looked around the familiar room. In one corner stood the upright piano, covered in a thin layer of dust. Bryony did not play the piano. The piano had been bought for Hannah. The photograph taken at Bryony's graduation was standing in pride of place on the dresser. Bryony attended King's College at Cambridge University, as did her father. Unlike him, she chose to study English. She did not have his passion for history. She had not wanted to take a subject that dealt with the past.

The day she graduated had been emotional. Her mother, dressed in a fashionable two-piece suit and wearing a large red hat, had cried with pride. Her father, like some eccentric professor, wore metal-rimmed glasses, bow tie and suit. He had beamed at her and yet the elephant in the room had been present all day. They had not mentioned Hannah's name even though they were all thinking of her on Bryony's big day.

Bryony's mother came into the room with a tea tray. On it stood a familiar china pot, pattern faded now but still serviceable. She gave a brave smile and wiped her husband's face with a handkerchief, removing the drool.

'Brought you some tea, Derek.' She spoke to him as if he were a child.

He nodded obediently and pulled at his blanket, fingers plucking at invisible threads as he waited, wanting to communicate but struggling to articulate his thoughts.

'Bryony's here.'

'Yes, Derek. She's brought another cake. It's your favourite – lemon drizzle cake. Isn't that nice?'

'Dad, would you like me to cut you a slice?' asked Bryony.

–

It was a depressed Bryony who unlocked her own door later that afternoon. It was becoming increasingly difficult to visit her parents and maintain a positive attitude.

Today's visit to her parents had been painful and tiring. The need to find her sister burned in her chest and was all-consuming. With the school holidays now in full swing she no longer had to worry about her students. She poured a glass of cold water and logged onto her laptop to start a new post for Hannah, but within seconds of sitting down her phone bleeped. She read:

> *Need a laugh? Come around. It was supposed to be a romantic night in but Sean is trying to light his new barbecue and we have several cows to eat. Please come help.*

Bryony could not help but smile. Melinda and Sean were terrific friends. Without doubt this had been planned. Melinda would have appreciated that Bryony would be downhearted after visiting her parents. Bryony logged off immediately and, in her haste, didn't spot the envelope icon flashing in the right-hand corner of the screen that alerted her to an email in her inbox.

Chapter Ten

Tuesday, 11 July – Evening

'Hurray, the cavalry is here!' Melinda cried, ushering Bryony through the front door. 'Thank goodness you turned up. I need some female support. Lewis called round to see if Sean fancied going running tomorrow and got roped into helping him out. They've been attempting to get it alight since half past four. It's taken several bags of charcoal briquettes, lots of matches and a few of cans of lager, so be warned.'

Melinda led Bryony through the kitchen and outside to the decking that overlooked a long narrow garden. It was a neat garden surrounded by high-panelled fencing painted in a dark green. Freshly trimmed and shaped beds in front of the fence were filled with colourful shrubs and flowers. Sean, dressed in a T-shirt, shorts and an apron bearing the torso of a scantily clad woman in only lace underwear and suspenders, was fanning the barbecue with a newspaper.

'Hi, Bryony. Just in time,' he shouted, racing over to plant a kiss on her cheek. He reeked of smoke, charcoal and lighter fluid and had a large, dark smut on the end of his nose. 'I'm about to slap some steak and chicken on the grill. It'll be more fun now we have guests.'

'Hi, Sean. Hi, Lewis,' she called to the figure hunched over the barbecue, tongs in hand, face scrunched up in concentration. He waved his tongs merrily. 'Where's Freddie?' asked Bryony. 'I'm surprised he's not helping you too.'

Melinda explained, 'He's staying overnight with Sean's parents. They took him to Drayton Manor Park today for a treat. I think the treat was really for Sean's dad. Charles can't wait to go on the rides with his grandson. He's a big kid at heart – like Sean,' Melinda added, hugging her husband from behind.

'Put me down, woman. I have a serious job to do here.'

'How's it going, boss?' asked Melinda, rolling her eyes at Bryony behind Sean's back.

'We're ready to put the goodies on the grill. Have you prepared the marinated chicken wings?'

'They're in the fridge. I prepped all the food and made the salad so I'm done for the evening. It's up to you to cook for us for a change.' Melinda poured two generous glasses of wine and passed one to Bryony.

'This *is* a man's job,' he answered good-naturedly. 'Come on, Lewis, you can be my trusty assistant. Can't let women barbecue.'

'Behave yourself,' Melinda responded. 'Or I'll go on strike and I don't only mean in the kitchen department.'

Sean's mouth turned down in mock sadness as he headed off in the direction of the kitchen to collect the food.

After several drinks each and a meal declared a success by all, Sean was in the mood for some silly entertainment.

'Time to enjoy ourselves,' he declared and darted towards the far end of the garden carrying a set of cricket stumps and a cricket bat. About 150 metres down the garden he banged a cricket stump into the lawn with his

73

bat, paced out a few steps to the side of it and banged in a second stump.

'Team game,' he announced loudly to his bewildered audience. 'It'll be Lewis and Bryony versus me and the ball and chain. Simple rules. First person takes a slug of their drink, runs down the garden to the stump, attaches their head to the stump with their fist.' He demonstrated by balling up his hand into a fist, lifting the thumb end to his forehead, bending and touching the top of the cricket stump with the other end of his fist. 'He or she must then circle the stump three times, run back to their team member, tag them and then they have to do the same.'

They lined up in pairs. Bryony was against Melinda. She took a large glug of wine and scooted down the garden where she attempted to hold her forehead as close as she could to the stump with her fist and circled it. She completed a second circle but became dizzy and lost count along with her sense of direction. The men cheered then yelled commands to encourage the women. 'One more turn, Bryony,' shouted Lewis. 'Keep going. You're almost done.'

'Another two circles, Melinda. Go on, girl. You can do it!'

Bryony lifted her head. The garden swam before her eyes and she stumbled back in the direction of Lewis, who urged her towards him, arms outstretched. She veered off towards Sean and had to correct her path, giggling all the while. Eventually she found Lewis's hand, tagged him and he raised his glass. Somehow, Melinda made it back to Sean, who gulped down an entire can of lager and hared towards his stump, overtaking Lewis.

The game became sillier and sillier, and before long they were tumbling into bushes, knocking into each other and laughing helplessly. Bryony ended up sprawled in a heap with Melinda, where they hugged each other, a tangle of legs and arms, and had to be separated before being escorted to the top of the garden.

Bryony hadn't enjoyed herself so much in a long time. After a ten-minute respite, Sean challenged Lewis to a wheelbarrow race and they staggered off, arms around each other's shoulders, to Lewis's house to collect a second wheelbarrow from the Shepherds' shed. Much to Sean's delight, they discovered it had a flat tyre, but Lewis was not thwarted by this setback and hauled it back to the party where he was greeted by Melinda and Bryony, cheerleading and pretending to wave pompoms.

Sean's new game involved each man wheeling his teammate around the stumps and back, draining a glass of beer and then following the course in reverse.

'You need a woman with some meat on her bones, like mine,' chortled Sean as he raced down the garden with Melinda bouncing up and down in his wheelbarrow. 'Good for stability and control,' he shouted.

'Shut up, big boy, and keep pushing,' commented Melinda.

Lewis could not control his barrow. Not only had it got a flat tyre but Bryony's long legs hung over the side causing more problems for them. They weaved their way down the course, chuckling loudly until the barrow hit a slight bump in the grass and shot off towards the borders where it tipped over and Bryony found herself plonked in a clump of marigolds, flat on her back, weak with laughter. Lewis attempted to drag her to an upright position but being worse for wear himself and somewhat unstable on his own feet, he too fell over, landing on top of her. All attempts to rise once more were abandoned and they sat back-to-back, propping each other up in the flower bed. Bryony discovered an old plastic flowerpot so she stuck it on Lewis's head, causing them both to laugh like braying donkeys.

Shortly after, Lewis fell asleep slumped against a cold barbecue. Sean lifted him into the broken wheelbarrow and together with a chortling Bryony they meandered off in the direction of Lewis's house.

Chapter Eleven

Wednesday, 12 July – Morning

A chink of light coming through the curtain woke Bryony. Her head hurt and the light stung her eyes, making the throbbing worse. She opened her left eye gingerly. Thomas the Tank Engine looked down from the poster next to the bed and gave her a cheery smile. Bryony groaned and attempted to hide underneath the Power Rangers duvet. She tried to remember why she was in Freddie's bedroom, and piece by piece the evening fell into place. Her thoughts were interrupted by the arrival of a text message on her mobile. She reached out, fumbled for it and peered at the screen through sticky eyes.

> *Why am I in a wheelbarrow in my shed and who replaced my tongue with a piece of dirty, furry carpet. You okay?*

She smirked and tapped out:

> *Head sore. We took you home. Hope you like the special cover I made you. Drink lots of water. Your tongue will reappear soon.*

The phone illuminated once more:

Classy – The Times. It kept me warm. Pity it smells of fish and chips.

Melinda was in the kitchen. She looked remarkably fresh-faced for someone who had drunk several bottles of wine and was already up and dressed at seven thirty.

'Morning,' she called. 'Tea?'

'Please. Is Sean in bed?'

'Goodness me, no. He got up an hour ago and went for a run. He muttered something about his body being a temple, said he was going to make a hair of the dog and left me in bed. He'll be back soon. He's got to go to a job in Harrogate later today. He's staying over. Hence the last-minute barbecue last night.'

'Work? Today?'

'Yes, not everyone gets two months off for summer.' She grinned and handed a mug of tea to Bryony. 'It was a good night, wasn't it?'

'Excellent although I have quite a few bruises from falling over so much.'

'I thought you and Lewis made a great couple.' She sighed heavily. 'Shame you're not exactly his type!'

'It doesn't really matter. I had fun and he's such a laugh. He sent a text a few minutes ago complaining about being left outside in a wheelbarrow. He really got into the games and boy, was he competitive!'

Melinda rubbed her sore bottom and said, 'He wasn't as competitive as Sean. I like Lewis too. He's an easy guy to like.'

Sean clattered into the kitchen, red-faced and perspiring.

'Talking about me again?' he asked.

'No, big head. We were talking about Lewis.'

'I knew I'd forgotten something. He asked me to tap on his door this morning. He's got to go to London and didn't want to sleep in. Maybe I should have invited him to come for a run first.'

'I don't think he'd have fancied a run. He's got a lousy hangover and he woke up still lying in his wheelbarrow.'

Sean grinned. 'My bad! He'll be cursing us for a while. I'll give him a call later. Got to grab a shower first. See you later, Bryony.'

'Bye, Sean. Thanks for a super barbecue.' She turned to Melinda. 'I'd better get off and leave you and Sean to it. You got any plans for today?'

'I could really do with a nice soak in the tub after all those drinking games. I'll try to encourage Sean to scrub my back. And then I'll go pick up an over-excited Freddie from his grandparents although I'll probably have difficulty in persuading him to come home. We're pretty boring compared to them. They're talking about taking him skiing with them later this year when they go to the Alps. I don't know where they find their energy.'

'I could do with whatever magic energy pill they take too. Thanks too for letting me stay the night and for such a laugh.'

'Did us all good,' replied Melinda, hugging her friend. 'It's good to be a bit crazy sometimes. I'd better go visit the neighbours later to apologise for the noise we made. I'll take them a couple of bottles of wine. That'll help ease the situation.'

Bryony sat back in her chair and switched on her laptop. She felt refreshed after some breakfast, a shower and a change of clothes. She was glad the school holidays had begun and she didn't have to go into work. The headache that had dulled her senses when she woke had now lifted and she was eager to recount the details of the night before to her sister. The memory of the events brought a smile to Bryony's face and she wondered idly how Lewis was feeling.

Her inbox flashed. She had three messages; the first was from Tim, a work colleague and friend who had sent her a photo of the house he and his fiancée Suzanne were renting, and a brief message that stated, 'If you find Mr Right, bring him here for a night!' The second message was from the Sydenham's chorea charity, reminding her about the fundraising event she had signed up for. She emailed them affirmation that she was participating in it. The last email caught her by surprise. She read it, blinked several times and read it again. A smile tugged at the corners of her lips.

> Hi Bryony,
>
> Congratulations! You have been successfully chosen as one of the first contestants on What Happens in…
>
> In the style of all the best game shows, we're continuing to keep the format of the show secret, but we can now reveal you won't be acting as an individual contestant on this show. You will be working alongside another successful applicant who attended the Birmingham audition yesterday, to win a whopping prize of £10,000.

Filming will take place over six consecutive days and all expenses will be paid by us, including accommodation and transport to and from a secret destination in France. As you were told at the audition, this is a last-man-standing show. That is still the case. Couples who fail in their challenges will be dropped from the show on a daily basis until we only have three pairs remaining for the final day.

As this will be the first show to be aired, we require bubbly, enthusiastic participants like you. We were all genuinely impressed by your charisma and energy at the audition in Birmingham and I hope you still wish to take part in what we believe will be a hugely popular show.

Please let me know as soon as possible if you are interested. You need to be available to travel on Sunday 23rd July.

If you still wish to be a participant, I'd like to arrange a time for a Skype interview with you as soon as possible to reveal more about What Happens in…

Kind regards,

Laura Perry Producer, What Happens in…

Bryony wriggled on her chair in delight. July 23rd was less than a week away. Bryony let out a squeal of excitement. It was going to happen. She'd made it onto the show and would be able to appeal to the whole country. Somebody somewhere must know Hannah, and if Anneka Rice was hosting the show, Hannah herself might even watch it. Now all she had to do was find out if Lewis had also received an email and was going to be taking part. Surely he'd succeeded. He might even be her teammate. Or Jim – the man who had an incredible general knowledge. Her mind flipped over the possibilities and she hoped it wasn't going to be Daphne, the woman who'd dried up in front of the camera, or purple-haired Tonya. She dialled his number but was greeted by an impersonal voice informing her Lewis could not be reached at that moment and inviting her to leave a message. Tempted as she was to blurt out everything to the answerphone, she decided it would be better to speak to him in person. It would best to find out if he'd got through before sharing her own success. She wouldn't want to rub his nose in it if he'd failed the audition. Bryony liked having Lewis in her life even if it was only as a friend. She would try his phone again later. Now she had to share her news with her best friend. The email had given her something she had not experienced for a long time – optimism. This might be the best opportunity she would ever have to convince her sister to come home – that was, if Hannah was still alive.

Chapter Twelve

Wednesday, 12 July – Afternoon

Melinda's front door flung open. 'Save me, Bryony,' shouted Melinda in mock horror, rushing outside and hiding behind Bryony's back. In the hall, Freddie waved a large plastic dinosaur and roared.

Bryony laughed and held up her hands in front of Freddie. 'You can't come outside,' she said. 'I'm Dinowoman and I'll transform your dinosaur into a teeny, weeny one if you chase my friend any more. Then, the cat next door will chase and eat teeny weeny T-Rex.'

Freddie looked at her in disbelief. 'You're not Dinowoman. You're Briny.'

'I'm definitely Dinowoman. Look.' She grimaced, bared her teeth and roared. Freddie squealed with laughter and ran off into the lounge, slamming the door shut.

'Phew! Come in, Dinowoman,' said Melinda, leading the way to the kitchen. 'We've been constructing a skeleton.'

'A real one?'

'Tempting as it was to head to the local cemetery and dig up a few bodies in search of a skeleton, I settled for a toy one.' Melinda sat down on a kitchen stool, motioning for Bryony to join her. 'So, come on. What's happened?

You only left here a few hours ago and you look very perky. Got a new date?'

'No. Better than that. I have news!' replied Bryony. 'I had to share it with you. I couldn't sit at home any longer.'

'What's happened? Was there a local earth tremor I missed?' asked Melinda.

Bryony took a breath and prepared to tell her best friend about the email. Since childhood, Bryony had relied on and shared every part of her life with Melinda. She was the only person who knew all the details surrounding Hannah's disappearance and who understood why it was so important she find her sister. She'd offered support and a shoulder to cry on numerous times and Bryony couldn't imagine how her life would have turned out if she'd never met her friend...

-

Bryony is eight years old and shaking with nerves. From this day she'll be anonymous in her new school filled with teenagers — teenagers who don't know about her horrible twitching episodes or her accident. Kids who won't know about Hannah running away or about her father who's been in hospital for months following a nervous breakdown. He's back home now and looks better. He isn't a headmaster any more. Bryony heard him talking to Mum about going back into teaching at a local school.

They now live in a small village where news of what goes on in Derby does not reach them. Everyone in Cobblestone seems more interested in protesting about the lorries that drive too quickly through the village and concerns over who will open the village hall so the senior citizens can do their art classes and the mothers and toddlers group can have their Tuesday coffee morning. The village gossips know only a little about her family. Her mother and father have remained tight-lipped about their past and gradually the gossips have lost interest in the quiet family residing at the end of the village who never go to church or the local pub and appear to be recluses.

She has to catch the bus to come to school. It stops at the edge of the village where she lives. She waits outside the house with her mother, who's being cheerful and keeps telling her it's going to be huge fun at the new school. Bryony is not convinced. She's fairly certain there'll be some problems and sure enough as soon as she clambers on board the bus they begin. There are quite a few children of all ages on board and she has to walk halfway down the bus to find a space, passing unfriendly faces that regard her with a vague interest as if she were a strange specimen in a jar.

A large boy sitting on the back seat starts whistling the theme tune to the film The Addams Family when he spots her and his mates begin to giggle and nudge each other. He is about two years older than her. His school tie is undone even though school has not yet started, his head is shaven like a convict's and a confident sneer rests across his acne-riddled face. She attempts to bluff her way out of the situation as she has done in the past by grinning amiably but it doesn't stop him. He continues whistling before commenting loudly that a mutant has boarded the bus. The other boys beside him snort loudly at his comment. She stares out of the window and fights back angry tears as the bus rounds the bend, leaving the sanctuary of the village.

A voice calls out from the seat opposite her. 'Take no notice. He's a retard!'

Bryony looks over. A short, plump girl with an open, friendly face, short dark hair and a sparkle in her brown eyes grins at her.

'I'm Melinda,' she says.

'Bryony.'

The girl nods before continuing an animated conversation with her friend.

The trouble really begins when they get off the bus. The boy who had been whistling pushes Melinda hard in the back, making her stumble to her knees.

'I'm not a retard, you fat cow.'

Melinda struggles to her feet, eyes blazing. She has grazed a knee and it is bleeding. Bryony summons up courage from within, steps behind the boy and prods him in the arm.

'You must be a retard. Only a retard would push a girl over like that.'

'You watch it, mutant!' he yells.

Before she can react, he grabs Bryony's schoolbag from her shoulder and holds it high so she can't reach it. The other boys join him and toss it from one to the other while Bryony hobbles from one boy to the other to try and get her bag back. Melinda yells at them to hand it over and kicks one of the boys in the ankle. Before long the commotion attracts the attention of a teacher.

They end up outside the headmistress's office, standing in a silent line against the wall waiting for her to call them in. The spotty-faced boy does not look as cocky and has done up his tie. The teacher who broke up the ruckus emerges and sends the boys in first.

'Don't worry,' whispers Melinda. 'She'll sort it out and they won't trouble you again.'

Sure enough, the boys emerge in silence. The spotty boy stands in front of the girls and apologizes for his behaviour.

The girls are called in next. Miss Turnbull is small, elegant and not at all fierce. She wears owl-shaped glasses, and her hair worn short to her shoulders is nut-brown. She is neatly attired in a smart blouse done up at the neck, blue skirt and matching jacket, attached to which is a brooch in the shape of a dog – a setter. Bryony immediately takes a liking to her.

'Melinda Clayton and Bryony Masters. Not a good start to the school year, is it, brawling like fishwives outside the school?'

Bryony isn't too sure what a fishwife is but daren't interrupt.

'Melinda, I understand from Mr Glover you were sticking up for Bryony. While it is commendable to stand up against bullies and to look after those who are more defenceless than us, it is also better to let the staff here deal with these situations. Please be mindful that you should not take matters into your own hands. You could end up injured.'

Melinda opens her mouth, thinks better of it and shuts it again. Miss Turnbull gives her a warm look. 'I would congratulate you on managing to kick Tyron – heaven knows he could do with a kick sometimes – but that would not be appropriate,' she adds, a twinkle in her eyes. Melinda smiles.

'Bryony, I talked to the head of your last school. He and the other teachers spoke highly of you. I understand life hasn't been easy, my dear, but it is advisable to ignore those who choose to be cruel. If it becomes unbearable then you must come and speak to one of the staff. Don't allow yourself to become one of the crowd. Think of how much you'll upset your parents if you don't fulfil the potential you have – and you have such potential.'

She leans back in her chair and it creaks. She steeples her fingers together and looks at Bryony over her owl glasses.

'Do you know what I see, Bryony?'

Bryony shakes her head. 'No, Miss.'

'I see someone who will make a difference in the world. Be yourself. Be proud to be yourself.'

She dismisses them and they leave together. The incident has cemented their relationship – a relationship that will last many years.

Melinda was ecstatic. 'You made it through! That's fantastic! They've come back to you so quickly. I thought it'd be ages before you heard from them. I suspected they'd choose you but for one of the later emissions, not the very first show. See, just proves what a great job I did on that application form.'

'Couldn't have done it without you. Oh, and I discovered it's probably going to be hosted by Anneka Rice.'

'Anneka who wore those amazing jumpsuits and raced about the country in a helicopter hunting for clues to help people win treasure?'

'That's her.'

'I wanted to be her when I was little. Pity I was short, fat and had dark hair.'

'Almost every young girl wanted to be like her. Hannah most definitely did.'

Melinda studied her friend's face. 'I think Hannah, like me, will probably have forgotten about Anneka Rice. It was in the eighties. We all had heroes and heroines then. I was in love with Billy Warlock from *Baywatch* but I wouldn't necessarily watch a show now because he was in it. You're not pinning your hopes on Hannah watching it because it's hosted by her, are you?'

Bryony shrugged 'She might.'

Melinda spoke gently. 'You have a good plan. You won't need Anneka Rice as a host. You'll get your chance to appeal for Hannah. Hang on, the show starts soon, doesn't it? You're going to be able to do this much quicker than we anticipated.'

'Next week. I'm leaving a week Sunday. I think the first day of live broadcast is Monday twenty-third of July.'

'Come on, tell me everything.' Melinda pulled out a stool and dropped down onto it. Bryony joined her at the table.

'It's going to be filmed in France and shown over a period of seven days. There'll be all sorts of challenges that will test us not just mentally. Every day the losing contestants will be thrown off the show, but the winners will remain in the spotlight. I'm going to win, Melinda. I'm going to win every challenge thrown at me and answer every quiz question correctly and make a name for myself, and I'm going to talk about Hannah at every opportunity and ask the nation to look for her.'

'I get it but as your best friend, it's my duty to caution you. This is a bit of a wild shot. What if you get booted off on the first day?'

'I won't.'

'Look, I know you're exceptionally smart and I'm one of your biggest supporters, but please don't pin all your hopes on this. I couldn't bear to see you disappointed. I know how important it is for you to find her and if this doesn't work out you get eliminated in the first round… well, I just don't want you to raise your hopes too high.'

'It'll work. Knowing Anneka Rice might be hosting the show, is even better news. I know Hannah will watch it.' She stared intently at Melinda, willing her to approve. Her friend chewed thoughtfully at her bottom lip and cocking her head to one side, spoke evenly.

'I agree there's a slim chance Hannah might watch the new show if she liked Anneka Rice as much as you say she did but I wouldn't bank on it. However, I think your best shot is to get the public supporting you and looking for and talking about Hannah. Remember the *University Challenge* contestant, Erik Monkman, who became a nation-wide favourite due to his eccentricities? You'll be like that only more so. What have you got to lose? You have great intellect and you're beautifully batty at times, so I think you could do this. People will love you. It's worth a go.'

Bryony released the breath she had unwittingly held. 'That's what I hoped you say... although maybe not the "beautifully batty" bit. You know what these shows are like for firing up public attention. If I can just capture the nation's heart, there are endless possibilities. There's one slight snag. I've got to team up with a partner.'

'Do you get to choose who?'

Bryony pulled a face. 'No. The production team will decide.'

'Hope they chose somebody good.'

'Me too.' She glanced at her mobile and checked the time. She spoke absentmindedly. 'I hope Lewis made it through.'

'Lewis? Whoa! Wind back a bit. Where does Lewis come into all this?'

'I bumped into him at the audition. Oh gosh, I shouldn't have said anything.'

Melinda barked a laugh. 'That's brilliant! You both went to the same audition for *What Happens in*... Neither of you mentioned it to us, your best mates.'

'We had no way of knowing if we'd be picked. Please don't say anything to him if he hasn't been chosen. I don't want to embarrass him.'

Melinda's mouth opened as a thought struck her. 'If he has been selected, you reckon *he* could be your teammate?'

'I suppose he could be.'

'It'd be pretty awesome if he is.'

'I wish I could get hold of him. I've rung him three times but I keep getting the message service.'

Melinda, lost in her own thoughts, honked with laughter. 'You two would be hilarious together. I wonder if one of the challenges would be for Lewis to wheel you about France in an old barrow with a flat tyre.'

'Unlikely. It's a quiz show.'

'There are challenges. You said so yourself,' Melinda said, her eyes twinkling.

'Even if there are crazy challenges, we'll face them sober not hammered out of our brains thanks to too much red Bulgarian wine.'

Melinda grinned at the memory.

'I'll try phoning him again later.'

'I think Sean mentioned something about him going to a technology exhibition or event in London. He's probably turned off his phone.'

'Oh! That's right! I'd better leave it until later then.'

Melinda clapped her hands together. 'I can't wait to find out. You *have* to be teammates. You'd be brilliant together. Can't you wangle it so he is your partner in this?'

'I don't see how. Laura, the producer wants to talk to me on Skype. I could mention Lewis, I suppose.'

'No. I've got a better idea. You convince Lewis to be your teammate first, then both of you persuade Laura.'

'He might not want to partner up with me.'

'Get out of here! Of course he will. You two are like Ant and Dec or French and Saunders or Phil and Lil.'

'Who are Phil and Lil?'

'Twins from *Rugrats*… never mind, you get the idea. You bounce off each other so well and you'd smash every challenge.' Melinda was becoming more enthusiastic with each word.

'How can you be so sure?'

'I just am. You'd be wonderful together. Bryony, you *need* Lewis for this. He'll win over every woman watching the show and between you, you'll get that opportunity you need to talk about Hannah on national television.' She squirmed in her seat. 'Find out and if he got through, ask him. Go on.'

'I'm not convinced…' Bryony began.

'If you don't, I'm going to.'

'No! Don't do that. I'll ask him.'

'Excellent.' Melinda rubbed her hands together. 'I have a good feeling about this.'

Bryony rubbed the back of her neck thoughtfully and decided Melinda might be right. With Lewis on her team, she'd be even more sure of getting through to each round. She just had to hope the producer thought he was an ideal contestant too.

Chapter Thirteen

Thursday, 13 July – Morning

The front doorbell emitted a feeble warble. Bryony felt awkward coming here but the part that was currently in control of her emotions urged her on. Hearing nothing from within, she rapped at the door again – rat-ta-tat-tat-tat-tat – a friendly knock. Nothing. She tried once more before deciding Lewis must be out. She plodded back down the path, her enthusiasm waning. She opened the gate. It made the same neglected whine it had made a few minutes earlier. As she fumbled for her car keys, she heard a shout. She turned. Lewis was hanging out of an upstairs window, his naked torso revealing sculpted shoulders and the upper part of a fine six-pack 'Don't leave!' he shouted. 'I'll be down in a minute.'

She grinned up at him and wandered back to the front door. Within seconds she heard someone rattling the door chain and Lewis appeared, his dark hair slick with water and a towel around his waist.

'I'm sorry. I'm disturbing you,' she stammered, trying hard not to gawp at his taut physique.

'I was in the shower. I didn't hear the doorbell. I was singing too loudly,' he replied with his customary grin. 'Come in. If you don't mind waiting a few minutes, I'll dry off and get dressed.'

He showed her into a sitting room and noted her expression as she took in her surroundings. 'I'm just staying here temporarily so don't judge me by what you see. Not my usual taste but it came fully furnished. I'm more caretaker and custodian than tenant. You should see what's been left in the attic,' he said with a grin. She stared at the shabby, red, patterned sofa, and collection of friendly pottery owls on display in a large glass cupboard – eyes watching her as she moved about the room. Among the many paintings that covered the walls was a framed photograph of the Shepherd family who owned the house: the two curly-haired children sat cross-legged in front of their parents, displaying toothy grins while the mother and father adopted more serious poses. The mother had one hand on her knee; the other held her husband's. Her large green-blue eyes were focused on her children, pride etched on her radiant face, her head tilted as if listening out for them. The father, a sandy-haired man, sat relaxed, one leg thrown over the other. The overall impression was of contentment. Bryony wondered what her own family portrait would have displayed had it ever been taken.

'There, I'm decent again. Coffee?' asked Lewis, his perfect physique now encased in a T-shirt and trouser combo that could only be described as a second skin.

'I'd love one. Thanks.' She followed him into the kitchen. A coffee machine stood next to the kettle. 'This is my favourite kitchen appliance,' he declared. His strong arms flexed as he brought the machine forward, grabbed a small capsule and fitted it into a slot. 'I don't object to using other people's settees, televisions or beds but I draw the line at their jars of instant coffee. I can't function until

I've had proper coffee. I treated myself to this machine. I'll take it with me when I find a more permanent place of my own.'

'This is only temporary then? Will you be moving away?' Bryony tried to keep the disappointment from her voice. She liked having Lewis in the neighbourhood.

'Not sure yet. Got quite a lot to sort out first. I like it in this neck of the woods, so I'll probably hunt for somewhere in the vicinity. I don't mind renting for a while but it's weird living with somebody else's memorabilia around you. Strong, medium, cappuccino?' he asked.

'I think I should stick to a medium coffee. I knocked back an entire cafetière at breakfast – Oromo Limu – so I'm hyper enough.'

'Aha! You know something about coffee. Can't say I know that one.'

'I can't resist decent coffee. It's the smell of the beans that does it for me. I discovered Oromo Limu by chance. It comes from the south-west region of Ethiopia, has a good body and is smooth with a long, chocolatey finish. It should really be drunk after dinner but I prefer it in the morning.'

The machine spluttered into life. Lewis waited for the water to heat and drip through, filling the cup beneath it. 'It's rare to find fellow coffee connoisseurs these days. So, what's brought you here? Although it probably is only for my fantastic coffee.'

'First off, sorry about all the missed calls you got from me yesterday. I was a little over-excited. I had an email from the *What Happens in…* production team.'

'I forgot to take my phone with me. I was so hungover I left it behind in the kitchen and the battery ran down.

It's been on charge since I got up this morning. I wasn't aware you'd phoned or I'd have called you back. So, was the email inviting you to participate in the new show to be filmed in France? As I recall, I was selected because of my "energy and charisma",' he added, removing the white Villeroy & Boch Newwave Caffe mug from the base of the machine and passing it to Bryony like a magician presenting the denouement of a complex trick. 'Voilà!'

Her spirits lifted. 'You got chosen too! Sounds the same wording as my email.' She admired the curved handle and breathed in the aroma of the coffee, taking her first sip, all the while collecting her thoughts. 'Ah, perfect,' she sighed.

'Superior coffee should always be served in proper coffee mugs,' he replied, pressing a button on the machine for his own coffee. It made a comforting burbling noise. As he waited, he placed his hands on the back of a pine kitchen chair and studied her face. 'Are you going for it?' he asked. 'The show?'

Bryony nodded. 'Definitely'

'What about work commitments?'

'School's broken up and I've nothing until September.' She opened her mouth to ask if he'd be willing to try and partner her but he spoke first.

'To be honest, I'm a bit hesitant now. Especially since I found out we get a teammate. I've just been propositioned by a new client – it's a lucrative contract – and I ought to get started on that project. I'm not sure I should spend time away.'

Bryony's face fell. 'Oh,' was all she could say.

Lewis took his cup and stared at the dark liquid. 'Are you disappointed?'

'Yes.'

He gave her a curious look. 'Why?'

'I was hoping you would consider partnering me. I thought we could maybe Skype Laura together and ask her if we could be teammates. After all, I need somebody else with the same amount of "energy and charisma" as me,' she said with a weak smile. 'It's okay. I understand. Getting work is important. I was being… selfish.'

'I don't believe that for a minute. You don't strike me as someone who is self-centred and I've met plenty of people who are. Come on, tell me why you want me to be your teammate.' He gave her an encouraging grin.

'No, it's not important.'

'It must be or you wouldn't have come over to find out if I'd been selected. You almost burst with excitement when you heard I had. Don't deny it.' He raised a finger to silence the protest she was about to make.

'I told you. I hoped we'd be able to be on the same team. Melinda thinks we'd be good together.'

'Melinda knows?' he laughed. 'Of course, she knows. She's your best friend.'

'I'm sorry. I didn't mean to tell her about you being at the audition. It slipped out.'

'I forgive you.'

'I was just so excited. I really *really* wanted to get onto the show.' She stopped. She was doing it again, saying more than she should. Lewis picked up on her words.

'Why's it so important? It's only a game show.'

She'd told everyone the reason at the audition, surely, he couldn't have forgotten already. Maybe he thought it was a silly idea, after all, he didn't know her very well, not like Melinda. Suddenly she felt embarrassed. Melinda had planted the idea of him partnering her in her mind and now it seemed vaguely ridiculous to be asking him. She'd got carried away believing she and Lewis could be a team on a game show, just because they got on well at Sean and Melinda's impromptu barbecue. He might not even want to be teamed with her. 'Forget it. It sounds a little crazy now I think about it.'

'I'm a terrific listener and I promise not to tie you up in a straitjacket – even if you do sound completely crazy. Go on. I'm all ears.' He flapped his lobes.

Bryony smiled at his boyish enthusiasm. He tapped the side of his coffee machine. 'We have all day and I have lots of coffee. I'll even crack open a packet of my best, most expensive, chocolate-covered biscuits. Surely you can't resist that offer?'

He emptied his coffee mug, pulled out a kitchen chair from under the table, brushed some imaginary crumbs from the faded cream cushion and said, 'Come on. Convince me. Tell me all the good reasons why I should nip off to France for a week. If you can sell the trip to me, I'll go along with it and we'll both talk to Laura, persuade her we're an ace team. Can't say fairer than that. Take a seat. I'll grab the biscuits.'

Somehow that seemed an easier proposition than going over the whole Hannah ordeal. Bryony brushed at an invisible stray hair and began. 'We get along well, so we should have a laugh doing this. It's an all-expenses paid trip. How many people go to France for free? It'll be quite an adventure because we don't know what to expect. We'll be on national television. We might even get our hands on the prize – £10,000. And,' she said hoping to produce her trump card, 'you told everyone at the audition you were considering buying a vineyard in France. Surely, you'd relish the opportunity to spend some time checking out pretty villages and potential areas to settle in?'

His smile widened. 'Got to stop you there. I only said that nonsense at the audition to stand out from the crowd. Most of the others wanted to win money for a holiday or to give to their children. I didn't want to appear to be the same as them.'

Bryony slapped her coffee mug onto the table. 'You lied! And I believed you. I honestly thought you wanted to head off to rural France, grow grapes, harvest them and turn them into bottles of Château Lewis. You were so persuasive and enthusiastic, I even fancied doing something similar. Does that mean you don't want to own a vintage Citroën 2CV either?'

'I prefer German-built cars like my BMW.' He shrugged an apology. 'So, you see, I'm not as keen on France as you thought.'

Bryony crossed her arms, suddenly irritated by his apathy towards her suggestion and towards being her team mate. 'Fancy lying to everyone at the audition. That's no way to carry on.'

'And you really wanted to win some money to buy shoes,' said Lewis, a smile of self-satisfaction now resting on his lips. 'I have difficulty believing that.'

'Why? Don't I look like a woman who likes nice clothes?' argued Bryony, her face flushing at being caught out.

'Nice as your clothes are, you don't look like a fashion mogul, and footwear is clearly not high on your radar,' he continued, nodding towards her comfortable trainers. 'In fact, I've not seen you in anything other than trainers or sensible flat shoes in the time I've known you.'

Bryony went scarlet. 'Okay, so I didn't want new shoes. As far as I'm concerned, my shoes need to be practical and durable. I spend most of my days on my feet teaching and I don't fancy getting fallen arches. As it happens, I'd give any winnings to a charity I have long supported. I have personal reasons for being involved with it and I try to raise funds for them in as many different ways as possible. That way, I'm not always dependent on the generosity of the same people each time.'

Lewis popped another capsule into the machine, a thoughtful look on his face. 'Is that why you went diving with sharks and did those other daredevil activities?' he asked after a while. 'You were sponsored to do them for your charity? I should have guessed. Difficult to imagine you actually wanting to abseil down buildings for fun, nuts as you are,' he added.

There was a fractional pause and then Bryony said, not wholly with conviction, 'Yes.' She pondered her dilemma. She really ought to confess that her charity interest was only a part of the reason she was desperate to be on the new show.

He sat down beside her. 'Tell me about this charity of yours and I'll stop behaving like an idiot,' he stated, placing a warm, comforting hand on top of hers. The contact reassured her. His eyes were compassionate and she felt a sudden longing to talk. 'It's not good to keep things bottled up inside you. Tell me all about the charity and why you support them.'

Convinced of his sincerity, she unburdened herself.

'When I was six years old, I contracted a streptococcal infection. Most children would have got over it but I didn't. The infection interfered with my basal ganglia – a collection of brain cells located deep within the brain that play a role in controlling movement and emotional responses. I developed what is known as Sydenham's chorea, also called St Vitus' dance. In essence, it's a horrible thing. Any child who contracts it loses control of their muscles – arms and legs jerk without the person having any control over them. I was like a marionette. One minute I'd be okay but the next, my arms would fly about as if being operated by invisible strings. My eyes would suddenly start twitching or I'd lose control of my hands. It was pretty scary at times.'

Lewis maintained his level gaze. His hand stayed on top of hers.

'Initially, I was so ill with the infection I was bed-bound for a few weeks. I recovered enough to begin to move about but I developed these tic disorders and would stumble or even fall over. You can imagine the reaction from other kids when I finally returned to school. I lost the few friends I had made. I was laughed at and bullied. Even little kids get bullied,' she commented, registering the look of surprise on Lewis's face. 'I didn't mix with the others after that and became withdrawn. I lost all self-confidence. I was so miserable. Sometimes, I'd sit in the corner and sob my heart out.' She took a deep breath. The memories always brought a lump to her throat.

Lewis patted her hand and Bryony dragged herself back to the present. 'My teacher often had to telephone for someone to come and collect me. Worse than that, I felt so tired all the time and I became needy. I didn't want to go outside. I wanted to stay at home with my family, especially my sister, Hannah. She was the only one I wanted to spend any time with. I became a really screwed-up, anxious child. Apparently, it's all part of the illness although at the time, it drove my mum mad. She didn't understand what was wrong with me. She tried to help and coax me out of my bad moods but I only wanted to be with Hannah.' She shook her head sadly at the memories.

'Over the years, I've learnt more about the syndrome and I assist in helping the charity raise awareness of it. I couldn't face standing up and telling people what I personally experienced but if I can help fund the charity, it will get the message out. Due to better sanitary conditions and the use of antibiotics to treat streptococcal infections and rheumatic fever, Sydenham's chorea is uncommon nowadays in developed countries but it still exists, and more so in developing countries. I don't want any other children to feel as awfully alone as I did. Contracting Sydenham's chorea was not only a horrible illness to deal with but the consequences of having it changed my life for the worst. It was part of the reason Hannah ran away from home. She's another reason – the real reason, I want to be on the show.'

'Hang on. Didn't you mention a sister at the audition?'

'That's right.'

'Ah, now I understand. Oh shit. You must think I'm completely cold-hearted. I actually missed some of what you said because the woman who was sat next to me chose that moment to hiss in my ear and ask if she should mention her swearing parrot. I only caught bits of what you said. Now I remember I heard you say "sister" and then you talked about shoes.'

She fumbled for a tissue in her pocket. Finding none, she sniffed noisily.

'I'm sorry. I shouldn't be getting so emotional about it.'

Lewis removed a box of tissues from a drawer and passed them to her. She pulled one out and blew her nose.

'You don't have to continue. I feel mean at not being more enthusiastic. You must have thought I didn't want to partner you. I was only teasing you. If we can get on the show together I'll be happy to go. If not, then I don't want to do it and I'll get on with my new client and cheer you from my armchair.' He replaced his hand on one of hers. 'We'll arrange a Skype call and do our damnedest to get on the same team. How can I refuse? Besides, it'll be entertaining and no doubt do us both good – I've not had the easiest time recently so it'll be an excuse to go away and let off steam.'

Bryony dabbed gently under her eyes. 'Melinda told me about your break-up with Maxwell.'

'In that case, I don't need to drag up all the sordid and miserable details.' He deftly changed the focus of their conversation. 'Let's both email the show's producers and say we are tremendously excited about the prospect of heading to France even though we have no idea what to expect once we arrive. I suppose you need me for my excellent linguistic skills.' He coughed then in a high-pitched tone said, '*Je m'appelle Lewis et j'ai dix ans. Merci.*'

Bryony managed a weak smile. 'I think you'd better leave the talking to me. Thank you.'

'Hey, that's what friends are for – handing out tissues, listening to troubles, making coffee and providing chocolate biscuits.'

A rush of warmth pulsated through Bryony. 'Thank you. You're a terrific friend.'

'I'd reserve judgment until we get back from France. You 'av not yet discovered ma fetish for zee saucisson and baguettes,' he said in a terrible French accent, twirling an imaginary moustache.

Chapter Fourteen

'Searching for Hannah'

Dear Hannah,

It's happening. I'm going to be a contestant on What Happens in…

Lewis wasn't keen to take up his own offer to be on the show and needed a good reason for doing so. I really wanted him to come too, so I tried hard to convince him. Then, he wanted to know my reasons for doing the show and I explained about my childhood illness. He hadn't heard of Sydenham's chorea or St Vitus' dance but was surprisingly compassionate when I told him about it. He assumed I wanted to be on the show purely to win the money for charity because he hadn't heard me tell everyone at the audition about you. He was most upset he'd not been sympathetic towards me once he found out the true reason for me being on the show and was then adamant we should email the producers immediately and arrange a Skype call to convince them to put us in the same team.

I firmly believe he really would be the best person for me to team up with. I can't imagine being paired up with somebody else, like the Helen

Mirren wannabe who sat next to me, or mad Tonya or any of the others at the audition. You know how I can suddenly lack self-belief and I need somebody like Lewis to keep me positive. I'd probably have been okay if it had been a game for individuals but working with a stranger is not something I'd find easy. I'd be much more relaxed with Lewis by my side. I hope the producer agrees or I'll truly be thrown in the deep end and I don't want to be partnered with somebody who loses me the chance to get through to the next round each day. I need to stay in the game as long as possible. I must be given the opportunity tell the nation about you.

There's little more to tell you at the moment, other than we're filming in two weeks' time and it'll be aired fairly soon after that.

With Anneka Rice hosting the show, I'm confident you'll tune in. You have to watch the show, Hannah. You have to see me on it and you have to come back home. Dad is still confused and so unhappy. Every time I visit he thinks I am you. You have no idea how much we all want you home.

Your loving sister,
Bryony

Chapter Fifteen

Friday, 14 July – Evening

'So, is everyone ready for this?' asked Melinda, drawing the Renault people carrier into a space reserved for the female golf captain and screwing about in her seat to look at her friends.

'Yes, ma'am!' shouted Sean who was seated next to her, clicking his heels together and saluting.

'Sean, you are a buffoon!'

'Yes, ma'am. I am a buffoon. Happy to be your buffoon, ma'am!'

Bryony looked out at the building that was the Bromley Golf Club clubhouse. It looked more like someone's bungalow than a clubhouse. A taxi pulled up next to them and a man wearing old-fashioned plus fours and long, vibrant checked socks leapt out of it. A woman in a luminous green tank top, short red skirt and yellow visor tagged along behind him, dragging an old golf bag.

Melinda's parents had invited her and her friends last-minute to make up a table at a golf fancy dress event, which was the reason Bryony now pulled at the brightly checked jumper, part of her costume. She and Melinda had bought the outfits at a fancy dress shop in Derby that morning but there had not been a great deal of choice, and Bryony had been left with an outrageous wig and visor affair along with the jumper and a golfing skirt that showed off far more of her legs than she was comfortable with.

'This has to be the most hideous jumper in the universe. Do these people actually wear jumpers like this?'

'You don't look as terrible as me,' moaned Sean, whose jumper was various squares of luminous green, orange and yellow. He also wore non-matching checked trousers in shades of plum and red. 'I look more like a clown than a golfer,' he continued.

Melinda gave him a stern look. 'Perfect outfit for you, then.'

'See that look, Lewis? Never mess about with a copper, ex or otherwise.'

'Why?'

Sean held up his ring finger. 'You end up doing time.' He guffawed loudly and Melinda hit him on the head lightly with her bright-pink checked visor. 'Ow! Ex-police brutality! You're both witnesses to it.'

'I was *not* a copper,' she said.

Lewis plopped a plain flat cap onto his head. Bryony decided it suited him. He was the only one who did not look ridiculous; he even managed to look sexy in his checked shorts and polo shirt. Lewis spoke again. 'Sean told me you both met when you were in the police force, Melinda.'

'She pulled me for speeding and I pulled her,' replied Sean before his wife could respond. Melinda groaned.

'He always says that. I did not. I wasn't even working with the traffic officers. I was office-bound at the time working in forensics. Sean came into the station to help identify some muggers who had attacked an old lady. He had fought them off single-handedly,' she added. 'He was very helpful and gave a clear description of the assailants. As he was about to leave, he asked about the old lady. He wanted to visit her in hospital to see how she was doing after the shock. I happened to overhear him asking which hospital she had been taken to. I thought he was like some sort of superhero.'

Sean shrugged his shoulders. 'Don't big me up too much, Mel. Anyone would have helped.'

Melinda ignored him and continued. 'He spotted me and said hello then asked me out.'

'Just like that?' asked Lewis.

'It was the flat black shoes and thick tights that did it, Lewis. I couldn't tear my eyes away from them.'

'Shut up, you silly thing! He was quite the charming gentleman, Lewis. I know that's difficult to believe when you see him horse-playing now. He was humble too. He didn't go for the usual crass chat-up lines. He scratched his chin and looked at me with his baby-blue eyes then coughed nervously and said, 'I don't suppose a clever lady like you would consider going to visit an elderly lady in hospital with a rough, scallywag electrician, would you?' I thought, *Why not?* And here we are, six years later.'

'That's very romantic.'

'Nah, I like a challenge. It's always good to punch above your weight. I was surprised when she agreed. More shocked still when she agreed to marry me. Still in shock that she cuffs me to bed every night and brandishes her rubber truncheon.'

'That'll do, Sean. For the record, I do not cuff him or brandish a rubber truncheon,' she announced.

Sean mouthed, *She does*, behind her back.

'That's enough about us. How did your Skype interview go earlier?'

Bryony's face lit up. 'We chatted about ourselves much like we did for the audition for *What Happens in…*'

Lewis joined in. 'Laura wanted us to explain how we met and if we thought we'd get on okay doing a treasure hunt. She asked which one of us was the bossiest and who spoke French. I told them I'd do whatever Bryony ordered me to do unless it was in French. Then I wouldn't be able to understand a word.'

'Lewis asked if we got sniffer dogs or a metal detector to help us locate the treasure,' continued Bryony, her cheeks dimpling at the memory. 'Poor Laura thought he was being serious and began to explain we would have to use clues and maps, then saw us trying not to snigger. She then told us we'd make a perfect team. We misbehaved a little but Laura seemed to like us being exuberant.'

'Of course, she did. We just have to wait and see if we did enough to convince her to pair us up because if I end up with somebody like that purple-haired girl, I'm getting on the first flight back home,' said Lewis.

Bryony grinned. 'We should receive the travel details later tonight or at latest tomorrow morning by email. Laura had a few other interviews to carry out, then she had to meet with the show's other producers and sort out final arrangements.'

'I think Bryony will swing it for us. She aced the French test. Laura asked all sorts of questions. It was gobbledygook to me so I gave her my best Gallic shrug and declared I was a dunce as far as the lingo is concerned and that was why I needed to be on Bryony's side.'

'They were only simple phrases, directions and so on. I think Lewis won her over completely. He impressed her with his family history. She asked why we wanted to be on the show together and Lewis told her about his love of all things French and passion for owning a vineyard, and then told her he'd always been a quizzing sort of person. His father, who's a retired scientist, used to make up clues for crossword puzzles for newspapers, and Lewis here sometimes helped him!'

'I had to trump you. How many contestants are modern language lecturers with degrees from Cambridge? And I bet no one else is a flipping member of MENSA! It took five minutes for me to drag my jaw back off the floor after that revelation.'

'Our Bryony may look dumb but she certainly isn't,' declared Sean, earning another thump on the arm from Melinda. 'Don't ever let her challenge you to a game of Trivial Pursuit. I swear she's memorized every card and answer in the box.'

'It comes from playing lots of games as a child,' she answered in a dismissive tone. She did not want to think about the happy afternoons playing with Hannah, her mother and father.

'I had a misspent youth – I wasted evenings riding about on my bike with a gang of no-hopers before hanging about outside shops trying to blag I was old enough to buy a few tins of beer. If I'd made more effort at school, I might have beaten Bryony at Scrabble last time we played.n It would also have helped if you'd let me play the words 'wotcha' and 'numbnuts'. Then I might have stood a chance,' said Sean to Melinda, who shook her head.

'Dream on, Sean. I've known Bryony since I was eight and I've never yet won a game of Scrabble against her.'

Lewis gave Bryony a steady gaze. She felt a warm stirring in her stomach. He smiled at her and announced, 'I reckon I could take down Brainy Bryony. I'm willing to brave it. I'm an ace Scrabble player. I have had lots of practice online. I sometimes play people all over the world.'

'Bring it on, Lewis,' Bryony replied, smiling at her new nickname. 'Playing the game for real is much tougher than playing the online version.'

'Now that's a proper challenge. You're on.'

Melinda opened the driver's door. Her parents were pulling into the car park. 'They're here. Time to go.' She waved at her folks.

Bryony checked her wig and golf cap in the mirror, pulled at the ridiculous jumper. Lewis picked up his golf club and gave it a mock swing.

'I don't think I'd ever get the hang of golf. It seems to involve a lot of walking and grumbling about missing your shot. I prefer running. It's easier. And you don't have to wear strange jumpers.'

–

The event was going well. Bryony, sat between Lewis and Melinda's father, Graham, was enjoying the banter and light-hearted conversation around the table. Melinda's father had entertained the entire table with golfing tales, and while they ate, drank and chatted across the table to each other, magicians had appeared and made cards mysteriously disappear only to reappear in odd places like under Bryony's plate.

The plates had now been taken away. The DJ was setting up. Soon they would all be jigging about on the dance floor. The golf captain rose and, tapping the microphone, welcomed them all.

'It's a little late in the proceedings but I hope you've all had a great time. Thanks to all the boys and girls who have been performing tricks at our tables while we ate. I'd like to ask, can I have my watch and wallet back now please?' The guests tittered politely.

'Before we start the dancing, I'd like to thank the caterers for the splendid meal.' Applause rang out. 'Thank you for coming along tonight and for making such wonderful efforts with your costumes. I'd love to see you lot playing on our course in these outfits on a regular basis!'

More laughs filled the room.

'Tonight, instead of the committee choosing the best fancy dress, we're going to do something a little different. Each table is going to nominate a "him and her" to come forward to do a beauty pageant and catwalk challenge, and you'll decide the winning couple.' A buzz filled the room. 'Come on, send up your contestants. The winners will take back a magnum of champagne for their table.'

Melinda shrugged her shoulders. 'I'm not going up.'

Sean shook his head. 'Me neither. I look far too ridiculous.'

'I can barely stand up, let alone do a walk on stage and twirl about. I'll fall over. Too much gin,' said Graham.

Bryony grabbed Lewis's hand. 'Come on, Lewis. We'll go and show these folk how to do it and bring them back a prize.'

'Go Bryony!' shouted Graham enthusiastically.

Bryony and a reluctant Lewis joined others on the stage. Lewis gave her a look of concern. 'I can't do this. There are so many people watching me.'

Bryony levelled her gaze at him. 'It's simple. Ever seen the film *Zoolander*?'

'That was the very funny film about male models. I've seen it.'

'Right, this is the plan. Think of Ben Stiller in that film and walk like he did, do a dramatic shoulder shrug at the end of your walk, adopt a hand on hip pose and then pout dramatically.'

'Pout? At these people?'

'Pout at Sean. Ignore everyone else here. You don't know them and they won't remember you after tonight anyway. Just pretend you are fooling about with Sean. Pout directly at him and make him laugh. We'll go on together. I'll be doing the same moves as you.'

'How can you do this? You're so calm. You're about to make a fool of yourself in front of a room full of strangers.'

'I'm a teacher. We're great actors. We act every day in front of unruly children. How else could we enthuse them to learn anything? The man who played Mr T in the original series of *The A-Team* was a teacher before he became an actor. In fact, some teachers become excellent comedians. Look at Greg Davies and Romesh Ranganathan. They were both teachers before they turned to stand-up. This will be a piece of cake. You only have to pretend to be someone you aren't. I do it all the time. You are no longer Lewis Scott. You are Ben Stiller performing the 'dance-off' scene with Owen Wilson and you're going to make Sean fall out of his chair laughing.'

The first two couples had already walked along the stage, showed off their attire and answered a couple of questions from the golf captain. It was now time for Bryony and Lewis. The DJ played the song 'I'm Too Sexy'. Bryony laughed and counted Lewis in. 'Ben Stiller... ready... three... two... one...'

They set off at exactly the same time, paced down the stage with exaggerated struts, heads high, then perfected a body swing to the right and struck a pose, both pouting memorably. The audience applauded. Sean wolf-whistled.

'You seem to have a following already,' said the golf captain, holding the microphone in front of Bryony.

'Thank you, everyone.'

'Now, tell me about your outfits.'

'Lewis is in his best golfing shorts in a fetching grey and black check with added wine stains from this evening. He brought two pairs of trousers with him tonight,' she said, straight-faced.

'Two pairs?' asked the golf captain as she had hoped he would.

'Yes. The shorts are a little tight on him and he was anxious he'd get *a hole in one!*'

'Nice one, Bryony,' whispered Lewis. The audience cackled. She bowed in response.

'Now, Lewis, I heard you don't actually play golf, do you?'

'Did a little *birdie* tell you that? No, I don't but after tonight and meeting this lovely audience, I have a *driving ambition* to become a golfer!' said Lewis after a moment's deliberation. Bryony rolled her eyes dramatically causing more merriment.

'You should have *put* that joke to one side,' she offered.

'Now, now. Golfing is serious stuff,' continued Lewis, a large grin spreading across his face. 'After all, it's people's bread and *putter.*'

There were more explosions of laughter and several people clapped. The golf captain turned towards the crowd.

'It's up to you all to decide if you think Bryony and Lewis should win.'

Bryony piped up, 'Please choose us. If you don't, it might put *a wedge* between us.' She twirled to show off her outfit and left the stage to further applause.

Lewis threw his arm around her as they left. 'You were brilliant and that was fun.'

Within minutes they were parading around the stage once more and puckering lips in exaggerated pouts before claiming the prize. Their table companions roared their delight as the pair returned with the magnum of champagne.

'You were fabulous, Lewis,' said Brigitte. You should consider going into male modelling as a career.'

'I might now Bryony has shown me all it takes is some acting and a killer pout,' he replied, pulling Bryony in to him and giving her a squeeze.

Chapter Sixteen

Sunday, 23 July – Afternoon

The aircraft, a swept wing business jet, was being marshalled into position as their taxi pulled up outside Wellesbourne Airfield, near Stratford-upon-Avon.

Bryony's mouth dropped open. 'No, surely not!' She reached for Lewis's arm in excitement and gave it a firm squeeze. 'We're going to fly to France in... a private jet?'

He beamed at her. 'We're either flying in the jet or in one of those!' he said, pointing towards a couple of small Robinson two-seater helicopters, blades rotating as they prepared to take off. 'If it's the latter, one of us is flying it and that someone won't be me.'

'Idiot. I suppose it's not likely we'll be going in that either.' She motioned towards the tiny silver-grey gyroplane headed towards the runway.

Lewis chuckled. 'I'm definitely not going if we have to pilot our way across the Channel in that. I'd rather fix feathers to my arms and flap like crazy.'

'Come on, let's find out what's happening,' said Bryony, pulling at her seatbelt like an eager child and snatching at the door handle. 'Sorry, I got a bit carried away. Did I hurt your arm?'

Lewis examined the area and shook his head. 'It appears there's no damage to be seen. I'm impervious to harm from sharp implements including female claws. I must be related to Superman.'

Their conversation was interrupted by a high-pitched squeal.

'Lewis!' shouted a familiar voice with a slight American accent. 'This is awesome! I thought it was you. Are you a contestant for this show too?'

A figure looking stylish in a linen jacket, pressed jeans, blue T-shirt and dapper canvas shoes appeared from nowhere. Lewis's face broke into an infectious smile when he spotted the young man hastening towards them. He pumped Oscar's hand.

'Hi, Oscar. It's great to see you again.'

'And you. And Bryony,' Oscar responded, catching sight of her and wrapping her in a warm embrace of cologne. 'This is mega. It'll be such a hoot, won't it? More so now I've discovered you're both going to be on it too. I had such a blast at our audition.'

'It was great. So, have you met anyone else from the audition?'

'Oh, how rude of me! I've left the poor man guarding our bags. We both arrived early and had a cup of tea at the Touchdown Café. There were a bunch of pilots hanging out there so we talked to a few to try and guess what plane we'd be flying in. Did you guys see the jet touch down? I came out here to take a photo then I saw you guys. Hang on a second, I'll go get him.'

Oscar scurried away only to return a few minutes later wheeling a small aluminium suitcase, a large tote bag over one shoulder. Marching behind him, carrying a holdall and dressed in dark trousers and blazer, and wearing a regimental blue tie with bright green stripes was Jim, the candidate with the large moustache.

'Good afternoon. I understand we're travelling in style today. I've been admiring the Avro Vulcan XM655 on the far runway. It's a beauty. A chap was telling me it was third from last of the Vulcan bombers produced for the Royal Air Force and was part of the UK's nuclear deterrent force throughout the 1960s and 70s.'

'Hello, Jim,' Lewis said, halting the monologue. 'What a surprise to meet you again.'

'Hello. Lewis, isn't it? You're the chappie who wants to own a vineyard in France.'

'Ah, yes,' replied Lewis. 'I might have been a little economical with the truth on that particular subject,' he confessed.

Jim shook hands and clicked his heels as he bowed forward towards Bryony.

'And I of course I remember you. Never forget a pretty face. Bryony, isn't it?'

'You're right, Jim. Lovely to see you again.'

A woman in her early twenties wearing a sleeveless pink cotton dress and wedged white sandals emerged from an office as they made their final introductions.

She welcomed everyone with a broad smile that revealed even, white teeth. 'It's great to finally see you all in person. I'm Roxanne, one of the researchers for the show. I was standing behind Laura during your Skype interviews so I've only seen you on screen. Jim, I have to say, you were hilarious in your interview.'

Jim straightened to his full height. Bryony half expected him to salute her. 'I had no idea what was happening. Thankfully, my wife knew what to do.'

Roxanne chuckled and revealed to the group that Jim had spent most of the interview tapping the screen to turn up the volume while asking if he was on the correct channel. 'I hope you're as excited about this as I am. I can see you've met each other. You'll have plenty of time to find out more about each other on your little jaunt to France today. Don't give away too much though. You'll be rivals tomorrow.'

The group chuckled.

'You might have guessed we've arranged a special treat for you and you'll be flying in the Citation 560 XLS aircraft—'

'Also known as the Encore,' Jim interjected.

'Interesting. I didn't know that. Anyway, the pilots are on board but they have been instructed not to communicate the whereabouts of your final destination. So, don't ask them,' she said, wagging her finger. 'We're keeping it as secret as possible until you get there for reasons that will become apparent. I can tell you though that you are currently standing next to your teammate.'

Bryony drew a sharp breath. Lewis threw her a wink. 'Bryony and Lewis, you'll be working together and Jim and Oscar, you too will be teammates. The other teams have been picked up from other airports and venues. You'll meet some of them later. I'll take you into the office to fill out the necessary documentation before we fly. First, I need to check you all have passports and driving licences.'

Bryony rooted through her handbag stuffed with paraphernalia required for the trip, and finally found her documents lurking under a bag of chewy mints. Looking up, she noticed Oscar was holding out two passports.

Perplexed, she was about to ask why he had two passports when a small, black, apple-domed, big-eyed, proud little face appeared from the top of the tote bag and stared at her.

'Is that who I think it is?' she said, putting her hand out to stroke the little pug dog.

Oscar beamed. 'Indeed. This is Biggie Smalls. Say hello to everyone, Biggie.' He allowed the dog to check out his travelling partners from the confines of the travelling bag.

'I couldn't leave him behind. He'd fret without me and probably demolish the apartment even if he had a dog-sitter. Besides, it'll be an ideal opportunity to take some new photographs of him to post on Instagram. Look, he's got the appropriate wardrobe.' Oscar rummaged in the bag's side pocket and extracted a small beret and a small striped jumper. He called his dog and plopped the beret on the animal's head, earning a round of applause from Roxanne.

'Isn't he adorable?' she cooed. 'I've been following him on Instagram. He's such a cutie. I loved the picture of him watching the Mercury Music Prize on TV wearing a mini COOGI hoody.'

Oscar flushed with pride. 'Biggie's got a few of those beautiful Australian COOGI sweaters. They're not actually real COOGI sweaters though – they're all exact replicas of the ones the Notorious B.I.G. used to wear. My Biggie's a proper furry homeboy.' He hugged the dog then released him from the bag. Biggie snuffled around their feet before sitting down to observe them.

Bryony took note of the pushed-in nose, expressive forehead wrinkles and the wide smile that Biggie was giving his new audience. He was a sturdy dog with small feet and a curly tail but it was his face that captivated her – his tongue lolled to one side making him appear comical. Biggie checked out everyone's footwear once more before settling back in front of his owner as if to ask him a question. Oscar crouched down and patted him.

'He loves being dressed up and is such a diva when he wants to be. However, he is a superb traveller. Come on, Biggie. It's time to go back in your bag.' Biggie reluctantly clambered back into the tote bag and observed the proceedings with a furrowed brow.

Papers checked, the small group led by Roxanne trooped towards the aircraft and up the steps.

'Wow!' exclaimed Lewis, eyes wide in surprise as he walked into the interior of the luxuriously appointed cabin.

'Who'd have thought we'd be travelling in such style? I thought we'd be going to France in a minibus or a coach. Never thought for a million years we'd actually be flying in a private jet,' stated Bryony, staring about the cabin. The executive interior was fitted with seven large individual seats in dark brown leather upon a chocolate-brown carpet. One was an individual seat near the cockpit, four faced each other and two were at the rear of the cabin. Highly polished walnut veneer accented by antique bronze plating complemented the colours.

'Oh my gosh!' exclaimed Oscar, bounding into the cabin and flinging himself into a seat at the back of the plane. He placed the tote bag opposite him on the floor. 'This is awesome – awesomely awesome. These seats are gigantic. Even better than the ones in business class on American Airlines and definitely swankier than the expensive leather armchair in my apartment.'

'And there's infinitely more legroom than I had on my last flight with one of those budget airlines,' declared Roxanne, dropping into the seventh seat. 'We've got everything we could possibly need for the flight. There's a refreshment centre and a toilet at the rear of the cabin. And there are even a few sandwiches,' she added, pointing to a tray covered with cling film. 'I'll pass them out after take-off. Now, before we get going, it's amnesty time. I have to confiscate all your mobile phones and any iPads or other tablet devices you've brought with you. As we explained during your Skype interviews, you are not allowed to use any electronic device to assist you in this game. You all received the emergency number for friends and family, didn't you? It'll be operational from now until you return to the U.K. so if your family need to talk to you, we'll make sure they can. Has anyone brought a device with them?'

Oscar shook his head. 'I left mine at home as asked even though I shall be helpless without it. I can't imagine what Biggie's followers are going to do without his daily updates. I'll have to get through the rounds each day so I can give them all news of him. I brought my camera along instead. That's okay, isn't it? I have to be able to take Biggie's photographs to upload when I get home.' Oscar looked down at the tote bag. Biggie had disappeared, no doubt for a nap.

'Cameras are acceptable. No one has a mobile device, then?'

Jim gave a small cough and twiddled his moustache. 'I'm afraid I'm guilty as charged, Roxanne. My Cathy insisted I bring my mobile with me. Of course, I would never use it to cheat on the show. That wouldn't be cricket at all.'

'Of course you wouldn't but you still have to hand it over, Jim. Sorry. Those are the rules. We can't have you sneaking online to work out clues or puzzles.'

'Fair enough, Roxanne,' replied Jim, extracting his mobile from the inside pocket of his blazer.

Oscar stifled a laugh. 'Jim! When exactly did you purchase that mobile? The 1980s?' he asked, his voice rising in amusement.

Jim looked at the large, old-fashioned contraption, a puzzled look on his face. 'I'm not too sure. It was while ago. It's a Nokia – one of the best-made mobile units.'

Roxanne burst out laughing. 'Jim, I ought to allow you to hang on to your phone. I seriously doubt you'd be able to use it to pull up the Internet. I don't think it will have 3G, 4G or Wi-Fi. Sadly, though, I have to take it. You can't have contact with the outside world while you are on the show.'

Jim looked bemused. 'I have no idea what any of that means, Roxanne. The Internet doesn't interest me so I don't know if the phone has that capability or not. I only use it to make telephone calls. I refuse to use the texting thing on it. I can't be doing with all this pointless modern technology. Why do people spend time writing out messages when they can pick up the phone and ask the question far quicker?' he continued. Then, sitting up straight, he asked, 'You take it though. I don't want to break your rules. I was only going to use it to phone Cathy to make sure she was okay.'

'I don't want you to worry about her, Jim, but I can't let you keep the phone. I'm sure if anyone needs to contact you they'll use the emergency number I gave you to pass to relatives. We'll make sure any message gets to you, whatever time of day or night.'

'I understand. Here. You take it.' He passed it across.

'Nobody else? Good. I'm not permitted to divulge much about what's happening next. When we arrive in France someone will be there to meet us. You'll be driven to your accommodation and tomorrow morning at seven o'clock on the dot, the team will meet you in the library and everything will become crystal clear. I know it's all very cryptic at the moment but it will make sense tomorrow morning. It all hangs on the element of surprise.'

'This isn't some hoax, is it?' asked Lewis. 'We believe we're going to France and we take off and fly about for an hour but then land in Wales or the Isle of Wight and then one of your team wearing a beret and carrying a Tricolour flag comes up to us and asks us questions in a phoney French accent?'

Roxanne thought for a second. 'Bother! You worked it out. You'd better all disembark then. No point in continuing.'

Seeing the looks of dismay, she gave a loud bark of laughter. 'Had you going, didn't I? You are definitely going to France.'

Bryony pulled at her seatbelt to ensure it was fastened. She said in awe, 'I feel like a celebrity. I bet they fly everywhere in planes like this.'

Oscar whistled softly before saying, 'Check out the seatbelt buckle. It looks like it's made of gold. I wonder if I could unpick the stitching and drop it in my bag.'

'Don't you dare. I'm sure the company that owns this jet accounts for everything. You'll get a bill if you steal it and, worse still, you might get thrown off before we even leave here.'

'Shame. It would make a nice souvenir.'

Lewis smiled across at Bryony, who had a faraway look as she stared over the airfield.

'Okay?' he asked softly.

'Totally okay,' she answered. 'I was wondering who might have flown on this jet before us. Someone very famous or very important could have sat on these very seats. They could have been politicians headed for meetings abroad, or musicians headed for music festivals, or even actors going to award ceremonies. Vital decisions that affect millions might have been made by politicians or all sorts of interesting business could have been conducted in this very cabin at thirty-seven thousand feet.'

The captain interrupted the conversation. He introduced himself and went through the safety procedure. Within minutes the engines started up and before long they had taxied onto the runway and were surging upwards away from the airfield, above green fields and into a clear blue sky. Bryony could feel her spirits soaring along with the aeroplane and hoped that this adventure would lead her to her sister.

Chapter Seventeen

Sunday, 23 July – Evening

It was early evening when the jet touched down and Bryony saw the large sign for *Aéroport Nantes Atlantique* over the terminal. They'd arrived in Brittany. A driver bearing a sign for *What Happens in…* was waiting for them as they came through the doors into the arrival hall. Roxanne raised her hand and greeted him in fluent French. They followed him outside and into the warm air. Oscar and Jim removed their jackets, slinging them over their shoulders.

'This is Philippe. He'll drive you to the hotel where you'll be staying tonight. I'm heading to a different venue to join the crew who are camped there at the moment. We've got lots to arrange for the morning.'

Biggie emerged from his bag and snuffled at his master.

'I have to take the little chap for a pee. I'll be back in a second. Don't leave without me.'

Oscar removed the dog from the bag and clipped a lead onto his collar. Biggie shook himself then trotted over to a nearby grassed area where he relieved himself against a sign marked '*privé*'.

Roxanne continued with her spiel. 'Could you wear the outfits we discussed with each of you on Skype?

We don't want you clashing with each other. Make sure they're clean and pressed. Cameras have a horrible way of making the tiniest stain stand out. That's everything for now. Sleep tight. You've got a big day tomorrow.'

'Roxanne,' called Bryony. 'Is Anneka Rice going to be on set tomorrow?'

Roxanne hesitated a second. 'Anneka Rice? She isn't the presenter. Whatever gave you that idea?'

Bryony's cheeks burned. 'A fellow contestant at the audition told me she'd overheard someone say it was going to be her.'

Roxanne shook her head. 'No. She was never considered. The person must have been pulling your leg. Don't worry. The presenter they chose is amazing. You'll love him.' With that and a wave, she shot off towards the taxi rank, leaving the group to follow Philippe.

Once on board the minibus, Bryony fell silent. It had been a long day filled with excitement and now she was overcome with fatigue. She was not sure what to expect over the next couple of days but the news that Anneka Rice would not be hosting the show was a severe blow. Without Anneka, Hannah might never tune in.

Lewis picked up on her mood and left her to her thoughts, chatting amiably to Jim and Oscar as they tried to guess where they were headed. Biggie kept his eyes on the road as if memorizing the route.

Little by little the conversation ebbed away and they sat in companionable silence as the minibus gobbled up the miles. Eventually it pulled up in front of a small château.

'Hotel Petit Château,' read Oscar. 'It seems we've not only travelled in a private jet but we're now going to spend a night in a château. Who's paying for us to enjoy the high life?'

'The production company is footing all the bills. Laura told me the French tourist agency is contributing a generous amount in an attempt to drum up interest in the region and to attract more British tourists to the country,' Jim replied.

'That's very generous and I for one shall do my bit to cement Anglo–French relations. I shall enjoy testing out their wines and rating them in my little black book of wines,' said Lewis.

Jim entered the cool foyer ahead of the others, who filed in behind him, heads turning to take in the elegant furnishings and walls in harmonious shades of greys and blues, decorated with paintings of dancing women. A tall, rangy, untidy figure of a man in a light-pink shirt, jeans held up by a pink and blue candy-striped belt, entered the lobby, arms wide open, and a large, gap-toothed smile on his face.

'Bonjour. I am Bertrand de Saint-Aldin. Welcome to my home, the Hotel Petit Château. You are the film people.'

'That's us,' answered Jim, setting his brand new wheeled bag onto the expensive marble tiles.

'I have your room keys ready. First, I must tell you, you are invited to dinner at eight thirty. There will be drinks in the lounge over there,' he said, pointing to a room along the hall. 'You must sample our famous wine grown here on the estate. It is,' he said, forming a circle with his forefinger and thumb and pressing them to his lips, '*formidable* – delicious!' he explained. Bryony suspected he enjoyed sampling the fine wine from various vineyards, and not merely his own. 'Now, can I have your names please?'

'I'm James Moore,' said Jim.

Oscar stepped forward, cuddling the tote bag. 'And I'm Oscar Brooks.'

'Ah,' Bertrand exclaimed, looking animated. 'You are the man with the big, small dog. Where is your big, small dog?'

Biggie chose that moment to make his entrance. He peered out from the bag, brow wrinkled, tongue out, and gave the man a quizzical look.

'That's him.'

'He is a fine dog – and he is wearing a little French beret,' Bertrand remarked. 'He is a *petit chien français* dressed like this, no? Monsieur Brooks you are sharing the suite with Monsieur Moore. You have one big bed and a separate room with two smaller beds – one for you and one for the dog, *n'est-ce pas?* Is that okay?' He handed them the key.

Oscar nodded enthusiastically. 'Thank you. Merci. Yes, that's fine. I hope you don't snore too loudly.'

Jim shrugged his shoulders and replied, 'Cathy says I keep her awake some nights. I snore badly if I eat cheese. If I don't eat cheese, I'll be fine. It must be the—'

'I don't mean you, Jim. I was talking to Biggie,' replied Oscar. 'I don't mind if you snore. I hope Biggie doesn't make too much noise for you. Did you hear that, Biggie? You get your very own bed to sleep in too. You'll be able to spread out in style. Come on, Jim, let's go and check it out and then you can phone Cathy to tell her all about the journey here. I want to take some photos of Biggie in the bedroom before I mess it all up with my gear. See you all downstairs in an hour,' he shouted, leaping up the stairs two at a time. Jim followed behind, admiring the décor and the exquisite wooden staircase as he climbed the stairs.

A telephone rang in the kitchen and Bertrand excused himself, leaving Bryony and Lewis waiting. The door to the dining room was ajar. Bryony stuck her head in. It was filled with dark period furniture, ornate in style and fitting for the château. A large portrait of a stern man hung above a dark chest of drawers. An oval table covered with a rich red cloth and set for five people occupied the centre of the room. Suddenly, she drew her breath. 'Lewis, am I imagining things or is there a painting of The Last Supper on the wall. It must be a reproduction,' she squeaked.

Lewis peered at the painting. 'It's definitely a reproduction and it's been expertly painted. The faces on it are slightly different to the original. Besides, it's highly unlikely anyone would own the original. That hangs in a convent in Milan and I shouldn't think anyone could steal it. For one thing, it's pretty large. Think it's about fifteen feet by twenty-nine feet. Bit difficult to sneak it into a handbag or briefcase. But more importantly, Leonardo da Vinci painted it on the dining hall wall.'

Bryony's mouth dropped open in surprise and she blushed at her ignorance. Lewis flashed a smile. 'Not a lot of people know that,' he said, emulating Michael Caine.

Bertrand reappeared and discovered them in front of the painting. 'This reproduction is by one of my ancestors. It is good, no?'

'First-rate.'

'It was painted around 1850 by a famous painter, reproducing the well-known *The Last Supper* from Leonardo da

Vinci,' continued Bertrand. 'Which of course was painted many years before that between 1495 and 1498. This, however, is a very fine painting,' he repeated, a smile of satisfaction across his face. 'I have your room key. You are in the Chambre Louis XVII. It is my preferred room and has a wonderful view of the garden and the pond. I hope you like it.' He held the key out to Lewis.

'Where am I staying?' asked Bryony.

The man's eyebrows furrowed together. 'With your fiancé.'

'I can't share that room with him because—' Bryony began.

She was interrupted by a bewildered Bertrand. 'All the rooms are occupied. The Chambre Louis XVII room is exquisite,' he added, wringing his hands together and misunderstanding her concern. 'It is my honeymoon room for couples. Everyone adores it.'

Lewis put a hand on her shoulder. 'Come on, darling. Don't confuse the gentleman. We'll be very happy with it. Thank you, Bertrand.' He took the key from the man, who seemed relieved. He offered Lewis a small bow in return.

'Just go upstairs,' he whispered to Bryony. 'We'll sort it out when we get there or tomorrow morning. I'll sleep on the floor if necessary.'

'Okay, maybe a room will come free tomorrow. If Jim can manage to share with Oscar and Biggie Smalls, I'm sure we'll cope.'

They headed upstairs and paused outside the room they'd been allocated. Lewis unlocked the door and Bryony let out a small gasp. It filled with antique furniture befitting of its name. The walls were papered in lavish cream and beige patterned wallpaper. A king-sized bed covered by a superb, handcrafted bedspread and matching cream pillows filled one wall. Two pillows embroidered in the same material were suspended from a brass railing above the bed. A period fireplace, over which hung a huge mirror, made the room appear larger and added to the feeling of grandeur.

Bryony placed her bag on the wooden floor and wandered to the open window, drawn by the sound of cicadas chirping in the garden below. The sky was deep shades of purple, orange and yellow, the colours so vibrant they were almost unrealistic. The delicate perfume of scented roses floated in with the warm evening air. From the dark pond that shimmered in the distance came the chorus of frogs, adding to the insect melody beneath the window. Their musical strains soothed her jaded nerves and she breathed in deeply before returning her gaze to Lewis. He gave her one of his mischievous grins, knocking her off-guard. He had placed an eiderdown and pillow on the floor in front of the bed.

'Ta-dah!' he announced. 'It'll be like camping only in the dry and it'll remind me of being in the boy scouts minus the woggles for holding up scarves,' he explained, 'And the camp fires singing 'Ging Gang Goolie'.'

'You were a boy scout?'

'Got my cook activity badge to prove it. I slaved over an omelette and some cornflake cakes to earn it. They were awesome cornflake cakes too. They became my speciality. My mum was so proud of that badge she sewed it onto a blanket for safekeeping. I think she's still got it somewhere. I didn't last long in the scouts. I wasn't cut out for life under canvas or doing outdoor stuff. I never got the hang of rubbing twigs to make campfires. Good thing we're not on one of those survival shows. We'd perish with me in charge. Give me a room, a cooked meal and a laptop any day.'

Bryony's mouth twitched. Lewis had also discovered and placed an old-fashioned twin bell alarm clock beside his makeshift bed.

'You can't lie on that uneven floor. It creaks and I'm sure it's uncomfortable. The bed's massive. If you don't mind sharing, we can both sleep there.'

'If you are sure. If not, I can always ask Oscar if I could use his spare bed.'

'Gosh no! Biggie Smalls won't like that. He's a dog used to his comforts. Also, it isn't fair to either Oscar or Jim. Sharing with one stranger is hard enough, let alone two. Poor Jim will be completely thrown out with two men and a dog in the room adjoining his. We're a team so we'll stick together. Besides, Oscar and Jim might try to nobble you in the night so we can't win, or tie you to the bed so you can't get to the meeting in the morning, or Jim will drown you in his vast fountain of knowledge or at least demoralize you.'

'My, you have a vivid imagination,' he scoffed. She pursed her lips to protest and he grinned. 'It is probably better if we don't separate tonight. We don't want them discovering too soon that you're the brains of our team and I'm only here to cheerlead. How about I place a pillow in between us if that helps protect your modesty.'

'I'm not exactly worried about you jumping on me in the night, if that's what you mean,' she laughed. 'After all, I'm not your type, am I?'

Lewis deftly changed the focus of their conversation. 'Any idea what to expect tomorrow, then?

'No. I am stumped. I looked at the road signs on the way here so I'm aware of where we are but I can't work out what the crew has planned for us. The only clue we were given was when Laura mentioned a treasure hunt during the Skype interview, so there must be one. Until we're told more, I'm as puzzled as you.' She paused for a second before saying, 'Sorry for being difficult about sharing a room. It's not like me to be grouchy. I was pretty disappointed to find out Anneka won't be hosting the show.'

'Is that all? What's the big deal about that presenter? It doesn't matter who's hosting, does it? You'll be on television, and if we play our cards right, you'll win a significant amount of money for your charity.'

'True. I need to stop being such a misery and get on enjoying this experience – after all, look at this place.' Bryony glanced about appreciatively, threw her travel bag onto the bed and unzipped it.

'Why's it so important that Anneka Rice hosts the show?'

'It's silly, really. I can't explain why.'

Lewis raised an eyebrow. 'You are shrouded in mystery, Bryony Masters.'

Bryony shrugged. 'I'm bagging the bathroom first – woman's prerogative. It's a fact that we take much longer to get ready than men,' she stated, bringing the conversation to an end.

Chapter Eighteen

Sunday, 23 July – Evening

Relaxed against a plump cushion on an extremely comfy settee, Bryony sipped her glass of wine. Bertrand stood proudly with a bottle in his hand, extolling the virtue of the grapes used to make the rather delicious, fruity Muscadet wine.

'Nantes is the capital of the Muscadet region,' he explained. 'And last year was an excellent year for the grapes.'

The wine was making Bryony feel mellow. She'd eaten little during the day and was now beginning to experience the warm, fuzzy feeling of the first stages of being drunk. She focused on the others, blocking out some of Bertrand's monologue. Jim's brown, button-like eyes shone. He was no doubt soaking up Bertrand's every word and committing it all to memory. He had a colossal capacity to recall information. In her opinion, the man was a human encyclopedia and his intelligence far outshone her own. Bryony reckoned she stood little chance of winning each day with Jim as an opponent. She might make it to day four or even five if she was lucky. Worse still, there'd be no Anneka. She felt downhearted at the futility of that part of her plan that had held so much promise. She glanced at Lewis, balanced on the edge of his stool. He too appeared fascinated by Bertrand's words and his eyes glittered with expectation. She scanned the room, taking in Jim's and Oscar's eager faces, and sensed the collective feel of anticipation. She mentally chastised her negativity and tuned back in to Bertrand.

Bertrand was talking about his home, arms outstretched as he gesticulated towards pieces of furniture and wall decorations. 'Hotel Petit Château is a fine dwelling dating from the time of the *Directoire*.' Bryony could not ingest any more facts. She had no idea who or what the *Directoire* was. Having listened to Jim for most of the journey to France, her brain was now full to the brim with facts. A gong sounded, interrupting Bertrand in mid-flow.

'I think now, dinner is ready,' Bertrand declared. 'We must eat.' Bryony registered they were moving, her nose picking up on the aroma of roast chicken that now wafted into the room.

'Biggie, you have to wait here.' Oscar wagged a finger at the small animal. 'Sit. Stay.' Biggie looked dejected and slumped onto the floor.

'He's not allowed at the table or to beg for food. He has a strict diet and I don't want him ballooning up. I'll never be able to carry him about if he becomes heavy and fat. Besides, it's not nice for anyone to have a salivating pug staring at them while they eat.'

'Quite right,' said Jim. The wine had gone to his head too and he had begun to slur his words. 'Discipline. That's the thing. We had plenty of discipline in the army. My, how I missed it when I came out into civvy street. It's difficult to quit the routine once you leave. And I missed the camaraderie even more. It was like leaving behind a huge family of brothers and uncles.' A wistful look played across his face. He did not, however, talk at length about the army. Instead he put a fatherly arm around Oscar's shoulder and complimenting Bertrand on his taste in furnishings, walked ahead with the pair, leaving Bryony and Lewis trailing in their wake.

'Anyone here need pinching to make sure this is all for real?' asked a deep voice. Bryony and Lewis turned towards it. It belonged to a colossus of a man dressed in cargo print trousers and an olive T-shirt that stretched over his barrel chest. At about six foot five, he towered over his partner and with his bald head, a large round face and merry, green eyes he resembled a friendly ogre.

Lewis was the first to speak up. 'I'm Lewis and this is Bryony. Nice to meet you.'

'Donald and this is my partner, Nicola. She's not my "partner", if you know what I mean. We're not living together.'

'Heaven forbid,' replied Nicola, smirking at the big man.

'She's my partner for this show. I'm actually happily married to one of her sisters, Eve. Eve and I always hold hands, even after twenty-five years together,' he said a wistful look in his eyes before adding, 'If I let go of it she shops.' His throaty laugh filled the air.

Nicola tried hard not to chortle at his remark. 'That's not true and you know it!'

Donald wriggled heavy eyebrows on his craggy forehead. 'They're all tough women in their family. Six women! I pity my father-in-law. Imagine what a life he had – all those nagging women to deal with. Even the dog was female. This one,' he said, pointing at Nicola, 'badgered me senseless until I agreed to audition for the show with her, then complained when we actually got teamed up. I wouldn't mind but I know naff all about France. Now, if it was about football...'

'I didn't badger you. You were really keen to get away for a few days and skip off work. Besides, it was never a given you and I would get through or be teamed up.'

'See,' mouthed Donald, pointing a digit at her. 'Bossy!'

'You eating with us?'

Donald shook his head. 'No, we arrived much earlier than you and went into town, so we've already eaten. Thought we'd opt for an early night, ready for tomorrow. Don't let us hold you up. See you tomorrow.'

'Competition,' whispered Lewis as the couple headed up the stairs. 'Deliberately being over-friendly when really he wants to beat us.'

'Really? How did you come to that conclusion?' Bryony asked.

Lewis tapped the side of his nose. 'Intuition. Don't worry. He might be broad and tall, but I have the secret weapon in my team – Brainy Bryony.' He gave a quiet chuckle and swept her into the dining room. A patterned casserole dish sat in the centre of the table. Next to it stood a polished, silver dish filled with perfectly golden roast potatoes garnished with rosemary. Bertrand lifted the lid of the casserole dish, allowing the aroma of garlic, herbs and chicken to escape. Bryony's stomach rumbled.

'This looks delicious but it's not what I expected,' enthused Oscar. 'I thought we might have a traditional French meal, like *confit de canard*.'

'Or, *cuisses de grenouilles*, frogs' legs, eh?' replied Bertrand with a smirk. 'This chicken is from the local farmer and my gardener grew all the vegetables that are in the casserole. This *is* a typical French meal. However, if you want something very French, I can bring you in some snails from my garden. They keep eating the vegetables so you can have them with pleasure.'

Oscar giggled. 'I'll pass on the snails, thanks, Bertrand.'

Bertrand gesticulated enthusiastically at the table. 'We also have a typical French dessert. It is a *tarte Tatin de pommes*. It is delicious. My gardener's wife made it so, of course, it is delicious.'

Lewis raised his glass. 'To Bertrand and to his gardener's wife for this super meal,' he offered.

Bertrand bowed his head. 'You are very kind.'

Jim helped himself to a large portion of chicken. He breathed in the aromas from his plate. 'I can definitely detect garlic and thyme in it. I always use thyme, bay leaf and plenty of red wine. Can't have too much red wine in a fine chicken casserole.'

'If you make casserole as good as this, I'm going to demand you write down the recipe for Mom,' Oscar declared. 'In fact, you should write a cookery book. I'd certainly buy it.'

'Lewis could give you his world-famous cornflake cake recipe to add to your collection,' offered Bryony, earning an exaggerated grimace from Lewis.

'Bryony's right. People would really want to know how to make those little beauties. They're very tricky to prepare.' Lewis took on a voice of one presenting a cookery show. 'Take one box of cornflakes. Open the box and tip approximately a quarter of the flakes into a large bowl, filling it to the halfway mark. Next, the tricky part.' His face became mock serious. 'Place a bar of top quality chocolate in a heat-proof bowl over a pan of boiling water and allow it to melt. Add the melted chocolate to the flakes, and mix in well. Roll small balls of mixture into round shapes using your hands and leave to solidify, then consume at will.'

Jim's moustache twitched as he suppressed a laugh.

'Any chocolate will do although I believe adding a rum-flavoured chocolate is not to be recommended, especially when doling out said offerings to small children.'

They all chuckled at his remark. Jim spoke again, more animated now. 'Cathy suggested the same idea about writing a cookery book but I never seem to have enough time and I can't see me sitting behind a desk typing all day. I used to spend hours preparing dishes. I especially love cooking pastry dishes or baking bread – I do enjoy that,' he added with gusto. 'After I left the army, I went to work in a local family-run bakery. I used to rise – forgive the non-intentional pun – at three o'clock every morning to warm up the bread ovens and prepare the specialist breads: olive bread, rosemary and oregano and so on. We won an award for our steak and ale pies. I came up with that recipe. I added a secret ingredient into them to make them extra-tasty.'

'What was it?'

'If I told you, it wouldn't be secret.'

'True.'

Jim's eyes twinkled. He leant forward in a conspiratorial fashion. 'Guinness. I added Guinness to the pies.' Satisfied he had impressed his audience, he finished with, 'I loved working at the bakery. The smell of warm bread or pies always brings back fond memories.'

'Did you not fancy starting up your own catering business?' asked Lewis. 'I'm sure you'd have been successful. You obviously have a penchant for cookery.'

Jim placed his knife and fork neatly on his plate. 'As it happens, Lewis, I did consider the possibility. I even started to save to buy my own shop. I fancied a small delicatessen that provided lunches. I thought Cathy could serve all the cheeses, breads and meats and I would do the catering in the adjoining restaurant, using some of the produce we had in the shop. Cathy was excited too at the prospect. It became our dream. I would work at that bakery, pummelling the dough and planning what I would cook when I had my own little shop. Then, out of the blue, my Cathy was diagnosed with multiple sclerosis. It was a terrible blow, I can tell you. She's a trooper. She didn't let it get her down and she fought to stay active but her condition deteriorated all too quickly and I chose to give up work altogether to help look after her. We got by on the savings and my army pension but there wasn't enough money left for any ambitious plans to set up a restaurant and shop, and besides, none of that seemed important any longer.' He looked off into the distance for a moment.

'The most precious thing we have is time, isn't it? I didn't want to spend all of mine working. Spending quality time with Cathy became my priority. It still is. I can't imagine my life without her. We go out every morning if she's feeling strong enough, and then in the afternoon, the little ones come around. It brightens our day. They always make us smile. I love seeing Cathy happy.' He paused for a moment; the memories of his grandchildren made his eyes shine.

'Our daughter, Susan, is looking after the old gal while I'm here. Cathy understands how much I enjoy a good quiz or game show. She insisted I audition for *What Happens in…* I get lots of quiz-like practice at home, watching the television and doing various puzzles while she's resting beside me on the settee. I suppose quizzing has become my hobby these days. Keeps my brain active.'

He picked up his knife and fork once more.

'Sorry to hear about Cathy,' said Lewis. Oscar and Bryony nodded earnestly.

'We've learnt to live with her condition. If I could win some money, then I'd really like to take the old gal to the coast for a long holiday. Maybe stay in a posh hotel. Treat her. Some sea air would do her good.' He blinked away tears and continued, 'Oscar, tell us about ballet dancing. I read somewhere that a male dancer lifts over one to one and a half tons' worth of ballerinas during some performances.'

'They certainly keep you on your toes.' Oscar snickered at his own pun.

The conversation moved on to France, the show and what they might expect in the morning. With full stomachs it was not long before they began to feel ready for bed.

Jim was the first to make excuses to leave. 'I'm not as young as I used to be and I usually turn in about nine o'clock. At my age, I need my beauty sleep. I had a super night thanks to you all. Thank you. It was good to chat and very nice of you to listen.' He tugged at his moustache

— a nervous gesture. Behind the disciplined, military man was a shy one. Bryony felt the urge to hug him.

'It was a pleasure, Jim. You'll have to give us some of your recipes before we part company, especially for your steak and ale pie.'

'I'll walk Biggie around the garden and come up in a minute, Jim. I won't be long. We've got a big day tomorrow. Night, everyone.'

Bryony and Lewis plodded up the stairs. From the room near theirs came the sound of someone panting and groaning. Bryony maintained a poker face and said, 'Probably someone doing late-night sit ups.'

With pursed lips Lewis agreed, all the while wrestling with a smile. He unlocked the door and they raced inside as the noise reached a crescendo and French voices moaning in ecstasy reached their ears.

'Or they're performing very energetic star jumps,' offered Bryony.

'I suppose that's a possibility. I once knew a bloke who would hang upside down off a bar in his bedroom for fifteen minutes every night before he went to sleep. He claimed it was good for his circulation. There's a saying that comes from the north about people being odd: "there's nowt as queer as folk". It seems to be accurate,' replied Lewis.

'I didn't know you were from the north.'

'I'm not but while I was living in London I once worked for a woman from Yorkshire. She had all sorts of little sayings and words that amused me.'

Bryony dropped onto a chair and removed her shoes. 'I have no idea what it is you actually do for a job. I've spent loads of time with you and know next to nothing about your actual life. Melinda told me you were into acting or something similar but that can't be the case. Even though you were accomplished at acting when we played the murder mystery game,' she added. 'You seem to return to London a fair bit, and didn't you go to some exhibition recently?'

'There's not a lot to tell you. Being a male escort isn't all it's cracked up to be.'

Bryony dropped a shoe in surprise. 'A male escort?' she repeated.

'I accompany wealthy women who need a partner for an event such as a charity gala dinner. They usually require the strong, silent sort who won't show them up, are polite, can look good in a dinner jacket and don't slop soup down their tuxedo.' His face cracked into a mammoth grin. 'Not really. I design websites. Nowhere near as exciting. I work from home which until recently was in London.'

'You almost convinced me then.'

'Almost?'

'You spilt a dollop of gravy down your shirt tonight. Male escorts wouldn't be so clumsy.'

Lewis pulled at his shirt, hunting for the gravy stain.

Bryony spluttered in glee. 'Ha! Got you back. You didn't spill any gravy.'

'Touché! I deserved that. Nice to see you smile. You've been unusually quiet this evening.'

'Sorry. Tired, I guess. I'll get ready for bed.'

'You sure you're okay about me sharing the bed?'

'Yeah, it's fine. You don't mind, do you?'

'I'm chill. As long as you don't snore or I'll have to ask you to decamp and join Biggie Smalls.'

Chapter Nineteen

Sunday, 23 July – Night

Bryony removed her make-up and stared at her bare-faced reflection in the mirror. After the euphoria of the day she now felt at a low, her brain befuddled by the wine. She hoped a good night's sleep would sort her out. She couldn't shake off the disappointment over Anneka Rice not hosting the show no matter how much she tried…

–

'I'm going to ride in a helicopter like Anneka when I grow up,' says Bryony. She's snuggled next to her sister. They're watching Treasure Hunt *and Hannah has hardly spoken. Bryony knows Hannah wishes she was the one in the helicopter in the red suit swooping over towns then jumping out and running across gardens or fields to the next clue. Hannah looks a bit like beautiful Anneka. She has large open eyes and long, golden hair. Bryony shifts in her chair. Maybe one day Hannah will go on television and dazzle other girls just like them.*

Hannah should not really be watching television. She has homework to do. Bryony wants to help her sister but the work is too difficult for her; besides, Bryony has her own problems. Today she got sent home from school again. She had been in Miss Lawrence's class finishing a picture of a chaffinch for a project. It had taken her ages to draw the bird and get every detail correct. She had watched the chaffinches in her garden each morning and knew she had captured the beak, the colours and the minute details in her picture. She was really happy with her effort and oblivious to the others in her class who sniggered behind her back when her shoulder suddenly jerked to one side, pulling her head with it. She loved the chaffinches with their merry song. She would like to be a bird and soar in the sky, free from the constraints of a rebellious body.

The painting was almost complete. Miss Lawrence had seen it and was astonished at the accuracy of the picture. It would definitely receive a gold star and that would make her parents proud. She didn't go into school very often these days. The doctor told her parents her illness came from 'chorea', a Greek word that meant 'dance'. The doctor told them it would get better in time but Bryony didn't know when. She hated it. She never knew when it would happen – when she might flinch or a shoulder might jerk or when she would suddenly blink her eyes or her face would tighten into a grimace. The more she got worked up about it the worse it became. And the children tittered and nudged each other even though they'd been told not to laugh.

Bryony dipped her brush into the jar of water. She needed to put some black onto the chaffinch's head. Without warning, her hand jerked open and before she could cry out, the jar of water tumbled over, soaking her beautiful chaffinch.

Bryony did not want to think about it any more. She had cried all afternoon. The teacher had sent her to the school nurse, who had phoned her mum to come and collect her. Her mother had not been as sympathetic as she hoped. 'It's only a picture. You can paint another.' She first became exasperated and then annoyed with Bryony. 'You're making a fuss about nothing,' she

*declared and left Bryony in her room where she sobbed and sulked
until Hannah came home from school.*

*Hannah had come into her bedroom, sat on the bed with her
and stroked her hair. 'It's okay, little sis. We'll paint a picture
together. You and me. We'll make the best picture ever.'*

*Bryony loves Hannah. She understands how horrible it is to
be the kid who is picked on. She never laughs when Bryony's
face suddenly contorts into a grimace or her eyes develop a tic.*

*Now she is next to Hannah on the settee and both are
absorbed in watching* Treasure Hunt. *Hannah catches her sister
looking up at her.*

'You okay, little sis?'

Bryony nods enthusiastically.

'I was thinking how you could do that too.'

*Hannah laughs a warm, happy laugh and squeezes her sister
affectionately.*

*'Why not? And maybe you could be the helicopter pilot and
together we'll find treasure.'*

Bryony's heart swells with pride. How she loves Hannah.

Gradually, she surfaces from her dream. The vision fades.

*A sudden wave of sadness washes over her as her conscience
interrupts the memory. Hannah will never be able to go on a
treasure hunt with her. Hannah has gone.*

*A chill seeps into her body and a familiar twitching sensation
begins in her face and then spreads to her shoulders. She cries out
in alarm.*

—

'Bryony, are you okay?' Lewis asked, leaning over to her
side of the bed and rubbing her arm gently.

Bryony snuffled. She had been crying in her sleep
again. Her heart felt heavy in her chest. Confused and

disorientated, she tried to place where she was, whimpering as she sat up.

'Hey, come here,' whispered Lewis. He drew her into his warm arms and held her, pulling her hair from her damp face, much as Hannah had done all those years before. The tender gesture made her sob further and she allowed the tears to flow, unable to stem them.

Lewis held her close until she gained control. 'I'm sorry,' she said in between sniffing and gulps of air.

'Don't be sorry. It must have been a doozy of a nightmare.'

'It wasn't really a nightmare. It was a memory – a bittersweet memory.'

'I'll get you some water and a tissue,' he offered, releasing her.

Immediately she missed his strength. She wanted him to return and cuddle her again.

'Here,' he said and shuffled back under the covers.

She thanked him, blew her nose and then accepted the water. She leant back against the hanging pillow.

'I dreamt about Hannah. It was so vivid. I could smell the apple shampoo she used and I could feel the warmth of her arm around me as we watched television.'

'Go on,' whispered Lewis.

'I went back in time to a point just before it all fell apart. My sister was with me. How I wish I could change what happened soon afterwards.'

'Do you think she might be dead?' he asked softly, holding her hand as he asked.

'Truth is, I don't know. I never gave up believing she was alive. Even after the police could find nothing to point to it. In my heart I feel she is alive. I wish with all my heart I could find her. I need to find her.'

'Have you tried a detective?'

'Yes, and I tried placing adverts in newspapers asking her to contact me. This was pretty much my last hope.'

'Tell me about it. How you hope this show will help to find her. Anneka Rice. Everything.'

'It's a long story.'

Lewis flicked on a small bedside lamp and opened the drawer beside the bed. 'In that case, do you want one of my secret supply of chocolate biscuits?'

She smiled, a weak smile, breathed in and began.

'Hannah loved watching game shows and in the eighties we used to sit in front of all manner of shows but her favourite programme was one called *Treasure Hunt*.'

'I remember that show. Go on.'

'When Daphne, the woman who sat next to me at the audition, told me Anneka Rice was going to host it, I got it into my head Hannah would tune in, and if she watched the show, she'd see me and get back in contact. The more I thought about it, the more it seemed plausible and I became over optimistic. As it is, she might not watch it and I'll have to rely on my original plan – to try and win the public's sympathy and interest.' She blew her nose and then, gripping the tissue, resumed her story. 'As you know Dad had a stroke a few months ago. He's recovering but the chances are he'll have another and next time he won't get better. Since the stroke, it's become imperative I locate Hannah. I have to try everything humanly possible and persuade her to come home before it's too late. I can't give up on her. Not now.' She shook her head in dismay. 'You see… I'm the reason she ran away from home.'

Lewis heaved a sigh that almost stirred the curtains across the room and placed his arm around her shoulders, pulling her towards him again. 'She might or might not have watched if Anneka had been hosting. She still might tune in. You can't become disillusioned yet. It was a slight setback, that's all. We'll both have to hope your sister sees the show regardless of who hosts it. It's never wrong to be optimistic, Bryony.'

'You're right. I got fixated on one detail. I shouldn't have got so carried away. When I applied for the show, I didn't know who'd be hosting it. All I knew was it was a last man standing show and guessed there must be times during the show when contestants can talk about themselves. I'm going to use every slot or opportunity to tell everyone watching the *What Happens in…* about Hannah. All I have to do is remain on the show and get support from the public. One of them might know her. That's one of the reasons I wanted to partner with you. I think together we could get through quite a few rounds, or days, and that'll give me time to mention her and my hunt for her.'

He left his arm in position. 'You thought I'd be good enough to get through?'

'Of course. You're really clever and up for all sorts of challenges. Look how you took on the murder mystery event, the daft fashion show at the golf club and pushed me about in a wheelbarrow. We'll be really good together. Melinda thinks we're the perfect team.'

'But you might have been partnered with Jim who's a genius! Or Oscar whose dog has gazillions of followers.'

'But that doesn't mean we'd get along. And they have different reasons for being here to me. They could easily take umbrage that I'm not on the show to win thousands of pounds but to ask for help in finding Hannah. You know the truth. Besides, I want to be with somebody I feel at ease with. Somebody who makes me laugh and lets me be who I am. I can be a little too intense for some people.'

A small smile tugged at his lips. 'You feel at ease with me?'

'Isn't it obvious?'

He sidestepped the question. 'So, Anneka Rice might not be hosting the show but there's every chance you'll be able to get your message out there. The more challenges we win, the bigger the name we create for ourselves and the better your chances of getting in the public's eye. Everyone loves a winner with a good story and you have a very special story to tell.' A heavy silence fell between them. Bryony thought he was going to remove his arm and accuse her of using him, but he didn't. 'You're right. We work well together and we can do this. I'll help you every inch of the way so we stay on the show and get those opportunities to appeal for Hannah's return.'

'Thank you, Lewis.'

'What for? You're my teammate. It's only natural I'd support you.'

'For supporting my idea – not laughing at me – and for being a good friend.'

'I wouldn't ever laugh at you,' he whispered, leaning towards her and kissing her lightly on the forehead.

Her stomach lurched and she wanted to drag his lips onto her own but sense kicked in. She couldn't ruin this friendship and Lewis might not take kindly to any advances.

Lewis broke the silence. 'While we're being open with each other, I ought to tell you about Maxwell.'

'You don't have to.'

'I do. It's only fair.'

She propped herself up on an elbow. Lewis lay on his back, staring at the ceiling.

'I haven't been honest with you. Maxwell is a woman – a woman with a peculiar name. She liked that – being different, being individual. She hated anyone calling her Max in case people thought it was short for Maxine. It was always Maxwell to everyone.'

Bryony held her breath.

'I let you assume she was male because it was easier than going through the wretched details of what happened, and part of me was amused that you believed I was involved with a man. I confess I overheard you and Melinda discussing me the very first time I met you. After I sneaked into the utility room with Sean, I earwigged your conversation. Melinda told you I wasn't your type. She hinted I was gay. I thought it was pretty funny, especially the whole "tonsil tennis" conversation.'

Her eyes widened and her mouth opened.

'Don't say anything. I can hear you're about to,' he continued. 'Let me speak first. Breaking up with Maxwell was the worst time of my life. I didn't merely lose the love of my life, I lost my own identity too. Overnight, I became invisible – a nobody. It's difficult to explain but Maxwell is gregarious, outgoing and draws attention to herself wherever she goes. It's who she is. She loves people and parties and staying up all night with crowds of friends, whereas I'm quieter, calmer and – believe it or not – more withdrawn. In truth, I don't really enjoy that type of social scene. I prefer smaller, friendly get-togethers.

'I was besotted with her. I would have walked over broken glass in bare feet if she had asked me to. It sounds silly when I say it out loud. I sound so… *pathetic*. It also made for a calmer existence to go along with whatever she wanted to do. It was easier to say yes when she wanted to go off out to a celebrity gathering rather than put up with the pouting, the sulks, the petty tantrums. Her beauty came hand in hand with a temper. She can be quite a spitfire when she's wound up. I admit I really loved being her boyfriend. I couldn't believe she wanted to be with me of all people – I was out of condition, scruffy and a bit geeky. Hardly a catch for any woman let alone a stunner like Maxwell. I'd spent my life behind computer screens and hadn't exactly taken time out for finishing school.'

The comment tickled Bryony and lifted the atmosphere.

'I never got used to that fact; after all, she could have been with someone better-looking or more exciting than me. When we went out together other men would give me sneaky, envious glances. I bet they were wondering what a bloke like me was doing with such a glamorous woman on my arm and I would think, *Yep, amazing, isn't it guys? She's mine.* It made me feel important – boosted my ego – and so I trotted along behind her like an obsessed fan or a faithful dog. It must have looked peculiar to people. We're opposites in many ways: She has stacks of showbiz friends; I'm more of a loner. She works with a huge variety of people; I work alone at home. Being with her meant I became visible to others and no longer the recluse I was before I met her.'

Bryony waited while Lewis struggled to convey how Maxwell had dazzled him and won his heart.

'The break-up took me by surprise and I fell to bits. Maxwell declared we were over and suddenly I couldn't bear to be in the flat a minute longer. I had to get away from her and so I did.'

Bryony waited for him to speak again. She could hear the hurt in his voice and wanted to hug him but refrained.

'I spent the first night on a bench by the Thames and mulled over everything. Come morning, I had a vague idea of what I had to do. I collected my car, stuck a pin in a map and ended up in Derby. Once I arrived there, I walked into a lettings agency and took a lease out on the first property they showed me. Life had lost all meaning. Might sound dramatic but that's how it felt at the time. Meeting Sean in the gym was the first bit of good luck I'd had for a while. Then becoming friends with you all and having a laugh helped me to recover. I'm better. I'm not over it completely but I'm much better.'

He paused to take a sip of water then resumed his monologue, his tone slightly brighter. 'Maxwell works in television. She's a researcher and it's due to her I applied for *What Happens in...* She got sick of me yelling answers at the television set whenever a quiz show was on so she applied to the show on my behalf. That was way before all the buzz surrounding the show, yet it was only after we'd split up and I'd moved to Derby, I actually got an invite to attend the audition in Birmingham. By then, I'd begun to change – both physically and mentally. I'd started taking control of my life at last. I'd even released some of the anger that replaced the tears and hurt. I'd met Sean, Melinda and you. I thought, *Why not*, and so I went along to that audition in Birmingham, thinking it would be a distraction – something to do. I'm so glad I did.' He stopped to let the subtext of his words sink in.

'And then there's you. You've been funny, full of life and a teeny-weeny bit bonkers. You made me smile again. You got me involved in stuff I might never have considered, including this trip to France that I'm really enjoying. However madcap this idea of yours is, it's worth pursuing and I'm more than happy to be a friend and help you find your sister. You might feel differently about me now. I should have told you sooner.'

Bryony remained silent for several minutes. She could hear his steady breathing as he waited for her to speak.

'You little shit,' she said at last. 'You knew all the time I believed you were gay. I even fancied the idea that you and Oscar might become an item. I thought you made a lovely couple.'

She heard a deep chuckle. 'Even funnier… Oscar's not gay either. He's a handsome, young man who is passionate about dancing. He's got a girlfriend called Lucinda who's also a dancer in New York. She plans to join him in London in a few months.'

Bryony smiled at him. 'And now I think you'd better put that pillow you suggested between us.'

'Spoilsport,' he replied, tugging it back into position.

Chapter Twenty

Monday, 24 July – Morning

The contestants gathered in the library. Bryony and Lewis were the last to arrive. Donald was perched on a stool looking uncomfortable, his thick legs protruded beneath a vibrant tartan kilt. His socks hung defiantly to his meaty calves. 'The first person to sing "Donald Where's Your Troosers" will be subjected to a terrible punishment. They don't call me Bravefart for nothing,' he boomed.

'Morning, Donald,' Bryony replied, catching Nicola wincing at the remark. 'You look very debonair today.'

'Thank you, Bryony. I have tried to make an impression and this kilt will certainly grab attention.'

'He's out to win,' hissed Lewis once they'd moved out of earshot. 'Why else dress like that?'

There were a couple of women that neither of them recognized in one corner. Laura was chatting animatedly to Oscar and Jim while Biggie Smalls was perched on Roxanne's knee, gazing into her eyes. She looked up as the pair entered the room.

'You look lovely, Bryony. You really suit green.'

'Thanks. I've got other outfits I prefer but they're patterned or too dull. It's been so difficult to choose something bright, plain and smart as requested. I think this one is what you'd call an opulent emerald.'

Lewis smiled widely and said, 'I had a similar dilemma. I couldn't decide between the outrageous-orange and the rose-pink polo shirt. It's been such a tough decision.'

Bryony shook her head in mock despair and said, 'The sad fact is that it's true. He's been flouncing about for an hour in a panic over his outfit. He brought along about ten different choices. In the end I couldn't bear seeing him in such a tizzy so I suggested he wear the bright blue polo top so we didn't clash.'

Lewis shrugged helplessly. 'What can I say? I don't normally think about what I wear for work, given I usually work from home. I grab whatever is clean.'

'It's okay, Lewis. My wife chose two outfits for me to wear. She laid out shirts, jackets and trousers on our bed and even added the shoes, socks and underpants in case I forgot them. She's been a little mischievous though. Look!' Jim lifted one leg of his pressed, dark grey trousers to reveal socks bearing tiny Mr Men characters. He chuckled warmly. Bryony felt a surge of affection for the man.

Jim studied Donald before speaking again, 'That's a very interesting tartan. I've never seen a mint green and yellow tartan. What clan is it from?'

Donald laughed. The sound vibrated around the room. 'It's a "WTF" tartan. A friend had it made up for me. It's not from any clan I'm aware of.'

'Doesn't your family have a special tartan?' asked Jim, oblivious to the nudge Donald gave Nicola.

'Families from Wimbledon don't generally have tartans.'

'Are you not of Scottish descent?'

Donald guffawed. 'No. I've no Scottish blood in my veins. My mates dared me to wear a skirt on television and since I've got fifty quid riding on it, I'm wearing the kilt.'

Donald tried to catch Bryony's eye but she looked away as Laura moved to the front of the room and coughed slightly to ensure she had their attention.

'Sorry I couldn't be with you yesterday. In case you don't remember me, I'm Laura and I'm the producer for *What Happens in...* You'll meet various other crew members over the next few days but for the moment you only need to recognize Roxanne, who you all know, and Nina, who's an assistant on this show.' A slim girl with deep auburn hair and almond eyes looked over from where she was sitting and waved at them.

'So, finally the mystery is about to be unveiled. It was somewhat cloak and dagger but I'm sure you understand why. We want this to be as spontaneous as possible. Today is a chance for the audience at home to get to know the contestants. It won't be too taxing and hopefully, it'll be a huge amount of fun. We're going to start with you doing a piece to camera. That is, where you talk about each other. You've had a chance to find out about each other on your trip here. Use all that information to put together a montage of your teammate, so for example, Jim, you might want to talk about Oscar's dog, Biggie Smalls, or what he does as an occupation. We only want a few sentences though, not the person's life story.'

Jim acknowledged her with a serious nod. She continued. 'After that, we have your first challenge. I can't say any more at this stage other than it is *awesome*. We'll film all morning but only an hour of footage, with the highlights of the day, will go out tonight on the first show. We're expecting massive viewing figures so wear your broadest smile and enjoy yourselves. You'll get the afternoon off to recover, and this evening at eight o'clock, we'll record a live segment here in this room, during which we'll announce the results and the losing team will have to leave the château, the show and France. The winners will then get a chance to do a private piece to camera about the day and say what they most enjoyed or disliked and how they felt it went. That will all go out live.'

Oscar spoke up. 'There are only three teams here. I thought there'd be more. It doesn't add up.'

'There are seven teams in total, the other eight contestants are staying the other side of Nantes at Grand Maison Bretagne. There was insufficient room at each hotel to accommodate you all together. They're doing their piece to camera too at the moment. Besides, it adds an extra sense of rivalry between the teams in each property. You'll meet the others later when we present you with your first challenge.'

Donald gave a loud guffaw. 'That's good, otherwise the last four days of filming would be pretty dull, what with no contestants.'

Laura ignored his outburst. 'If everyone is happy with what I've said, we'll have breakfast, and afterwards, our make-up lady here – Mattie, also known as the hairspray lady – will give you a quick dusting of make-up, powder and hairspray.' A stout, middle-aged woman smiled at them all. 'After that, you'll be miked up and we'll call you back here a pair at a time, to interview you. I'm looking for lots of energy today, people, so eat plenty of croissants now and vive *What Happens in… France!'*

–

Appetites satiated and excitement mounting, the teams were in high spirits as they waited to be made up. Bryony patted her freshly coiffed hair, now stiff with hairspray. Lewis paused to admire his reflection in an antique mirror hanging above a Louis XIV desk. I've never had such magnificent eyebrows,' he stated. 'They make me look intelligent and, dare I say it, a little younger. I'll have to buy an eyebrow pencil and have a go myself. They make such a difference. I could even get a little creative and put them on at an angle when I'm feeling cross or draw them high so I look surprised.' He raised the penciled eyebrows up and down for effect.

Bryony chuckled at his comical expressions. 'I'd leave them alone if I were you. They make Sean's eyebrows look almost sparse. He'd be over the moon if you turned up at the gym with those thick babies.'

'He does have bushy eyebrows, doesn't he? He was trimming them in the changing room last week. I ignored him. Didn't want to draw attention to him. So, I should forget the idea of male make-up then?'

Bryony appraised him once more. 'I prefer you the way you are,' she said and blushed. 'What are you going to say about me?' she asked, changing the subject

'I honestly have no idea. I thought I'd wait to see what came to me when we're in front of the camera. It would be more natural that way.'

'It's tough, isn't it? We don't want to come across too confident or too wacky.'

'I think Donald's bagged that angle,' said Lewis.

'He's a larger than life character, isn't he?' Oscar said, arriving in time to catch the end of their conversation. 'You should hear the joke he was telling the make-up lady. She could hardly keep a straight face. Almost drew a third eyebrow on poor Jim. 'I've no idea what to say about Jim. He's a lovely man but I can't say that, can I?'

'Talk about his passion for baking and being a full-time grandfather,' suggested Bryony. 'The viewers will love to know about his family.'

Oscar threw her a grateful look. 'Thanks. I'll do that. I don't want to let him down. I'm so nervous I'll mess up and say something ridiculous.'

'You won't,' said Lewis. 'Just be yourself and chat as if you're talking to us.'

Their conversation was interrupted by Roxanne. 'Lewis and Bryony, you okay to start?'

'Break a leg,' said Oscar.

'Ready?' asked Lewis.

'As I'll ever be.'

They followed Roxanne into the library and sat down on the two chairs, placed in front of a camera. Laura, by the window, waited as the cameraman adjusted his lens and confirmed he was ready to film.

Laura gave one of her famous grins. 'I'm going to start by asking you to tell me a few interesting facts you've discovered about Lewis and vice versa. If you could sum them up in only a couple of sentences, that would be ideal. We need to keep it snappy and fun. Then I'll ask you, Bryony, why you think Lewis and you are a good team. You okay with that?'

They nodded. Outside, the sky was a perfect cobalt blue and Bryony gazed at it for a moment, calming her nerves. Laura gave the signal and then spoke. 'Bryony tell me a few fascinating facts about Lewis.'

'I've not known Lewis long but during that time I've discovered he's modelled golfing attire on a catwalk and helped murder a bad-tempered chef. When he's not working as a business web designer, he's online, playing scrabble with anyone who is willing to take him on.' She stopped and looked earnestly at Laura who gave her thumbs up.

'Murder?'

'At a murder mystery event. Not in real life. Not that I know of, anyway.'

'Lewis, can you tell us something about Bryony?'

'Bryony is a champion puzzle solver. She puts her heart and soul into every challenge life throws her and she's faced a few. The biggest is trying to find her sister, Hannah, who ran away from home when she was sixteen. Bryony is desperately trying to locate her because their father is very ill and desperate to see her again.'

Bryony's jaw dropped. Had he really just said all that?

Laura cocked her head. 'Hannah?'

'Hannah Masters. She left when Bryony was only six and she hasn't seen her since. If anyone knows Hannah, please tell her to watch the show, and to contact Bryony. She needs you back home.'

Laura gave a brief nod and moved smoothly on to the next question. 'Bryony why do you think you and Lewis are a good team?'

Bryony swallowed hard to keep the tears at bay. She had to win the hearts of the nation. Lewis had given her that opening. 'We connected from the first moment we met when I discovered him dead in a pantry, then found out he wasn't dead and chased him around the kitchen with a wooden spoon. We're both ready for this challenge. And anyone who can wheel me about in a wheelbarrow with a flat tyre and not collapse in a heap afterwards, is the best partner I could wish for.' It was gushing and too much but it was all she could think of.

'Thank you both.'

The camera was switched off. Bryony sat in stunned silence as Laura checked the footage. Lewis stood up and walked across to the window.

'That looks good. Thank you both. If you'd like to wait in the dining room, I'll be there in a short while to explain the first round.'

'Was it okay?' asked Bryony.

'Super,' said Laura, waving at Roxanne as she spoke. 'Next team, please.'

They passed Jim and Oscar in the hall as they left. There was no time to do anything other than exchange glances with them. Back in the dining room, Bryony opened her mouth to speak. Lewis put a finger to his lips and pointed at the microphone clipped to his shirt. Every word would be heard. She mouthed, 'Thank you' and received a small smile. He held up crossed fingers.

Chapter Twenty One

Monday, 24 July – Morning

With interviews completed, the contestants soon found themselves being addressed again.

'Time for your first challenge. It's a pretty basic one but will test your communication skills and determination. If you'd like to follow me.'

The contestants trooped after Laura to the front of the château.

'You're joking!' Lewis exclaimed. Lined up on the drive stood three Citroën 2CVs. The first was covered in orange and black zigzags, the second had bright yellow and black panels and the third was covered in fur fabric so it looked like a woolly car.

'You cannot be serious!' exclaimed Donald in a fair impression of tennis star John McEnroe. 'There is no way on this planet I'm getting into the woolly one,' he stated, folding his chunky arms and pouting. 'It will ruin my macho image.'

Laura held out three cards to Nicola. 'Pick a card.'

Nicola took the middle card, turned it over and read, 'The 2CV Tabby.'

'Is it that orange one? A tabby cat. At least it doesn't have ears and whiskers,' grumbled Donald, taking the key from Laura. 'But it clashes with my kilt.'

'Jim, your turn.'

Jim selected one and passed it over to Oscar, who read, 'The 2CV Bumblebee. Has to be the yellow and black one.'

'That means we've got the beautiful furry one,' said Bryony. She accepted her card. 'It's called the 2CV Furby.'

'What does 2CV mean anyway?' asked Oscar, picking up a prancing Biggie, who was keen not to be left out.

'The 2CV name is an abbreviation for *Deux Chevaux Vapeur*, "two steam horses", which is actually a technical legal term from the French tax code,' explained Jim. 'The 2CV was designed to fall into the second horsepower tax class. It did not mean that it had only a two-horsepower engine,' he added.

'So it's got more poke than a lawnmower,' said Lewis.

'I think it has a little more "poke", as you put it, but it's no Ferrari,' replied Jim. 'Or "Fur-rrari", Lewis.' He chuckled. 'It was designed for country roads not grand prix circuits.'

'Jim, you have more knowledge in your brain than there is in an entire series of *University Challenge*. Is there anything you don't know?' Oscar asked, head cocked to one side.

Jim thought for a second. 'There's lots of things I don't know,' he mused before adding, 'yet.' His shoulders rocked with silent laughter at his quip, making Oscar snigger.

Laura spoke again. 'You'll have fifteen minutes to get used to driving your cars up and down the lane, and then face your challenge. One of each pair will drive. The other will give instructions. The person driving will be blindfolded and completely in the hands of the person directing them along a purpose-built course. The idea of the challenge is to drive to the far side of the course without knocking over the obstacles. For every one of those knocked down, ten seconds will be added to your final time. When you reach the end of the course, the person issuing instructions, must get out of the car and collect a basket of eggs which they are to put in the car boot. You must then both return to the starting point. The driver is to keep on their blindfold until the end of the game when they pass over the finish line. Every egg found broken on arrival will add ten seconds to your time. The winners will be the team who completes the course in the fastest time.'

Donald rolled his eyes. 'The horror of it – blindfolded and dependent on Nicola who doesn't know her left from her right.'

'It's slightly more complicated than that, Donald,' said Laura with a smirk. 'All instructions must be given in French.'

Oscar let out a horrified squeal. 'I don't know many driving commands. What's French for reverse?' he asked in a panic. He looked around for help. Bryony came to his assistance.

'*Reculer* means to retreat.'

'That'll do. Jim, once we get those eggs, we'll retreat.'

'Sounds like a good plan.'

'I'll leave you to work out your strategies and get used to the cars. By the way, they're all fitted with cameras which will be filming you and I must remind you, you're wearing microphone packs which are constantly recording you, so no swearing and no cheating! When you're ready, return here and we'll head off to the very first *What Happens in… France* challenge.'

'Are you ready for your chariot, m'lady?' Lewis asked Bryony. 'Unless you fancy driving it.'

'I'm more inclined to stroke it and fetch it a saucer of milk or something.'

'I don't think we're supposed to feed it before midnight.'

'That's gremlins not Furbies.'

'Same thing, aren't they? Hairy and cute but can turn nasty if you don't look after them properly. Or is that women?' said Lewis with a wry smile.

—

'You happy with the commands?' Bryony asked.

'Left is *gauche*, *droit* is right, *tout droit* straight on and *recule*, reverse. Got it!'

'Great. How's the car to drive?'

'Beastly.'

'You know they were built with farmers in mind and due to their flexible suspension were expected to cross field with a basket of eggs safely in the boot?'

'So that's how they came up with this challenge,' said Lewis.

'I'm guessing the course will be across a field.'

'Really? I thought they might let us loose on the main roads around here. Could be great fun in our blindfolds.' He grinned.

'Idiot. I meant a field as opposed to a driving circuit.'

'I know what you meant. Just pulling your leg. You looked so serious for a minute.'

'Sorry. It's become real, hasn't it? I want to win now and stay on the show.'

He pointed subtly at his own microphone, reminding her to be careful of what she said. They'd drawn back up outside the château and were lined up with the other cars waiting to follow Laura, Roxanne and Nina who'd jumped into a people carrier, along with some of the crew. It pulled away.

'Allons les enfants de la Patrie,' Lewis sang.

'You know the French national anthem?'

'Picked it up from watching the European football matches. I only know some of the words to a couple of the national anthems – Germany and Spain.'

'Ha!'

'What do you mean, "ha!"?' He smirked.

'There *are* no words to the Spanish national anthem.'

He beamed at her. 'Correct Brainy Bryony. Let's hope that comes up as a question. Got to concentrate now. This little furball requires careful handling.'

They trundled down the lane and turned onto a main road, flanked by poplar trees, and then beyond them, golden fields of sunflowers bursting into bloom, their huge heads upturned to the brilliant sky. Bryony couldn't quite believe she was bouncing along in a typically French car taking in such beauty. For a minute she forgot she was participating in a show and lost herself in the stunning countryside as they continued past the sunflowers and climbed a twisting road that afforded panoramic views across endless fields, dotted with rolled hay wrapped in pink and white plastic like giant marshmallows. In the distance stood a town, with a tall church spire poking out from apricot-tiled roofs that glinted in the sunshine; ahead lay hamlets of grey stone-built dwellings each with coloured shutters in hues of green and blue, and as they followed the convoy of strange Citroëns they caught sight of open-mouthed faces peering from windows, marvelling at the small procession. A small dog chased after the black and yellow car in front of them, tail wagging, until called off by a man in blue bib and braces trousers, who acknowledged them with a wave.

Gradually the houses disappeared from view as the cars snaked upwards through increasingly narrow lanes, lined with tall hawthorn bushes whose branches reached out as if attempting to touch the cars. Finally they peeled off into a vast field, where four more outrageously painted Citroëns were parked. They'd arrived at the venue.

Ahead was the course, little more than a close-cropped wide path flanked by square hay bales, that twisted and turned and headed down the hill towards a large trestle table, containing seven baskets. At various points along the route stood gaily-painted cardboard cows – the objects to be avoided.

They clambered out of their car and joined the other contestants, now milling around Laura. She broke off the introductions with some news. 'Sorry guys, but our host has been held up and won't be here today. We were hoping he'd be able to chat to you before you got started.'

'Who is our host?' asked a woman wearing overalls and a scarf tied under her chin.

'I can't tell you that. It's a surprise. A very pleasant surprise. Okay, everyone. Time to get back into your cars. We'll go in order of parking so Declan and Avril, you'll go first.' The woman in the scarf nodded in affirmation. 'Once you complete the course, park back up in the same spot and wait in your vehicles until all the contestants have finished. You all clear on the rules? All drivers must wear blindfolds. Nina is handing those out now. No cheating. The cameras are on you and be careful what you say. When you wear the microphone packs, we can hear everything. This is a family-friendly show and we don't want to spend all afternoon editing out any bad language. Passengers, you can only use French to instruct your drivers. We'll time each team but the results won't be released until tonight during the live segment of the show. Good luck everyone. Remember, lots of energy folks and… enjoy yourselves.'

Lewis accepted his blindfold and held up a thumb to Oscar as he and Bryony returned to their car, both ignoring Donald who'd put his blindfold on over his ears and was being playfully smacked by his partner. Bryony climbed into the furry 2CV and sat in silence as they watched a fluorescent pink CV bound off from the start line and weave into the first cow. Bryony winced.

'I hope we don't do that.'

'That's up to you. All damage inflicted on any cows will be down to your navigation. I'm simply taking orders. Which is rare, so make the most of it.'

—

With eyes completely covered, Lewis clung onto the steering wheel and pressed the accelerator pedal gingerly. The car lurched forward. Bryony, on the edge of her seat, issued commands steadily and with confidence. Years of teaching had given her the ability to appear calm even when her heart was slapping against her ribcage. The car bounced up and down in the ruts, causing her hair to flop over her face. She brushed it away.

'Tout droit, tout droit, tout droit… gauche!'

'We miss the cow?'

'Oui,' she replied. 'Droit, droit.'

They weaved and stuttered, accelerated and slowed. 'Gauche. Non! Gauche.'

'Oh la la,' said Lewis. 'This is probably the hardest thing I've ever done. I'm sweating here.'

'Tout droit.' Another cow was looming up and the course veered to the left. 'Gauche. Ack! Merde!'

'Did you just swear in French?' he asked, grinning.

'Oui. Stop!'

She threw the car door open and scampered towards the last remaining basket of eggs, then charging around to the boot, lifted the lid and placed the basket as far back as she could. Diving back into the passenger seat she began instructing once more, arms waving even though Lewis could see nothing. 'Recule.'

The furry CV was turned around and they retraced their journey, hitting the first cow and flattening it.

'I hit it?' he asked, as they bounced over it.

'Oui. Dead cow.'

'Okay, c'est le moment pour le Plan B,' he replied. The car sped up.

'Too fast!' shouted Bryony in horror. 'The eggs. Gauche! Droit!' She inched closer to the windscreen to navigate.

'We have to make up time.'

'Tout droit. Slow down.' She hung onto the door handle as the car bounced up and down and jiggled them from side to side. 'Lewis!'

'Non.'

'Slow down… cow!'

They hit the second cardboard cut-out and it toppled over. Lewis kept his foot down and they swerved dramatically to the right then left and made it around the bend without further incident. Bryony screeched commands all the while clinging to the handrail with both hands.

At last they reached the finish line where Lewis removed his blindfold and dropping both arms onto the steering wheel, placed his head onto them and drew a deep breath.

'Why did you speed up? We nearly collided with every bale of hay there. I thought we were going to end up in the next field. We'll lose loads of points for hitting the cows and the eggs will be broken.'

'It was the only thing I could do.'

'Really? I thought taking the course steadily and not incurring penalties might be the thing to do. I don't remember being told to bump into everything we could possibly hit. You almost crushed a cameraman!' Bryony unclipped her seatbelt and threw him a bewildered stare.

'Trust me,' he mouthed.

The fight went out of her in an instant. He'd had a plan, one she'd not been party to. It had been deliberate.

Laura arrived to check the basket of eggs. 'One egg broken. Eight dead cows. We'll have to add ninety seconds to your time. Nice driving Lewis. If I didn't know better, I'd say you weren't wearing a blindfold.'

'I was definitely wearing it, Laura. I might keep it. I obviously drive better with it on than off.'

Each team was stripped of their microphones and once again the convoy of cars made their way back down towards to the main road. This time the cameras were not watching them.

'Spit it out. What was this great plan of yours,' said Bryony. 'I have a right to know, given I almost died in a fur-covered Citroën today.'

'You were safe. I was pretty confident I knew where I was going and I knew you'd yell at me if I steered off course. At worst we'd have hit a hay bale. I've got a pretty decent sense of direction, even in a blindfold. I noticed all the other cars before us took it really slowly on the return journey to make sure they didn't break any eggs, but you told me these cars were designed with exactly that in mind – they have super springy suspension and if farmers could drive over rutted fields and still bring back their eggs safely, I figured we would too, no matter how fast we went. The others were unnecessarily cautious, so as I watched them complete the course, I figured we should go for the opposite tactic – drive as fast as we dare and the eggs would be fine. I knew I'd kill a few cows but even with the penalties added to our time we ought to be in the top three.'

Bryony studied him. His forehead was still damp with sweat and the make-up on one of his eyebrows had rubbed away. She couldn't be annoyed given he'd tried so hard. 'You're right. I should have realized the eggs would be okay. Thanks for taking a chance, and thanks for what you said this morning at the interview.'

'That's what being a teammate is all about. You have each other's backs. Just need the gamble to pay off now.'

Bryony recognized the lane they'd been up and down earlier that day when they'd first got into the furry Citroën. It led to the château where they were staying. It was already mid-afternoon and they only had three hours until they'd find out who had made it through to the next round. She was counting on Lewis being right.

Chapter Twenty Two

Monday, 24 July – Evening

The library seemed tiny with all the contestants and film crew crushed into the space. There was not one but three cameramen filming each of the teams. Roxanne wasn't with them. She'd gone to join the other teams at their hotel and now all that connected them to her was a television screen which currently showed her sitting with the other four contestants. Laura and the crew were making sure the link stayed live and were waiting to be counted in. The public had already been watching the very first episode of *What Happens in…* and had no doubt already decided on who they liked and wanted to win. In two minutes, all their anxious faces would be beamed out on national television and one pair would be sent home. The thought was terrifying. She shifted in her seat and pulled at her blouse. Lewis, next to her, sat with a concentrated mien. She wondered if he was as nervous as her.

Bryony had spent the last half an hour trying to dispel anxieties that had appeared as she'd prepared for the live show. Lewis had gone for a walk around the grounds to give her space to get ready. She'd wished he'd stayed because left to her own thoughts she could only dwell on their dismal performance and speculate as to how badly they'd done. Back in the UK people were now glued to the show and would see her clinging to the grab handle of the car. She shuddered at memories of her screaming at Lewis to slow down. People would hate her.

Laura lifted a finger. One minute to go. Oscar, to her right, appeared to be as nervous as her. His knee bounced up and down rhythmically as he waited for the result. Biggie Smalls had decided he didn't want to be on camera and had disappeared under a chair for a snooze. On the television screen in front of them, the other four teams looked to be equally nervous.

Somebody said, 'Action' and a deep voice that came from the television, spoke. 'It's Monday evening and the end of day one of the hugely anticipated show, *What Happens in…* Our fourteen contestants are waiting eagerly to hear the results of today's challenge and find out which of them has made it through to day two, and the next round of *What Happens in…* Coming live from France on this sunny Monday evening, we have all of our intrepid contestants staying in not one but two châteaux. Bonsoir, contestants!'

'Bonsoir,' everyone chorused back.

'Laura do you have the results for your three teams, over there at Hotel Petit Château?'

'I do. Oscar and Jim, you completed the course in eight minutes, fifteen seconds. You incurred only thirty seconds of penalties which means you did it in eight minutes forty-five seconds.'

'Is that good?' asked Oscar.

Laura smiled a reply. 'Donald and Nicola, you completed the course in nine minutes and incurred fifty seconds of penalties which means you did it in nine minutes fifty seconds.'

Nicola squirmed in her chair and glanced at Donald who gave a confident nod. Laura stopped talking and the voice on the screen took over.

'Thank you, Laura. Now let's go across to Grand Maison Bretagne.'

Bryony interlocked her fingers to prevent her hands from shaking. Having flattened so many cows, they'd gained ninety seconds of penalties. It was too much. It was unlikely they'd beaten the others. Laura had not disclosed their results because they were last. Now on the large television screen were the faces of the other contestants in Grand Maison Bretagne sat in a room not dissimilar to theirs at Hotel Petit Château: Avril and Declan, a couple in their forties, who'd started the game off, then Evan and Thomas, two men from Wales both with beards and glasses who looked like brothers but weren't related, next, Hugh and Terri, who'd travelled from Scottish islands to be on the show and finally, Deepan and Mira, a cheerful couple from the south of England. Bryony watched as one by one the teams learned their times and faces broke into smiles of relief and she guessed it was over for her and Lewis. She fought back disappointment. They'd not even made it beyond the first day. She couldn't look at Lewis who'd tried to win the game for them but who'd in fact, lost it with his outrageous tactics.

'And so with all the times in for the contestants at Grand Maison Bretagne, let's return to Hotel Petit Château, and find out how our final team, Bryony and Lewis, got on.'

She lifted her head at the mention of her name and looked at the camera, willing viewers to remember her and Hannah. Laura read from a white card. 'You completed the course in six minutes twelve seconds and having squashed all your cows on the return journey, had ninety seconds added to your time, giving you a total of seven minutes forty-two seconds. Which was an *incredible* time. Congratulations Bryony and Lewis, you are actually tonight's winners!'

The room filled with applause like the soft wings of a thousand butterflies lifting as one towards the sky. Bryony's mouth dropped open and she found herself swept in an embrace. She barely registered the television screen now showing the disappointed faces of Avril and Declan, over in the other château. Heart racing, she turned her full attention to what was happening, sorry for the pair who were leaving and relieved it wasn't her and Lewis.

'Sadly, we have to say goodbye to one team and tonight we'll be saying au revoir to Declan and Avril, our couple from Liverpool.'

Avril, wearing similar overalls and scarf to those she'd worn during the day, wiped a tear from her eye, then she and Declan stood up and shook hands with their fellow contestants Grand Maison Bretagne and waved to the camera before walking away. The screen changed again as they began broadcasting from Hotel Petit Château. A cameraman moved silently towards Lewis and Bryony. Laura stepped forward to join them.

'Lewis would you like to say a few words?'

He squeezed Bryony's hand. 'It's thanks to Bryony we won. She gave me the lowdown on Citroën 2CVs and how they were built for farmers. We took a chance, based on her logic and it paid off.'

'Bryony, have you got anything you'd like to add?' Laura asked.

Bryony swallowed. Out of the corner of her eye, she could see herself on the screen above the fireplace, eyes wide and cheeks flushed with success. 'I have but it's not to do with France. I'd really like to put out a request or a plea, even. My sister, Hannah Masters, ran away when I was a kid. I've missed her every day since. I need her to get in touch with me, so if anybody knows her, please tell her I'm on this show and I love her. That's *Hannah Masters*. I don't know what surname she uses today, or even what she looks like now, but she used to have blonde hair and grey eyes similar to mine, oh, and she's forty-five years old.'

'How can they get in touch with you, Bryony?'

'Via my blog, *Searching for Hannah*. My contact details are there and photographs of Hannah as a child, so please look at them as see if they remind you of anyone you know.'

'You think you and Lewis can stay in the game and beat the others on *What Happens in…*?'

'I hope so. We're determined to do our best. We want to be able to ask the public for their help every day and if that means winning all the challenges, no matter how hard they are, then that's what we'll do,' she said, smiling at Lewis, who nodded his accord.

Bryony and Lewis, thank you and we look forward to seeing how you get on tomorrow, day two, on *What Happens in…*'

The cicadas chirped late into the night. With the windows wide open and an agreeable light breeze wafting into the room, Bryony and Lewis lay on the bed and reflected on the events of the day. It had been more exhausting, mentally and physically than either had anticipated and soon she began to drift to sleep.

'Nice here,' Lewis mumbled. 'I could live here.'

'I could stay here forever,' Bryony replied. 'Maybe I could move into the château next door. Then I'd know where to come if I wanted a decent cup of coffee and cornflake cakes.'

Chapter Twenty Three

Tuesday, 25 July – Morning

'Morning, everyone. Did you all sleep soundly?'

'Good thanks, Laura,' said Lewis.

'I hope you all got a sheet explaining what's happening today. I asked to have them delivered to your rooms early this morning so you wouldn't have time to confer with each other or try and work out the route we'll expect you to take. Apologies again for keeping you in the dark, for confiscating your phones and for banning tablets but we couldn't have you searching online for everything ahead of today and tomorrow, especially as this part involves logic, map-reading and intelligence.

'Rules me out, then,' said Oscar with a nervous giggle.

'It's going to be a busy couple of days. I'll read through the game rules with you and make sure you're all clear on them.

'As you've now discovered, this challenge is a car-rally scavenger hunt. Anyone ever done a scavenger hunt similar to this before? No? It's huge fun. Roxanne is going to hand out the vital packs of information that will help you solve clues and get you around the route. There's also a map and, of course, you'll get to drive your fabulous vehicles.' She paused to allow Roxanne to pass the packs to the contestants. Donald, once again in his kilt, was looking less rambunctious than the day before. Nicola wasn't next to him but had chosen instead to sit near Oscar.

'It's actually quite simple. On top of each pack is a red envelope. Don't open it yet. It contains the clue to your first destination and to a treasure you need to collect along the way. You can use the packs of information to help you decipher the clues. The answers are in there somewhere.'

She stopped to check everyone understood and once satisfied continued, 'When you decipher the clue and reach the first destination, you'll discover one of us waiting there. We'll then ask you a question relevant to the destination. For example, if you had worked out you needed to go to Paris, I would greet you there and I might ask you, "What did Gustave Eiffel build?" No, Oscar, you're not going to drive to Paris,' she added, seeing his mouth flap open.

'Mind-reader,' he retorted.

'Tell us the answer and we will hand over the clues to your next destination and the treasure you will need to collect en route, and so on, until you reach the final destination. If you don't guess the answer, you pass it. You'll still receive your clues but you'll have a point deducted from your final score. Please, no swearing, no cheating and no heated arguments. Actually, you can have heated arguments. In fact, it'll be more entertaining if you do argue.'

'We'll be bloody hilarious then,' mumbled Donald, earning a cold stare from Nicola.

Jim spoke up. 'Let me get this right. We're given clues to a destination and to a *treasure* we have to find along the way. Once we have worked out both clues, we head to the destination, collecting our treasure as we go. We meet you. You ask us a question about the destination in order to receive the next set of clues. If we don't know the answer we can pass on it, incurring a penalty point.'

'You got it, Jim. Are the rest of you clear on the rules?' The others nodded.

'Who gets to drive? Same as yesterday?'

'You decide which one of you is going to drive. Once you have figured out your destination, you need to plan your route using the map.'

Jim nodded his head in approval. 'Maps. The old-fashioned way,' he murmured.

'Your partner needs to read the file to find out as many facts as he or she can about each destination. It's been laid out in easy-to-read sections for you.'

'What if we all arrive at the first destination at the same time?'

'It's unlikely, especially as you have to pick up a treasure on your way to the destination. Also, you'll be starting from different locations equidistant to the first endpoint. We'll go with you to the starting points and will tell you when you can open your first envelope. First team to each location wins three points while the second to arrive wins one point. These points will tally up at the end of the day. The team that reaches the final destination the quickest will win an extra three points and the other team will win one point. They will also be added to your final scores.'

Jim scratched his ear thoughtfully. 'So, the first team to a destination wins three points and the fastest around the entire circuit wins three points?'

'Correct. You receive one point for every item or trea-sure you find on the hunt too. It might be an actual item or you might be asked to photograph a monument, a statue, a building or something different. You can use the phone in the glove box for this purpose too. It has a camera.' She checked that everyone understood the brief.

'Teams have been issued with a picnic in the boot of the car. We're allowing you one hour for your lunch. You can take the hour whenever you want. It will not be docked from your final time.' Laura scanned the faces of the group. Satisfied there were no other questions, she continued. 'Finally, there's a huge surprise at one of the checkpoints. You'll know what it is when you get there,' she announced, a smirk spreading on her face.

'Today, it's all about finding your way around the region, answering questions about what you discover and having an enjoyable time. By the way, there's to be no speeding to get to the destinations. You must stick to speed limits. Remember, we have cameras in your cars and we shall be watching your every move.'

The room was filled with exuberance as contestants wriggled on seats, eager to get going.

'After breakfast, please come back here to let Mattie check you over and wait for the tech guys to check your microphone packs are working. Once we're ready, Jim and Oscar, you'll head off with Roxanne to your starting point. Donald and Nicola, you'll be with Nina and Lewis and Bryony, you're with me.'

The contestants bustled out of the room, chattering loudly. Biggie picked up on the excitement and scuttled beside his master, his claws pitter-pattering on the tiles.

Chapter Twenty Four

Tuesday, 25 July – Morning

'This cursed car!'

'Now, now. There's to be no swearing in this car,' Bryony said, smirking at the look on Lewis's face. The engine churned again before the two cylinders kicked in. The engine trembled, screeched then whizzed and popped at idle.

'Just when I think I've got it, I forget where the gears are. Okay, come on, you little furry pain, let's get going.'

'It's quite minimalist in here, isn't it?'

'That's one word to describe it. I can think of a few others that aren't suitable for prime-time viewing,' he added as the Citroën lurched around the car park.

'The seats are comfortable though. They're really wide and softly sprung. I'm slumped in mine like it's an overused sofa.'

'They have to be large and comfy to soak up all the bumps and bounces. Aha! I'm sorted now. I'm going to drive this tin shed like it's never been driven before. Are you sure you don't want to have a go at driving?'

'I'll drive if you don't fancy it but I am probably the best person to read the files and sort out the clues. I can speed read – it's one of the skills I picked up while studying at university. I'll be able to get through the information quickly.'

Lewis pursed his lips and let out a slow whistle. 'Brains, looks and can speed read. I'm impressed. Of course, I've driven around Silverstone Grand Prix circuit so clearly, I'm more suited to driving.'

'Did you really?'

'I took an Aston Martin around the circuit on one of those track days where lots of petrol-heads turn up wanting to screech around the track like racing drivers. You could almost taste the testosterone in the briefing room before we went out onto the circuit. I managed about three laps in ten seconds. At least, that's what it felt like. It was probably ten minutes. I was terrified. I think I drove the last lap with my eyes shut! Which pretty much accounts for why I was so good at yesterday's challenge. Can you read out the first clue again? I'm ready to tackle the road.'

'Locate the flying flea then search for the elephant to discover your first clue.'

'Wasn't the flying flea some sort of aeroplane?' asked Lewis, furrowing his brow.

'Known as "*pou du ciel*" in French,' replied Bryony. 'They were home-made aircraft built in the 1930s, I believe.'

Lewis shook his head and laughed. 'You never fail to astound me. How do you know all this stuff?'

'Too much time spent with my nose in a book. Although, you can never have too much time reading,' she answered. 'I'm not sure where I picked up that particular piece of information. Dad enjoys watching documentaries on television, especially those about history.' For a second an image of her father filled her head.

Bryony relegated the memory to the back of her mind. 'I expect it was something I learnt from one of those. He was invariably glued to one documentary or another,' she added absently as she chewed her lip. The pair worked through the file and bandied about ideas until finally Bryony tapped her head with her forefinger.

'Got it!' she exclaimed, eyes alight with excitement. 'It's mentioned in these notes. "*Les Machines de l'île* built within the once-decaying shipyards of the Isle of Nantes." I bet we'll discover a flying flea there along with a few other strange creatures. Come on, chauffeur, let's go!' she shouted waving her notes.

'Go to the top of the class, Bryony,' Lewis replied, and pressing the accelerator pedal to the floor, they exited the car park towards Nantes.

–

Thanks to some excellent signage, Lewis and Bryony had no difficulty in finding the old shipping area which had become a tourist hotspot. No sooner had they exited the car than they found themselves trailed by a cameraman, one of a group of three, who'd been waiting for their arrival. They followed the queue of visitors into the world of *Les Machines de l'île*, towards a carousel unlike any other Bryony had witnessed.

Lewis read out the leaflet picked up at the ticket office. 'My goodness, this place is incredible!' he declared, his nose buried in the leaflet. 'It's full of mechanical marvels. Aha! Here it is. It's as we suspected. Get this,' he continued, '"Pay attention when you enter the *Galerie des Machines* for an enormous heron will swoop over your heads. Dodge the giant ant scurrying past you – and try not to scratch and squirm at the sight of a giant flea,"' he read. '"The wind tunnel flight simulator used to test all the amazing flying machines is unique in the world. You can watch as a machinist takes the control of a flying flea, straps on a seat belt, helmet and goggles, and flies at speeds of more than one hundred kilometres an hour." This is both amazing and weird. It's like *Avatar* meets Disneyland.'

Bryony was no longer listening. She stopped in her tracks and reached for Lewis's arm. 'There!' she gasped. Emerging from the vast old steel and glass warehouses of the island's past, eyes blinking in the daylight, trunk spraying water and packed with amazed joyriders, was a gigantic mechanical elephant.

The elephant raised its enormous trunk and trumpeted. Parents and children stood agog as the lumbering beast advanced, placing each enormous mechanical foot deliberately on the ground. Bystanders as small as beetles in comparison to the huge creature snapped away at it with cameras and phones.

Some thirty or so passengers seated the equivalent of four storeys high under a canopy on the elephant's back were taking in the view of the former shipyards from their lofty position while others stood either side of the animal, where a saddle might fit, and observed the ogling crowds or the gears being operated by a machinist.

'That's where we'll find our next clue,' she shouted and tugged at Lewis's arm. They approached the behemoth with caution as it ambled towards the carousel where it stopped, trumpeting loudly. The tourists began to disembark and headed towards the carousel while others waited to fill their places. The crowds filled with excitable children and parents eager to entertain them clustered around the beast.

Lewis threw up his hands. 'What now?'

'Climb on board and see if there's a clue hidden up there,' suggested Bryony.

'I'm game for that. This is the coolest theme park I've been in and not a Mickey Mouse in sight.'

'No Mickey Mouse but guess who I can see?' replied Bryony, a large grin spreading across her face. Laura stood near the carousel. She was brandishing an envelope. A girl holding a reflective dish that resembled an umbrella without its handle said something to her and along with a third individual, they advanced towards Bryony and Lewis. Without being instructed, the girl angled the dish and received mumbled thanks from the cameraman. A shaven-headed young man carrying a large furry microphone held it over the pair.

Laura beamed at them. 'Congratulations! You're the first team to work out the clue and arrive here. Isn't it an amazing place?'

Lewis offered her a broad smile in return. 'It certainly is. I hope there'll be time to explore before we leave.'

'You could stay here and enjoy all that it has to offer or you could carry on to the next checkpoint ahead of the others,' she joked. 'The choice is yours.'

'Next checkpoint,' said Bryony. 'Definitely. We want to win, don't we, Lewis?' Lewis nodded obediently while pulling a face like a reluctant child. Bryony nudged him in the ribs.

'It's like being married,' he complained. 'She's such a taskmaster.'

'No comment. Did you find the treasure on the way here?'

'Oh yes, although we were tempted to scoff them ourselves,' replied Lewis, extracting a packet of chocolate biscuits from a carrier bag.'

'Aha! You've brought a packet of LU Petit écolier – the little schoolboy,' said Laura, eyeing up the red box. These are my all-time favourite French chocolate biscuits.'

'And mine too. It was an easy clue for two biscuit lovers. Bryony eats her own weight in chocolate biscuits per day,' said Lewis, grimacing as he received a sharp prod in the ribs from his teammate.

'I think you're the chocoholic biscuit-muncher in this team. Who travelled here with three packs as emergency rations?'

Lewis raised his hands. 'Guilty.'

'Okay, folks, to earn your second destination clue you must answer the following question: once a knight and lord from Brittany, a leader in the French army, and a companion-in-arms of Joan of Arc, this self-confessed serial killer of children, believed to be the inspiration for the 1697 fairy tale "Bluebeard" by Charles Perrault, was hung in the city of Nantes. Who is he?'

Bryony beamed. 'Reading the file in the car paid off. It was Gilles de Rais,' she answered with confidence.

Lewis held up his hand and she high-fived it.

'Good thing I wasn't driving and had plenty of time to research a little.'

'It was a good thing you weren't driving. End of sentence,' said Lewis, earning himself a friendly punch on the arm.

'That's the correct answer, Bryony,' said Laura and handed them a white envelope. 'Here's your second clue. Open it when you're back in your car. Good luck.'

They raced out of the park as quickly as they possibly could all-the-while avoiding huge groups of people headed towards them in a steady flow.

Lewis stuck out his bottom lip. 'Shame. I'd have liked a quick ride on that gigantic elephant.'

'I'll treat you to an entire day here when we win. Now, let's get this envelope opened and on the road.'

Back inside the Citroën, Bryony waved the envelope at the camera secreted in one corner of the car before ripping it open. '"We three queens are still sailing today but where was the flagship of the Cunard Line built? Your next clue will be at the old submarine base,"' she read, lines of concentration furrowing her brow.

'I think the question refers to the ocean liners the *Queen Elizabeth*, *Queen Mary II* and *Queen Victoria*,' declared Lewis. 'Which one of them is Cunard's flagship?'

'I have a feeling it's the *Queen Mary II*. She replaced *Queen Elizabeth*. She was designed for transatlantic cross-ings and at the time was the largest liner ever built.'

'Don't tell me. You watched a documentary about cruise ships.'

Bryony nodded. 'You got it. I have my dad to thank for that piece of knowledge too.'

'This is turning out to be a breeze for us. Hope all the other clues are as easy. We now need to work out whereabouts it was built. Pass me the map. It must be along the coast somewhere.'

Heads almost touching, they examined the map together. She could feel the warmth emanating from his body. He smelt of lavender and oak moss – a heady woody and herbaceous scent – reminiscent of her parents' garden and a fleeting memory of being a young girl curled up on a blanket beside the well-tended borders, reading *Alice in Wonderland*. The memory vanished as Lewis stubbed his finger against the map, making it rustle and fold under the pressure. 'Saint-Nazaire,' he cried triumphantly. 'It's a large French port. I bet that's where we need to go. Check in the file.'

Bryony thumbed through to the appropriate page and skimmed through the notes:

'"Chantiers de l'Atlantique yard, Saint-Nazaire,"' she recited. '"Located at the mouth of the Loire, it is one of the world's largest shipyards. The iconic *Queen Mary II* was floated in 2003."' And, get this, there's a huge submarine active during the cold war that is open to the visiting public and a museum that's set up like a liner. We've worked it out. We are the A-team!' she shouted. Her victory was short-lived as she spotted the arrival of the black and yellow Citroën.

'Quick. Get going. Oscar and Jim are hot on our tails. We don't want to lose our lead. Foot down. Don't spare the *deux chevaux*.'

'*Oui, madame!*' shouted Lewis in response, as he put the car into gear and drew away into the traffic.

Chapter Twenty Five

Tuesday, 25 July – Late Morning

The furry Citroën puttered into the large car park at the old submarine base in Saint-Nazaire and drew up in front of the Escale Atlantic, an ocean-liner experience, where a small group of people was gathered. Roxanne waved at their car and spoke to the men standing next to her. Each of them wore a beret and matching striped red, white and blue T-shirts with *What Happens in… France* written across their chests. Two cameras on pivots were trained on the car as it drew up.

Bryony had once more worked out the clue and announced that actor Jacques Tati had holidayed at Saint-Nazaire in his famous film *Monsieur Hulot's Holiday* that had been filmed on a beach nearby. In return they received a card containing the written clue for the treasure they had to collect. Bryony read out, "'In which of the twenty-three books does the character Tintin, along with his sidekick Captain Haddock and Snowy the dog, come to Saint-Nazaire? This is your second treasure. You must find a copy of the book and take it to the third location.'"

'We'll have to locate a bookshop and quickly. They all shut for lunch at twelve o'clock on the dot. We'll have to hang about until three if we don't find it before then or forfeit the point.'

Bryony checked her watch. It was half past eleven. 'We should have enough time. Let's go.'

The pair hastened back to their car and ripped open the envelope.

'"Pass the salt and head to main gate of the capital of Morbihan."'

'Guérande,' said Lewis before Bryony had even reached for the file. 'It's renowned for its salt marshes and peat bogs and the sea salt known as Fleur de Sel de Guérande. It can be used as bath salts and also in cooking. It's found in butter too – little crystals of it rather than grains. Maxwell used to buy it from a delicatessen shop in the town. I don't know why she couldn't buy ordinary butter,' he commented, transported for a moment back to his penthouse in Camden. He shook himself free from the clutches of the memory.

'You can work out the rest of the clue while I drive in the direction of Guérande. There must be a bookshop or a newsagent around here somewhere. With Tintin as famous as he is in this town, there's sure to be somewhere that sells the books. I'll putter along. Ignore anyone who toots at us. I'll wave at them and look lost.'

As he was speaking, Bryony noticed an elated Oscar skipping back to his vehicle, a blue envelope in his hand. 'Go, go, go!' she yelled, and the furry Citroën rattled out of the car park, leaving behind a bemused cameraman.

Bryony chewed at her bottom lip, head turning left and right in search of a bookshop. The car moseyed down the road, rapidly gathering a line of traffic behind it as it dawdled along streets. An irritated driver in a Renault blasted his horn as he finally overtook them. Unfazed, Lewis waved merrily back. Yet another angry driver soon overtook the car. This one yelled something unintelligible out of his window. Lewis blew him a kiss.

'This is way more stressful than I anticipated,' Bryony grumbled. 'My brain is whirring too fast.'

'If you want to swap, you can drive,' Lewis offered as a van honked at them and overtook at speed.

'I'll stick to being flummoxed if you don't mind. You're far better at driving than me. You're calmer than me. I'd be a gibbering wreck by now.' She peered out of the window, scanning left and right. 'I can't see a newsagent or… whoa! Hold up. There's a *médiathèque*. That's a multimedia library. Stop the car and I'll go and check to see if they have any Tintin books.'

Lewis pulled to the side of the road, allowing several grateful motorists to pass him. Bryony clambered out of the car and, dodging the oncoming traffic, dashed across the road into the large building. Ten minutes passed before Bryony emerged again. She held a brown wrapped parcel. She jogged towards him, arms waving in triumph, jumped into the car, threw her arms around him and planted a kiss on his cheek.

'I got the last remaining copy of *The Seven Crystal Balls*. If it hadn't been for you driving around and around so patiently, we wouldn't have discovered the *médiathèque*. You're an ace teammate.'

Bryony hunched forward and rifled through the notes again, deciding on the route for their next destination 'The capital of Morbihan is Vannes. It looks to be approximately eighty kilometres away. I'll read up about Vannes. You can admire the scenery.'

'Or maybe you'd like me to sing a French song to get you in the mood.'

'What French songs do you actually know?'

'What about 'Fade to Grey' by Ultravox? There are some French lyrics in that. And, of course, there's that Serge Gainsbourg song – the one with all that heavy breathing in it. I don't know the words but I can do the heavy breathing for you.'

'Camera, Lewis. You're being filmed. You can't do heavy breathing on this show. They'll have to edit it.'

'Can't think of any other songs. Do you know any?'

'Promise not to snigger? I really enjoy Jacques Brel's music. 'Ne Me Quittes Pas' is one of my favourite songs. It's poignant. It means, don't leave me.'

'Don't leave me,' Lewis repeated and cast a quick look in her direction. She had her head lowered, engrossed now in studying the file. He gripped the steering wheel, murmuring, 'Impressed. Seriously impressed.'

–

An hour later they'd almost reached the walled city of Vannes. Bryony was fidgeting in her seat. Her hip was aching like mad.

'Can we stop before we reach the town and the gate?' she asked. 'I really need to have a stretch and a walk.'

'Sure. I could do with getting out too. I'm beginning to feel like I'm getting cramp all the way to my toenails.'

They pulled over into a lay-by and vacated the car, breathing in the scent of meadow flowers. Each slipped off their microphone pack that attached around their waists and left them on the car seats. Lewis raised his arms and stretched, luxuriating in the warmth of the sun, then circled his shoulders to ease the stiffness that had accumulated in his muscles. Meanwhile Bryony dropped onto the grass and, in a seated position, pulled her spine erect then brought the soles of her feet together, clasping them tightly with her hands. She took a deep breath in and then, breathing out again, she pressed her thighs and knees downward towards the ground. She sat with eyes closed for a few seconds before flapping her legs like the wings of a freshly hatched butterfly, rhythmically and slowly. After a while, she straightened her legs. Lewis was watching her.

'It's called the butterfly pose,' she explained. 'Also known as "Badhakonasana". It helps with fatigue when you've been in one position standing or sitting for a long period and it helps with flexibility and discomfort. I usually practise yoga positions like this every day but I haven't since we left the UK and my hip's beginning to grumble.'

'How did you hurt your hip?' Lewis asked.

'A nasty accident when I was a kid. I got hit by a car,' answered Bryony. 'My pelvis took the worst of it and I fractured the left iliac wing badly. It was fortunate I was so young – I was only six at the time – and could heal. The surgeons stuck me back together with a mixture of metal plates and screws and I had to use a walker to get around for quite some time but I recovered. I had a limp for many years but exercise and physiotherapy have helped, and as you see, I'm fine nowadays. The hip niggles some days. I seem to suffer most when I sit for too long or if I'm overactive. I suspect it's down to ageing. The doctors told me I could expect to get arthritis when I was older and I'm older now.'

'I'm sorry. You didn't have much luck as a child, did you?'

'There are many people worse off than me. The accident wasn't important, nor was the treatment that followed it, but it *was* the reason I lost my sister Hannah.'

'How come?'

'I think my parents blamed her for my accident. I remember her sneaking into hospital to visit me. She looked so dreadful – scared, shocked and white-faced, like a ghost.

'Hannah changed in the months following the accident. She withdrew from us all. Mum took personal time off work to look after me, and Hannah didn't babysit me any more. I missed our time together. Hannah began studying for her exams so she was invariably too busy to watch television or play with me. She spent most of the time in her bedroom and only appeared at mealtimes when she would push food about her plate and hardly eat anything. Mum got really annoyed about that. I remember her raising her voice, which she never used to do. Hannah would sulk and say she wasn't hungry, and Mum would insist she ate to keep up her strength.

'There were a few arguments too. Mum would tell Hannah she was becoming a moody little madam and Hannah would stomp off to her room. Hannah used to sneak out at nights too. I never knew where she went but I didn't tell my parents what she was up to. She was having a hard enough time.' Bryony paused, looked out at the golden fields beyond filled with sunflowers and sighed.

'She disappeared on a Friday. I can recall it so clearly. I was watching *Crackerjack* – we usually watched it together but she'd gone straight to her room after school. I remember hoping she'd come downstairs and join me. The Krankies were on at the time and I was laughing at something they'd done – really laughing, you know when you can't stop? Then Mum suddenly came rushing into the room in a wild panic, clutching a note, saying Hannah had gone and asking if I knew anything about it. Of course, I didn't. The note was from Hannah. I didn't read it until later, after the police had been called. It was in her best handwriting and on pale blue notepaper with animals along the bottom that I'd chosen for her as a Christmas present. It was brief and cryptic and I memorized every single word of it: "I'm so very sorry. I can't carry on any more. The guilt is ripping me apart. It's best if I leave. Please don't look for me. Goodbye. I love you all." That was the last we heard from her. I don't know how many times I've wished I could turn back time and change the sequence of events that caused my sister to feel she had no other option than to run away from home. If I hadn't had that accident, she'd be there now.'

Lewis spoke, his voice soothing. 'I don't know what to say to make it better for you, Bryony.'

'You're helping already. You've come on this crazy adventure with me and you're doing a great job helping me to get people on board and look out for her. Now, I can't sit here being maudlin. We have a town to reach and a clue to work out.'

Lewis put out his hand and helped her to her feet. They stood facing each other, the warm breeze caressing them. For the longest minute, he held her hand before pulling away.

Chapter Twenty Six

Tuesday, 25 July – Afternoon

Lewis cheered her up with some light-hearted banter and a terrible joke. Bryony pulled such a comical face that he almost drove into the side of the road laughing at her expression. The mood changed again and each entertained the other with ridiculous jokes until, chuckling loudly, they arrived at Vannes.

'Is that the bumblebee car near the gate?' asked Bryony.

Lewis looked over and groaned. 'There can't be two cars with that design.'

'And that's the tabby car and that one over there looks like one belonging to another team,' she added, pointing at one covered in stars.

'How did they all get here so quickly?'

'Must have worked out the clues before we did.'

They parked and searched for the crew at the gate Porte Saint-Vincent Ferrier that led into the well-preserved medieval streets of the walled town of Vannes.

'It looks stunning. We really should stay on in France after this show and come back to explore these places more thoroughly,' Lewis suggested. A smile tugged at Bryony's lips. It was an appealing thought. Lewis caught sight of Nina standing with a television crew and nudged Bryony. 'Cameras at two o'clock.'

'Roger, I have eyes on them,' Bryony replied and they hurried towards the crew. 'Bryony! Lewis!' yelled a high-pitched voice. Bryony turned and located Oscar waving his arms like a windmill. He beetled over to them, Biggie Smalls trotting by his side.

'Wait till you see,' he gushed. 'I couldn't believe it.'

'What do you mean?' asked Bryony.

'I know what he means,' said Lewis, a dark cloud flitting over his face. A fair-haired man in tight black jeans and a short-sleeved Lacoste shirt with his back to them was doing a piece to the camera. He faced them and Bryony gasped.

Oscar was at Bryony's elbow. 'Isn't this a surprise and a half? I'll see you later. We're going to grab a late lunch. I spotted you arriving and wanted to see your reaction. It was exactly the same as mine. I was speechless. I went all giggly and shy. Jim had to do all the talking. Must go. Have fun with the professor!'

Professor David Potts, the delicious host of *Mate or Date*, was in his thirties, fresh-faced and slim. He had an air of boyish enthusiasm as he pointed out various landmarks beyond the gate yet his dark-blue-framed glasses gave him a sense of gravitas. He turned in their direction. 'And here come the other pair of contestants who have correctly guessed their clue. Welcome, Lewis and... Bryony,' he said smoothly, taking her hand, flipping it and planting a kiss on the back of it. Bryony's knees went weak; her mouth flapped open but she was unable to articulate any words.

'So, you worked out that Vannes was the capital of the Morbihan,' read Professor David from his autocue. 'But did you also know the Place des Lices, which once hosted

202

jousting tournaments, is now the venue of an open-air market on Tuesday and Saturday mornings? This is a truly beautiful town and we're lucky to all be here on such a wonderful, sunny day.'

He looked away from the camera for a moment and frowned. 'Can we change that last bit? It sounds too twee. Can we say, "This is a truly beautiful town and not to be missed if you come to Brittany?"'

'Okay, Prof,' replied the man behind a large microphone.

Another man stepped forward. 'Take it from "So, you worked out that Vannes was the capital of the Morbihan."'

Professor Potts spoke his lines once more. A crowd of tourists and visitors had gathered and was watching the filming with interest. Bryony had recovered a little. She could see Oscar, a sandwich in one hand and Biggie's lead in the other. Obviously, Oscar was another fully paid-up member of the Professor David Potts fan club.

'And I have a question for you. Are you ready, Bryony?' he asked. She tried to drag her attention away from his sparkling blue eyes that seemed to be searching her thoughts. 'What are the citizens of Vannes called?'

Bryony's throat was dry. She could not concentrate for a second then the answer flashed into her mind.

'They're called "Vannetais",' she replied, wanting him to be pleased with her response.

'Excellent! You certainly know your stuff, Bryony.' Her insides turned to liquid at each mention of her name. He had a way of making her feel there was only the two of them in front of the gate. She smiled. He returned it and her stomach somersaulted once more.

'Would you like your next clue?' he asked, as if hoping she would say no and stay with him here, in this moment.

'Yes,' came a gruff reply next to her. She'd forgotten about Lewis. She'd been so enchanted by Professor Potts her mind had ceased to function.

Professor Potts ignored Lewis and pressed a card into Bryony's hand. 'I'm sure you'll work out what the treasure is. And here's the envelope containing the clue to your next destination. Good luck.'

Bryony took the card as if in a daze. 'Thank you,' she stammered.

'And cut!' shouted a man dressed in black.

Professor Potts turned away from her. 'All okay?' A voice in his ear responded. 'Great. Time for lunch then,' he added with a beaming grin. 'Don't suppose you fancy joining me for coffee at one of the cafés here, do you?' he asked Bryony.

'We need to get to our next destination,' Lewis said through gritted teeth.

'We're allowed an hour for lunch,' she reminded Lewis. 'We can get a coffee and then eat our picnic. You were the one who said Vannes was a beautiful place to visit. We should see some of it before we move off.'

'Yes, Lucas,' continued Professor Potts. 'You should visit some of it while you have the chance.'

Lewis threw him an angry look at this obvious attempt to rile him. 'Bryony, remember why we're doing this show,' Lewis hissed in a low voice while Professor Potts removed his earpiece and prepared to leave.

'But this is Professor David Potts! I know women who'd kill me to go to lunch with him.'

'He's no one special,' Lewis covered up his microphone with a one hand and whispered, microphone. 'He's only a presenter. You and I need to work out the clue and get to the next destination if we're in with a chance to win this competition.'

Bryony bit at her bottom lip. She could imagine what Melinda would tell her to do. Lunch with Professor Potts might lead to something special. She wrestled with her conscience. She was in a quandary, thrown out by the arrival of the delectable Professor Potts. Lewis had been good enough to come on this game show and she acknowledged she had feelings for him too. However, she was unsure if there would ever be anything deeper between them, especially as Lewis was still hurting over Maxwell. She concluded that even if their relationship was platonic, Lewis had supported her wholeheartedly and she owed it to him to stick to the agenda.

Bryony sighed. 'Thank you for your kind invitation, and coffee would be lovely, but we really must get going.'

Professor Potts took her hand again, sending another shiver through her body. 'My loss,' he murmured. 'Next time,' he added. 'Don't let me down twice.'

Nina hurried up to him. 'Roland wants to do the piece to camera again, if you don't mind.'

Professor Potts shrugged. 'Whatever Roland wants. But let's get it right this time. I haven't got all day.'

He released Bryony's hand. 'Good luck, sweet Bryony. See you tonight at the live event.'

-

'Did he flirt with me or was I dreaming?' Bryony asked as they returned to their car.

'He flirted with you. He has a reputation for it,' said Lewis darkly, opening the car door, clambering in and slamming it shut. 'What's our next clue?' he asked in a flat tone.

'What about lunch? Our picnic?'

'I'm not hungry. Come on, let's get this hunt over with.'

Bryony detected a distinct shift in mood and decided to leave Lewis to sulk. He was probably cheesed off that he was not the object of her attention any longer. *Men!*

'The clue for the treasure reads, "Head back in time to the stone age and take a photograph to prove you have visited this site."'

Lewis pulled out the map. 'Check the file while I look at this.'

Bryony skimmed through the sheets. The atmosphere was less light-hearted than before and she could not work out what had changed.

'Carnac.' She read, '"It is the site of more than three thousand prehistoric stone monuments."'

'Then that's where we're headed.' He worked out the best and fastest route to the new destination. After a few minutes of silence, he raised his eyes to her. An apology rose in his throat, halted by the cool regard she gave him. 'If you're hungry, get something out of the hamper now and we'll eat it as we drive,' he said, hoping to ease the tension.

'No, I'm okay. I seem to have lost my appetite,' she retorted, wondering if they would still be friends by the end of the day.

Chapter Twenty Seven

Tuesday, 25 July – Evening

In spite of the coastal views, stunning scenery and agreeable drive, both lapsed into silence as tiredness and frustration replaced eagerness and fun. It was only once they reached Concarneau and collected a Breton cake as a treasure that the sour atmosphere altered.

'It's called Kouign-amann,' Bryony explained to a somewhat sullen Lewis, 'and it is a specialty of the area made of bread dough, layers of butter and sugar. Try a piece. It might cheer you up. It might even make you smile a little bit,' she continued, wafting the cake in front of his nose until a small smile cracked his face.

Lewis's mood lifted and he insisted they stop for some coffee and to enjoy the picnic before heading to Quimper. They removed the mike packs again, found a spot off the main road and set up camp beside a field of golden sunflowers.

Lewis immediately drained a bottle of water and then wolfed down a ham-filled baguette. After a moment he spoke. 'I ought to apologize.'

Bryony had decided she didn't like falling out with Lewis. It was far more enjoyable when they were friends and the atmosphere lighter. She wasn't one to hold a grudge or be off with anyone for long. Whatever had upset him had passed. 'We all have our moments. I had mine yesterday. Want to tell me what upset you? Was it me?'

Lewis pushed his sunglasses back onto his forehead and fixed her with a forlorn look. 'Gosh, no! Well, sort of. It's complicated,' he said with a sigh. 'I can't tell you in the car because the damn camera is on us all the time and we haven't got sufficient time now so I'll have to explain later.'

She chewed thoughtfully on a piece of cheese. 'No problem,' she replied. 'Isn't this fabulous? Sunshine, countryside and not a soul around apart from us.'

'It's superb. Can you hear that?'

She cocked her head and located the low humming of hundreds of bees. 'Bliss!'

'You know, I think after this experience, I almost could be tempted to move to France and buy a vineyard after all. It's a world apart from our own hectic lives. It's serene, filled with bounteous nature, few people and wonderful roads to drive along for mile after mile.'

'Or kilometre after kilometre,' she said with a laugh, glad that their relationship was back on an even keel. 'Seriously, it would be wonderful. I can see you settling here and tending to your vines, then popping into town for a small aperitif before a lunch of cheese and fresh bread. Can't think of anything nicer at the moment.'

He sat quietly, reclining on his elbows, sunglasses perched on top of his head, and his eyes closed. Bryony decided the French way of life would suit him. This trip might be the catalyst he required to kick-start a new life. The moment passed and with a sigh, she stood preparing to continue their journey and leave behind this idyll.

The final legs of the journey were not filled with the same tension they'd experienced at Vannes but when Bryony requested a stop on two more occasions to stretch her legs, there were no more moments of intimacy. By late afternoon they reached Rennes, the capital of Brittany and their final destination, somewhat exhausted. Fortunately, the crew was on hand to provide sufficient enthusiasm for the final shots and within minutes, amidst noisy cheers from those involved in the filming, the black and yellow car came into view and drew to a rapid halt outside the Palais Saint-Georges, a medieval abbey now housing city offices.

'You beat us!' Oscar cried, leaping over to congratulate the pair. Biggie snuffled around Lewis's ankles with renewed interest.

Lewis bent to pat the animal. 'Hello, Biggie boy. How did you enjoy your trip?'

'He slept through the majority of it, the philistine. How many dogs get to go on a cultural journey around Brittany? He spent most of it on his back zonked out. How about you?'

'It was interesting and tiring,' Bryony replied.

'What about Professor David Potts?' Oscar babbled. 'I couldn't believe he was at Vannes. I thought he might be one of those lookalikes until he spoke. He's got one of those dreamy voices, hasn't he? My mum thinks he's cute. Mind you, she thinks everyone under the age of forty is adorable. I think he's dead hunky and yet sensitive and charming. No wonder he's on the list of the UK's top ten sexiest men. I got my photograph taken with him and so did Biggie. Biggie's his latest fan. See, the man is a god. Even my dog loves him.'

Lewis muttered something unintelligible and stormed off in the direction of the abbey.

Bryony watched him depart then decided to join him. 'I think Lewis needs to stretch his legs and so do I. We'll be back in a moment.'

She caught up with Lewis, who was studying the building, arms stiff by his sides.

'Come on, let's walk and talk.' She took his arm and guided him into the palace gardens, strolling past wide beds of geraniums and marigolds and along the path before stopping in front of a wooden bench where they both sat.

'It's Potts. Potts is the problem,' he said at last.

'Why?'

Lewis sucked in a long breath, tipping his head back as he searched for the words to explain. 'He's the reason Maxwell and I split up.'

Bryony digested this information and chose to remain quiet while he clearly struggled with his emotions.

'Maxwell had an affair with him,' he suddenly blurted out. 'She was working on one of his programmes and like every female I've ever known, she fell for his smooth patter. He is ridiculously charming, isn't he? All that hand kissing and holding your gaze, making you feel you're the most important woman in the universe. And he's got that easy Irish charm. Women love that – looks, charm and intelligence. It's a heady mixture. Maxwell was like an over-excited puppy the day she found out she'd be working on the show with him. I humoured her. At that point I wasn't jealous in the slightest. I honestly believed our relationship was solid. I didn't have any reason to think she'd be bowled over by Professor clever-arse Potts.'

He spat out the words and clenched his fists, his eyes narrowing.

'I shouldn't have been so bloody complacent. There I was, parked at home dressed in trackpants every day, tapping away at a keyboard, thinking everything was ideal in my world. Meanwhile, Maxwell was falling head over heels for a suave, good-looking dude. I should have anticipated it. I should have made some effort before she jumped into bed with him.'

He shut his eyes and continued speaking. 'I let myself go. It's easy to do when you're happy in a relationship. You don't notice it to start with – a few pounds here, a few pounds there. Then one day, you've put on a stone. You tell yourself you'll make an effort to lose it but you don't. Work gets in the way and you go out almost every weekend and drink and eat all sorts of crap. Then you buy clothes in larger sizes and convince yourself it doesn't matter because you think you'll lose it when you finish your next project. Of course, you don't because you've been eating takeaways while your girlfriend is out at night, and when you do get time off you don't feel like jogging or going to the gym. Besides, you don't want anyone to laugh at you at the gym. You'll be the fat bloke while everyone else will be pumping weights and showing off six packs.' He paused, opened his eyes and gave a sharp laugh before shaking his head.

'So, there I was, an eighteen-stone idiot. I didn't imagine Maxwell would have an affair, let alone with someone like Potts. I was a fool. She is beautiful. I knew that. Of course other men are going to find her attractive. I believed she was as happy with our relationship as I was.

I didn't suspect for a minute she would give up on me and everything we had – our home, our life, our future.'

He dropped his head into his hands. Bryony felt helpless. She wanted to comfort him yet he had now erected an invisible shield. He still loved Maxwell. That much was obvious. She toyed with the idea of putting an arm around him but he raised his head and with a weary sigh said, 'I walked out the day she told me about the affair. I didn't argue. I didn't fight for her. I didn't stand up like a real man. I skulked off like a kicked dog. I ought to have convinced her to give us another chance but I didn't. My own self-worth was at a low. I helped cause the breakup. She would never have had an affair if I'd been more attentive to her, to our relationship, and been in better physical shape, or just simply shown her how much I cared about her. I was as much to blame as she was.'

'No, Lewis. I understand you might feel that way but you're wrong. No one deserves to be cheated on.'

He gave a small nod. 'Anyway, I licked my wounds, chose a new destination and got a grip on my life.

'I shed the weight. Stress played its part along with resolute determination. I moved out to another flat in London. I ran every single day and once I'd dropped the first stone, I started working out at the gym. The rest of the blubber fell away pretty quickly in fact. I worked hard at it. Spent endless hours on the cardio machines and then working out with weights. I was like a man possessed. I not only lost the weight I put on, I lost more and more. I kept at it. I had a crazy notion that if Maxwell saw me looking more like my old self or even better than that, she'd fall for me again.'

He looked across at a couple wrapped in each other, walking down the path, oblivious to his pain.

Bryony broke his silence. 'She didn't want to give it another go?'

In a hoarse whisper he replied, 'She'd moved on too. Potts was a fixture in her life. He moved in with her, into our old flat.' Lewis shook his head, eyes filled with pain. There was a catch in his voice. 'How could I ever compare to the wonderful, clever, macho Professor David Potts? She'd never choose me over him. The rest you know. I gave up and moved to Derby.'

'How can you think that way? To start with, you're macho too, but people don't get together with people just because they're macho. You're more than that. And you're buff. I've seen you with your shirt off and Melinda commented on your bum last time you visited. Said she wanted to take a bite out of it.'

He offered her a small smile.

'You have so much more to offer – you're entertaining, witty and massive fun to be with. Even Melinda agrees on that score and she's really difficult to please. I've loved being with you here in France. And you have plenty of intelligence. Look how we got on today and a lot of that was down to you. You knew things I didn't know. Potts may know stuff about science but I bet he wouldn't have been able to navigate French streets in a rickety French car. And I think you'd even stand a fair chance of beating me at Scrabble,' she added gently, smiling at him. 'After all, you did win the UK Under 13s Scrabble competition. I think Maxwell is a prize chump. She had something special – a wonderful man who loved her – and she threw that away.'

Lewis nodded. 'Thanks. I shouldn't let Potts get to me but seeing his smug face bought it all back.'

Bryony thought for a second before saying, 'It's not fair to put you through this. You shouldn't have to put up with Potts as a presenter. I'll tell Laura we don't want to continue and we'll pull out. They'll have to find someone else.'

Lewis gave her a thoughtful look. 'You would pull out, wouldn't you?'

'Too right I would. I'd much rather we throw in the towel than you have to face that man. Sometimes it's best to walk away from the past.'

Lewis held out a hand. She took it and he squeezed hers lightly. 'Thanks, but I'm no quitter. Potts may have won Maxwell but you and I are going to win this contest and you're going to get every possible chance to appeal for your sister. Come on. Let's get back to the others. We have a contest to win.'

She slipped her arm through his and they sauntered back towards the group.

'Did Melinda really say she liked my bum?' he asked.

Chapter Twenty Eight

Tuesday, 25 July – Evening

'Welcome to the live edition of *What Happens in…* It's Tuesday evening and we've reached the end of day two in the contest. Who will be sent home today and who will continue their journey in France? We'll find out in a moment. The teams are gathered beside me in the gorgeous city of Rennes, known for its beautiful half-timbered houses and its magnificent cathedral, on a gloriously sunny evening. What a day it's been! The contestants have been on a lengthy treasure hunt that saw them cover 256 kilometres and take in some wonderful sights this outstanding region in France has to offer.'

David Potts was doing what he did best – schmoozing the audience. Roland and the crew were watching him, faces tense in case he made any errors, but tonight Professor Potts was on form. All the contestants were lined up in front of him, waiting to learn the results. A crowd of locals had also gathered on the square where the filming was taking place and were watching the proceedings with interest.

'It's been a day of drama, tears and tantrums. We've seen laughter with Jim and Oscar when Oscar's dog, Biggie Small, decided to chase after a poodle, and witnessed Nicola and Donald's full-blown row outside Vannes, which saw Nicola hitching a ride with a rival team from Grand Maison Bretagne, Evan and Thomas – our dynamic Welsh duo. Tonight, all the teammates are back together and waiting to discover who won the treasure hunt challenge, and who will be going back home tonight. Those who stay will be treated to a top meal at the fabulous Galopin restaurant here in magnificent Rennes… and the losers, a sandwich on a Ryanair flight back home.'

He smiled affably at the contestants, his eyes resting on Bryony a fraction longer than on anyone else. 'Without further ado, let's find out who won today's challenge.'

He pressed a finger to his ear and spoke. 'Nicola and Donald…'

Nicola swallowed back tears.

'You are… staying in France.'

Nicola sobbed loudly and threw her arms around Donald's waist. 'Sorry I lost my temper,' she said.

'It's fine. It's okay,' Donald replied, hugging her fiercely.

'Terri and Hugh. You are also remaining on the show.'

The contestants from the islands in Scotland, dressed in striped jumpers and both wearing false moustaches jumped up and down in delight and one broke into a Highland dance at the news.

Potts beamed his bright gaze onto the next team. 'Deepan and Mira… you are… staying!' The young, quiet couple beamed and high-fived each other.

Potts turned towards Oscar. 'Oscar and Jim, and Biggie Smalls, you are…' He lifted his head and waited several seconds, allowing the tension to mount, before he finished his sentence. 'Staying.'

Lewis edged closer to Bryony. The warmth rising from his body did little to comfort her. They'd done everything possible. They'd collected their treasures and got their clues correct. Had it been enough?

'Evan and Thomas…'

Her stomach flipped. Surely not? She reasoned if Nicola had joined them after leaving Donald, they might have had help interpreting the clues and beaten her and Lewis. Was that fair? She ought to challenge it even. Beside her Lewis was holding his breath. Potts continued.

'I'm sorry to say, you will not be staying tonight. You must return to the hotel and pack your bags. Bon voyage. Give my love to Wales.' He waggled fingers at the disappointed pair before facing the camera and revealing his white teeth again.

'We now have six teams remaining but which of them won today's challenge. Let's look back over the highlights of today's challenge as the contestants raced around this wonderful region, and then I'll reveal all.'

'Cut!'

Nina charged forward with a bottle of water for Potts. He swigged it greedily then shouted, 'Make-up! I need some of this sweat wiping from my brow. Christ, it's bloody hot here. How long have we got?'

'Five minutes.'

'Mattie!' Potts bellowed. She raced forward and powdered his face.

The contestants shuffled from foot to foot. It was impossible to speak with microphone packs on. Lewis stepped forward and shook Evan and Hugh's hands. The others followed suit, wishing them a good journey. The pair left the set with Nina.

'Back to your places please. We're going live again in a minute.' Laura's voice was loud.

Bryony glanced around her. The park was huge at about ten hectares but retained an elegant, romantic feel with immaculately landscaped gardens, awash with colour. Ahead was a bed of vibrant oranges, yellows and reds – plants and flowers she didn't recognize – and set between them, exotic grasses and yuccas. The grey blue lamppost adjacent to them was from a bygone era and she found herself wondering what it would have been like to have visited the gardens in the nineteenth century, attended the open-air theatre here, or listened to a concert while seated around the ornate bandstand. Her mind drifted to an image of ladies in crinoline dresses with bouffant hairstyles. Laura's voice brought her back to the present.

'Four… three… two… Live!'

'Today, our teams were on an elaborate treasure hunt that saw them collecting objects and clues. It's been tricky adding up all the scores in such a short time, but our production team have managed it and I can reveal that it was close – very close indeed, and the winners are… Oscar and Jim!' Potts pointed at the pair and applauded.

Laura's eyebrows furrowed and she whispered something into her microphone. Potts pressed a finger to his ear to hear what was being said in his earpiece, shook his head slightly, and then glided forwards to congratulate the teammates. Oscar leapt up and down, clapping his hands together before grabbing hold of Jim and wrapping him in an embrace.

Lewis squeezed Bryony's hand. 'Can't win them all,' he said.

The recording ended and as they handed in their microphone packs, Bryony noticed Laura stalking towards Potts. Although she couldn't hear what was being said, Laura was clearly annoyed with Potts who lifted both hands in a submissive gesture and kept smiling and shaking his head. In the end Laura stormed off, clipboard under her arm.

'Come on. Let's go and join the others for dinner. At least we're still in the game,' said Lewis.

Bryony nodded. She'd have to try harder the following day if she wanted to get in front of that camera again. They meandered across to the other contestants, waiting to go to the restaurant. 'Did you hear the goss?' said Deepan as soon as they joined them.

'Hear what?'

'Potts screwed up the results. One of the technicians told me. Apparently the top two teams were extremely close – there was only one point in it, and Potts gave out the wrong result.'

'Who was the other team?'

'No one knows. Potts said it was an honest mistake and the production team are going to have to let it go because it was broadcast live, but Laura is furious with him.'

'I don't suppose it matters who won,' said Mira, a gentle-faced woman with wide amber eyes and dark hair scraped from a beautifully calm face. 'We all got through. It's only a few minutes in front of the camera. It's not like we lost the money or anything.'

Deepan shrugged. 'True but let's hope he doesn't get anything else wrong.'

Oscar and Jim returned to the group. 'The Prof let Biggie Smalls say hello. He waved a paw at all his fans! It was so exciting, wasn't it, Biggie?' The pug wrinkled his eyebrows. 'And Jim said hello to his grandchildren and wife. I'm sure they're very proud of him.' Bryony smiled. Mira was right. The winners only got a few minutes camera time, and Oscar had clearly relished his time in front of the lens. It was just a shame she hadn't had another opportunity to mention Hannah.

Chapter Twenty Nine

Wednesday, 26 July – Morning

The group was assembled once more in the library at Hotel Petit Château. Donald had given up on his kilt and had chosen a white T-shirt and jeans instead. Nicola and he were once again on friendly terms and had been guffawing together with Oscar when Bryony had appeared for breakfast.

Laura stood, back to the wall, and smiled winningly at them all. 'Great job, everyone. We got some superb footage of you on the treasure hunt, and you'll be pleased to know a whopping three point four million viewers tuned in to watch the show yesterday! Pretty awesome stuff, eh?'

The teams burst into spontaneous applause.

'At this rate, you'll all become household names and there's been a lot of activity on social media,' she said, looking pointedly at Bryony. Before Bryony could probe further Laura read from her agenda. 'Today's tasks are less arduous. You won't have to drive hundreds of kilometres around the countryside in your friendly cars.

'Shame,' said Oscar. 'I'm getting used to Bumble.'

'Today we're splitting you up.'

There was a collective intake of surprise. Bryony threw Lewis a look of concern. He shrugged a response and waited for an explanation.

'One contestant in each pair is going to be tested on their observational skills while the other person in the team will be challenged physically. It isn't going to be too arduous, not a Ninja-style assault course or anything like that,' she added, sensing the panic in the room. 'All will be revealed at the destination. We'll leave in the minibus in fifteen minutes so decide who's doing what and those participating in the physical challenge, you'll need trainers.

The contestants scurried from the room in pairs, urgently deciding who was doing what. Lewis spoke first. 'There's no question about it, I'll take the physical part. You're way more observant than me.'

'You reckon?'

'Without doubt. I'm not in perfect shape but I can probably hold my own. I just hope I don't let us down. I might be okay in the gym with Sean but some of the other teams look pretty fit. Deepan definitely looks like an athlete.'

'Don't be silly. Just treat it as a bit of fun. Remember how much you enjoyed strutting about on stage once you decided to playact a bit? Pretend you're a top athlete or a Ninja Turtle or Superman. You'll ace it. Can't imagine either Nicola or Donald excelling in the physical side unless it's tug-of-war and Donald is up for it – then we're stuffed.'

He chewed at his bottom lip. 'Yeah, okay. I'll try that *Zoolander* playacting thing again. Better get changed into my trainers and joggers. Meet you at the minibus.'

Bryony headed outside and joined Jim. 'Oscar's going to take on the physical challenge. He's such a nice lad. I'm thoroughly enjoying his company. In fact, I'm having quite a good time all round,' he said. 'Not had this much fun since I was in the army. We took on some difficult physical challenges back in those days. I detested the assault courses. There was one where we had to surmount an enormous wall at the beginning of the course. It was at least nine foot high and impossible to get over unless you helped each other. One of us would interlink our fingers like this,' he demonstrated so his hands were palm upwards, 'and give one of the lads a hoist up, then he'd clamber onto the wall, hang down and help the rest of us. It was the only way. The chaps who tried to run and jump and pull themselves up alone never made it. That's what it was about – aiding each other. Same in this show, isn't it? You can't really succeed without your teammate. Imagine me doing a physical challenge now! I'd be lucky if I reached the finish line. Yet with Oscar on my team, we're in with a shout. Ah, talking of my teammate…' He caught sight of Oscar pulling at a reluctant pug.

'He won't come,' he wailed. 'Biggie, come on!'

The little dog remained firmly on his haunches and looked sadly at his owner, refusing to move.

'Come on, Biggie,' said Roxanne, crouching to pat him. 'Look, I've got some ham from breakfast. Do you like ham?' The dog took the tidbit and allowed her to fuss him and then pick him up. 'I'll look after him while you're filming, if you like,' she said.

'Would you? You're an angel.'

'Of course. I'm one of his many fans. Can I take a selfie with him?'

'Sure you can. There you go, Biggie, another adoring slave to add to your collection. Aren't you lucky?'

Donald emerged last from the château, red-faced and in trainers and shorts which once again exposed his trunk-like legs, and a T-shirt emblazoned with the logo *Keep Calm and Drink Beer*. Nicola trailed in his wake.

'It appears Donald's attempting the physical challenge,' said Oscar quietly to Lewis. 'If it involves tossing a caber or similar, he'll breeze it.'

Laura jogged over to the assembled group. 'Everyone here? Let's go. I've been informed the other teams have already left Grand Maison Bretagne and are on their way to the destination. Oh, one last thing, there are cameras set up in the minibus. No dozing off on the trip.'

Bryony felt slightly wistful at leaving behind the furry car, now parked in the car park with the other vehicles, and wished she was alone with Lewis, but rules were rules and although everyone settled back and occasionally smiled or spoke to each other, it wasn't as relaxed an atmosphere as it had been in the car with just the two of them.

The bus headed out of Nantes, threading its way through the busy streets filled with scooters, cars and bicycles. In spite of the traffic, Bryony felt an affection for the vibrant yet elegant city, once a busy seaport and historic capital to the dukes of Brittany that offered incredible architecture and history as well as a taste of modernity that appealed to her. It was a place she'd never tire of if she lived here, and as she watched a young woman with long dark hair, on a sit-up-and-beg bike, dressed in a pretty yellow dress ride into a park alongside a young man on another bike, she decided it would be lovely to spend more time here alone with Lewis.

Their route took them out of Nantes along the main road, and as conversation dried up, she wondered where they were going. She didn't have to wait long. Within ten minutes they were entering the gates of an amusement park and had drawn up beside a small roller coaster with brown tracks, lifted high into the air on green supports. Bryony stared as empty carriages tore down the tracks and turned this way and that. The cartoon face of a large yellow owl attached to the first carriage – shot by her at speed.

'No!' Oscar's voice had risen an octave. 'What have they planned for us here? Please not the roller coaster. I hate roller coasters. I can't do heights. I'm not doing any challenge that involves one.'

'No roller coasters,' said Laura, coaxing him from his seat with an outstretched hand.

Bryony jumped from the minibus and joined the other two teams who were watching the carts dart around the track.

'Looks fun, doesn't it?' said Decpan. 'Might bring the kids here one day. They'd love it.'

'You have children?'

'Four. Two sets of twins. Lucky, eh? They're four and six. This would be right up their street.' His eyes sparkled as another carriage, this time with a painted duck on its front tore down the track and disappeared again.

'There are no passengers,' Bryony commented.

'They're probably just testing it out before they let anyone on it – safety checks and whatnot.'

'Not sure I'd enjoy it.'

'You never been on one?' Deepan asked.

'Never been to an amusement park,' Bryony replied, grateful that Laura and the others were approaching. She didn't want to have to explain about her childhood.

'The challenge will take place just over there.' Laura pointed to an enormous brightly coloured inflatable fort. Potts was waiting for them, a set of cards in his hands, rehearsing his words to no one in particular. 'So, if you could go and join the Prof by the entrance, we'll get the cameras rolling. Everyone ready? Energy people... energy.'

Chapter Thirty

Wednesday, 26 July

Stood beside what could only be described as an inflatable assault course, consisting of artificial rocks, trees and a number of structures to navigate and cross, Professor Potts was dressed in a polo shirt the same colour blue as his eyes. He faced the camera.

'We still not ready to do this yet?' he asked a lean-faced man. 'Come on, folks. I've been here since eight.'

There was a flurry of activity then somebody called, 'Rolling.'

'It's Wednesday, the middle of the week, and day three of *What Happens in...* France. You join us outside Nantes at a fabulous amusement park which has seen thousands of families through its doors since it opened way back in 1971. The Parc des Naudières has so much to offer, and you'd be crazy to miss out on it if you pass through this wonderful region. We've mixed things up a little for our hopefuls today and each team member will have to pull their weight if they're going to win the challenge we've got planned for them. Brute force will not be enough to get through, nor will smart knowledge. This time we've devised a dastardly test for both members of each team.'

He pointed towards the quintet consisting of Bryony, Jim, Nicola, Mira and Hugh.

'These are our spotters. They'll be given a photograph and using their powers of observation, they'll determine what is odd about the picture. Once they identify what it is, they must write it down on the notepad they've been given, then tag their teammate who can begin their challenge.'

He held up a hand to halt proceedings. 'Honestly, guys, can we please keep the damn children out of the way. I know this is an amusement park for families but we're trying to shoot a show here.' The two children who'd strayed close to the filming, along with their parents, were ushered gently away and Potts resumed his monologue.

'The second part of the task requires the other team member to complete a series of challenges on these fabulous fun inflatables,' he said, indicating the giant structures and the other five team members on a huge bouncy castle. 'The first game is called *touchdown*. As you can see, each participant is attached to the wall of the bouncing deck by a stretchy cord. The idea of the game is for the contestants to touch the circles on the floor with the rugby ball they're holding. There are three circles in total, each a foot from the last, and participants must touch each circle once with their ball. All the while, they'll be restrained by their cord. They'll gain a point for each circle touched. At the end of the round the spotter must tell us what they thought was peculiar about the picture. If they get it wrong, they'll lose all their teammate's points. Once we've completed this round, we'll move onto round two and repeat it with different pictures and a new course. Contestants, you only have five minutes to complete this challenge. Are you ready?'

'Yes.'

'I can't hear you. Are you ready?'

'Yes.' The reply was louder this time.

'Then trois… deux… un…' A klaxon sounded and the game began. Bryony, Jim, Mira and Hugh all studied their first photograph. Bryony was quick off the mark to scrawl an answer, scamper across to castle wall and tag Lewis who inhaled deeply and surged forward, rugby ball in hand as if he were about to score a try in an international match. His efforts were thwarted as with each stride, he bounced higher and higher until the cord yanked him backwards and he landed on his backside.

'Oh dear, it seems Bryony's partner has taken a tumble at the first attempt,' said Potts.

'Go on, Lewis! Go, Lewis!' yelled Bryony who'd now returned to her original position. She didn't want Potts to get any satisfaction from seeing Lewis fail.

Lewis picked himself up and powered forwards again, this time reaching out and forcing his ball onto the first circle.

'After a weak start, Lewis has managed to score his first touchdown,' said Potts, commentating on the game in an amused voice. 'And, what's this? Jim has the answer and is tagging his teammate, Oscar.'

Oscar gave a low growl, bent his knees and charged ahead only to be yanked back immediately.

'Oh dear, I think he'll have to try a little harder if he wants to score.'

Potts's sarcastic tone was irritating Bryony. 'Go on, Oscar,' she called.

'And Oscar has acquired a cheerleader from a rival team,' Potts added smugly. Bryony ignored him.

Lewis was ahead of Oscar, attempting to hit the second target but was yanked backwards, sent flying upside down and ended up flat on his back, chest rising and falling as he gulped in air.

Potts barked a loud laugh. 'It appears Lewis is trying to reach his target using back crawl. Might need to rethink that method, Lewis.'

'Lewis. Think catwalk,' Bryony shouted.

Potts gave her a curious look but quickly readopted his host-like expression as Donald suddenly took off and charged like a bull down the bouncy track. 'Look at Donald go. And, yes! Donald scores his first touchdown!' he shouted excitedly.

Lewis had heard Bryony. He stood up on wobbly legs and, squaring his shoulders, ran full pelt towards his second circle and smashed the ball onto it.

'Second touchdown for Lewis,' said Potts. 'Although I don't think he's any energy left for the third one… and Oscar has made his first touchdown… and here comes Donald again. My goodness, I'd hate to be in a scrum with this man.'

Donald, with ball in outstretched hands pulled hard against the ever-stretching cord. The muscles in his neck stood out as he strained against it and steadily planted one foot at a time. He leaned forward, grimacing as he did so. He was losing his grip and being hauled back little by little. He gritted his teeth and let out a might roar, reached out with his arm and tapped the ball against the second circle. The horn sounded, signalling the end of the game. The three men, now slumped against the inflatable wall let out exhausted breaths. Potts summed up the situation.

'Unfortunately, two teams have scored no points, having not got off the starting line. Bad luck folks, but don't worry, this is only the first round. Oscar has won one point and Donald and Lewis both have two. Now it's down to the spotters. If they were accurate and noticed the anomaly in the photograph, their fellow contestants can keep their points.

'The contestants were given this photograph of a lovely French chapel, not too far from where we are, called *chapelle de Bethléem*, or as we'd know it, the Bethlehem Chapel. Spotters, please turn over your pads and tell us what was uncharacteristic about this picture.'

Jim, Bryony and Nicola revealed their notepads to the camera. Potts tilted his head this way and that.

'Jim you noticed "unusual gargoyles that aren't typical representation of chimeras but are from American films". Bryony you've written, "Two of the gargoyles are from the film *Gremlins*: one an evil gremlin, the other Gizmo." Both answers are correct. The chapel was renovated in the nineties when a local stone cutter, supported by the town, decided to base the replacement gargoyles on popular creatures from films – *Gremlins* and *Alien*, television and Japanese animation. Nicola did you get that answer?'

Nicola hugged the notepad to her chest, eyes damp with unfallen tears. She shook her head and slowly turned the notepad towards him. She'd written *The front door is too small to walk through*. 'It looked so tiny on the photograph compared to the shuttered windows,' she stuttered. A tear escaped and trickled down her face. Potts spoke kindly, 'Never mind, Nicola. I'm sure Donald won't mind… too much.' He threw Donald a toothy smile.

'Cut!'

'Oh, Nicola, don't take it to heart,' said Bryony. 'There are another two rounds. Just brush it off. The other teams didn't win any points either. Focus on the next photo. That one was really tricky. You needed to be into films to get what it was about.'

Nicola sniffed. 'Yeah. You're right. I just felt so bad for Donald especially after he did so well.'

'He'll get over it. He doesn't even look puffed out. Lewis, on the other hand, looks like he might stay there for the duration of the game or at some point require mouth-to-mouth.' She glanced at her teammate, who'd managed to sit up but had yet to achieve an upright position. The game might have looked amusing to those watching, but it had drained the participants. Heaven knew what state he'd be in by the evening if the next round was as gruelling.

Donald hauled Lewis to his feet and helped unhitch him, then both assisted Oscar. As they clambered off the inflatable, Laura arrived to issue them with new instructions. She pointed at the crew who were moving across to what looked like a giant inflatable rodeo bull. Bryony rolled her eyes. It was going to be a long day.

–

Donald, Nicola, Oscar, Jim, Bryony and Lewis all clustered in the library at Hotel Petit Château. Thanks to retakes and a problem with one of the cameras, they'd spent most of the day at the amusement park.

The games had been demanding and taken their toll on those who'd participated in the physical challenges. There'd been no time to discuss the outcome or the events of the day in their room, and a weary Lewis had tumbled into the shower then dozed off on the bed for half an hour until Bryony had gently woken him for the evening live performance at eight o'clock. The results of the last game of the day had been withheld. Nobody knew how many points had been scored during a ridiculous assault course that had required the participants to scramble over inflatable hills and objects in search of large red, white and blue feathers. The finale had been a difficult clamber up inflatable steps onto a huge bouncy slide. It had been a tight contest with all the men jostling for space that had led to a collision between Donald and Oscar, and had resulted in Deepan winning. Now it all hinged on their teammates, the spotters, and whether or not they'd accurately worked out what was wrong about the photograph of a French motorway they'd been given.

Laura was remaining tight-lipped about the results. Oscar had attempted to prise them out of her to no avail. She was now focused on the television set, waiting to cue in the contestants as Potts spoke to them through the medium of the screen.

Potts, in white trousers and a lemon shirt that showed off his tanned face was commentating on the day's events that had already been broadcast to the nation. 'It's Wednesday evening and the third day of *What Happens in...*, the phenomenon that's been gripping the nation. Yes, over four million of you tuned in yesterday to discover what happened here in France. Thank you all.

'Now, I have four very nervous contestants standing beside me here in Grand Maison Bretagne, all dying to find out who will spend another night in luxury and take on a new challenge tomorrow, and who'll be hitching a ride back home on the overnight ferry.' He flashed his teeth briefly before continuing. 'Well, you didn't have the greatest start in today's challenge, but Deepan and Mira, you... will... be staying.' Deepan held up two thumbs. 'Over in the library at Hotel Petit Château, we have six participants all equally concerned about the results. Oscar and Jim. Well done. You are... staying. Bryony and Lewis. Congratulations. You will also be staying another night. No need to pack your suitcase just yet. Now then... Hugh and Terri and Donald and Nicola. I'm sure you are all eager to know the results.' He heaved a dramatic sigh as if it were almost too painful to continue, his face now doleful. 'You put up a truly magnificent performance today and nobody will be able to forget the sight of Donald and Oscar entangled on the slide... However, I'm sad to say, Terri and Hugh here with me...' he indicated the men with matching beards before looking immediately back at the screen, 'And Donald and Nicola there, in Hotel Petit Château, you will *all* be leaving tonight. It's time to pack your bags and say goodbye.'

Nicola's mouth dropped open. She shouted at the screen. 'We did well in the last round. Donald came first. That can't be right.'

Donald added his voice. 'There's been some mistake.'

Potts gave a small smile that didn't reach his eyes and ignoring the outburst snapped back to presenter mode. 'What a dramatic turn of events. Four contestants leaving today. Who'd have expected that? Coming up after the break, we'll reveal the results of today's activities and discover who was the yellow jersey winner and who took away the wooden spoon.'

The television screen cut away to show highlights of the day and Donald hauling his frame over a giant toad-stool. He was still complaining about the result. Laura had hastened across to them and was speaking in hushed tones to the fuming couple. Bryony looked back at the screen.

'And Potts, that last sentence didn't even make any sense,' shouted Donald as he strode from his chair towards the door. 'Yellow jerseys and wooden spoons. You're an idiot. A useless presenter who keeps screwing things up and the show is a fix.' Laura walked outside to join him.

Nicola burst into tears, shoulders shaking. Bryony stood up and hugged her. 'Don't cry. It's only a game.'

'Donald's so angry.'

'He'll calm down. Laura will speak sense to him. He's annoyed, yes, but he'll recover and remember the fun parts. At least you didn't go out first round and have had some fun.'

Nicola nodded and sniffed back her tears. 'Yes. It's been a laugh.'

'We'll come and say goodbye before you leave the château,' Bryony whispered before Nicola was escorted from the room by a technician. Laura re-entered the library.

'Donald's fine. Just a bit upset. I explained why they're leaving. Right, we're going live again in a minute so places people.'

Potts returned on screen. He wore a doleful expression. 'What an absolute shocker of a day here on *What Happens in…* Not one but two teams are out of the show and on their way back home. How could this have happened? The answer is simple. Unfortunately, Nicola and Hugh who were the spotters, didn't work out the correct anomaly on their photographs and as a consequence, our losing teams drew with zero points each. The producers took the tough but fair decision to eliminate both teams, leaving us with only three remaining pairs in the running.'

He gave a shake that rearranged his features and beamed once more at the camera. 'I'm sure all of you at home are dying to find out who won overall today, and I can now reveal that up until the last round, Deepan and Mira had four points, while Oscar and Jim, and Bryony and Lewis, had five points. Once again, it's down to the spotters. Did they identify the deliberate mistake on our photograph? Here it is for viewers at home. It's a picture taken on the Bordeaux to Nantes motorway. Looks normal enough, doesn't it? Vehicles, speed restrictions signs, overhead signage. What was weird about this picture? The answer is one of the cars is a right-hand drive vehicle. The number plate on the Renault overtaking the lorry is French but the steering wheel is on the wrong side of the car for roads in France. Did our teams get it correct?' Mira lowered her gaze as Potts turned towards her.

'Mira you thought the mistake was in the speed restriction sign. Unfortunately, you were wrong and therefore we have to deduct the two points Deepan won in the last game, bringing your final score for today down to two. Let's cross to Hotel Petit Château and see how the other teams faired.'

Bryony didn't look up at the screen even though it now showed the four of them sitting in the library. If Jim and Oscar won, she wouldn't get the chance to talk about Hannah again.

'Oscar, do you think Jim got it right?'

'Absolutely. I have faith in him.' Oscar beamed at Jim who gave a small shake of his head.

'Regrettably, on this occasion, Jim didn't get it right. He thought the mistake was to do with road markings. That means you lost the point you gained in the last round, dropping your final score from five to four.'

Oscar gave a light shrug. 'It's no big deal,' he whispered to his teammate.

'Congratulations, Bryony. You spied the error and therefore that makes you and Lewis today's winners. Thank you to all our contestants and all our wonderful viewers at home. Who will stay and who will go? Will Jim and Oscar beat tomorrow's challenges or fall at the last hurdle? Will Mira and Deepan race ahead, or will Bryony and Lewis hold onto the winner's jersey for two days in a row? Tune in tomorrow for day four of *What Happens in…*'

Laura gave Bryony a wide smile. 'Here's your chance, again,' she said. 'Go spread the word.'

'What word is that?' asked Oscar.

'Bryony's trying to win each round so she gets a few minutes in front of the camera to tell everyone about her missing sister,' said Laura. 'With over four million viewers now watching, I hope one of them knows where she is.'

'Of course. I remember you said so at the audition,' Oscar said. 'Tell me afterwards. I want to know more about it.'

Laura steered the men away, leaving Bryony and Lewis to face the television screen and tell them why it was so important for them to stay on the show.

Chapter Thirty One

Oscar was wide-eyed. 'What a terribly sad story,' he said finally, when Bryony had finished telling him about Hannah.

The cicadas were chirping in the garden and the evening air was filled with the smell of honeysuckle. Bryony rested her head against the sunbed cushion and sighed. Biggie, lying on the floor between the two loungers, licked her fingers. Oscar snapped a photo of them as she stroked him.

'Thanks, Biggie. I think he just gave me a doggie version of a kiss.'

'He's intuitive. He'll have picked up on you feeling sad. He does it to me, when I'm down.'

'I'm not really sad as such. I suppose this is my last chance to find her. Dad is so ill and I don't think he'll be with us for much longer. I want him to see her one last time...' Her words hung in the air and she swallowed back the lump in her throat. She'd given it her all in front of the camera this evening. She and Lewis had both appealed for help to find Hannah.

It had been an exhausting day. The garden was a haven and respite from the frantic activities and filming.

Bryony had got used to the cameras, microphone packs and constant visits from Mattie the make-up lady to dab powder onto her cheeks or move a single hair away from her face. She'd become accustomed to the waiting when no one could speak until the crew was ready to continue. It had been interesting and fun. Meeting Oscar and Jim and being with Lewis had been wonderful, yet sat in the shade of the beautiful walled garden, she wished she could pause time and stay here for longer, away from her normal world, her day-to-day existence and the ever-present guilt that enveloped her like some toxic cloud. If only she had some idea of what was happening back home. Were people listening to her pleas and had anybody checked out her blog, *Searching for Hannah* and left her a message?

'Can I ask you something, Bryony?' Oscar said as Biggie leapt onto his lap.

'Sure.'

'I'm getting really worked up about winning. I only came on the show for a bit of a giggle. I thought it would help raise my profile as a dancer, like celebrities who go on dancing shows or eat nasty stuff in the jungle. But after spending time with Jim, I really want to win the prize. Not for me but for him. He's such a nice man. His family means everything to him. He could do so much for them with the money.'

He paused and stroked Biggie's soft head.

'I wouldn't worry. Just being here has been a real tonic for him. I don't think winning holds as much importance for him as you may think.'

Oscar stopped to rub Biggie's tummy. 'I don't want to let him down.'

'You definitely aren't letting him down. Look at the difference in him. He's completely rejuvenated and a lot of that is down to you. He obviously loves having you as a teammate.'

He gave a smile and after a moment spoke again. 'Thanks, Bryony. I wish I had a sister like you. I'd be able to ask you all sorts of things.'

Bryony flushed. 'Are you an only child?'

'No, I've got a brother, Joe. He's three years younger than me. We're not very close and we don't have much in common. He takes after Pop. He's a doctor. Pop's an obstetrician and Joe's a medical doctor. You call them general practitioners here.'

'You didn't fancy the medical profession yourself?'

Oscar let out a honk of laughter. 'Heck, no. I'm no good at any science. I don't have Pop's brains, which is no surprise as he isn't my real father. But he is, if you know what I mean. He's always been my "real" father. He was always there for me when I was sick or needed anything. He tried to teach me baseball and soccer. He took me out to films and even sat and watched *Billy Elliot* with me. He's terrific. Always interested in everything and everybody. You'd love him. He's awesome.'

He waved his arms theatrically as he spoke. 'I don't know my biological father. He left us before I was born and then Pop came on the scene. Mom told me it wasn't worth me tracking him down. He didn't want anything to do with either of us and Pop is everything to me. What's the point in searching for someone who can't possibly be better, kinder or nicer than your own father?' He fussed Biggie some more then closed his eyes and tilted his head back.

'I was going to insist and track him down a few years ago but Mom looked so unhappy about it, I figured it wasn't worth it. You know, I sometimes fantasize that my real father is a world-famous ballet dancer – someone like Joaquín Cortés perhaps – except I look nothing like him with my blonde hair and pale skin so it couldn't be him. Or Ethan Stiefel. Unlikely, I know, but it would explain my love for ballet. In reality, my real father is probably nothing at all to do with dancing and is a middle-aged accountant with a bald head who likes drinking and playing darts and who has a stout wife who nags him all the time,' he said with a chuckle.

'I've loved dancing since I was tiny. Pop's been great about my choice of career too. Not every man would be happy to take his son to ballet lessons. Both my parents have helped me every step and pirouette along my path. I'm very fortunate.'

Biggie fidgeted on Oscar's knee. 'I'd better take some photographs of him here to upload onto Instagram. I seriously can't wait to get back online. It's awful having no access to Wi-Fi. I keep fumbling for my mobile then remember I don't have it with me. I don't know how everyone managed before they were invented. Thanks again, Bryony. You're a doll.' He gave her a peck on the cheek.

'Any time,' she replied.

As he meandered away, Biggie by his side, Bryony stared up at the darkening sky and silently sent a message to the universe. *Please send Hannah home.*

Chapter Thirty Two

Thursday, 27 July – Afternoon

'Come on, Furby!' Lewis pumped the accelerator pedal. The sunshine streaming in through the windscreen was causing him to squint. At last the car sputtered into life and they made it onto the starting line.

La Pommeraye was a 2.5 kilometre hill climb and the trio of bizarre cars and film crew had attracted a large crowd of supporters who lined the closed circuit, cheering for each of the contestants as the cars raced by. Lewis and Bryony were the last to attempt the climb.

They waited by the lights, currently on red. It seemed to take an age for them to change.

'Go… go… go!' Bryony yelled as they tore up the hill past the spectators who waved at them. 'Right bend!' The car bore to the right, past a house outside which stood three children holding a sheet marked *Allez Furby*.

'We have fans,' said Bryony, clinging to the grab handle as they rejoined the main road and hastened past more fields. The circuit was an ordinary D road with some sharp bends and twists, railings to one side and all exits blocked off. It made for an exciting circuit although the furry Citroën was nowhere near as fast as the cars that usually competed in the annual hill climb.

Bryony adjusted her racing helmet. The strap was tight under her chin and she had to shout so Lewis could hear her commands. He could see the bends but it helped if she warned him of them too, given he had enough to manage with handling the vehicle.

There was no time to take in the fields of meadow flowers or the cows lazily grazing or the high banks of grass filled with people. Lewis was committed to finishing the race in the fastest time possible without crashing, and Bryony to holding on for dear life.

A bend to the left, another sharp one to the right and an inflatable bridge across the road bearing the name of the show. Cameras to the left and the right and cheering French people. They crossed the line.

Bryony high-fived Lewis. 'Great driving.'

'Bit different to that track day I did but not bad at all,' he replied.

They climbed out of the car hoping they'd done enough to win the challenge.

–

Laura gave a tired smile. 'Congratulations again, Oscar and Jim. I'm very pleased you got through too, Bryony and Lewis. It is a shame to say goodbye to Deepan and Mira on day four of this contest. I'll miss them, but I'm also pleased the finalists are the people I've got to know the best. Right, we're down to the last two teams. Tomorrow we'll begin filming at the Château du Torquet, listed as a historic monument and built in the seventeenth century.'

There were appreciative nods from Jim.

'You'll be there over the next two days and take part in two quizzes. The first is a general knowledge quiz and the second is a category round. I'll go through it tomorrow morning.'

Oscar yawned and stretched. 'That's good. I can't take in any facts tonight. My brain has officially checked out and left the building and I smell after all that driving. I need to shower and change.'

Laura looked at her watch. 'I won't be joining you tonight for dinner but Roxanne will and so will Professor David Potts.'

Oscar let out a high-pitched squeal. 'Really?'

'Really,' replied Laura. 'He wanted the opportunity to get to know you a little before tomorrow. He's not like a lot of celebrities who want to hide in their own hotel and get away from us all. He actually enjoys meeting people. I expect that's one of the reasons he has such a tremendous following.'

Bryony threw a look at Lewis. His face was unreadable.

'I'll see you tomorrow. Have a good time with David. We're so pleased he's hosting the show. It's certainly helped boost ratings.'

Chairs scraped back and the room emptied, leaving only Bryony and Lewis.

'Fancy getting a taxi into town and going to a café instead?' asked Bryony.

'That's really nice of you but no thanks. You go to dinner. I'll head off on a run. I've been sitting too long today. Some fresh air and a shower will make me feel better.'

'I'll bring you up a doggy bag then?'

He made a non-committal noise and went upstairs.

Bryony meandered through the back door and into the garden to drink in the evening warmth and reflect on the events of the day. She discovered a charming wrought-iron seat partly concealed by climbing roses and clumps of lavender, and she sat surrounded by peace. The heat from the late sun soaked into her body, easing her aches. She shut her eyes and sighed contentedly. She could definitely stay here forever.

'Oh, I'm sorry. I didn't mean to interrupt you.'

She opened one eye. Oscar was standing on the twisted path, camera in hand. Biggie, wearing a baseball cap back to front, urinated contentedly in a flower bed. He spotted Bryony and trotted over, tongue out, sitting obediently for a pat.

'You're not interrupting.'

'Sorry you didn't win today. I was mega surprised we won the hill climb. I'm normally not a speed merchant at all. I honestly believed we'd be going home and I was so shocked when we found out Deepan and Mira were leaving. I'd got used to them being around. They were really chilled out about everything.'

'Honestly, I'm happy for you. Jim was euphoric. I loved that little dance you did together when you found out you'd won. We couldn't have lost to nicer contestants,' she replied. Lewis had taken the defeat badly. He'd been convinced they'd won the hill climb and been very quiet since the results had been announced. Professor Potts hadn't helped matters. He'd made several barbed comments about Lewis's driving and needled him further. It was little wonder he didn't want to spend any time with the man. They'd not spoken again about Maxwell but she was sure it ate into Lewis every time he set eyes on his rival.

'Look, I don't want to be out of order but when we gave our interview tonight, I asked all of Biggie's fans to look out for your sister. It might help. Maybe one of them has seen her or knows her.'

Bryony was dumbstruck.

'I wanted to do something to help. I hope you're not offended.'

'No. No. Not at all. That was so sweet of you. Thank you.'

'It was nothing. I love happy endings and I so hope you get one. That's all. I better get changed now. See you at dinner.'

He jumped up and with a breezy gesture disappeared around the corner of the building. Bryony decided she too ought to change for dinner and wondered if she could persuade Lewis to join them. It would be much nicer if he were there.

Chapter Thirty Three

Thursday, 27 July – Evening

By eight o'clock Lewis had still not returned from his run. Bryony gave up waiting and decided to join the others. Laughter rose to greet her as she descended the staircase.

Jim, dressed in beige trousers, desert boots and a perfectly ironed short-sleeved shirt, was standing next to Professor Potts, resplendent in a white shirt, blue Victorian Jacquard waistcoat and Armani jeans. Roxanne, sitting by the window, was chatting amiably to Oscar. Biggie was wearing a gold pendant and a black baseball cap. He grinned at Bryony but remained fixed on Roxanne's lap.

Professor Potts downed the contents of his glass and boomed. 'Bryony, so glad you made it. Where's your teammate, Lucas?'

'Lewis, not Lucas,' she replied, feeling her smile tighten.

'Ha! Of course. I keep getting confused. Is he not joining us?'

'He's gone for a run. Driving all day made us both stiffen up,' she answered.

'He seemed a bit of a stiff,' he joked, raising eyebrows at Roxanne to draw attention to his quip. Roxanne smiled in acknowledgement. 'I'm sure Lucas, oh dear, there I go again, I mean Lewis, will feel much better after a long, sweaty run,' said Professor Potts. 'There's little point in waiting any longer for him. He'll probably be gone ages and we don't want the food to go cold. Shall we go and eat? I'm ravenous. Bryony, why don't you sit next to me and we can chat? I haven't had the chance to find out much about you and you seem such an enchanting creature.'

Bryony cringed at his smarminess. Professor Potts was clearly not as charming and pleasant as she had initially thought. They drifted through to the dining room where Bertrand was waiting for them, a bottle of white wine in his hand. He circled the table. A middle-aged woman, white hair swept back in a bun and dressed casually in jeans and shirt covered with an apron, brought in a large tureen of soup. Bertrand stood to attention and announced, 'French oyster soup, a typical Breton dish. I hope you enjoy it. Bon appétit.'

'One of my favourite dishes,' Professor Potts enthused, reaching for the serving spoon and ladling some into Bryony's bowl. 'They use the smallest oysters to make this soup. That's what gives it the extra creamy texture and, of course, oysters are an aphrodisiac,' he added, his eyes glittering. His hand brushed against hers as he set the bowl down and he glanced at her meaningfully. She thanked him and deliberately looked away.

'So, did you all enjoy today?' he asked.

'It was a blast!' said Oscar.

Roxanne took a sip of her soup and remarked, 'This is good. Very good indeed. I bet my brother-in-law would really enjoy this soup. He's from Marseilles.'

'You should ask Bertrand to pass you the recipe for your sister to make it for him,' said Potts airily.

Roxanne shook her head. 'I think my poor, long-suffering sister has enough to do holding down a full-time job and looking after four children without preparing oyster soup. I try to help her out when I'm around. That's what sisters do, isn't it?'

Bryony felt the room swim as her words echoed in her head.

'Earth to Bryony.'

'Sorry. I drifted off.'

'Fatigue,' Professor Potts declared. 'You were cooped up with Lucas for a long time. Must have been tiring.'

Bryony placed her spoon back on the table, preparing to correct him once and for all. Oscar saved her from speaking.

'Lewis,' he said quietly. 'His name is Lewis. Not Lucas.'

'Silly me. Oscar, tell me all about Biggie Smalls' outfit. Is that a replica Jesus piece pendant he's wearing or did you, like the rapper B.I.G. purchase it from Jacob the Jeweler?'

'Hardly. This is a replica. I couldn't stretch to an authentic pendant. My little Biggie wore it for a music magazine photo shoot last year and the magazine let us keep it. They dressed up several pugs to look like famous rap artists. Biggie had such fun and made lots of doggie friends. This Biggie Smalls prefers wearing jumpers to pendants. He only wears this piece on special occasions.'

'Looking good, Biggie,' commented Professor Potts, hiding a smirk behind his serviette.

'Can I ask you something rather personal?'

'Fire away, Oscar.'

'Have you got a girlfriend?'

'I haven't had much time for relationships recently. I was pretty busy filming abroad for a new show about the natural world, and the last series of *Mate or Date* was demanding.'

'You haven't got a girlfriend. I find that very difficult to believe,' Oscar continued. 'I don't mean to be nosey. It's just I hang out with lots of ballerinas who'll be insanely jealous when they find out I've had dinner with the handsome Professor David Potts, and the first question they'll ask me will be about his eligibility.'

'You can tell them I'm not dating anyone at the moment,' replied Professor Potts, finishing his soup and wiping his mouth with a serviette. 'Nor do I have any love interests. I'm young, free and single. What about you, Oscar?'

'I have a girlfriend – Lucinda – who's also a dancer. She's a Brit but is working in New York. It's one of those easy relationships at the moment – not too serious because we're both so busy but she's moving in with me in the fall and we'll see how that works out.'

Bryony heard the creak of the front door as it opened and caught a glimpse of someone passing the dining room. It was Lewis. She suddenly felt the urge to share the news with him. If Professor Potts was indeed not seeing Maxwell then Lewis might stand a chance of rekindling his relationship with her. She thought about following him upstairs but a small voice fixed her in her seat. Did she really want him to rush back to Maxwell?

Oscar was now talking about his family in the States.

'Why didn't you stay in New York? There must be lots of companies and productions there,' Roxanne asked.

'I was born in London but we moved to the States when I was a toddler so I don't have many recollections of time in the UK. As I got older, I became curious about England – afternoon tea, red post boxes, double-decker buses, the royal family, Buckingham Palace – they all seemed so romantic and very *British*. I took up ballet classes in New York from an early age at one of the best schools – Joffreys. I was a natural and ballet fast became my passion. I could have stayed and enjoyed a career there but Europe seemed much more alluring so I cajoled my folks into letting me study in London. My ballet tutor suggested I apply to the Royal Ballet School and to cut a long story short, I was accepted and came over here. Mom and Pop helped me find an apartment and made sure I had enough money to start off. They were great about everything. I stay in touch with them all the time. They plan to visit London this year and come to see *Swan Lake*. It'll be such a buzz to see Mom and Pop sitting in the front row looking proud. I'm a lucky guy.' He gave a wide smile.

Bertrand removed the soup tureen and returned with warmed plates for everyone. The woman placed a large dish of fish in tomato and covered with sour cream in the middle of the table.

'This is called *la lotte à l'Armoricaine*. You call it monk-fish in American sauce. It is a traditional French recipe from coastal Brittany.'

'Delicious,' murmured Jim, licking his lips.

'Bon appétit!' Bertrand bowed before leaving the group once more.

'Truly awesome,' agreed Oscar.

Jim's eyes twinkled as he regarded the dish. 'Did you know monkfish is also known as poor man's lobster? I haven't had monkfish for years. I enjoy a nice piece of fish but I don't like cooking fish much. It's the smell. It pervades the entire house and sends the cat crazy.'

Roxanne sat up with interest. 'You have a cat? I've got one too. Mine's a Persian. A right pampered puss.'

Emptying his mouth first, Jim continued, 'Our cat's a stray. It found us. It sat outside our back door one wet afternoon a year ago and cried for over an hour until I let it in, then it made a beeline for Cathy and jumped onto her lap where it spent the rest of the day purring. Poor little creature is as bald as a coot. It's called a Sphynx cat and it's got no fur, only a pelt the same colour as skin. I've never seen an uglier cat but my goodness, it is affectionate.'

'Is it an Egyptian breed?'

'No, it's a breed from Canada. Apparently, they're becoming increasingly popular. I'm not that fond of it but as I said, Cathy adores it and the little 'uns love it too.'

'How old are your grandchildren, Jim?'

'Poppy's ten, Daisy's eight and little Rose is six. They're cracking kids. Would you like to see a photograph of them?' asked Jim. He replaced his cutlery onto the plate, wiped his mouth and moustache with his serviette and, twisting around, extracted his wallet from the pocket of his blazer hung tidily on the back of his chair. He gazed at the photograph, adoration etched all over his face, and passed it to Professor Potts.

Professor Potts glanced at it briefly, mumbled 'Lovely,' and gave the picture to Roxanne.

She was more enthusiastic with her praise. 'They're so cute. I can see why you're so proud of them.'

'I'm blessed,' said Jim. 'They're such clever girls too. I'd like to get some money together to help them through university. I'll have to try out for a few more quiz shows before I'd be able to do a lot to assist them but I have time, so who knows.'

'I think they're equally blessed to have such a loving grandfather,' Oscar added.

Jim took the photograph from Roxanne, studied it once more with a blissful look on his face. 'Those little girls are my world. And Cathy's too. They make both our lives worthwhile. Hearing them laugh is worth more than all the diamonds in a diamond mine. You really can't beat family,' he said with heartfelt sincerity.

With those words, Bryony was suddenly overwhelmed by sadness. She could not face any more of this conversation, and the wine she had just sipped tasted sour.

'I know it's mid-meal but would you mind if I left you all? I'm suddenly ever so tired. I can hardly lift my fork and I'm not hungry any more.'

Roxanne threw her a concerned look. 'You okay?'

'Yes. It's been a long day. See you tomorrow morning.'

'Night, Bryony,' called the others.

Professor Potts picked up his wine glass and gave her a cursory wave. 'See you tomorrow, Bryony. Hope Lucas enjoyed his run.'

Chapter Thirty Four

Thursday, 27 July – Evening

Lewis was staring out of the window, his shoulders bowed. He turned towards her and gave her a tired smile. His wavy hair was damp with perspiration and the light stubble on his chin enhanced his good looks.

She dropped onto the chair. 'Hey!'

He rubbed his chin. 'Shouldn't you be at dinner?'

'I couldn't eat any more. Besides, I have some news for you. I've discovered that smarmy Potts is no longer seeing Maxwell.'

'I know,' he replied flatly.

'How? I've only just found out from the horse's mouth.'

'I went for a run down a road that led to the town. I stopped to catch my breath and spotted an Internet café. I didn't want to turn around and run back immediately so I went in and logged onto my emails to see if I'd got any more contracts or enquiries. There was an email from Maxwell.'

Bryony stared at him, eyebrows raised.

'She wrote that she'd broken up with Potts and wished she'd never met him. Her email was full of remorse and regret. She wants me to visit her and discuss what to do about her staying in the flat – it's up for sale at the moment

– and possibly make amends. I didn't get much time to read it through properly. The café was closing and I was asked to leave.'

Bryony felt a wrench in her stomach. She ought to be delighted for Lewis. He had been through so much but she did not feel Maxwell deserved to have him. What if she discarded him again when another celebrity or similar crossed her path? Lewis might not cope with rejection a second time.

'Are you going to see her?'

Lewis looked out towards the pond. The sun had disappeared. The sky had turned a deep navy studded with stars. The moon high and full was reflected in the waters of the garden pond. 'I'm not sure. I'll have to give it some thought,' he replied. 'Circumstances have changed. I've changed and Maxwell has probably changed too. I need to consider a lot of things.'

Bryony drew her knees up and clasped them with trembling hands. It was not for her to interfere even though she wanted to scream out for him to let Maxwell get on with it alone. She recalled his face earlier that day – the pain etched across it – and decided she was being selfish. She was letting her fledgling feelings for him get in the way. Lewis should do what would make him happy. If he wanted to give it another go with Maxwell, then he should.

'I really hope it works out for you, Lewis,' she said, hoping he heard the sincerity in her voice. 'You deserve to be happy. You're a terrific friend and a really cool guy. And it doesn't matter what you look like, what you wear, whether you put on weight or not, you are huge fun to be with. I hope she recognizes that fact. She was dumb to not see it before.' She avoided his eyes and rose. 'Did you eat at the café?'

He shook his head.

'Would you like something? I can nip downstairs and ask Bertrand for some cheese and bread and maybe a bottle of cider. Don't want you fainting with hunger tomorrow. I need all your brain synapses firing on full power. I can't do this without you.'

She stood expectantly like a puppy eager to please. Creases appeared around his eyes.

'Thanks. I am a little peckish after that run.'

'Grab a shower and I'll sneak back down and collect some grub from the kitchen.'

'You're a star!'

In a robotic voice, she announced, 'Stars – hot bodies of glowing gas that start their life in nebulae. Next question, please.'

Lewis laughed out loud. 'Funny lady. You can test me on my general knowledge when you return. My grey cells need igniting in readiness for tomorrow.'

She put her hands together and bowed before leaving the room and tiptoeing down the stairs once more. The door to the dining room was shut but she could make out Oscar's exuberant giggle followed by Jim's hearty chuckle. She had developed a fondness for the other contestants and knew she'd be genuinely pleased for them if they won the competition.

She ducked into the kitchen and whispered her request to Bertrand, who scurried about the kitchen preparing a tray for Lewis. She thanked him and left as quietly as she could. There was less laughter to be heard in the dining room now. A soft cough alerted her to someone on the stairs behind her. She turned to see Oscar standing at the bottom of the staircase, cradling his dog.

'Lewis okay?' he hissed, concern arching his eyebrows.

'He's fine. I'm going to make sure he eats and gets plenty of rest before tomorrow,' she replied.

'I had to go. I was getting so cheesed off with Professor Potts. He keeps making inane remarks and he's hitting on Roxanne. He's not as cool or witty as he comes across on television,' said Oscar in a hushed tone, motioning towards the dining room. 'He only reads out what's written for him on the autocue, and he mostly gets that wrong,' he continued in a conspiratorial fashion. 'None of it is from him at all. He's a fake. I shall have to tell Mom she needs to find a different celeb to drool over.' Biggie wriggled out of his arms and snuffled at the wooden banister. 'Got to take this little bad boy out for a wee, then I'm going to grab some sleep. The professor's leaving soon. He's waiting for the driver to collect him and Roxanne. I think he's gotten bored with us. He keeps yawning and checking his watch. Jim seems very relaxed though. You were right. He's having a good time just being here.' He blew her a kiss and left her to take the tray upstairs.

–

Bryony prepared for bed in the en-suite bathroom while Lewis ate his food. She removed her make-up, careful not to drag on her skin around her eyes and the scar that jagged upwards from her right eyebrow into her hairline – a permanent reminder of the accident. She'd become accustomed to seeing it and over the years it had become less angry, less raised and slightly less noticeable. Nowadays, practised use of concealer and a lengthy fringe that hung over that side of her face ensured the scar was not visible to others. Nevertheless, she was conscious of it. She had many other scars on her legs and back, and a long one over her hip into her right thigh. They were now pale in colour, and since she invariably wore trousers, they bothered her less. She tugged on a long T-shirt and returned to the bedroom.

Lewis was propped up on the bed, a look of concentration on his face.

'I've been thinking,' he stated.

'About tomorrow?'

'Of a fashion. I was trying to work out if there was anything more we could do to help you to find your sister. That is if this plan doesn't work. If we fail the task tomorrow, we won't be able to get in front of the camera again and speak up about Hannah. My expertise is in website design and social media so I could drive traffic to the Facebook page you set up for finding Hannah. I also thought Oscar and Biggie Smalls would help with it. They must have thousands of fans on Instagram and Twitter.'

'He's already appealed to his fans. He did it during the winners' interviews.'

'Has he? That's great news. We could tweet major television stars to help out. I know quite a few of them thanks to going to events with Maxwell. I would expect they'd remember me. I'll draw up a list and set to work on it when we get out.'

'Really?' she answered, dropping onto the bed and facing him.

'Social media is a perfect medium for this. I know you've tried to get your message into cyberland but it needs more impetus and I'm probably the person to give it that push. We should put up a new photo of you, a description of Hannah and maybe a picture of her too. Do you have one?'

'I have a couple. There used to be lots of pictures of her about the house until dad had his breakdown. Gradually, they disappeared from view and now my mum keeps them in a box in her wardrobe. They both lost faith in Hannah ever returning. Mum is convinced something dreadful happened and she's dead, and Dad, he's so confused these days he often thinks I'm Hannah. It hurts to see the pain in his eyes when I correct him.'

'It must be really difficult for you,' he replied. He studied her distraught face, reached out to her and placed a comforting hand on her shoulder.

'I never really got the hang of the whole social media thing. I've only got about fifteen friends on Facebook and I don't spend much time on it. Melinda tried to help me out but she's not into it much more than I am. She suggested the blog for Hannah which is essentially a series of letters to her, reminding her of our life together and letting her know how much I miss her...' She faltered. Lewis waited for her to continue.

'I thought she might stumble across it. I had such high hopes for the blog but nothing has come of it. I've no idea if more people have been visiting it since I came on the show or if they're completely disinterested. I'd love to know if anyone's tried to contact me about Hannah. All I can do is keep saying the same thing, night after night and hope people begin to talk about her.'

Lewis's face changed. 'Oh shit, Bryony. I'm so sorry. I ought to have looked on your behalf when I was in the café, not logged onto my emails. What was I thinking of? I was so pissed off about Potts and messing up the challenge today for you and losing you the opportunity to speak again about Hannah, it didn't cross my mind. What a total shit! I logged onto my emails when I should have Googled the show to read the reactions to it or find out how your appeal was going. I could go back down to the village first thing before the challenge begins. The café might be open then.'

Bryony wasn't at all upset with him, in fact, she was touched by his genuine dismay at not thinking of checking up for her. 'No, don't do that. It's really not an issue. It's Friday tomorrow and we'll soon be going back home. I can wait a couple of days to find out what's been happening. Besides, I don't want to mess up my perfor-mance on the show. We've got general knowledge quizzes next and I'll be completely thrown if hardly anyone's visited *Searching for Hannah*. I won't be able to concentrate and I don't think I could bear to know this has all been in vain. If this hasn't worked I'll try anything else, Lewis. I have to give everything a go. I'm scared I'll run out of options and then what? I can't face the thought of failure. This is all my fault and I have to get her back, especially now when Dad needs her more than ever. It tears me apart looking at my parents' faces every time I visit them, knowing I'm the root of their misery. Some days, I wish I hadn't survived the accident and then maybe Hannah would never have left.'

'No. That would have been much, much worse. You poor, sweet girl.' He rubbed her shoulder gently. His eyes travelled her face and rested on the scar. He lifted a finger and traced it ever so gently. Bryony held her breath. He seemed completely unfazed by this deformity. She sensed rather than heard the electricity between them as it fizzed and crackled and filled her body with heat. Time stood still, then he leant into her and brushed the scar with his soft lips. He pulled back slightly. She felt his breath on her skin. His finger descended to her cheek, then to her jaw where he pressed slightly to tilt her face towards his. Their lips touched without any sense that either had initiated it – a soft, satisfying kiss full of tenderness. She drew back a little. 'Are you sure about this?'

'Very sure.'

A gentle moan escaped from somewhere inside and she surrendered to his warmth and passion, allowing each caress to dissolve the pain she had carried inside for so long.

Chapter Thirty Five

Friday, 28 July – Morning

'Come on, sleepyhead,' she heard. 'Time to smash this contest.'

She looked up. Lewis was washed, dressed and leaning over her. He kissed her, his breath minty and fresh. She responded eagerly.

'Oh–oh, better stop that or we'll never get downstairs in time,' he said, grudgingly pulling himself up from her. 'I'll fetch you a croissant and you can get ready while I'm downstairs. That way, I won't get so distracted I'll have to make passionate love to you again.'

He blew her a kiss and left the room. Her face, still rosy from their lovemaking, broke into a wide grin. She eased herself from the bed and collected the T-shirt discarded the night before. She could smell him on her skin and taste him on her lips. She had never felt so contented. The first time they had made love, it had been the desperate, frenzied affair of two lonely souls who needed to heal. Afterwards they had lain side by side, legs entwined, holding hands. They had talked about their lives, their likes and France, but mostly they had enjoyed silence – the contented calm of two people who have exorcised demons. He had run his hands over her stomach and down her hips. Then he had followed the pale lines left by scars with his lips and the second time they made love, it was with a delicious passion. Afterwards he had kissed her goodnight and wrapped a protective arm around her. For the first time in years, she didn't endure a night punctuated by anxious dreams and moments of wakefulness. She benefitted instead from a deep, dark slumber that left her body revitalized and a sense every cell was buzzing with life.

Lewis rushed back into the room as she was putting the finishing touches to her make-up, face contorted as she brushed her lashes with a second coat of mascara. He placed a cup of coffee and a croissant on the shelf above the sink.

'Get that down you, Brainy Bryony. The minibus is outside. I'm pumped and ready to win this quiz!' She screwed the top back on her applicator and replaced it in her make-up bag. Before she could reach for the coffee, he grabbed both of her hands in his own. 'I've been thinking. It'd be best if no one suspects we're *together*. I don't want "us" to overshadow what you're trying to do. It's not that I don't want to shout out about it, I just think it would be prudent to keep it quiet for now. We have to keep the public focused on finding Hannah. It might be better to keep this under wraps... just until we've won.'

It seemed logical to her and his concern was appreciated. 'Sure. That makes sense.'

He kissed her on the forehead. 'I'd really like to throw you over my shoulder and march you downstairs, shouting, 'I've found a woman!'

'Would you really?'

'Or you could carry me over your shoulder. I'm not sexist.' He kissed her again, this time on the lips, before pulling away.

She returned the smile he gave her and slipped on kitten-heeled black shoes that complimented her red and black dress.

'Wow! You look every inch a winner,' he said.

'You'll have to stop giving me compliments if you want to keep this quiet. People will soon suspect.'

I told Donald he looked nice in his kilt. Didn't mean I fancied the pants off him.'

Bryony laughed then drank her coffee in one, stuffed the croissant in her bag for later and grabbed his arm in hers. 'Ready, partner. Don't want to be last down.'

Outside, an over-exuberant pug was prancing around his master's feet. Biggie was sporting a new multicoloured jumper and a tiny fedora hat.

Oscar hopped excitedly from foot to foot, narrowly avoiding stepping on his dog. 'I'm so excited I could explode,' he squealed.

'Hold the bus. Wait for the winners to arrive,' yelled Lewis as he and Bryony bustled outside.

'We'll see about that,' said Jim good-naturedly.

'You don't stand a chance, mate,' replied Lewis, patting Oscar on the shoulder as he eased past him and stepped over Biggie. 'I have Brainy Bryony on my team.'

'And I have Ingenious Jim,' Oscar replied, a gleam in his eyes.

'Touché! So, it's anybody's game. May the best team win.'

They climbed onto the minibus, and in an atmosphere soaked with excitement and tension, they pulled away from Hotel Petit Château.

—

Forty-five minutes later they arrived at their destination. They passed through a pair of magnificent wrought-iron gates and down a lengthy drive, accompanied by the sound of gravel crunching under the tyres of the minibus. Bryony caught a glimpse of the Château du Torquet as the sweeping drive opened out onto a vast lawned area behind which stood an imposing building, fifty times the size of the one they had been staying in. She gasped in amazement, a sound echoed by her fellow passengers as one by one they feasted their eyes on the château facing them. The grandness of the building was all-encompassing, the sheer size of it was impressive.

Oscar was the first to break the stunned silence. 'Wow! That's like the Palace of Versailles. It's humungous. I wonder how many rooms are in it.'

'At least forty or fifty,' said Lewis.

Jim nodded in agreement. 'It's a superb seventeenth-century example of design and architecture. I'd love to bring Cathy here. I can't wait to see what's inside. Do you think they'll let us take photographs, Oscar?'

'We can always ask Laura. I've got my camera with me. I've been using it to take pictures of Biggie since we arrived. Maybe they'll let us use it inside. If so, I'll take some photos for you to show Cathy.'

Bryony spoke up. 'There are about thirty black vans with blacked-out windows lining the drive. It's like some sort of major political convention has tipped up. Judging by the activity around them I'd say they belong to the film crew.'

Oscar's excitement was mounting. He clutched the headrest of the seat in front of him and stared outside. 'There are *so* many people. How many does it take to film a quiz show?'

'Unless there's something else going on as well as the filming, I'd say about a hundred. It's so exciting! All of a sudden I feel like a celeb.' Bryony clapped her hands together, eyes wide. Lewis picked up on her enthusiasm.

'It makes you feel really important, doesn't it? All those people just for the four of us.'

The minibus pulled to a halt in front of the château and its doors slid back automatically. The contestants began to disembark, scrabbling for their bags as they left their seats and stumbled off the minibus in a daze where they were met by Roxanne.

'Hi, everyone. It's a bit mental at the moment. We're still setting up. You wouldn't believe how complex it is to film in a place like this. We have cables and lights and technicians everywhere. We've completely taken over four of the rooms with our kit.'

The group trailed after her into the huge entrance and stood while several members of the film crew, dressed identically from top to toe in black, weaved around them carrying stands, boxes, coils and other mysterious objects. Once the kerfuffle had abated, the contestants travelled in single file along a dark tiled hallway and into a cavernous room with enormous windows affording a superb view of gardens, magnificent stone fountains and flower beds befitting of the estate. Mattie had set up camp in here, her palettes of make-up and brushes spread out on a cloth on a large wooden table. The far wall was filled with a free-standing clothes rail containing ironed shirts and suits of various colours for Professor Potts. She faced an enormous gilt-framed mirror and was busy applying liberal amounts of make-up to a pasty-faced Potts.

'Morning, contestants. Hope you're all on form today and didn't glug too much wine last night.'

'Once you left, the party ended,' Jim replied. 'Oscar and I turned in for the night.'

'Yes, apologies I couldn't stay for dessert. Roxanne and I had to get back to the hotel to go through today's agenda.'

'I slept like a log,' said Jim. 'I must say, the wine we had at dinner was excellent. I fell asleep as soon as I hit the pillow.'

Mattie stood back to admire her handiwork. Potts swiftly removed the white cloth protecting his bright blue shirt and, with an airy wave of his hand, dismissed her without thanks.

'I'll see you all later. I have to do my introductory pieces to camera. My, you do all look delightful. And Bryony you are positively glowing today,' he added, his eyes appraising her. 'Looks like you had a very good night's sleep.'

Bryony could sense Lewis's hackles rising. She thanked Potts and, summoned by Mattie, slipped into the vacated seat to have her hair styled. The others waited their turn in awed silence, admiring the ornate furnishings in the room.

Once ready, Bryony waited in the corridor for the others to join her which brought back memories of her schooldays and Melinda. She wondered how her friend was getting on without her. It was strange not to be able to talk to her. Although they didn't chat every day, she'd never been out of contact like this for so long. She thought about her parents and hoped they were both alright then comforted herself in the knowledge that had anything awful happened, Melinda would have phoned the crew's emergency number and got hold of her. Melinda was the sister she'd never lost and she loved her. In spite of that, Bryony sighed and wished with all her heart she could have prevented Hannah from running away. She had no way of knowing if this crazy adventure had been successful and people were looking for Hannah. All she knew was she wanted to win and have another opportunity to ask everyone watching the show to assist. There would be new viewers who hadn't yet heard her story and one of them might know something. This was probably going to be her last opportunity to put right the past.

Chapter Thirty Six

Friday, 28 July – Morning

'Right, if you could all follow me and watch out for the cables,' bellowed yet another man in black. With his headset and microphone clamped to his head, he resembled some strange alien. Bryony was having trouble working out who was who. With similar fork-shaped beards and short dark hair they all looked similar.

The contestants trooped behind him into the château restaurant used by the public on open days. Pots of coffee stood on a long, wooden table pitted with knotholes. Laura was looking youthful, dressed in snug-fitting black trousers and a loose, lacy black top. Her long, dark hair scraped back into a shining ponytail enhanced the impression of youth and took ten years off her face.

'Morning, everyone!' she said in a breezy voice. 'Excited? It is going to be hugely enjoyable, so come on, teams, let's get some energy going! Roxanne will run through the rules for today and then you'll be getting your microphones and packs fitted and head off to be filmed.'

Roxanne came forward. 'These next challenges are going to be really easy, fun rounds all filmed here over the next two days. Today, we're set up in the Gallery Room where you'll take part in a general knowledge quiz consisting of one hundred questions. Professor Potts will start with an introduction to the château then invite to you to say a little about yourselves once more, in case some of our millions of viewers don't know who you are yet,' she added with a grin. 'He's got all the information we gathered from you when we interviewed you on Skype plus whatever he found out about you over the last few days and at dinner last night. He might, for example, say, "I understand you have a famous dog, Oscar?" and you'll be able to talk about Biggie Smalls.' She scanned their faces to ensure they all understood. 'Then the actual quiz will begin and he'll ask you one hundred general knowledge questions. You buzz in when you know the answer. First pair to buzz in and answer correctly will win the point. It's all very simple. Enjoy it, be yourselves.'

'Remember, plenty of energy, people,' Laura added.

'Energy,' whispered Lewis to Bryony. 'We've got stacks of it.'

'Okay, the techies will make sure you have discreet microphones. They're not the same as the ones you've been wearing on past challenges. However, like those, these are switched on at all times, so once again, don't speak if you're not being spoken to and no swearing. You must all be dab hands at this by now.'

Bryony recognized some of the young men from the days before, now dressed in black shirts and black jeans. They unplugged wires from packs and deftly threaded them through clothing, reattaching them to sound packs. A young man with a small goatee beard and black-framed glasses dropped a wire down the back of Bryony's top but struggled to attach the pack.

'You're too tight,' he chided. 'I can't get it in,' he continued, causing Oscar to snort loudly.

A man with three days' stubble, huge dark patches under his eyes and the look of a man who was being hassled, entered the room and rubbed his hands together.

'Morning, folks,' he called. 'I'm Terry. I'm what they call the floor manager, which is just a title for "stressed bloke who needs a fag". No doubt you've been told already but please watch out for cables. They are every-where and some are hidden under raised covering. Try not to stare at the cameras. It's different filming inside to outside as the cameras are closer to you, but pretend they're not there, and enjoy yourselves. Now, how do I get outside this place to get a cigarette?'

Both Roxanne and Laura carried walkie-talkies, which now babbled into life.

Laura responded quickly, 'Roger that. I'll bring the teams through.' Turning to them, she gave another of her infectious smiles. 'Okay, guys. This is it. Break a leg.'

'I might do that if I trip over any of the cables,' muttered Jim to himself. No one acknowledged him. Nerves had kicked in and they followed Laura out of the restaurant, along the corridor and into a magnificent room. It was immense even filled as it was with about forty people. Six cameras pointed in the direction of the plinths while a seventh concentrated on Professor Potts, who stood staring at the autocue, a sour expression on his face. Mattie fussed about him spraying strands of hair and patting them down. Four men, arms folded and wearing headphones and microphones, communicated with invisible members of the team. Camera crew were positioned behind their apparatus awaiting commands. People rushed in and out of the room. Cables stretched around the floor like dark, coiling snakes.

'Hi, guys!' yelped a short, chubby man with a smile that stretched across his face.

'Bryony and Lewis, could you please stand here?' He walked them to two red crosses marked out in tape on the floor in front of a plinth. 'Lewis, stand slightly behind Bryony, please. You need to squeeze right in behind her so we can get a tight shot of your faces. That's it. Now Jim, Oscar, please can we have you at the next plinth? That's it, Jim. You stand in front and Oscar behind. Great.'

Terry reappeared from his cigarette break and shouted, 'Okay, everyone. We're ready for the take. Prof, you ready?'

'If someone shoos off Hairspray Mattie,' Potts answered, fiddling with his earpiece.

She pulled a face at him and joined the crew to observe the proceedings.

'Cameras?'

'Rolling,' replied each camera operative.

A figure came forward with a clapperboard. Bryony could feel her heart hammering with anticipation.

'Action!'

Professor Potts faced the camera, plastered a smile on his face and began, 'Hello and welcome to Friday and day five of *What Happens in...* We're standing in the remarkable Gallery Room at Château du Torture—'

'Cut! Prof, it's Torquet not Torture.'

Potts scowled. The cameras rolled and he tried again. 'Hello and welcome to the final day of *What Happens in...* We're here in the remarkable Gallery Room at Château du Torquet, a room filled with outstanding sculptures and artwork and where we can discover portraits and pictures from as early as the sixteenth century.' He smiled winningly.

'Our teams have been tested on all manner of challenges but today it's all about their general knowledge. Have our remaining teams got what it takes to become champions and win ten thousand ponds—?'

'Cut! Ponds? However did you come up with that?'

Potts grinned boyishly. 'Misread the autocue. The light was shining on it.'

'Take it again starting from, "Our teams have been tested",' shouted a grumpy voice.

'Miserable sod,' mumbled Potts, winking at Bryony.

'I heard that!' said the voice.

'You were supposed to. Loosen up, Roland.' He faced his camera. The autocue was rewound and he began again.

'Our teams have been tested on all manner of challenges but today it's their knowledge—'

'Misread it again,' grumbled the same grumpy voice.

'It's the light, Roland. Move the wretched autocue. I can't see the words.'

'Move the autocue for the professor,' yelled another voice.

Oscar fidgeted on his spot. Bryony knew how he felt. They hadn't started the quiz yet and already she was feeling too stressed to put up a good performance.

Mattie shot out from near the cameras, can in hand, brushed a hair back from Professor Potts' face and sprayed his hair liberally, causing him to cough.

He waved his hands at her. 'Go away. I have enough hairspray already. If anyone comes near me with a match I'll go up in flames.'

Bryony heard someone muttering, 'Anybody got a lighter?'

At last, the autocue was in the right place and Professor Potts managed to read the introduction without any errors. He turned to Bryony and Lewis.

'So, our first contestants are Bryony and Lewis.' He gave them a brilliant smile. 'Bryony, Bryony, Bryony,' he repeated in an affectionate manner. 'How are you, darling? Bit nervous?'

'A little,' she confessed.

He walked over to her and held her hands between his. 'You have no need to be. You'll be fine. Now, I understand you're searching for your lost sister, Hannah.'

She wanted to yank her hands away. His felt clammy.

'Yes, she ran away from home when she was sixteen and my family tried everything to find her; they even hired two detectives but they had no success and said she'd fallen completely off the radar. Many children run away from home, never to be heard of again. They have their reasons for going but they leave behind a terrible hole in people's lives – a hole that can't be fixed. Certainly, none of us ever got over losing Hannah. My father took it the worst and last month, he suffered a major stroke. It's now more important than ever I locate her and beg her to come home. We all want to see her so badly. If anyone knows anything at all about her, or has contacts with people from missing person's agencies, or anything that could help us track her down, I implore them to get in contact via the blog *Searching for Hannah*.'

Potts stared at the camera, eyes wide, sincerity oozing from every pore. 'If *you* know Bryony's sister, Hannah, please get in touch with her and tell her about what you've heard. It would be wonderful to know that this incredible show has provided a happy ending. Now Bryony, I understand you're a teacher. What subjects do you teach?'

Bryony was surprised by the sudden change in the conversation but answered all the same. 'I teach English and help children and young adults with learning difficulties. It's extremely rewarding.'

'And do you have any hobbies or interests?'

'I like learning languages. I can speak French and a little Russian.'

Professor Potts dropped her hands theatrically. 'Get out of here! That's incredible. Isn't that amazing?'

Bryony ignored the overdramatic reaction and smiled again.

'Can you say something in Russian for us? How about, "I'm very happy to be on the show?"'

Bryony obliged and earned a round of applause from the crew.

'What about that, eh? Russian. You'll be a formidable force today. And this is your teammate, Lucas.'

'Cut!' yelled the grumpy voice again.

'Sorry. My mind wandered.'

'Go from, "What about that, eh?"'

Bryony could feel Lewis tensing beside her. She nudged his hand with her own and looked up at him, willing him to concentrate on the quiz and not the feud that was developing.

'How about that, eh? Russian. You'll be a formidable force today. And this is your teammate, Lewis. Lewis, what's this I hear about you wanting to purchase your own vineyard? Bit of a wine lover, are you?'

Lewis rubbed the back of Bryony's hand with his own and fell into the role of enthusiastic contestant.

–

'And at the end of that quiz, I can tell you Jim and Oscar have won by only two points!'

The men in black, lurking in the shadows applauded and as footage was checked, the teams had their microphone packs removed and were led back to the dining room. Last to leave, Bryony felt Lewis's lips caress her ear as he whispered, 'You were brilliant. We only just missed out and you got to talk about Hannah. Don't worry, we'll smash it tomorrow.'

Once in the dining room, he headed directly towards Jim who with head held high, seemed even taller and straighter than usual. 'Well done. You deserved to win. There were some tricky questions and you nailed them.'

'Bravo. You too, Oscar, you both deserved to win,' agreed Bryony, dropping a light kiss on the man's cheek. He flushed pink and then beamed at her.

'Thanks. It was ridiculously close though, wasn't it?' replied Oscar, waggling a biscuit at Biggie, who scuttled over and immediately sat in front of him, lavishing him with undivided attention. 'I thought you were going to beat us. Talk about neck-and-neck. I sweated so profusely in there, I swear I've lost several pounds.'

Laura clapped her hands for attention. 'Okay, everyone. Great job. Sorry about all the delays. It took far longer than we expected. The driver should be here soon to take you back to the hotel. The crew are now relocating to the library for the second part of the quiz which takes place tomorrow, so I'll have to leave you for now. Chill out, read a magazine, have a coffee and Roxanne will come and fetch you shortly.'

Bryony picked up a magazine and reclined on a seat. She didn't want to engage in further conversation with Jim and Oscar, nice as they both were. She really wanted to talk to Lewis about their night together but that would not be possible in front of an audience. Bryony spotted the date on the front page of the magazine. It was a current edition that ran to the third of August. She sighed. It would soon be the fourth of August again and she would have to visit her parents for the annual ritual...

–

'Happy birthday, dear Hannah, happy birthday to you!' Bryony sings in a reedy voice. She hands Hannah the present wrapped in pink tissue. She has drawn hearts on it in crayon.

'It's lovely, Bryony,' says Hannah, ripping the paper apart and holding the heart-shaped silver necklace to the light.

'Mummy chose it with me,' says Bryony. 'I wanted to get you something nice. It's got your name engraved on it.'

Hannah attaches the chain around her neck and fingers the heart. 'It's beautiful. Thank you, little sis. I shall treasure it forever.'

–

Lewis stood behind her chair and leant forward. 'What are you reading?'

'Not reading anything in particular. I was reminiscing. It's Hannah's birthday in a couple of weeks. She'll be forty-six years old. I was wondering if she's around to celebrate it.'

'Hopefully so, and I shall make sure we find her,' he said in a low voice before heading towards the toilets.

'Any juicy gossip, then?' Oscar asked, pointing at the magazine.

'I wish I knew but I don't recognize half of these so-called celebrities.' She handed the magazine to Oscar, who slipped into the seat beside her.

'That's Lucy Mecklenburgh from the television show *The Only Way Is Essex*.' Oscar continued to flip casually through the pages making comments. 'Ooh, that's a gorgeous outfit. I wonder if I could get away with that jacket. Is that his mansion? Wow, amazing! Here's Alex Jones the television presenter and her husband Charlie Thomson. I think she's got the loveliest Welsh accent. It's like music when she speaks. I love that dress she's wearing. Red really suits her. You'd look lovely in that too, Bryony.' He turned another page and pointed at the woman in the photograph. 'This is Taylor Swift – surely you must have heard of her?'

'She's a singer, isn't she? I obviously need to take a diploma in how to stay in touch with modern society.'

'Oh pur-lease,' he said in an exaggerated fashion. 'You're perfectly fine as you are. You don't need to keep up with celebs. You know plenty of other stuff and lots of interesting facts that I don't know. Go on, teach me how to say, "Your bum looks too big in that tutu," in Russian.'

Chapter Thirty Seven

Friday, 28 July – Evening

'Unusually, you already know the results from today's challenge and are aware that nobody is leaving, so tonight we won't be putting you through that anxiety during a live broadcast. We have a surprise for you, instead,' said Roxanne.

Oscar looked up from feeding Biggie Smalls some sausage. 'I love surprises. What is it?'

'It wouldn't be a surprise if I told you,' Roxanne quipped.

'Where's Laura this evening?' asked Jim, sat on the settee near Bryony. 'She's usually here to talk us through the live event.'

'She's still on set with the technical crew. They've had some difficulties and are working late. That's why you've got me. I'm going to make sure you're all settled and enjoy the evening.'

'Biggie's already enjoyed his. What was that you got for him?'

'*Saucisson Sec*. It's from the butcher in town.'

'I'll have to buy him some more to take home with me. What do you reckon, Biggie?' The pug licked his lips in appreciation. 'Ah, at last.' His comment was directed at Lewis who entered the library.

'Dozed off,' said Lewis. 'Bryony woke me up before she came downstairs.'

'You moved into Nicola's old room now?' Roxanne asked.

'Yes. Thanks. It's very nice,' Bryony replied.

'Sorry about the mix up and you having to share with Lewis. I don't know how that happened. You were really good not to make a fuss about it.'

'It's okay. We got along fine,' said Bryony. She didn't want to let on just how well they'd got along, although she feared the smile on her face might give it away. She hadn't been keen to move out of their double room but it would have looked odd if she hadn't agreed, even if it was for only one night. Lewis had insisted she took up the offer to move rooms. Once again, he'd voiced his concern that should anyone discover they were having a relationship, it could well put the message about Hannah that Bryony was trying so hard to get out, in the shade. She'd agreed albeit reluctantly.

No sooner had they returned from the filming than Bertrand had pounced on her, full of apologies at the misunderstanding that had led to her and Lewis sharing a room. He'd not only insisted on carrying her packed bags to the freshly cleaned room, now vacated by Nicola, but had filled the place with fresh flowers from the garden as an apology.

Packing up to move rooms and dealing with the overwrought Bertrand who'd invited her to join him for a drink to make amends, had meant she hadn't spent any time with Lewis that afternoon. She was hoping to rectify that after the live event.

The screen erected on the wall was switched on. Day five of *What Happens in…* had already been broadcast in the UK so the audience at home had seen the one hundred question quiz, and it was time for the live chat element of the show. Professor Potts appeared to be broadcasting from where they'd been filming earlier in the gallery at Château du Torquet. He'd changed his outfit and now wore jeans, combined with a very pale blue shirt and a turquoise sweater draped over his shoulders. His suntanned face was as handsome as ever; his penetrating blue eyes twinkling in the lights. Bryony wondered how many women would be watching him and yearning to be on the show if only to be near him. Melinda would be positively green with envy. To be fair to him, he had let her talk about Hannah and had even made an appeal on her behalf. That could only be a good thing. Maybe between them, they'd triggered a thought, memory or response in somebody who was even now writing to her. Oscar hissed at Biggie Smalls who was scratching noisily and Bryony turned her attention again to the set. Potts opened his arms in a welcome gesture and spoke.

'So it's the fifth day of *What Happens in…* and we're down to the final two teams. Because no one will be sent home tonight, our live event is going to be a little different. I see our four contestants are all gathered in the library at Hotel Petit Château. Good evening everyone, or should I say *bonsoir*?'

'Bonsoir, Professor,' they duly replied.

'The viewers at home have watched today's electrifying one hundred question quiz. It really was a nail-biter, wasn't it? It went right down to the wire. This is the part of the show where ordinarily we'd give you the results and send one of the teams back home but not tonight. No, tonight we have a surprise for each of you. You've all been locked away without internet, television or phones since you arrived five days ago. You haven't been able to talk to your loved ones, friends or find out what the public think of your performances so far. Well, tonight we're going to change that. Oscar, look at the screen. Recognize anyone?'

Oscar's eyes widened. The screen had changed. Potts had gone and, in his place, sat a beautiful girl with dark eyes and hair scraped back from a porcelain complexion 'Lucinda!' he gasped.

'Oscar, we're all so proud of you, honey. We've been watching all the shows on YouTube, here in New York. You've been totally awesome so far and you did so well in all your challenges, especially that inflatable one. It looked so difficult! Hope you're enjoying France and Biggie is behaving. All his fans are rooting for you too. The show was trending on Twitter yesterday and I think they all kept tweeting about it. You can win this. Love you.' She blew a kiss. He raised an open hand and caught it and returned one of his own.

'Love you too, Lucinda.'

Lucinda disappeared to be replaced by a frail lady in a large faded armchair. On either side, sitting on the arms of the chair, were two adorable girls who Bryony identified immediately as the two girls in the photograph Jim had passed about at the dining table. He released a soft sigh and spoke his wife's name. 'Cathy.' The little girl, Poppy, sitting on the right arm of the chair, twisted at a curl of dark hair and spoke assuredly.

'Hello, Granpops. We've been watching you on telly and you're the best. We love the bumble bee car too. Can you bring it home from France with you? We love it too and the bouncy things at the park. Can you take us there one time?'

Cathy whispered something to her. The little girl continued. 'Granny says you will win and we think so too. We love you and good luck tomorrow.' She finished her sentence in a rush and grinned. The other little girl waved wildly and Cathy gave a warm smile that made her eyes sparkle.

Jim sniffed back tears but a sob caught in his throat and his eyes reddened. He lifted a hand and nodded at the screen, unable to speak. Before anyone could say a word, a face that Bryony knew so well, appeared on the screen and beamed.

'Hi, Bryony! Everyone here is totally behind you and Lewis. What an incredible team you make! The internet is awash with clips of the pair of you and appeals for Hannah. I know that's why you went on the show and wanted to let you know you're doing great. I've been monitoring the blog, *Searching for Hannah* and it's getting hundreds of hits *an hour*. You're a winner, Bryony. Good luck for tomorrow. Massive love from us all.'

Bryony's stomach flipped. Melinda had used her interview time to tell Bryony what she needed to hear. People were supportive and were behind her on her quest to find Hannah. Her lips were tugged into a smile that froze the instant she saw the woman on the screen. Lewis, sat beside Bryony, tensed instantly. She looked briefly at his face which showed no emotion, only the clenched fists gave it away. The woman fluttered long eyelashes and smiled seductively.

'Lewis, you are… incredible. Truly fantastic. I couldn't be prouder of you. You've performed amazingly in every single challenge and come out top in most of them. I knew you could do this. You've always lacked confidence in yourself but I hope this will help you to believe in yourself, like I do. I'm so glad I convinced you to apply for this show. I've got everything crossed for you for tomorrow's final. You can win this.'

The stunning dark-haired woman, with a perfect pout, who ran her elegant long fingers through luscious hair in a sultry manner as she spoke, could be none other than Maxwell.

Bryony couldn't move. Why was Maxwell on the screen? Why had she been chosen to talk to Lewis? Why not another friend or even a relative? This woman was talking as if she and Lewis were still an item, not like they'd had an acrimonious split. Up until now, Bryony had been under the impression Maxwell had treated Lewis like dirt, yet the gorgeous creature on the screen who gave a flirtatious wink as a goodbye gesture, still seemed to carry a torch for him. Had Lewis kept something from her?

Potts was back now, his white teeth on full display. 'What a treat for our remaining contestants who have made it through to the final. I think the viewers can all see how deeply they've been affected by seeing and hearing from their loved ones. Oscar, Jim, Bryony and Lewis, you have a huge amount of support and plenty of cheerleaders waiting for you back home, who'll all be glued to the set tomorrow evening. Good luck for tomorrow when I'll see you all again for the finale of *What Happens in…*'

The screen went blank.

'Cut!'

The crew stopped filming the contestants' reactions and began the regular practice of packing away the equipment. Roxanne crossed the room and put a hand on Jim's arm. 'That was so lovely.'

Jim wiped at the tears that had streaked his face. 'I'm such a lucky man. I didn't think I'd miss them as much as I do, and I'll be glad to get home. It seems longer than six days since I left them.'

Oscar was in high spirits. 'Didn't Lucinda look fab? What a babe. Talking of babes, who was that, Lewis?'

'A friend.'

Oscar pulled in his chin and wrinkled his nose. 'Really?' He stretched out the word.

'An ex-friend,' said Lewis. 'Bryony, we need to talk.'

Bryony blinked. 'We do?'

'Yes. Now.' He ignored Oscar's furrowed expression and stalked out of the room.

'Back in a min,' said Bryony to Oscar who nodded thoughtfully.

'Take your time.'

–

It was cool outside in the car park. Bryony wrapped her cardigan more tightly around her and shivered. The two remaining Citroëns were parked side by side. Her legs so heavy she could barely trudge to where Lewis was standing, next to the Furby 2CV.

'Before you ask, I've literally no idea what she was doing on that screen. I don't know who contacted her or why she even agreed to be interviewed and send me a message unless it's part of Potts' crackpot plan to piss me off. At the moment, he's succeeding. I've put up with all sorts of crap from that bloke ever since I got here and seeing Maxwell has been the sodding icing on the cake.'

She hadn't seen him so agitated. He flexed his fists and marched up and down the gravel alongside the car. 'Bryony...'

'You don't need to say anything.'

'I do. I want you to understand I had no idea Maxwell would pop up today. As for all that "I'm so proud of you" shit! What must you think? I can't fathom out why she agreed to do that piece to camera.'

'I believe you.'

'You do?'

'Of course. Look at you. You're totally wound up. You wouldn't be like that if you'd expected to see her. You were as shocked as me when she flashed up on the screen. At first, I couldn't work out why she was there either, but then I thought it over and wondered who else knows you're on the show apart from her? Well, Sean and Melinda, obviously, but who else knows?'

He shook his head.

'That's what I figured. So, who could they have invited to speak to you? You said yourself, she put your name forward for this show. She probably even knows half of the production team. It's only logical they'd invite her on.'

He stopped his pacing and held her gaze.

'Thank you. I couldn't make sense of it and was blowing it out of proportion but you've put it in perspective again. You're not angry with me?'

'Why would I be? You didn't invite her to cheer you on.'

He lifted both hands up in a submissive gesture. 'I don't know why…'

She stepped forward and, placing her hands either side of his face, pulled him into a long kiss. After they drew apart she said, 'Now, forget it and come and have dinner with the others before they suspect we're more than teammates.'

Chapter Thirty Eight

Saturday, 29 July – Morning

Roxanne issued instructions. 'Listen up because there's a lot to take in. The first quiz is going to be based on what you might have learned and seen while you've been here in France, called *What Happened in France*? After that, there'll be a break followed by a second quiz, the category round, during which you will answer a selection of questions that come under the title of the category you've chosen. All happy so far?'

'What are the categories?' asked Jim.

Laura shook her head. 'I'm not allowed to tell you that. You'll find out later. Everyone clear on what's happening?'

There were consensual nods.

'Are both quizzes going out on air tonight?' asked Oscar.

'No. *What Happened in France* will be aired tonight as day six of the show. The second quiz, the category quiz, will be aired tomorrow evening as day seven. The viewers will assume you are still in France but you won't be. If all goes to plan, you'll be back home by then.'

'Cool.' Oscar, stroked Biggie's head. 'Back to your tiny bed. No more loafing about in a castle for you, Biggie boy.'

Laura continued. 'There'll be another short break while we shift across to the Louis XIV room for that, during which time, you'll come back here for refreshments. Once we're ready, we'll be filming Sunday's grand finale show which will be transmitted at 7 p.m.'

'That's the usual time the live events are aired,' said Jim.

'That's right, but obviously it won't be live. You'll record it later today.'

'Understood,' he replied.

'Professor Potts will do a round-up of what you scored over the week and your cumulative points will be totalled. There's a specially made scoreboard showing the results in the room. That'll be when we want to see all those emotions. We want lots of oohing and aahing. We want visible disappointment. We want tears, cheers and lots and lots of energy.'

Lewis gave Bryony a wink. She interpreted its meaning and gave him a warm smile. Maybe there'd be time to be energetic with him later.

–

'Bear with us, folks,' said Laura for the umpteenth time in an hour. 'We're almost ready.' The teams had drunk enough coffee to keep them hyped for a month and were desperate to complete the second round of the day. The first quiz, *What Happened in France*, which would be beamed into sitting rooms in the UK later that day, had been another hard-fought quiz with Lewis and Bryony only just snatching victory from Oscar and Jim.

The room they'd been recording in had been stuffy, more so with all the crew members in there with them, and now the teams were hot and tired. The constant filming and efforts of the week were taking their toll, and not even the magnificent building they were filming in, or the buffet-style breakfast of an array of charcuterie and pastries, cheeses and fruit seemed to cheer the contestants.

Roxanne had brought along a couple of games for them to play while they waited but the wooden blocks had long since been packed up and Oscar and Lewis were discussing football versus American soccer. Jim, alone for a moment in a corner of the room, was studying the photograph of his grandchildren. He returned it with care to his wallet and leant back in his chair, head propped against the wall, eyes closed.

Bryony was beginning to wonder if they would actually manage to complete the filming that day or if they'd have to stay over an extra night. The thought made her face glow.

'You understand the rules?' Laura asked again.

Jim looked up. 'This quiz is being filmed for tomorrow night's show, right?'

'Yes, that's right.'

Jim continued, 'The winners receive five points which are added to the total number of points the team has won over the entire week. You calculate how many points both teams have won this week and the pair with the highest score, that is the greatest number of points in total, wins the prize money.'

'That's spot on.'

'So, if we win this category round, we haven't necessarily won the entire competition?' Oscar still looked uncertain.

'That's right. We'll work out which team has won the greater number of challenges, received the most number of points and that couple will win the ten-thousand-pound prize.'

Oscar nodded. 'I think I've grasped it. Sorry. I'm so out of energy. I've no idea how my brain will manage yet another session of grilling.'

A burst of static from the walkie-talkie and some garbled dialogue got Laura animated. It was time to start recording. They trooped down the labyrinth of corridors and into yet another room where they faced Professor Potts, who was muttering his lines as if reciting a crazed monologue.

The cameras rolled once more and the last round began.

'It's Saturday, day six... Shit, it isn't, is it? It's day seven. Who decided to make this so complicated?'

'Cut! We're filming for *tomorrow* night's show, Prof. It'll be day seven. Sunday, day seven, okay?'

'Yes... yes... I've got it. It's been a bloody long week, you know?'

'Don't we know it,' came back the reply.

Potts shook himself like an athlete and tried once more. 'It's Sunday, day seven, and the *final* day of *What Happens in...* We're once again at the *magnifique* Château du Torquet and are gathered in the library of this grand building, where you would need several months to browse through the impressive collection of over three thousand books.' He swept his arms wide so the camera could take in the floor to ceiling shelves filled with volume after volume of hard backed books each with intricate lettering on aged spines.

Bryony pursed her lips and raised her eyebrows. That was a remarkable collection of books.

'Our teams are almost at the end of their mammoth adventure. Seven days of gruelling challenges that made them pit their wits against each other, and physical challenges that sorted the men from the boys, and now we're exhausting our contestants' brain power. Oscar – delightful Oscar – slave to Biggie Smalls, you and Jim lost the round yesterday entitled *What Happened in France*?' Potts moved forward to address the pair more intimately. 'You therefore have the right to select the first of our two categories in this, the final round of the competition. Oscar, what do you fancy: "Pieces of Eight" or "Masterpieces"?'

'I reckon "Masterpieces" will be mostly about art and that's not one of my strengths,' murmured Jim. Oscar agreed. 'If we choose the other category, it could be about coins or currency.'

'If it's currency, we'll be fine. Oscar, you've been a splendid teammate, a real trooper and I trust you implicitly. Let's go for it,' said Jim, slapping Oscar on the back. 'We'll take "Pieces of Eight", please, Professor Potts.'

'So, you're answering questions on "Pieces of Eight," Professor Potts confirmed. 'The time will begin as soon as I finish asking the first question...' He paused for effect then read, 'Before the introduction of the euro, which country used the drachma as its currency?'

'Greece.'

'Correct. Whose portrait appears on the US two-dollar bill?'

Oscar waved his hands in excitement and squealed, 'Thomas Jefferson.'

–

'"Money Makes the World Go Round" comes from which musical?'

'*Cabaret*,' shouted Oscar, bouncing on the balls of his feet.

'Correct. What—' A buzzer sounded. Professor Potts looked at the men, who were now eager to know the outcome of the round. 'I can't finish that question. We're out of time. At the end of two minutes, you have scored eleven correct answers, giving you a total of thirty-three points. Some of those fell in your lap, eh, Oscar?'

Oscar's head bobbed up and down and he clung to Jim's arm.

'So, Bryony and Lewis. You have been left with the category "Masterpieces" in this, our last quiz of the entire competition. Are you ready?'

'As we'll ever be,' said Bryony.

'Time begins at the end of the first question. Which French artist, born in 1834, was best known for his paintings of ballet dancers?'

'Toulouse-Lautrec,' answered Lewis with gusto before Bryony could open her mouth.

Bryony shook her head. 'No, he painted cancan girls at the Moulin Rouge.'

Lewis whispered, 'Sorry.' She smiled back at him.

'That's right, Bryony. The answer is Edgar Degas.'

–

'Which artist is famous for his statue, *The Thinker*?'

'I think he created *The Kiss* too,' said Lewis, giving Bryony a meaningful look.

She called out, 'Auguste Rodin.' A rush of warmth tinted her cheeks a light rose.

With each correct answer Bryony had been gaining in confidence and now she knew she was within a heartbeat of beating Jim and Oscar's score.

'Correct. When was the iconic painting *The Last Supper* painted?'

Bryony tipped her head back with relief and blessed the fact they'd looked at and talked about the painting in Hotel Petit Château on their first day. She opened her mouth to answer and caught a glimpse of Jim. His eyes were shut, his face contorted, and he clung onto Oscar's arm. She knew in an instant she'd been wrong when she'd told Oscar she thought winning wasn't important to him. It was as clear as day that winning the show meant *everything* to the man. The vision of Jim looking at the photograph of his grandchildren and the way his face had glowed when speaking about his family, flashed in front of her eyes. She recalled the excited, proud faces of his grandchildren on the television screen in the library, and the warm smile his wife Cathy had given him, and she knew Jim had to win.

'1850,' she said flatly. Lewis shot her a look. The buzzer sounded. It was the end of the round.

Professor Potts shook his head at her as a parent might at a wayward child before saying, 'Oh Bryony, bad luck. You were well out with that last guess. *The Last Supper* by Leonardo da Vinci was painted between 1495 and 1498.'

He turned towards his autocue and the camera, beamed at it and announced, 'We've come to the end of the final round. It was a close-run thing. Bryony and Lewis, you scored ten correct answers, giving you a total of thirty points. Good job, Bryony. Shame about the last answer but I think you showed you know a lot about art. And,

Lewis, Rodin sculpted many pieces including the iconic *The Thinker*, *The Burghers of Calais* and, of course, *The Kiss*, which is believed to have been inspired by his assistant, lover and muse, Camille Claudel,' he added, a smug expression plastered across his face.

Behind them an ecstatic Oscar pirouetted before hugging a beaming Jim.

'Congratulations, Jim and Oscar! You are the winners!' Potts drew a deep breath. 'Thank goodness. We managed it all in one take. Everyone happy out there?' he asked the film crew. A man in a headset nodded at him. 'Terrific. Looks like we're on for an early lunch then.' He pulled out his earpiece, handed it to a member of the technical team and walked off without speaking to any of the contestants.

Once again, they trudged back into the restaurant. Oscar raced off to walk Biggie, accompanied by Roxanne and floor manager, Terry, who needed another cigarette break. Laura chatted to an elated Jim, face alight with pleasure.

'You threw the last question,' Lewis hissed quietly. 'Why?'

Bryony raised her face to his. 'I realized this competition was hugely important to Jim. He's a proud man. Jim needs that feeling of accomplishment, of satisfaction, of self-worth. Oscar told me as much the other evening in the garden, but I didn't believe him until I saw the desperation on Jim's face earlier. I don't need to win this competition but he does. I've had a chance to tell everyone watching about Hannah and that's really what I wanted to do. I'd have only given my half of the winnings to charity but in reality, I can raise money in other ways. I can do a sponsored skydive or shake a tin at strangers in town but winning is important to Jim. I felt I had to give him an edge in the competition. By my calculations, they should walk it now. They've won more rounds than us: day two they won the treasure hunt, the hill climb on day four, and two of the quizzes.' She looked away to make sure she'd not been overheard. 'I'm sorry I've robbed you of the chance to win the money. I hope you don't mind,' she whispered. She felt Lewis's hand on the centre of her back, its heat penetrating her skin. His lips were close to her ear.

'You're a very special lady,' he murmured before pulling away.

Jim wandered over. 'Bad luck,' he said kindly. 'I didn't know the answer to your last question.'

'That's the way it goes. So, you're one step closer to winning the contest. Excited?'

'My dear, I can't explain how I feel at this moment. It's a mixture of anxious suspense tinged with sadness that we can't all win. I've had a marvellous time here, and whatever the outcome is, I'll still feel like a winner. I've met all you remarkable people and relished every moment of the last week.' He leant forward and whispered, 'I even like that funny little dog. I've had my photo taken with it. Oscar is going to put it up on "Instant Gran" or whatever it's called. My granddaughters are into all that modern stuff. It'll be a surprise for them when they see me with a gangsta dog,' he chuckled, his face crinkling.

Bryony warmed further to the man. He was older than her father but being away in France and being in Oscar's buoyant company had revitalized him no end.

'Talking of which, there's my partner in crime. Must go and congratulate him on some of those responses. He's a remarkably bright young man.'

He scurried off to backslapping and chuckling from Oscar as both relived the last round and Biggie danced about with a happy grin on his face.

Chapter Thirty Nine

Saturday, 29 July – Afternoon

Laura stood next to the door waiting for confirmation that all was set to go. She was sporting a headset and microphone much like a pop star or an exercise class teacher would wear, and she looked even more tense than the contestants, her fingers drumming against her clipboard. From time to time, a crackle of incoherent voices erupted from the walkie-talkie strapped to Laura's waist.

Oscar performed some stretches against a chair with grace. Lewis sat opposite Bryony, elbows on the table. They glanced at each other from time to time and smiled but neither spoke. It wasn't the time or place to share what was in their thoughts. Following the live event and the shock of seeing Maxwell on the screen the evening before, they'd eaten dinner with Oscar and Jim, a meal that had stretched late into the night and, after consuming too much wine, she'd turned in before Lewis, leaving him in a semi-drunken stupor with Biggie Smalls curled up in his lap, deep in conversation with the others about New York at Christmas. There'd been no opportunity since to talk in private and they'd have to wait until the filming was over.

He glanced over and gave her a wink that she returned. The ringtone of a mobile phone fractured the silence. It was the emergency phone. Jim glanced up at the sound, a look of panic spreading across his face. Roxanne retrieved the phone from the table and spoke quietly. 'Sorry, you're not making much sense. Okay, that's better. Can't it wait? He's about to go onto set,' she said. 'No, don't cry. I'll fetch him but please be quick. We're expecting to get called very soon.' With a grave look on her face she handed the phone to Lewis. 'It's Maxwell. She says it's important. She sounds very upset,' she added quietly.

A jolt like an electric shock raced through Bryony. She tried to catch Lewis's eye but he ignored her, strode towards Roxanne, took the phone and headed to the toilets to speak in private.

At the same time the walkie-talkie sprang into life babbling commands and unintelligible sounds. Laura listened to the voice in her headset. 'Cool. We're on our way. One moment. We're waiting for one of them. He won't be a minute.' She clapped her hands in excitement, and her ponytail swung from side to side as she scanned the room to speak to everyone. 'The moment you've been waiting for is here at last. This is the grand finale. Good luck to you all and don't forget, let's see loads and loads of energy. This will be broadcast instead of the live event tomorrow night, and we're anticipating well over five million viewers or maybe more.'

The sound of scraping chairs filled the room. Biggie jumped up at Jim's leg, his tongue out. Jim bent and patted the little animal. 'I hope you're my good luck charm,' he whispered. Oscar put his arm across Jim's shoulders and spoke softly to him. Bryony turned. Lewis marched towards her, lips thin, face set, eyes blazing.

In a gruff tone he said, 'Let's go.'

There was no time to talk to him. She silenced her thoughts and concentrated on the instructions being issued by Terry.

'We're ready to shoot,' shouted a voice.

'Waiting for the professor,' replied Terry.

'I'm here,' called a voice from behind them. He snatched his earpiece from a technician and stuffed it in his right ear. 'Had to nip to the little boys' room. Hope I've not held you all up. Bet you're all nervous. So am I,' he added, looking anything but. He wandered up to the front of the line and coughed dramatically.

'Prof's here. Get ready, cameras.'

'Rolling.'

'Action!' The board snapped loudly.

The door to the Louis XIV room opened and Bryony's eyes fell upon ornate framed paintings hanging on the walls and huge wooden cabinets filled with porcelain objects and china. With its high ceilings and opulent wallpaper, it was very grand. It even smelt grand – the aroma of aged wood and polish filling the vast space. She halted beside the others. Potts squinted at his autocue. He coughed then began. 'Bonsoir from la belle France and welcome to what is normally the live event but tonight is the grand finale of *What Happens in…*, coming to you from the Château du Torquet in Brittany. We began the week with eight teams of enthusiastic contestants and now only two remain, but which pair has won the key to the treasure chest? Who will be walking away ten thousand pounds richer? Let's invite the contestants, Oscar, Jim, Bryony and Lewis to stand by their pedestals for the last time.'

They moved in silence, aware of the blinking lights and a large group of people watching from the darkness. A large board in front of them lit up. At one end of it were two cartoon cars waiting at a starting line. The first was yellow and black and the other brown. At the other end was a finish line and behind that, a treasure chest.

Potts began his speech. 'And here we have our special board. On it we have the little Citroëns our contestants drove for some of their tasks. Thanks to the magic of technology, we're going to be able to see who has won the *What Happens in…* prize.'

He stopped to wait for the autocue to move. 'It's stuck. Come on, guys. We need to wind this up. It's been a long few days and I have an important meeting after this.'

'Yeah, in the hotel bar,' whispered a voice in the shadows.

The autocue started again.

'And thanks to the magic of technology, we're going to be able to see who's won the *What Happens in…* prize. Jim and Oscar, you won the general knowledge quiz. Let's translate those points you won onto our board.

The yellow and black car moved in a jerky fashion towards the finish line. Oscar clapped his hands together again in excitement as he watched the car inch forward until it came to a halt almost a fifth of the way across the board.

'That's a good start, isn't it?'

Oscar tapped his knuckles together, face alight with expectation.

'Let's see how the other car did – 2CV Furby, start your engine!'

The other car lurched across the board and stopped a short way behind the first car.

'Bryony and Lewis, you won the *What Happened in France* section. Let's see where that takes your car.'

The brown car edged forwards, past the black and yellow, stopping ahead of it.

'Gosh this is close. I can feel the tension in the room. Jim and Oscar, you won the category quiz earlier today. Can your car overtake theirs?'

The yellow and black car eased away again. The crew encouraged the participants by making 'ooh' noises. Oscar joined in vociferously. The car puttered close to the halfway point and came to a stop.

'Let's add Bryony and Lewis's points. The little brown car shuddered onwards, failing to reach the lead car.

'Bryony and Lewis, what can I say? It was a shame you got your last question about *The Last Supper* wrong in that round. A correct answer might have brought you almost neck and neck with Jim and Oscar.' Potts waited for a reaction but Lewis stared unblinking at him while Bryony looked at her feet. He turned back to his autocue.

'Earlier in the week, the team completed other challenges that saw them physically challenged on inflatables, driving blindfold around a course with eggs in the boot of their car, up a hill climb circuit and the fastest time around this beautiful region on a treasure hunt. Once again, we've converted all their points into distance. Will either of the cars cross the line and reach the *What Happens in…* treasure chest? Let's see.'

The little cars set off at the same time. The furry car continued advancing and was soon right behind Oscar and Jim's car. The bumblebee car stopped. The brown car overtook it and also stopped. Oscar's hands flew to his mouth in surprise. Potts raised his eyebrows and opened his arms in mock surprise.

'This is a such a close contest now. Let's add in final points for collecting treasures during the treasure hunt challenge. Could the cars rev their engines for the last time?'

The cars crept forward almost neck and neck. Oscar began to bounce up and down muttering, 'Come on, come on.'

Both cars were within two spaces of the finish line when the furry car drew to a standstill and the yellow and black car hopped over the line. Oscar squealed and threw his arms around Jim, whose eyes were wet with tears.

'We did it!' cried Jim. 'We did it!'

Bryony's heart lifted at seeing their excited faces, and she cheered and applauded loudly along with the crew. Lewis stuck his thumb up. 'Congratulations!' he yelled.

Potts waited for the kerfuffle to calm and then adopting his by now familiar grin, he waved a large key at them and said, 'Oscar, Jim, please come forward and unlock the treasure chest. You have won the bounty inside. Hats off to you both and, of course, commiserations to the other team. It's been enormous fun having you on the show and I hope you've all enjoyed being part of *What Happens in…!*' he proclaimed.

Jim's vision was blurred with tears of joy, and with a trembling hand he unlocked the chest. The crew and contestants cheered. Together with Oscar, Jim pulled out handfuls of notes, waving them at the camera, grinning like crazy.

'Cut!'

Laura emerged from the darkness and embraced the winners. 'I'm genuinely happy for you. Congratulations. You were amazing. Jim, I don't think I've met anyone who knows as much about all sorts of things as you do. Of course, you can't keep hold of that cash. It's fake. We'll ensure the real winnings are deposited into your bank accounts. I'll get the details in a minute.'

'Okay!' barked the man with the grumpy voice. 'It's all looking good. We're happy with the shots. We're done. Time to clear out, everyone.'

'Thank goodness. I must get off,' Potts said, checking the time on his Patek Philippe watch. With that he removed his earpiece, barked instructions at a technician and marched off.

The group gathered in front of Laura for the final time.

'I'd like to thank you all once more. You've been superb contestants. You were really fantastic. I've really enjoyed working with you and thanks for making the show such a success.'

She spotted Roxanne in the doorway and nodded at her. 'I've got to get off but I'll leave you in Roxanne's capable hands. She's got the details for your return journey. The jet is on standby and you'll be driven directly to the airport from here. Remember nobody will see the final show and the grand finale until tomorrow night when both will be broadcast, so you must keep the results quiet. You can tell your loved ones but nobody else. It must remain secret until the show and the results show both air. We don't want the press to find out before then. Have a good trip back, everyone, and thank you for being such wonderful contestants. Hope to meet you all again on another show in the future.'

'Where's Potts?' Lewis asked the floor manager.

'Changing room. Getting his make-up removed.'

Lewis turned on his heel and stomped in the direction of the make-up room – Bryony not far behind.

'Lewis,' she called.

He ignored her and strode through the open doorway into the room where Potts was standing, hands on hips, an arrogant sneer on his face. Mattie was searching through the clothes rail. Bryony drew to a halt by the door and watched the proceedings, heart thudding.

'Ah, it's Lucas the Loser. Have you come for my autograph?' Potts asked.

Lewis's face reddened and he leant towards Potts, close enough to speak to him with vehemence without causing Mattie to turn around and stare.

'I've come to give you a message, from Maxwell.'

Potts maintained his smirk. 'What does that stupid tart have to say?'

'This,' Lewis replied and raised his fist in readiness.

Bryony anticipated the movement and punctuated the air with a wail. 'Lewis, no!'

He paused, fist in mid-air. 'He deserves it,' he growled.

'Don't do it. He's the sort to bring charges against you for assault. You could get into all sorts of trouble. He's not worth it.'

Mattie looked up briefly at the commotion then ducked out of the room into a side room, to leave them to it.

Potts scoffed. 'Bryony's right. I'll make sure your face is plastered across every newspaper in the UK. Can you imagine the outrage when my adoring fans hear that a Neanderthal like you hit me because of jealousy over a woman – a woman who lost interest in you because you were such a loser?'

'I'm no loser, Potts. You were living with her in my luxury penthouse flat – losers don't own property worth a few million. I'm better than you any day and not because I have money. I have standards and decent morals. I wouldn't break up with a woman because she thought she was pregnant – pregnant with my child. I wouldn't tell her I wanted nothing to do with any baby and tell her to get rid of it. I most certainly wouldn't then slander her and ensure she was fired from a job she was good at. I ought to expose you for the heartless bastard you really are. Still, maybe I won't need to. I was wearing my microphone when Maxwell called me and told me what happened between you and her. I'm sure someone here will have picked up on the conversation.'

Potts paled. He puffed out his cheeks in a show of bravado and squeaked, 'I'll make sure you and anyone who takes me on is sued for libel if anything untoward comes out.'

'One day, Potts, you'll get what's coming to you. Bryony is right. You're not worth it.' He poked Professor Potts in the sternum with his forefinger, causing the man to take a step back. 'I'll be waiting and watching to see you tumble from your lofty, sanctimonious position because you will fall one day. People like you always do.' With those words he turned and strode towards Bryony.

'Sorry you had to witness that. He really did have it coming.'

She shook her head in confusion. 'Why, Lewis? Why would you consider hitting him?' She backed away into the corridor.

'Maxwell—' he began.

'No, don't try to justify it. Maxwell is no longer your girlfriend. She was horrible to you and left you for that beastly man. It's good you want to stand up for her regardless of what she did to you, but are you doing it for the right reasons? Do you still have feelings for her, Lewis?'

His mouth opened and shut again. She took it to mean he still liked Maxwell in spite of everything she'd done to him and everything he'd said about her. Bryony's heart sunk at the look of confusion on his face. How could she have been so foolish as to think he'd prefer her to the stunning beauty who'd pouted and winked at him on screen and told him how proud she was of him? She'd been such an idiot to think he'd choose her over Maxwell. It was a no contest. Maxwell was now a free agent and wanted her man back. Bryony couldn't compete with her. She bit back bitter tears. 'You shouldn't feel the need to rise up like some shining knight when she beckons you – unless she means more to you than I believed she did. I thought after what happened between us, we had the beginnings of something special. Apparently, I was wrong.' She rushed down the corridor towards the restaurant.

'Bryony, hold up,' he called. 'I need to...'

Roxanne approached from the opposite direction, slowing Bryony to a halt. She called out, 'Lewis, there you are. I've managed to change your flight home as requested. You'll be able to catch the three o'clock Ryanair flight to London. I've booked you on it.'

Bryony shot a look at him. 'London. To see Maxwell?'

Lewis opened his mouth to speak but she walked off once more. She couldn't listen to any excuses. He'd made his decision. Lewis attempted to follow her but Roxanne was blocking his path as she stood with paper and clip-board, waiting for his signature for an airline e-ticket. He sighed. Bryony would have to wait.

Chapter Forty

Saturday, 29 July – Afternoon

Bryony headed directly to the boot room where they'd left their luggage and dragged her bag outside, where she sat down on the steps of the château wishing she could spirit herself home. She'd made an idiot of herself. She'd allowed her guard to drop. How could Lewis have broken through her defences? She thought they were two of a kind – both nurturing secrets and hurt. He'd convinced her of his affection. He'd caressed her unlike any other man and had made love to her in a way that surely had been more than purely sexual. Then less than twenty-four hours later, he had dropped her unceremoniously to race back to his ex-girlfriend. She concluded theirs had been no more than a trifling holiday romance, a distraction, and a passion born from being together in beautiful France. She shouldn't have allowed it to happen. Life had been so much better when they were just friends.

She chewed the inside of her cheek, admiring the garden laid out in front of her – it was like taking a step back in time. It was the perfect place for sanctuary and peace. She wanted to hide here and cry – cry for a very long time. Her adventure, so full of promise and excitement, had terminated abruptly and unhappily. The emptiness she now felt had nothing to do with the competition ending or Jim and Oscar walking away with the prize. She'd lost more than that. A rustling alerted her to the arrival of someone and a wet tongue licking her leg made her look up. Biggie Smalls snuffled beside her then sat on her feet, gazing at her with a furrowed brow. Oscar, who had followed the animal, dropped down beside her with a contented sigh.

'It's beautiful here,' he observed. 'I'd love a garden like this and a château, of course.' He glanced over at Bryony. 'You look like someone who's lost a fortune. I hope you're not depressed about losing the game. I would hate that.'

'Far from it. I couldn't be happier for you and Jim. You were right and I was wrong. Jim needed this more than any of us. The look on his face when you won was priceless. I just fancied some "wind down time". It's been hectic the last week and I had to collect my thoughts before we return home. It's come to an end so abruptly and we'll all be going on our separate paths again.'

'I'll miss you. It seems sort of stale now the show's over. I've said my goodbyes to the crew and judging by the clearing up going on in there, it'll soon be as if none of this ever happened. Jim's on his way out too. He's got his phone back and is probably having a quick chat to Cathy. There ought to be a party or some other way to celebrate having been part of this experience. It shouldn't end so flatly. I've got all your numbers though, so I'll ring you and maybe we could all meet up in Birmingham for a post-show celebration.'

'I'd really like that. Thank you.'

Jim emerged. 'The minibus is on its way,' he said. 'Only the three of us are going home in the jet. Lewis is returning on an ordinary plane. He'll miss out. A taxi came for him a couple of minutes ago and he left via the back entrance to catch his flight to London. It's manic in there now. They're running about gathering up cables and whatnot. It's like we were never there. That is apart from that nice, fat cheque that'll go into the bank eh, Oscar?' He gave a hearty chuckle.

Bryony gave Jim a smile in spite of the hurt that burned in her chest. Lewis had left without so much as a goodbye. How could he, after all they'd been through? She seemed to be making a habit of losing people who meant something to her. Suddenly she wanted nothing more than to get home and be with Melinda. Melinda would laugh and joke and shake her out of her mood. Thank goodness she had Melinda.

Chapter Forty One

Saturday, 29 July – Late Evening

Freddie, with his large eyes shining, offered a cheeky smile exactly like his father's, opened the door to her and shouted, 'Briny! Come and see my animal park.' He clasped her hand and tugged at it, leading her to the sitting room where Sean sat cross-legged on the carpet surrounded by hundreds of Lego bricks. He jumped to his feet and yelled for Melinda before wrapping warm arms around her. Melinda peered around the kitchen door and yelped.

'What are you doing here? We were watching you on telly only an hour ago. The final show isn't until tomorrow evening. You should be in France. Nothing serious has happened, has it?'

Bryony shook her head. 'We've finished filming. It's a recording tomorrow.'

Melinda surged forward and grabbed Bryony by both hands leading her to the settee.

'Come on. Tell us, did you win?'

Bryony adopted the cheery look she'd practised on her way over. 'No. We lost.'

'Oh, what a shame! You were absolutely brilliant, wasn't she, Sean?'

He nodded. 'We were sure you'd ace it. Where's Lewis? I suppose he's unpacking or unconscious. Must be worn out after all those challenges. You really were fantastic. My goodness, we couldn't stop laughing at that game on the inflatables. I thought he was going to strangle that wretched inflatable rodeo bull. Melinda's recorded all the shows for you so you can watch them.'

Bryony gave a restrained grunt and was grateful when Freddie spoke.

'Look, Briny. This is my animal park. The people are going on the train around the park.' He chugged the train from the house to a squared-out area containing the bear. 'Daddy and me made *enclosures*,' he pronounced the new word with care, 'for all the animals, and a special house for the snakes so they don't get out.' He pointed towards a small red-brick house. 'And this is my dinosaur.' He picked up a multicoloured stack of bricks and roared.

Bryony smiled at the boy and marvelled at the power of a child's imagination. To an adult eye it was nothing more than a scattering of green bricks and houses but to Freddie it was a magical park where people could visit dinosaurs and snakes in a blue train.

Sean and Melinda exchanged glances. He leant across and ruffled his son's hair. 'Come on, champ. Time for bed. It's very late. How about I read you a bedtime story while Bryony and Mum have a girlie chat?'

His son chuckled – a musical sound that filled the room. 'They're not girls,' Freddie laughed.

'Oh, they are. Trust me, son. They are. Come on.'

'Night, Briny. Night, Mummy.' He hugged both in turn. Melinda planted a kiss on his forehead. 'Sleep well, love you.'

'Love you too,' He raced away. Sean winked at Bryony.

'For what it's worth, you were spectacularly good. I'll let Melinda tell you what's been happening while you've been away. It's all pretty mind-blowing,' he added.

Once he'd left the room, Melinda shifted closer to her friend.

'It must have been a close contest. You should have won. The other contestants seemed nice though.'

'They were. We got on really well.'

She studied her friend's face and grinned. Words tumbled excitedly. 'Come on, girlfriend, what was it *really* like? You looked fantastic all the time, by the way. I thought I'd just tell you that first. Apart from when you were screaming at Lewis to slow down in the furry car. Jeez, that was hilarious! You wait until you see it. I recorded everything although the best bits are on YouTube. Hang on. We need celebratory wine.' She jumped to her feet and beetled off into the kitchen returning with two generous glasses. She passed one to Bryony and clinked hers against it. 'Right, now you must tell me all about what really happened in *la belle* France. Oh first, have you checked your emails and blog yet?'

'Not yet, I came straight here.'

'Wait until you see what's been happening. There've been YouTube clips and tweets about the show and the contestants. It's mental. There have even been articles in the national newspapers about you all and you got an extra mention because of looking for Hannah. I'm surprised you haven't been mobbed on your way here. It seems everyone online is looking for Hannah. Hashtag #SearchforHannah even trended on Twitter after Oscar mentioned it during his interview. You need to write a post for the blog cos people will probably go and look at it once the final results are announced tomorrow. It might be your last chance to get so many people interested now the show is almost over.' She cocked her head. 'I know. I'm talking too fast and giving you no time to digest it all. I'll shut up.'

'No. It's just – amazing,' said Bryony, tears springing to her eyes. 'I should go home and see if Hannah has tried to contact me.'

'You should but you look done in and you can't leave here until you've told me all about it. Come on, dish the goss.'

Half an hour later, Melinda was looking as confused and glum as her friend actually felt. 'So, let me get this straight: you flew in a private jet, made new friends, stayed in a remarkable château, drove about the French country-side having a good giggle, lost the quiz to two people you really liked and had dinner with the delicious, I-wouldn't-kick-him-out-of-bed Professor Potts. I understand full well I'm an ex-policewoman who possesses extraordinary skills when it comes to detective work but even an idiot can see you are unhappy about something. You don't fool me with your phoney enthusiasm,' she remarked, leaning back in her chair to better study her friend's reaction.

Bryony gave a deep sigh. 'I knew I wouldn't be able to hide anything from you. You're like one of those sniffer dogs.'

Melinda pulled a face. 'That'll be my large nose that can snuffle out trouble.'

'Hardly. It's not large at all. You have great instinct.' Bryony shoulders slumped. 'Lewis has returned to his girlfriend. He's gone back to London to make up and start again.'

'Girlfriend? I thought he lived with Maxwell. Isn't that a man's name?'

'It turns out Maxwell can be a girl's name too. She was the person who cheered him with a personal message like you did for me.'

'That was Maxwell!' Melinda's mouth dropped wide open for a second. 'Oh fuck! I wondered who she was. Sean and I thought she was some relative or just a good friend. Shit, she's a real hottie.'

'That was *his* Maxwell, a woman that meant so much to him that even after she dumped him, wrecked his life and broke his heart, he took her back.'

Melinda's eyes narrowed. 'You've slept with him, haven't you? Years of experience and I can spot the things that are left unsaid. Besides, you have that injured look in your eyes.'

'I did sleep with him. It was wonderful and I thought I'd found my prince at last but I'm still plain, old, scarfaced, wonky-hipped Bryony, not a princess. Nor am I a glamorous television researcher who has the power to twist any man around my finger. Maxwell has convinced him with only one email and a telephone call to race back into her arms. He flew off to London immediately after the recording rather than catch the jet back with the rest of us.'

'How did she contact him? I thought you were all banned from using phones and if anyone wanted to contact you we had to use an emergency number.'

'He must have given her the number. He accessed his emails one evening and I suppose he replied to the one

Maxwell sent. She phoned immediately before the final recording. Her timing couldn't have been worse. It took the edge off the whole experience and, well, you know.'

Melinda reached out her hand and squeezed Bryony's. 'That sucks but look at it this way: you had a great time together and I've no doubt you had plenty of laughs too. From what you've told me it was a once-in-a-lifetime event. You got to race about Brittany in a proper French car, stay in a château of all places, be on television and you met the wonderful Professor David Potts.'

'I'm about to pop that particular bubble too. Firstly, the professor's not as good-looking as you might think – layers of make-up help make him look healthy and handsome. Secondly, he's a bit smarmy and even rude at times. And thirdly, he isn't one bit funny. And from what I gathered, he's definitely not the sort of person you'd want to get involved with.'

'No! That can't be. You've shattered my illusions.'

'Good thing you hadn't made any plans to abandon Sean and run off with Professor Potts then.'

'I'll go unpack my bag immediately,' Melinda said, chuckling. 'You want another glass of wine?'

'Thanks, but no thanks. I'd better get off. I came here directly from being dropped off at home. I needed to get it all off my chest.'

'I'm glad you did. For what it's worth, I wouldn't worry about Lewis. You've got friends, a great job and family. You're better off without him. It's his loss and I hope Maxwell pisses him about again. Nobody gets to hurt my friend like that. I feel totally responsible for this. I introduced you to him and encouraged you to go on the show with him.'

'You didn't make me sleep with him.'

'No, but it's still a shame. Bloody Lewis! Wait until I see him again. He doesn't get to mess with my bestie's feelings like that. Look, forget about him for now. I know that's easier said than done but you ought to see if anyone has contacted you about Hannah. That's far more important.' She paused to slug her wine then spoke again.

'I'm going to say this, because you're my friend and I think you need to hear it. I don't want to upset you but if nothing comes of this, you're going to have to accept you probably won't find her. I don't mean to be cruel but I'm starting to worry you're becoming consumed with this quest to find Hannah for your father's sake. Don't let it take over. How about you come over one night in the week? Sean's going to be away again and Freddie goes to bed at seven on a weekday. We can watch a film, eat crap, get drunk and gossip about things like we did in the old days when we shared the flat.'

Bryony decided that an evening together might be the medicine she needed to help get over Lewis. 'Thanks. I'd love to come over. Now I'd better go. I need to lick my wounds and unpack my bag, and I should phone Mum to let her know how I got on.'

'She's been watching the show. I spoke to her yesterday. She's so proud of you, Bryony. It doesn't matter about winning or losing. We all know why you did this and you couldn't have asked for a better platform for telling everyone about Hannah. I'd wear sunglasses when you go to the shops tomorrow. People will be clammering for your autograph.' She beamed again. 'Your face when Lewis was thrown from the inflatable bull. It was a picture. You'll have to watch the show.'

'Maybe when I feel up to it.'

'Come and watch the last episode with us tomorrow.'

'Yeah, maybe I'll do that.' Her words felt hollow. She wasn't sure she could watch her and Lewis together on screen.

Melinda embraced her friend. 'Get some sleep and replenish your energy levels and forget all about Lewis. Treat it as a one-off fun affair. There are plenty more fish in the sea.'

'Always the voice of reason,' Bryony replied with a tired smile.

Chapter Forty Two

Sunday, 30 July – Afternoon

Sat in front of her laptop, Bryony pulled up her blog on the screen. Back in her apartment with familiar surroundings and after a long night's sleep, the trip to France seemed to have been no more than a poignant dream.

Although she had a huge number of emails, none were from Hannah or anyone who knew her sister. Most were congratulatory ones from friends and work colleagues and one from her friend, Tim, who invited her to bring Lewis along to the holiday cottage he was renting. Melinda had been right about the online interest in her search for her sister. Typing Hannah's name into the search engine, she found hundreds of tweets and video clips. There were stills of Bryony, taken from the television programme along with captions, stating she was searching for Hannah and asking if anyone had seen her. She was impressed by the number of people involved but no one had located her sister. It had been a fruitless exercise.

Lewis's idea about using the power of social media was a decent one. She'd have liked his help to get it right – it was his field of expertise after all – but given he was no longer around, she'd have to tackle it alone. It wasn't beyond her if she set her mind to it. Maybe now she'd been on television people would follow her online and share the news. She'd ask Oscar to tweet to Biggie Small's followers. The more she considered the idea, the more she felt she could manage it without Lewis. She had, after all, created a blog without too much assistance other than from Melinda.

She'd been occupied all day, setting up Twitter and Instagram accounts and redoing the page on Facebook for Hannah, loading pictures of her and her sister and a contact email address. Finally, she turned her attention to her blog and put together a positive post that told of Oscar, Jim and Lewis while avoiding the truth of her relationship with Lewis and the heartache that had ensued.

Once she had posted her tale of *What Happens in…*, she read over the introduction to her blog:

> *My sister Hannah left home at the age of sixteen never to be seen again. She left a goodbye note and took a small bag of clothes with her so I can only assume she wanted to leave us.*
>
> *She left shattered lives, broken hearts and sadness in the wake of her departure. Tears, too many, have been shed time and time again. We tried to find her but she remained and still remains hidden, unable or unwilling to return to us.*
>
> *I carry the burden of guilt with me because I know I was to blame for Hannah leaving. Even now I cannot forgive myself for causing her so much misery that she felt her only option was to run away.*
>
> *Hannah, if you read this, please find it in your heart to contact me using the address on this blog.*

We all miss you so much. More than you can ever
know. There isn't a birthday or occasion that passes
without tears as you are not with us. Dad is most
unwell and calls out for you daily. To see him and
our mother suffer all over again is tearing me apart.
Please, Hannah, I beg you. Please come home.
   Your loving sister,
   Bryony

A quiet voice that sounded exactly like her mother's, whispered ominously that she was merely chasing shadows. Bryony reprimanded it. She either needed to be more proactive in this hunt for Hannah or, as Melinda had suggested, she ought to finally let go of the past.

The final show was due to be broadcast in less than an hour. She picked up a book and settled down with it. There was no way she was going to turn on the television. Watching herself and Lewis on screen together would be too much for her to bear.

Chapter Forty Three

Monday, 31 July – Morning

'So, can you make 5 p.m.?' The voice was assured.

'Yes. 5 p.m. I'll be there.'

'That's terrific. Look forward to meeting you.'

Bryony sat up in bed. It was quarter past eight and she hadn't been in the mood to get up and hang about the house alone. The day was bright but she'd felt down-hearted. Post-competition blues? Or more likely she was suffering from post-Lewis blues. The call from the television studio had chased all that away. ITV wanted her to appear on an aftershow with her fellow teammates to discuss what really happened behind the scenes in France.

They'd be able to chat in depth about their reasons for being on the show and what they'd got from it. There was huge public interest following the last episode shown the evening before, and the production company had decided to capitalise on the sensation of *What Happens in...* and arrange for the four finalists to be interviewed together. It would be one last chance to talk about her long-lost sister and she was going to grab it.

The only fly in the ointment was Lewis. The studio had rung and left a message but not heard back from him. They might have to do the interview without him, but Bryony knew from what she'd read online that many people would tune in just to see him. He, like the others in the teams, had won over thousands of people who wanted to know everything about him.

She jumped from her bed, threw on a loose top and jeans, scrubbed her teeth and pulled back her hair. Catching sight of her reflection, she wondered if Hannah looked at all like her. Certainly as children they had little in common other than the same colour hair, delicate nose and calm, grey eyes. She wondered idly if Hannah's hair was still golden-blonde or if, like her own, it had darkened over the years.

–

Melinda opened the door before she rang the bell. Bryony grabbed her by the hand and hustled her into the kitchen.

'You'll never guess what's happened.'

'They've signed you up to be the face of a famous cosmetics company? You're going to host the Royal Variety Performance this year? Ed Sheeran has written a song about you entitled *Brainy Bryony, a Girl in France*? Am I close yet?' She dropped onto a kitchen stool.

'Funny! I've been invited to Birmingham for an after-show this evening. All the finalists are going to get the chance to chat about the show – the highs, the lows, and I'll be able to speak about Hannah again. I'm going to take photographs along and all my new social media links.'

'That's incredible. Good for you. I told you there'd been a crazed interest in the show. Is Lewis going?'

'I don't know. They hadn't managed to get hold of him when I spoke to the producer.'

'Really? He's back. His car's outside his house. Why don't you nip round, find out, see how he got on with Maxwell and make up with him?'

'There's little point in being friends if he's going to leave the area and move back in with Maxwell.'

'At least there'd be no bad feelings between you. If he goes on the show this evening, you need to be able to spark off each other like you did during the challenges. That's what the public want to see. You'll lose sympathy if you freeze him out. You need them on your side.'

'Sorry, I can't be false. I'll be civil but I'd rather put what happened between us behind me. He made his choice. I'd better ring Mum and tell her. I had planned to visit her and Dad later. I'll have to put it off now.'

She made to leave. Melinda scooted off her chair and accompanied her friend to the door. 'I'll be watching. Is it live?'

'Going out at 6 p.m. We have to be there at an hour before.'

'I'll spread the word and… break a leg!'

They hugged and then Bryony strolled back towards her car parked on the road near the house. As she did so, she spotted a figure racing from the opposite direction. She quickened her pace, hoping to reach the car before he caught up with her but Lewis sprinted quickly and drawing to a halt in front of her, seized her arm.

'Bryony, I have to talk to you. Don't go. It's important.'

She let out a sigh. 'Lewis, look, it's okay. I get it. What we had was a holiday fling and Maxwell has come back into your life and—'

'For goodness sake! Maxwell is *not* in my life. You are. You most definitely are.'

Bryony's brain could not fully process the meaning of his words but a burst of adrenaline coursed through her veins. She took a sharp intake of air and her hands began to shake.

'Maxwell was never going to worm her way back into my affections. Not after you. You and me, well, we're *close*.' He spoke the last word in such a way that Bryony felt a surge of elation course through her body.

'Are we?'

'Of course, we are,' he replied, pulling her towards him in a tight embrace and kissing her full on the lips. Reluctantly he released her.

'Maxwell…' she began.

'Maxwell is sulking and throwing tantrums and behaving like a spoilt child but she'll survive.'

'You didn't go back to her?'

'Why would I do that now I've found you?' he asked, caressing her cheek with his fingers. 'Maxwell tracked me down through her contacts. She discovered I was on the game show with Potts and after doing that piece to camera at the live event, she wheedled the emergency number out of one of the film crew. She knows me too well. She worked out that no matter what had happened between us, I'd stand up for her, especially against Potts. She was incredibly upset with him. The bastard not only split up with her because he thought she might be expecting a child – it was a false alarm – but he also put out the word that she was clingy, self-centred and destructive, and thanks to him she was dropped from a new show she was working on.' He held Bryony's gaze. 'She may have her faults but she didn't deserve to be treated so badly. That callous pig told her there was no way he was having children and she could do what she liked but he'd have no part of it. I'm afraid I went off the deep end. I'm sorry for almost thumping Potts. If you hadn't been there I don't know how much damage I'd have inflicted on that shit. I planned on giving him a broken nose at the very least. You must think I'm a complete thug.' He shrugged an apology. She shook her head at him.

'After the telephone call, I had to see her in person. Maxwell was in a terrible state, tearful, talking seriously about taking her own life. She came out with all that "I should never have been so stupid to let you go" nonsense. I'd have explained if I'd had a chance but you walked off and I couldn't find you anywhere, then Roxanne suddenly hustled me into a taxi which was at the back door before I got a chance to speak to you. It all happened so quickly. I went to London to set the record straight and tell Maxwell, face to face, that I was seeing somebody I really, really liked. She isn't one to give in easily so it was best she could understand how much I've changed and see how happy I've become. With Maxwell, seeing is believing. We talked for an age. We worked things out. She understands she and I will never get back together and once the flat sells she'll move into another one with a friend – a girlfriend. I returned really late last night. I rang your mobile a while ago but there was no reply, then I spotted your car. I've been hanging about, twitching the front curtains waiting for you to emerge. I can't begin to tell you what you mean to me, Bryony, but I hope you'll let me show you. In a short space of time you have literally spun me around 360 degrees and I don't want to be with anyone other than you. It's up to you now. You need to decide how you feel. Take your time. I'm not going anywhere – well, not without you. But I want one thing before you make a decision.'

'What's that?' she asked tentatively.

'This,' he murmured, wrapping his arms around her body gently, drawing her face towards his own and then pressing his lips against hers with a passion and urgency that made her heart soar.

—

Lewis rapped on Bryony's bathroom door and called, 'Taxi will be here at three o'clock which give us loads of time to reach the television studio before five. Oscar's on the phone. He wants to know if we'd like to join him for dinner at a Japanese restaurant on Broad Street after we've done the show. He raves about the place. It's very trendy. Fancy going?'

Bryony, naked in front of the bathroom mirror, was towel-drying her hair. 'Great. Let's do it.'

'Bryony says yes, mate. See you later. Look forward to it.'

Bryony emerged from the bathroom, her tousled locks framing her face and cascading over her shoulders.

Lewis crossed his arms and whistled. 'You going to do the chat show like that?' he asked.

Bryony put her hands on her hips. 'It's a new look I'm perfecting. I'm calling it the Lady Godiva look.'

'I'm calling it the "duvet" look.'

'Why?'

'Because it makes me want to drag you back to bed and smother you with my lips,' he answered, pouncing in her direction.

She shrieked playfully and attempted to scurry away but found herself enveloped in his arms. She breathed in his scent and willingly tilted her head towards his.

'I love all this,' he said as they lay together on the rumpled sheets. 'A beautiful day, and a beautiful woman by my side. I consider myself very fortunate. Oscar and Jim might have won the money on *What Happens in…* but I got the first prize.' He kissed her again.

Chapter Forty Four

Monday, 31 July – Evening

Glowing lanterns hung from the wooden pagoda bar in the sushi restaurant while the clean angles of the tables were softened with little touches from Japanese fans, duck-egg-blue crockery, bamboo blinds and a giant print of a Japanese fir forest. There were kitsch touches too – a half-hidden, life-size Kendo warrior among other quirks – that all added to the charm of the thirty-seat restaurant.

Bryony and Lewis kicked off their shoes to take a seat at one of the low-lying zataku tables and were immediately joined by an exuberant Oscar.

He shrugged off a light jumper draped over his shoulders and appraised them both, noting the fact they were holding hands. 'Well, don't you look the perfect couple? I so hoped you'd get together properly. It was obvious you were mad about each other while we were in France. All that sexual chemistry bubbling every time you were together. Even Jim noticed it and asked if you were "courting". Pity he couldn't join us after the interview.'

A small figure in a bright yellow jumper and matching beret edged closer to Oscar and plopped down next to his feet.

'Biggie, you look like a small sunflower,' said Lewis.

Oscar laughed. 'The outfit's from a fan. Biggie has gained even more notoriety since his appearances in France. His fans have sent loads of outfits and as for messages from female dogs! It's bonkers. I can't keep up with all the interest in him. He'll be demanding his own television show next. I thought being on *What Happens in…* would raise my profile not his.' He laughed good-naturedly.

'He was well-behaved during the chat show,' said Bryony.

'That was because he was completely worn out. I took him to the park earlier and he chased after ducks for an hour until he exhausted himself.' He seized the menu, glanced at it and said, 'I recommend everything on the menu but I especially like the miso soup as a starter because it isn't too filling followed by a mixed sashimi. That was fun, wasn't it?' He was referring to the chat show. It had been an intense hour of questions from a genial host and a live audience. Bryony had been asked over and over about Hannah and felt she'd finally done as much as she could. It was now up to the universe. If Hannah was out there she must have heard about Bryony by now.

'It was really good. Lovely to see Jim looking so happy,' said Bryony.

'It really was. Cathy's already chosen a top hotel for them to stay at by the sea. They're taking the grandchildren too. Jim's over the moon about it all.'

The chef interrupted them to serve beer and lead them in a clink and toast in Japanese before declaring, 'Your soup is arriving,' as a little train snaked around the bar counter, trucking three bowls of miso behind it. Bryony almost wanted to applaud its entrance.

'It was huge fun but I suppose it's back to normality again now, isn't it? Shame, I've really enjoyed all the attention,' said Oscar.

'You still get that when you perform.'

'Oh sure, it's not quite the same though. That game show was intense. I couldn't believe how popular it was. Even Mom and Pop watched the YouTube clips. Some of them were hilarious. My favourite one is when Donald and I collided on the bouncy slide. It wasn't funny at the time but oh my, watching it, it was a different ballgame. We resembled a weird, giant octopus – a mishmash of arms and legs and I had no idea I could shriek quite so loudly.'

'I've not watched any of the episodes,' said Bryony.

'You haven't? You must. They're gold dust. Honest to goodness. I had no idea we were all so comical.'

'It'd give us something to do later,' said Lewis, lifting one eyebrow in her direction.

Oscar missed the flirtatious look and continued talking. 'Oh, I put that photo I took of you and Biggie up on my Instagram page. It's such a divine picture. He looks like he's trying so hard to comfort you in it. I mentioned it was of the lovely Bryony who is searching for her sister, of course. It's had literally thousands of likes. I know you're still looking but haven't you had any news at all about her? Surely somebody out there must have seen her or know of her.'

The chef collected the empty bowls and returned with a sashimi starter. They picked up chopsticks and tucked into the food.

'No. I've had hundreds and hundreds of goodwill messages and people who've also got stories of missing family members or loved ones but nothing from her or anyone who knows her. I'd pinned my hopes on her seeing the game show. Now, I'm hoping she was watching the chat show we did earlier. There's so much about it in the press and online and everywhere. She can't possibly have missed it.'

'That's true. *What Happens in…* is the hottest show on television and millions of people know about you and Hannah. Maybe she doesn't want to be found,' said Oscar with a sad smile.

'I'm beginning to think that too. I'll keep trying. I've updated my blog *Searching for Hannah.*'

He popped some food in his mouth, chewed and after swallowing said, 'I love the name Hannah. My Nan on my Mom's side is a Hannah too. I once bought her a really neat key ring for Christmas. It was one of those that tell you about the origins of the name. Apparently Hannah means favour or grace which suited Nanna perfectly. And all Hannahs are unique, creative individuals who tend to resent authority, and are sometimes stubborn, proud and impatient. Nanna was definitely a lady who wouldn't listen to anyone, especially Grandpops and he was a law enforcement officer. Does that description fit your sister too?'

'Some of it,' said Bryony. 'She was definitely stubborn and impatient and certainly unique.'

Oscar smiled. 'I really hope you find her. I'll keep my fingers firmly crossed for you.'

The evening passed pleasantly with Oscar telling them stories about the other ballet dancers and ballerinas he'd met and about Lucinda, who was joining him soon. They delighted in a main course of teriyaki roll of salmon in a coil of rice, topped with slender slices of avocado, a sprinkling of crispy onion and Japanese mayonnaise before declaring they could eat no more and settling down with some tea.

Bryony felt like she'd known Oscar all her life. He was enchanting and entertaining in equal measures. He had them in fits of laughter about his dog's exploits during a photo shoot and made Bryony splutter tea at some of his impressions of overzealous performers.

The bill paid, they decided to call it a night. Oscar shrugged his sweater over his head and smoothed it over his lithe frame. A taxi pulled up outside and the owner signalled to Oscar.

'Oh, that's for me. It's been wonderful to see you both. We must do this again. Maybe in London next time if you like and I'll bring Lucinda along. She's dying to meet you.' He kissed Bryony on both cheeks and gave Lewis a hug.

'Okay. Bye-bye, lovebirds. See you soon,' he chirped as he climbed into the taxi, Biggie in his arms.

Once the taxi pulled away, Lewis dropped a kiss on her head. 'Don't be too disappointed if nothing comes of the chat show. You really gave it your best shot. Oscar could be right. Perhaps Hannah doesn't want to be found.' He put an arm around her and pulled her into his body.

She sighed deeply, relishing the comforting gesture. This part of her life had turned a corner. She'd found somebody she could trust and love. If only Hannah could be found, then life would be perfect.

Chapter Forty Five

Thursday, 3 August – Evening

With a furrowed brow, Bryony typed the post to be scheduled on *Searching for Hannah* for the following day – Hannah's birthday. The blog was still getting in excess of 500 hits a day. The Facebook page had been shared hundreds of times and she was now being followed by thousands of people on Twitter and Instagram but there was still no news of Hannah.

Bryony felt she could do little more. The hopes she harboured were fading, and having spoken to her mother again, she was now anxious because her dad seemed to be fading fast. Time really was running out.

The post was ready for the blog. She uploaded it along with a photograph of them all as a family and one of Hannah blowing out the candles on her sixteenth birthday cake. She wore a flat expression and looked embarrassed by the camera. Bryony thought she looked underwhelmed by it all and wondered if Hannah had felt happy that day.

> *I once dreamt you were aboard a sumptuous yacht sailing in some exotic location; aquamarine seas sparkled beneath you as you sat on the edge of the boat, your golden hair flowing freely behind*

you, a smile on your lips. You lifted a crystal flute of champagne to the wind and sipped its gilded contents. The dream was so realistic I believed I could reach out, touch you and talk to you. When I awoke, I was overcome with the sense that my dream had been a sign and that you were alive and deliriously happy.

Today, I shall imagine you are on that yacht and I shall raise my glass to you.

Happy birthday to my beautiful sister. I wish we could celebrate with you.

Tomorrow she'll visit her parents. She always goes to see them on this date. Each year they hold a tea party. It is a mockery, celebrating the birthday of someone who is no longer part of their lives, but it has become their ritual and she won't let them down, especially with her father being so ill. Her mother will be tearful and her father will call her Hannah as he has been doing ever since the stroke. There will be no true celebrations.

–

She slipped in between the sheets and snuggled against Lewis. Since his revelation about wanting to be with her, they had not been apart one night. Lewis said he preferred her flat to the rented house and they were considering what their next move should be.

She and Lewis were a good fit. Even though they had only been together a short while, she knew this relationship was going to have a happy ending. It only needed time.

336

Lewis turned towards her. 'Hello. What have you been doing? I've been here ages waiting for you.'

'Writing a post for the blog. It's Hannah's birthday tomorrow.'

Lewis stretched himself awake. 'I wonder if she'll read it.'

'I'm not so sure anymore.'

He kissed her on the nose. 'That isn't like you. Think positive. Anything's possible if you believe in it.'

'Is that a line from a film?'

'Not sure. It sounds as if it might be.' He chuckled.

She wriggled to get comfortable and Lewis threw his arm around her. She smiled to herself. Her life was changing quickly for the better. If only she could get hold of Hannah… That would be the icing on the birthday cake.

Chapter Forty Six

Friday, 4 August – Morning

'Are you seeing Melinda today after you've been to visit your parents?'

'No. I'll come back here and you can cheer me up instead. Melinda's out all day shopping with her mum.'

Lewis was propped up in bed on one elbow. 'Pity you have to go.' He grinned at her wickedly.

'You have a meeting with the accountants so forget it, Romeo. I'll put the coffee on while you get showered and we'll pick up where we left off later,' she murmured, pressing her lips against his neck.

'You're on.'

Bryony strolled down the corridor of her flat. She could hear Lewis humming as he got ready. She smiled to herself. Maxwell was already a distant memory. Bryony had mended that particular hurt. She stooped to pick up a postcard and a large envelope on the doormat. The postcard was of a beach scene from her work colleague, Tim. On it he said the offer was still open. Bryony smiled. She'd ask Lewis if he fancied a few days on the coast and maybe surprise Tim and Suzanne. The large envelope was a puzzle. It had come from Paris but there was no sender address on it. She ripped it open and pulled out a maroon, leather-bound diary. She opened it, read the first few lines and gasped. Flicking through the pages she lighted on a lengthier entry and read...

Dear Diary,

Today was one of those days that you know is going to change everything. After school I headed off to town as usual. Mum was collecting Bryony from school so I said I was going to the library but instead I nicked some sweets from Woolworths and managed to blag I was eighteen and bought a pack of Player's Number 10. Everyone seems to think butter wouldn't melt in my mouth. Stealing stuff is a real buzz. Part of me wants to get caught and see the look on my parents' faces when they find out – it would be such a shock to learn the headmaster's daughter is a common thief.

I ended up by the Mecca Bingo Hall and lit up. It's one of the few places I can go and not get spotted by someone who knows me.

God how I hate being goody-goody Hannah! Some days I want to scream at all the teachers and the neighbours and all the kids at my school. 'I'm not the perfect schoolgirl you all think I am. I'm normal like you. I want to have friends like you do and do stupid stuff like you do.' One day my mask will slip and they'll see the real me.

Today I was leaning against the wall thinking about what a shit life I have when a boy came up to me. He was so handsome it was untrue. He had dark black hair and brown eyes with the longest eyelashes I've ever seen. He was dressed fashionably in Levi jeans and a turtleneck jumper over which he wore a bigger jumper. He had a cigarette between his lips and asked if I had a light. I fumbled about in my jacket pocket and drew out my disposable lighter. He lit his cigarette and instead of clearing off, joined me leaning against the wall. He spoke after a few puffs.

I didn't know what to say to him so I nodded. I felt all hot and yet excited. He seemed interested in me. He's so different to Rob who's just a friend but wants to be more than that. This guy looked and acted grown up, not like Rob who has spots and wears sweatshirts with cartoon characters on them.

He gazed into my eyes at one point and I thought my knees were going to give out. I didn't want him to leave.

He told me he'd spied me in the local supermarket trying to steal some sweets. My heart started hammering and I wondered if he was a security guard. I got ready to protest but he smiled, a lazy, handsome smile, and said something like, 'If you're going to nick stuff, make it expensive and worthwhile.' Then he winked at me and walked away.

I don't know if I'll see him again but I hope so. I'll go to the same place tomorrow in case he passes by. I'm tingling with excitement. I met someone who knows who I really am and seemed to like me for it. I don't want to be the Hannah everyone expects me to be and maybe I don't have to be. I can't explain what's happened but this experience

has triggered a switch in my mind. I don't have
to stay and be this person if I don't want to. I
can be who I want to be and be liked for it. I feel
different. I feel lighter knowing this. It's like being
free at last.

Bryony turned the pages of the diary quickly, the coffee forgotten. There were more entries. With her ability to speed read, she raced through each neatly handwritten page, searching for the answers that were hidden in them.

Dear Diary,

I feel truly horrible about what's happened. I'm so angry with my mum. I didn't want to take Bryony to the park but she insisted. She shouldn't have made me take her. If she hadn't, Bryony would be okay. I'm even angrier with myself. I should have looked out for my baby sister. She's only six and I'm sixteen.

My mind was on other things that morning. I just wanted to scream for everyone to leave me alone. Everything's so messed up in my head. I've got exams coming up and Dad keeps going on and on about me getting into university. I haven't even taken these exams yet, let alone A-levels. I needed space but instead I had to take Bryony to the park and look what's happened. Bryony's seriously injured. She may even die. Oh God! Please don't let her die.

I can't think about anything other than leaving now. I don't care where I go. I must get away from here and go somewhere where there are no expectations to be the golden girl, and no parents nagging me to work harder; no one to stop me doing normal teenager stuff; no one to judge me and no one to hate me for what's happened to Bryony.

Everything went wrong when Rob turned up unexpectedly outside our house. I've been avoiding him for three weeks ever since I told him I didn't want to be more than friends with him.

He must have been hanging around near the house because he rushed up to me when I left with Bryony. He wanted to know why I was avoiding him and asked if I didn't want to go out with him because I fancied the boy in the turtleneck jumper. He'd been following me and spying on me and I was furious about it. We got into an argument about it all. I let go of Bryony to face him and tell him to go away and leave me alone. That was all it took. It was no more than two minutes and suddenly I had a sense of impending doom. I turned. It happened like in films. Everything slowed. I could see Bryony running across the road towards that stupid puppy that is always escaping. It was staring at her, a small plastic pot by its feet. From the left I spotted a large car. I knew in an instant I would never reach Bryony in time. I screamed at her but as soon as the sound left my mouth there was a horrible screeching of tyres followed by a crunching, sickening thud and Bryony flew into the air before landing like a rag doll on the road. Her limbs went in all directions and I thought she was dead.

Everything happened at once then. First came the noise – a babble of sounds as cars drew up and neighbours raced from their homes. People cried. I couldn't make any sense of what was happening. Someone covered Bryony with a blanket. Someone else banged on our front door until my mother came outside, a look of sheer panic on her face. I shook and shook, unable to move from the spot. Rob turned away and was sick all over the pavement. My mother howled like a wild animal. It was a sound I'll never forget and I could only think that I had killed my sister. The woman from two doors down held me against her chest and told me over and over again it would be all right.

My parents were at the hospital all day and most of the night. The woman from two doors away stayed at our house and made me cocoa but I couldn't drink it. Dad came home some time this morning, his eyes red. He said Bryony would be okay. She'd broken a few bones but she'd live and recover. I broke down then. He held me by the shoulders and told me it wasn't my fault but I know it was. We both knew it was.

Neither of my parents have any idea of what a bad daughter I truly am. They imagine I am a golden creature who is good, kind and clever. I'm not. I shoplift. I smoke. I've even dabbled with drugs. I can lie convincingly but I'm never going to be able to live up to their expectations. This episode proves it. A good daughter wouldn't have been arguing with an ex-boyfriend because she didn't want to sleep with him. A proper daughter would have kept an eye on her little sister who's been sick and who suffers from St Vitus' dance. I'm not a proper daughter.

I have no choice. I'm going to run away. They'll be far better off without me. I'll move far away and change my appearance and my life. I'm sad but not afraid to leave. I'll manage alone because I'm an expert in pretending to be one thing when, in fact, I am another.

Water like a heavy drizzle was running upstairs, occasional louder plops as it cascaded down the plastic screen and into the tray. Lewis was getting ready for his meeting. She had time to learn what happened next to her sister all those years before. She read on, absorbing every detail of the diary.

Dear Diary,

I haven't written for a long while because so much has happened since the day I ran away.

It all happened so quickly. One minute I was lying on my bed thinking again about leaving home, the next, I'd written a note, grabbed my bag, stuffed with what I thought I'd need, and was out of the door. I headed into town where I stole some hair dye and reading glasses with the weakest lenses in them from Superdrug, and then I cut my hair over a sink in the public toilets. It was the hardest thing imaginable and I cried as I did it, but it was for the best. I needed to become someone else – a person who wasn't a dreadful daughter and a rotten sister, and not somebody who felt suffocated by parents who wanted her to be something she could never become. I had to get rid of the headmaster's daughter who was never going to be the brilliant student he wanted her to be and disguise myself so I attracted no attention. I left the toilets a different girl. I instantly became almost invisible. No one turned to look at me in my baggy tracksuit bottoms and coat with my hair cut like a boy's and my plain-framed spectacles.

I hitchhiked to London and found a youth hostel. I'd taken enough money, saved over the months, to last a few weeks and I'd hoped to find work and better accommodation before it ran out. My luck was in and I discovered an advert asking for a flatmate in a newsagent's window.

I now live in a tiny bedroom on the first floor of a shabby Victorian house. My room's next to the bathroom so it's a bit noisy when the others who live here have a shower or bath but I won't be here forever. I'm going to save up and rent a place of my own in time.

I share the house with another girl, Vienna, and two guys, Rich and Fraser, along with various girlfriends of theirs who stop over for the night or hang about here for a few days. They're all musicians and perform in the same group. They seem to have accepted me without knowing anything about me. I told them I'd been in a long-term relationship that had broken up and was looking to start over again. They've no idea I'm only sixteen. That's one good thing about being here in this huge city;

nobody knows anything about you. You can be whoever you want to be.

Some days I get very depressed and wonder what I've done. I hope my parents and Bryony are okay. I tell myself Bryony will be fine. She's such a tough little girl and so intelligent. She's far cleverer than me. My parents were really proud of her over the way she dealt with having St Vitus' dance and she was recovering from the accident when I left home. Bryony is strong and she'll be a far better daughter to Mum and Dad than I could ever be. She won't turn out like I did and be a huge disappointment to them.

I sort of wish I could see them all again but I wouldn't be welcome. By running away, I've only made matters worse. They'd never be able to trust me again.

I hope Bryony can walk properly once more. I couldn't bear it if I knew she couldn't. I still have nightmares about that day. I wish I'd looked after my little sister as I was asked.

I got a job this week at a dry-cleaning shop. I'm out the back where the clothes and machines are and the job is pretty boring. It's hot in the shop and very noisy and there's no chance to talk to anyone, not that there are many people to talk to. It suits me. I don't want to chatter and I certainly don't want to have to divulge too much about myself.

At least I now earn enough to keep paying rent and for food. I no longer feel suffocated. I am trying hard to make this work. I don't want to be the bad old Hannah Masters any more.

Each entry was a piece of the jigsaw puzzle of Hannah's life. At last Bryony was beginning to understand why her sister had taken off and relief that she wasn't solely to blame had flooded her body, warming it.

She shifted from one leg to the other. She'd been stood in the same position for too long, bent over the kitchen table, eyes glued to the diary. She glanced at the digital display on the cooker. She'd been reading for fifteen minutes, and her head was jumbled by emotions and the knowledge she now possessed.

Lewis appeared at the kitchen door, hair damp from the shower. 'Hey, where's this coffee you promised me? You haven't even put the machine on. Bryony, you okay?'

She looked across at him, her face a mix of emotions and burst into tears. He rushed to her, held her tightly and let the tears flow. Eventually, she pulled away and said, 'It's okay. They're happy tears. I understand why Hannah left and why she hasn't contacted us before. It's all in this, her diary.'

'Her diary?'

'I think she posted it to me. I've read half of it and I understand why she ran away. Listen, here's one of her entries about a couple she lived with who ran a café. She lived above it and became very friendly with them:

They invited me to their house last night for a meal and were so kind to me I felt really sad. I've lied to them about who I am. They believe I'm an orphaned young woman who has no family. Josie gave me some curtains and matching cushions she'd made especially for my flat and hugged me. Their generosity really touched me.

'When I got home, I wept for me and I wept for my parents and then I cried for Bryony who I deserted. I ought to be eating

dinner with them and sharing my news, not with two kind strangers. As time's gone by I've come to understand I let them all down. I wasn't there to support them when I should have been, and worse still, I abandoned Bryony who adored me. I should have been braver and gone home, maybe after I left the house rather than try again on my own, or soon after I realized I'd been stupid. I should have faced up to my parent's disappointment or anger and admitted my mistake but I buried my head in the sand and convinced myself staying away was the best course of action. I ignored what my heart was telling me and too much time has passed. I created this situation. I may have terrible regrets but now, it's too late and I can never go back.

'In spite of Tomasz and Josie, I feel so alone. I wish I'd never run away. Nevertheless, I can never go back. I have broken every rule and moral code installed in me. They'd never forgive me. I'm not the person they hoped I'd become.'

Bryony looked up at Lewis, eyes still damp with emotion. 'She convinced herself we didn't want her back.'

'She's sent you the diary to help you understand how she felt. Maybe she's also testing the waters and wants to see how you respond once you know.'

'I think you're right. She says in this section: "*It's been almost two and a half years since I left my family and there's not been one day when I haven't thought them and wonder how they're doing without me. There were so many times when I almost rang them, just to hear their voices but chickened out at the last minute, then last week, I made the call only to find their number is no longer in service. They've given up on me.*

"*It was only to be expected. I left them a note asking them not to look for me and they haven't. They've probably erased me from their lives. I don't know why I'm so upset about it after all, that's what I wanted them to do.*" Then there's a bit about meeting a new man and wanting to tell him the truth about herself and she goes on to write, "*You can't run away and expect to be forgiven and welcomed home with open arms after two and a half years. I've been fooling myself to think I could. I'm going to have to try harder to forget them all and just be Hannah.*"

'I must tell her I forgive her, that we all forgive her and persuade her to come home but I don't know how to contact her. She may have found out my address and posted her diary to me but I've no idea how to get in touch with her. It was posted in Paris.'

Lewis shook his head, eyebrows furrowed. 'Check your blog again. She must have left you a comment. She wouldn't send you the diary without any explanation or contact details. It makes no sense. She's clearly paving the way for a return. Want me to look at the Facebook page in case she left a message to you on it?'

'Have you got time?'

'The accountants can wait for me. This is way more important. You want to carry on reading while I look?' He picked up his mobile and trawled through the sites.

'No. I'll read it later. I'll check too.' Bryony fired up the laptop on the kitchen table. The blog came into view immediately. 'Stacks more comments,' she mumbled.

'And on the Facebook page.'

A hiatus fell as both concentrated on the numerous messages, some lengthy, offering advice, names of agencies Bryony could get in touch with to help her quest, and others sympathizing with her or wishing her luck. She rubbed her forehead. There were so many missing people in the country, some who'd been gone for decades and some for weeks. It was heart-rending to read the comments from those, like her, who'd been searching for loved ones: a mother looking for her twelve-year-old daughter, a family hunting for their father, another parent whose son had disappeared leaving no note. They were all heart-breaking stories written in a few paragraphs but all the commenters shared one thing – they all had hope.

Lewis, scrolling through the numerous comments on the Facebook page, looked up. 'Nothing,' he said.

Bryony wasn't surprised. She'd decided Hannah or somebody who knew her had sent the diary to help Bryony understand why Hannah had left home, but her sister was either dead, or didn't want to come home.

She was about to log off when she noticed an unread comment flashing on the administration page. It hadn't been placed under her last post as all the others were. It had been written under the information about Hannah. Her eyes skimmed over it and she gasped.

'Lewis.'

He turned to face her.

She read out loud. 'Mouse. Birthday. Birmingham airport. 2 p.m. flight from Paris.'

Bryony felt incredulity, a surge of love and immense excitement.

'It's Hannah,' she cried. 'She's coming home at last. It has to be from her.'

'It's a bit cryptic, Bryony,' Lewis cautioned.

'No. It's her. No one else could possibly know my nickname, Mouse.'

A large grin cracked Lewis's face. 'Mouse?'

'I was very small as a child and incredibly quiet so my family called me Mouse. No one else could know other than my parents and Hannah. It's definitely Hannah. She's coming *today* on her birthday. Oh-my-gosh, this is actually happening. And it's all come about because you and I went to that game show audition and then you agreed to partner me in France!' She yelled and jumped up and down, holding onto Lewis's hands. He threw his arms around her. She hugged him then drew away, still holding onto his hands.

'This is amazing. Melinda. I must tell Melinda. Ah, she won't have her phone turned on. She never does when she goes shopping. Could you visit her when you finish at the accountants? Tell her Hannah is coming home. Tell her about the diary.'

'Of course I will. Do you want me to come with you to the airport? Be your support team? I can wait outside.'

'As lovely as that is, I'd rather go alone.'

'I figured as much. Go on, then. Get ready. Got to look your best. I'll be here when you get back.'

'You have no idea how glad I am to hear you say that.'

'I'll always be here, Bryony.'

He drew her into his arms again and they shared a tender kiss.

'Now. Go!'

Chapter Forty Seven

Hannah

Hannah had finished loading the dishwasher and wandered through to the sitting room where her daughter, Belle, was curled up on the settee staring at her mobile.

'You fancy watching any telly?'

'There's nothing on worth watching. I looked. What time's Dad back?'

'Not until late.'

Hannah picked up the control and was about to turn the set on when Belle let out a squeal, 'Aw, isn't he the cutest?'

'What's that?' she asked.

'This dog.' She lifted the phone to show her mother a picture of a pug dog dressed in a beret and striped T-Shirt with a comical expression on his face that made her laugh out loud. Encouraged by her reaction, Belle flicked through some more photos.

'He's really cute,' said Hannah, smiling at the various outfits and poses.

'He's called Biggie Smalls after a rapper. His owner's a ballet dancer. I've been following him on Instagram for ages. He's here in France at the moment, near Nantes, filming a quiz show.

'The dog's on a quiz show?'

'No,' said Belle, pulling a face and swiping though some more pictures of the animal. 'His owner is. It's being shown in the UK *but there are a few clips of it on YouTube. It's really funny. Look this is one of the other contestants.'*

She lifted the phone so her mother could see the photo of a striking woman with grey eyes, sitting on a sunbed. She had the saddest face Hannah had seen. Next to her was Biggie Smalls, licking her hand. Belle read out the caption. "'This is my new best friend, Bryony Masters, who's on the show with my owner. She's a lovely human who's trying to find her long-lost sister Hannah. If you know Hannah, please tell her about this. Thanks. Biggie." Isn't that cool? Biggie's helping her. Weird, isn't it? Her sister has the same first name as you.' The girl carried on happily swiping at the screen unaware of her mother's reaction.

Hannah's heart stopped.

—

Hannah watched her daughter, eyes fixed on her mobile and long fingers deftly typing out messages. She smiled to herself. The girl was very different to Hannah at that age.

It'd been thirty years since she'd left home – a third of a century they'd lived without her and still she thought about them. Had Bryony married and got children? Her daughter looked up from the screen.

'You okay?'

'Yes, just thinking.'

'You had that weird expression you sometimes get.'

'Lost in the past. It's an age thing. It'll happen to you when you are older.'

She moved away and stared out of the kitchen window onto the small front garden filled with rose bushes and watched as a blackbird chased after a blue-winged butterfly. It escaped and flew off into the brilliant blue sky. That was how she felt some days, like the butterfly who'd escaped and yet other times, she felt like one caught in a net. The past never left you no matter how hard you tried to forget it, she mused. It had a knack of sneaking back, catching you unawares and reminding you of your mistakes.

She took off to the main bedroom – a spacious, uncluttered room with large windows that overlooked the back garden and swimming pool outside – and raked through the bottom drawer of a modern unit. She found what she was searching for and removed the diary she'd written in her teens. She swept one finger over the lock that prevented anyone from opening it and stroked the maroon leather cover, seemingly innocuous but Hannah knew what horrors the diary kept hidden within its pages. She extracted a pillbox with a mosaic lid from her bedside drawer and felt for the tiny key that would unlock the diary – a veritable Pandora's box of shocks.

She sat on the edge of her king-sized bed and for the first time in many years read the first entry, once more remembering the sixteen-year-old Hannah who'd written it…

–

Hannah put the diary aside. Her eyes were sore with reading and her heart heavy for the girl who was too selfish to see what was in front of her eyes and who'd made such a monumental mistake.

She clicked onto the video clip she'd watched several dozen times already and wiped away the tears that fell yet again. Was it too late? She now knew Bryony wanted her back but could her parents forgive her? Hannah clicked onto the information she'd found, carefully copied the name and address onto a large envelope and slipped the diary inside.

CHapter Forty Eight

Friday, 4 August – Afternoon

Bryony ran her fingers over the page and tried to imagine how hard it had been for Hannah. She'd read the diary from cover to cover and now waiting in the car park for the flight to arrive, she looked again at one entry that had touched her deeply.

> *Dear Diary,*
>
> *I'm feeling very dejected today. Last night I had a dream about the events that happened exactly one year ago when Bryony was hit by a car, only this time, she didn't recover. I woke up in a sweat, fearful that the dream was some terrible message telling me she'd died as a consequence of that accident.*
>
> *I wanted to make sure she was alive. I wanted desperately to tell my parents I was sorry and more than anything I wanted them to all forgive me but I know I've left it too long.*
>
> *Twelve months have passed and I haven't made any contact with them. They'll probably have begun to push me out of their thoughts by now and be carrying on with their lives.*

Recently, I've been thinking about why I ran away. I got drunk with my housemates a few days ago and burst into tears for no apparent reason. Vienna asked me what was wrong and I told her some bullshit lie about my boyfriend I'd left behind and how I was just having a low moment because I missed him. After she'd gone, I thought about the real reason I'd broken down. It was because finally, after several months of being a different Hannah, here in London, I actually thought about the consequences of my actions. I suddenly had a vision of Bryony's sweet face and in that moment, I missed so her badly it felt like my heart was actually on fire and I wondered if it might burn out and I would die.

I should have waited longer before leaving. I could have managed to live the lie, been the diligent daughter for a few more months until I'd at least taken my exams or until Bryony was a little older and needed me less.

I was so desperate to escape the cage I was trapped in: the endless days of torturous pressure to succeed and the perpetual looks of disappointment when I didn't reach my father's lofty expectations, and creeping around the house like a shadow, wishing I could be like normal kids and go off with friends to town or off to the cinema, not spend day after day with my stuffy parents and sister who, as lovely as she was, was only a little kid. I hated being shunned by classmates because of who my parents were, and I was so lonely it was unbearable. I thought the loneliness would kill me if I didn't get away.

I'm such an awful person. No matter how much I hide behind this new Hannah image, I'll never forgive myself for leaving Bryony. I hope she doesn't hate me for everything I've done. She can't possibly hate me any more than I hate myself for such selfish actions.

She tucked the diary away in her bag and checked her face in the rear-view mirror. She'd forgiven Hannah a hundred times over. She needed only to prove that to her sister and convince her to visit their parents.

–

Bryony hopped from foot to foot. Birmingham airport was jammed with people heading off to sunny climates. She fought through the ebb and flow of holidaymakers towards the arrivals exit where she stood outside the Marks & Spencer store with others awaiting loved ones. The screens showed that the flight from Paris had landed on time. Her heart hammered against her chest, threatening to burst through her ribcage. The arrivals doors swished open, allowing several people to emerge. None were female.

The doors opened again. A young couple with deeply suntanned faces and pulling matching purple suitcases appeared before the waiting people. Next to her, a middle-aged man in a suit held a sign marked 'Mr Chiltern'. He wore the look of someone who was used to waiting. He thumbed his mobile with his free hand, oblivious to the crowds surging past him. She checked her watch. Surely, it couldn't be much longer.

The doors slid apart again with a soft *whoosh*. A family of three with a young child came through, their cases piled high on a trolley. The toddler broke free from his mother's hand and yelled, 'Granddad!' An elderly gent wearing a cricket hat scuttled forward, scooped up the boy and smothered him with stubbly kisses. Bryony smiled at the chuckling child who batted his grandfather's smooches away.

Then her focus shifted to the open door once again. Time slowed as a woman walked through it. Bryony took in the slim face, snub nose and ash-blonde hair cut into a fashionable bob that shimmered as she walked. Her grey eyes skimmed over the faces in front of her and alighted on Bryony's. Rooted to the spot, Bryony knew at once it was her sister and recognized the heart-shaped silver necklace hanging at Hannah's throat. It would be engraved with her name. There was a sudden welling in her chest, and a release of hot tears cascaded down her cheeks. She held out her arms and Hannah walked into them. Sisters finally reunited.

Chapter Forty Nine

Friday, 4 August – Afternoon

Bryony reached for her sister's hand and gripped it. There were so many questions but they had time.

'It seems so stupid now when I look back on it all. Time twists memories, fuzzes the corners of them, so now all I can recall is the sensation of pressure – the constant need to behave as they wanted me to behave, be as successful as they wanted me to be and knowing all the while I couldn't do it. I was fighting the Hannah inside me who wanted to be somebody completely different. The accident was the catalyst that sent me spiralling into a descent I couldn't control. I had to get away. The guilt was unbearable, Bryony.' She squeezed her sister's fingers.

'I've been haunted by memories of that day since. You know, I hated myself for running away. I regretted leaving my little sister.' She fingered the small heart on her chain. 'I thought about you often. There were times when I almost tried to contact you but bottled out. There were so many times I wanted to get back in touch but I'd left it too late. I couldn't crawl back and face you all. I couldn't have stood the look of disapproval or the cold treatment I feared I receive from Mum and Dad for being so stupid.' She faltered and fought a rebellious tear as it broke ranks and balanced on her eyelashes.

'I'd no idea you blamed yourself for my disappearance, not until I watched you on YouTube and heard what you had to say. I had to come back to set the record straight. I was so selfish and naïve to think I wouldn't hurt anyone.'

'You saw me on YouTube? How did you find out about the show? You live in Paris. It wasn't transmitted in France.'

'It's a long story. My daughter follows a cute pug dog on Instagram called Biggie Smalls. She was showing me photographs of him and there was one of you with him and a caption saying how you were searching for your sister. She told me about the show and I found clips of it online. There was one when you were interviewed and asked for everyone who knew me to beg me to come home. I was overwhelmed. I found out more about you and your address came up in one of the searches from the national register. I thought if you read the diary it would help explain some things before you met me.'

'You have a daughter?'

'Belle. She's fifteen. You must meet her, and Larry, my husband. He's an American. So much to tell you. I've wasted so much time. It all seems a lifetime ago. For someone who was supposed to be clever, I really have been incredibly stupid.'

Bryony saw to her horror that her sister's eyes weren't just sad but full of tears. Hannah clutched at her hand and said in a hoarse whisper, 'I've so many wrongs to put right. Bryony, I'm scared.'

'Don't be. The past is exactly that. It's the past. This is what matters. You must come back with me.'

'But I've left it too long.'

'None of that matters.'

'You sure?'

'I know so.'

Hannah lowered her head and chewed at her lip. For a second she looked like the teenager Bryony remembered, concentrating on a difficult piece of homework or glued to a passage in a book. Bryony wanted every detail of her life and to meet her family and spend hours in her company, getting to know her again, but this wasn't that moment. It was far more important she join her and visit their parents. She waited quietly, pulse beating in her ears. This decision was up to Hannah. People rushed by them in a blur. Bryony saw none of them. Eventually Hannah looked up. 'Okay. Let's do this. Let's go and see Mum and Dad.'

–

Bryony tapped lightly on her father's study door. Her mother was engrossed in a book, her reading glasses perched on her nose. In front of her sat the old china tea service and a tiered plate of cupcakes, each decorated with pink and white icing. Each year she baked the small cakes especially for Hannah's birthday. There was always one they kept aside for her. Her father was dozing in his chair, a checked blanket over his knees. His face was shaven, his hair had been combed and he was wearing a clean shirt. Her mother looked up expecting to see Bryony, words dying on her lips as she noticed the woman standing by the door. She took in the grey eyes so like her own and Bryony's.

'Hannah,' she whispered. Her trembling hands released the book and it clattered to the floor. Bryony moved aside to let her sister enter the room. Her mother stood up in one swift movement and lurched towards her daughter, holding her, then pulling away to look to her and then drawing her towards her again.

Her father roused by the sound of soft sobs opened his rheumy eyes. He squinted hard. 'Is that you, Hannah?' he asked in a reedy, wavering voice.

Hannah released her mother and crossed the room to kneel down beside her father's chair. She dropped a kiss on his head, lighting up his eyes.

'Yes,' said her sister. 'Yes, Daddy. It's Hannah.'

A Letter from Carol

Thank you so much for buying and reading this book. I hope you enjoyed meeting the characters and buzzing around France. I am a complete Francophile and have spent many years living and working in France. It was wonderful to be able to write about perfect Summer afternoons and the stunning countryside – all of which I remember with nostalgia.

I draw quite a bit of material from real life and this novel was no exception. As part of my research for it, I applied for and was accepted on various televised game shows, including *Decimate* with Shane Ritchie and *Tipping Point* presented by Ben Shepherd. I met hugely entertaining characters on set and at auditions like those at the audition for *What Happens in…*

Much of the inspiration and traits of the characters for this novel came from sitting in a country manor house in Essex waiting to film a game show called *Masterpiece* with Alan Titchmarsh. We began filming at seven in the morning and did not finish until almost ten o'clock. We were also all put up at the same hotel so we had much time to kill as we waited for our pieces to camera and plenty of opportunities to learn about each other. I have to say that Alan Titchmarsh is nothing at all like Professor David Potts and he did not need to retake once.

So, who was your favourite character? I'm torn between Melinda and Oscar both of whom I adore. It's been wonderful having them in my life and hard to wave them goodbye. I wonder if Bryony and Lewis will see a lot of Jim and Oscar and I hope Biggie Smalls the Second will gain an even bigger following than he already has, and Oscar will become a famous ballet dancer. I'm also curious to know where the next edition of *What Happens in…* will be filmed. In brief, I am sorely tempted to write more about them all, especially if it means I get to spend more time with the utterly delicious Lewis.

My thanks again for reading. If you enjoyed *What Happens in…* could you kindly leave a review no matter how short it may be? It would mean such a lot to me.

Acknowledgments

Much research goes into my books and there are many who help me on my journey in writing *What Happens in…*.

My mother who has sadly passed away since the writing of this book helped me understand what Bryony would have gone through as a child suffering with Sydenham's Chorea. My mother contracted the illness also known as St Vitus Dance in her childhood. She shared her experiences of it with me and revealed how it affected her relationship with her older brother, her education, and how it rocked her confidence. Those who suffer can become very clingy hence Bryony looks up to her sister more than an ordinary sibling might.

I am grateful to all those involved in filming "Masterpiece" and game shows "Decimate" and "Tipping Point" for helping me discover what goes on behind the scenes, in particular Laura and Helen the shows' producers for inviting me to be on the shows, Alan Titchmarsh for being such a wonderful host, Shane Richie for making me laugh so much on game show "Decimate" I couldn't concentrate on the questions, and Ben Shepherd who made me blush like a love-struck teenager.

I thoroughly enjoyed researching for this book, after all who wouldn't love travelling around stunning French countryside and staying in small chateaux? I did however drive my husband demented watching endless quiz shoes and racing off to attend auditions for television shows. I met some incredible people at those auditions – too many to name but I have to shout out thanks to Mitz Patel, Pauline Yong, Pete Thomson, Becky Smith, Craig Ansell and my lovely friend Michelle Marriott who has been successful on other shows since we met on set. Being on a game show is addictive. Once you've done one, you'll want to do another.

I really couldn't have written this book without the help and advice of my superb editor Hannah Todd who kept my ramblings under control and lifted my spirits with her enthusiastic emails and cheerful editing notes. Thank you, Hannah and all the team at Canelo.

And finally, my thanks to you, my readers. Your messages, emails and support keep me writing long into the night.